REGRETTING
THE RAINBOW THIEVES

— WORLD OF PAERRIES SERIES | BOOK 1 —

A NOVEL
BY DAN SLONE

To My Wonderful Daughters:

Amanda Leigh Slone & Jocelyn Courtney Slone

Regretting the Rainbow Thieves
By Daniel K. Slone

WorldOfPaerries.com.
Follow the author through
Facebook at Daniel K. Slone.

Book design by SparkFire Branding, LLC
Cover illustration by Timothy D. Thomas
Printed in the United States of America.

ISBN 978-1-73265 18-0-7
Library of Congress Control Number:
2018909360 Paper Edition

*"In all things of nature,
there is something of the marvelous."*

— Aristotle

*"Everything we see hides another thing,
we always want to see what is hidden
by what we see, but it is impossible."*

— René Magritte

*"Alas for those that never sing,
but die with all their music in them!"*

— Oliver Wendell Holmes

CHARACTERS

SILTH

Called "Paerries" by the Trow and, sometimes, themselves

ARAN
Storyteller who becomes a
shaman, also called "Heartless"

MERIT
Battle leader for Fortress Colony,
also called "Dawn Defender"

SHRA
Teacher, Aran's lover

CASIUS
Aran's brother, high priest
of New Faerie, member of
Kawran Council

STORNG
Shaman, also called
"Storm Rider"

QWERT
Young Silth

NADARA
Leader of Tiki Crew

ANULI
Shaman, member
of Kawran Council

DON, MARINA, VIC, KIRSTN, NICK, LOANA
Tiki Crew members

TELLICK
Leader of Kawran Council

CHARACTERS

HUMANS

Cowboy, Quaker

Costa Rican parrot poachers

Jocelyn ("Joss")

Eco-activist, biologist

Stanley Ryder Brophy,
Chilen, Juan

Twenty-something eco-activists

Kate

Joss's friend, New Orleans
curio store owner

TROW

Called "Faeries" by the Silth

Faelen

Former general of Trow army,
son of Xafar

Demest

High-ranking Trow officer,
married to Thest

Thest

Current general of Trow army

Xafar

King of the Trow

Fod

Spy for Thest

Hepler

Son of Thest and Demist

Angeles ("Angel")

Trow pretending to be Human

GLOSSARY

COATI:

A raccoon-like mammal native to Costa Rica.

COLONY

A place where larger numbers of Silth live. Typically surrounded by villages, each of which is centered on an extended family.

GLAMOUR

As a verb, the act of disguising the true appearance of a Silth or a Trow. As a noun, the particular appearance projected by a being.

HARVEST

The annual process of Silth gathering Human products for their own use.

THE LAND

The home world of Trow. Also referred to as "Faerie" by some Humans and Silth.

HATHER

The hair-like feathers of a Silth.

SILTH

The progeny of Trow and parrots. About the size of a large parrot. Humanoid, with the arms, legs, torso, and sharp features of a Trow, but with wings and the coloration of a parrot. The Trow call them "Paerries" as a derogatory term, but when they apply it to themselves it is meant as a show of defiance.

TROW

A race of interdimensional beings who have visited the Earth since mankind's early days. Some Silth call them "Faeries" because of their place in the Silth mythology, but the Trow hate the name and use it to refer to their lesser animals.

CHAPTER ONE

Scene 1

Aran (Silth)

"Do you think that Humans know they are evil?" Aran asked Storng in his croaking voice as they flew over the sprawling parking lots and laydown areas surrounding the cargo ship berth. As he looked at the asphalt and hardscape spreading out below him he added, "Do you think grass ever dreams of being concrete?" He shivered beneath the sunless morning sky, pulled the many-pocketed shaman cloak tighter around him, and glanced back over his shoulder. The one-eyed Trow was nowhere in sight.

Cranes unloaded the container ship, their home for the past month since leaving Costa Rica's Puerto Limon for Panama City, Florida, with a brief stop in Progresa, Mexico. Aran flinched at the sharp metal-on-metal clang below.

To his surprise he missed the rainforest noises. Human sounds abounded in the port's unfamiliar landscape as well as barking dogs and a few birds. But morning in the rainforest elbowed its way into the day with the whoops, hoots, clicks, grunts, and chuffs of legions of birds in addition to lilting birdsongs. Most mornings churned with the growls of howler monkeys and the grunts of wild pigs foraging through the jungle.

He was used to colony-hopping and settling for the

night wherever he happened to land, instantly establishing new relationships—Silth with whom to pass the time, but seldom friends. The Silth colonies were calm and peaceful refuges in the rainforest, with plenty of food. In the rainforest every shadow hid a jaguar or puma. A moment's inattention resulted in a snake squeezing the life from you. Forget to look before you put down your hand, and a spider bite or a bullet ant sting reminded you to pay better attention. The pigs would kill you on sight. Still, he knew what to fear there and how to be safe. Now he looked around, seeing nowhere safe to land.

"I don't think grass dreams of being eaten, though half the world's creatures eat it," Storng answered, nodding his head toward a large oak in a parking lot beside a marina filled with fishing boats. For any Humans watching from below, Aran and Storng were glamoured to appear as cattle egrets, common birds in this area. Aran, however, saw Storng as he appeared behind this secondary glamour, but surrounded by a slight bluish glow.

They landed and squatted in the tree branches. Storng went on, "But grass adapts and learns to thrive when grazed. Its roots get stronger. There's no thriving beneath concrete." He fixed his black eye on Aran, while the other white one looked off into the distance, the milky white of the skin between his face's black tattoos luminescent in the branches' enclosure. Below, Humans walked from their cars and trucks to the boats, waking them up for their day's work.

"And Humans are not evil as a people. Only as individuals." He ran his hands through pockets of his cloak. "I have to take care of a few things before we join the crew. Promise me you won't kill anyone while I'm away."

Aran looked down at the Humans. "How long will you be

gone?"

"No more than an hour."

"I can restrain myself that long."

Apparently Aran's smile did not reach his eyes, because Storng regarded him a long moment before standing up. As he launched himself from the branch, Storng's shaman cloak gave a quick flap, but his wings, bright blue on top and an even brighter yellow beneath, made no sound.

Aran closed his eyes. He'd trained hard every day aboard the ship, in the little space they'd created at the forward top of the containers, high enough that no crew ever came there. He'd forgotten how physical shaman training was. In the ten years since he'd left the training, he had lost none of the knowledge—he remembered the magic, potions, dream casting, even the fighting moves—but his body had forgotten the sheer physical endurance that magic required. He drifted.

Soaring above Shra, looking down at her silhouetted against the rainforest tree canopy, the reds, yellows, blues, and greens of her hather and wings rainbowed above the deep green treetops, and the only sound was the rush of air. The curve of her hips excited. As she glided without flapping her wings, he was certain she knew he was there, but she gave no sign.

A loud clank and grinding of gears woke him with a start. He wiped the wetness from his face and eyed the big truck pulling into the parking lot, piled high with wire cages. Men rushed out to move them to the boats, talking and joking loudly as they worked. Aran told himself this was different. These cages were for some sea creatures such as crabs. The casual way these Humans brought capture and death to the world wasn't meant to be disrespectful. But he was inching along the branch to get a better line of sight, and almost involuntarily his hand reached into his pocket for the lighter—the spark that would allow him to rain fire down on the heads of these men.

He tried to calm. He closed his eyes. But instead of drawing up some vison of the peaceful ocean his mind betrayed him; he was back in the poacher's camp as night fell, holding his broken lover in his arms.

She smiled at him. "Heartless, ask me ... to stay."

"Stay."

"Tell me you'd do anything to keep me."

"Anything ... anything." He swiped at his tears.

"Ha, I won the heart no one thought could be won."

"Always."

As the darkness spread around them, she lost consciousness again. He whispered urgently for her to hang on, that someone would come for them, that he loved her. With more kisses, he transferred all the energy he could to her while still maintaining his own glamour.

Soon her labored breathing slowed. Pause ... gasp ... a longer pause ... another gasp. Two hours after the sun disappeared, she stopped breathing. For Aran the moment seemed completely unreal. It could not be happening. Or ... he must be watching it happen to someone else.

A Human in a big hat was working his way down the rows of cages checking the occupants, and numbly Aran slid Shra off his lap. The Human's flashlight lit up her lifeless body and reflected up into Aran's face. Aran glared, his glamour barely a mask for his hatred.

The Human called to the others, "Hey, this poco is dead."

"Okay, Cowboy, we'll eat her. Sell the feathers," came the answer. "But come here, help pull the tarp over these first."

As Cowboy turned away, he didn't see the rainbow-hued body disappear from the cage. The only items left were the metal fasteners from her clothes and the large silver bracelet she always wore. Aran grabbed the bracelet before it could fall through the cage floor and slipped it on his own wrist.

Aran regained his focus, pointed the lighter at the truck, and muttered the incantation. As four men returned for another load of traps, sparks tumbled from Aran's other outstretched hand. Suddenly his branch bucked, throwing Aran off balance and breaking his concentration.

Storng settled in beside him, looking at the men below. He pulled out a small, woman's pocket watch and handed it to Aran. "I realized you didn't have a watch, so you wouldn't know how long an hour was."

Aran's mind dully picked at the words. An hour? "Ahhh," he said, staring as the last traps were pulled off the truck and remembering his promise. He took the watch. "Well, now there'll be no mistakes."

Scene 2

ARAN (SILTH)

"We need to be gulls," Storng said.

He and Aran flew as egrets into a low, wispy cloud, and when they emerged, they appeared to the world as two large, handsomely-patterned seagulls. Below, a few ships were docked in the Panama City port, unloading containers or loading wood pallets or other items back into ships. Aran was gliding low enough to hear the beep, beep, beep of backing forklifts and trucks.

Aran dropped back slightly, following Storng, barely registering where they were going. A couple of days earlier, Storng had told him that his direct instruction and shaman training were finished. Though it took place years earlier, Aran had forgotten nothing from his earlier training, and because he'd almost completed his studies in Amazonia before abandoning them, it had taken only the last few weeks to refresh his memory and bring his body back into shape. Had his life really changed so radically mere weeks ago? Just one night had taken him from a traveling singer and storyteller back to his shaman studies.

Their gentle argument of that morning had turned into planning their future. The sun rose high enough to burn off the morning's clouds, and it was time to return to Kawran. Heads up, hands by their sides, Aran and Shra flew a few feet above the cloud forest floor, down a path leading to the rainforest below. Shra took the lead, laughing as she dipped and swooped along.

Without warning she jerked to a halt, suspended in air. He had no time to react before he too hit the mist net. He recognized the net as soon as he collided with it, having watched Human biologists catch birds, bats, and other creatures for banding, seeing the light net give way and wrap the terrified victim in its web-like hold. Struggling merely caused the mesh to bind even more, but Shra twisted and pushed.

"Shra, stop! You're making it worse."

Four men rushed out of the bushes—they didn't look like biologists.

"Ahh, a couple of lovely parrots. Puera Vita! Load them into the travel crates."

From prior experience with Humans, Aran wasn't surprised he could understand the man, just as he understood the languages of other animals. About half of the Silth had this skill—Shra didn't.

"Hey, Cowboy, this one bites." The man holding Shra grimaced and moved his big gloved hand to avoid her mouth.

The damp ground squished as a large, grey-haired man moved forward. Clean-shaven while the others had several days' beard growth, he lifted bushy eyebrows and eyed Shra. "Move them into the travel cages." His voice was deep, his pronunciation crisp. "You two carry those cages back to the camp while we check on the other nets."

The man referred to as Cowboy said, "You heard Quaker. Move it."

Aran feared he wouldn't get a better opportunity, so he bit the hand holding him. Cowboy swore but didn't relax his grip, and he shoved Aran into a cage on back of an ATV hidden in the bushes. Another man stuffed Shra into an adjoining cage, where she looked at Aran wide-eyed through the wire. While the team moved on to check other nets, Aran shook the cage door and eyed the latch. Having watched poachers in the past, he knew what would happen next.

"Shra, we have to get out now. Before they load us into heavier cages with locks."

The noise of the five ATV's starting up and the men's constant movement around the trailer had Shra flipping around in her cage, watching whomever was closest to her. "No, no. We should wait, Aran. They're too close."

Three of the ATV's took off along the path, and with a whine of its engine, the ATV holding them started moving the other direction. They struggled to maintain their balance.

He reached through the bars of his cage, lifted the latch on Shra's, and swung open the door. "Hurry, fly!"

As she started out of the cage, the ATV driver glanced over his shoulder, shouted "Ojo! Ojo!" and hit the brakes hard. Aran's cage tumbled over with a loud clanging of metal. Shra, almost free of hers, slid back inside, but she rose and tried again as Aran struggled to open his latch. Just as Shra was almost clear, Cowboy pulled alongside on his ATV and pinned her with the door. She screamed. Aran rushed to the side of his cage and craned his neck, but his view was blocked. As Cowboy turned and laid her crumpled figure in Aran's cage, he said, "Sorry, little one."

They were moved into the heavy cages stacked with many others under a canvas shelter next to the clay road at the edge of the poachers' camp. The din of the panicked birds filled the air. Fear had its own smell, overwhelming Aran. He rocked back and forth, formulating and discarding escape plans. The sun dropped below the lip of the canopy opening. Darkness would soon follow. She'd never make it through the night if he didn't find a way out.

Silth were taught from the time their colony took them in not to *show themselves to Humans—it was drilled into them until maintaining a glamour and appearing to others as some type of bird became as natural as breathing. Do not reveal yourself, they were told. To do so would expose their people. The Humans had forgotten them, and the Silth didn't want to be remembered.*

When he tried to move her wing to a less painful angle, she cried out, her eyes fluttering open. He shifted his position to between her and the men.

"Aran, I hurt so bad," she gasped.

"I'm sorry. This is my fault. I thought we could get away before—"

When she put a finger on his lips to shush him, her secondary glamour winked on and off more obviously. One moment she was a macaw, the next a diminutive beautiful Faerie-like creature with parrot wings and tail.

"I can't ... hold my glamour. They'll see me."

He leaned over and kissed her. As he held the kiss, the flickering of her glamour first slowed and then stopped altogether. She appeared steadily as a macaw.

She pushed at him feebly. "What are you doing?"

"Giving you some of my ...my energy. A skill left over from shaman training."

"Not far," Storng said, bringing Aran back to the present.

Now he would apprentice for six months. An additional six-month probationary period would follow, during which he would function as a colony's shaman under Storng's supervision. He would then be a "one-feather" shaman. For high ceremonies the shamans wore headdresses with harpy eagle feathers—one small under-feather was worn for each year he or she served as shaman of a colony.

They neared a long building a few miles from the port. The building was a single-story structure with a second story on about one-third of it. The shimmer Aran saw indicated that it was glamoured, probably protected by stay-away spells and other enchantments as well. They landed on the first-floor roof, on a patio covered by a lush garden and facing a metal door. The bright green of the banana trees, palms, and other plants, and the trickling sound of water a stark contrast to the surrounding landscape just awakening from winter.

Storng flew up and pulled hard on the big bar in the center of the door. As it opened, Aran thought, this will be the first time I've met Silth as a shaman—well, almost a shaman. Nerves fluttered deep in his belly. He held himself more erect and entered with what he hoped was a solemn gait. A few steps inside, his mouth fell open.

The place was bedlam, with assaults on Aran's every sense. Raucous screams, profane shouts, and an eruption of crashes blurted from the room as plates and furniture flew through the air. The noise overlaid an orchestra playing exotica on an overstrained boom box. The smell of the place welled up, with sweat, pheromones, and the scent of liquor and sweet fruit blending into a clearly several-days-old perfume of party. Aran instantly began perspiring from the heat.

A small group of Silth, only slightly younger than Aran, were spread out in the room and in constant motion. Two wrestled across the floor, their wings periodically unfolding for a quick flap to gain leverage. A female zipped through the air to tackle a male with his back to her. Before he recovered, she took off and flew into another couple grappling among the tables of an eating area. As they collided, they knocked over the table, sending dirty dishes crashing to the floor. Across the room a wobbly male was throwing darts at what looked like a hand-drawn picture of Storng, with dozens of darts sticking out of both it and the surrounding wall. An equally unsteady female danced nearby. Although there was some height variation, none was more than eighteen inches high, and even with wings spread, the Silth were still in danger of being lost in the cavernous room. No one seemed aware Aran and Storng were present.

Aran suppressed his laughter. He glanced at Storng, who seemed neither surprised nor angry but was studying each Silth in turn with fondness in his smile.

As the chaos continued, Aran examined the room. Cinderblock walls covered with forest murals, the space was about a hundred feet long, fifty feet wide, and perhaps twenty feet from floor to the struts holding the roof. On the longest wall hung three parallel levels of hammocks, a set of storage trunks below. A series of industrial windows about ten feet off the floor covered the other long wall. Near it a long wooden table sized to Silth scale was overturned, most of its low stools flipped over as well. A Human-sized kitchen and bar occupied the corner to Aran's right.

Storng had told him that most harvesting crews adopted some theme—wild west, baseball, nautical—that would both distinguish and unify them. Aran eyed the décor of unlit tiki torches, blowfish lights, shrunken heads, and tropical flowers draped over the thatch covering the bamboo bar. The mostly open center of the room held several wood chairs, also Silth-sized, and a couple of Human-scale couches covered in loud floral prints. A huge black-velvet picture of a hula girl hung on the far wall, flanked by tiki masks, and a four-foot-high moai stood in the corner. Aran had used tiki themes in some of his performances, so he recognized many of the icons.

Even though Aran and Storng had been standing there several minutes, the rollicking mob showed no sign of noticing. Storng rolled his eyes at Aran and marched to the center of the room. "Raak! Raak! Stop, you flock of toucans!"

Silence instantly fell, except for the orchestra straining out of the small speakers. The Silth on the floor remained locked in their holds but unmoving, while the bright blue-hathered female froze with her hands on a red-and-blue-hathered male's shoulders, pinning him against the wall. When she released him and straightened up, he slid down the wall to sit on the floor. The two by the dartboard stood as though turned to stone, and a head peeked over a nearby stack of bags and boxes.

Storng's white eye shone like a spot light, and his black one seemed to suck all light from the room. As Don Tiki's "Hot like Lava" boomed in the background, Storng shouted, "Shut that monkey scat off. Who used to be in charge here?"

Head lowered, the blue female quickly wound around obstacles until she stood before Storng. "That would be me," she said to the floor.

Aran's lips parted in astonishment. Most Silth, males and females, presented themselves as "beautiful" in his experience. Their beauty was not an accident of nature, in fact it wasn't natural at all. It wasn't even real. Silth had the ability to present layers of glamour. They could present a secondary glamour to appear to Humans and other animals as a bird, but they could also present a primary glamour amending their personal appearance. The majority of Silth adjusted their image to appear as they wanted. Mostly this resulted in a beauty that became routine. They were well-proportioned in their foot-and-a-half size, with their Faerie lineage apparent in their sharpened features—nose and ears more pointed than Humans, and thinner faces. Their hather, wing feathers, and tail feathers were the bright colors of their parrot mothers. No one knew the actual appearance of most of their friends, acquaintances, parents or even lovers, because they would maintain their primary glamour throughout their lives. Over the course of their three hundred years of life, of course some would get fat or thin and other distinctions would evolve. There was a joke that all Silth went through the "squash machine" in the course of their life. They appeared to be tall, thin and beautiful through most of their lives, and then when they finally got so old that they couldn't be bothered with the primary glamour, their actual appearance was short. Sometimes fat, sometimes thin, sometimes ugly and sometimes handsome. But always short. Because of the uniformness of the socially accepted glamours, small distinctions assumed large significance. A young Silth might distinguish himself or herself by the quality of their clothes, the cadence of their speech, or their skill at some undertaking.

Standing in front of Storng was a Silth female unlike any Aran had seen. Her predominantly blue hather had been rendered blonde at the tips. Her earrings were small, shrunken heads, and her nose and belly-button were pierced with small spears. She wore a black halter and a tropical sarong. Almost every visible inch of her body was covered in blue tattoos with orange highlights.

"Nadara? What is going on here?" Storng's gravelly voice deepened even further so that each word came out stern and disappointed, and Aran hid his inappropriate grin.

Nadara's head snapped up, and a tangle of words gushed out. "We were having dinner when Vic started talking trash about Martin Denny's music and how it was nothing but monkey scat and then—"

"Stop," Storng inserted softly. "Breathe. Look at me. How would a leader speak to me?"

With a start, Aran realized Nadara too was a student of Storng's, and perhaps the others were as well.

Nadara's eyes widened as if she was realizing a serious mistake. She held Storng's gaze, thinking hard about her response. Struggling not to look away from the disconcerting eyes, she squared her shoulders and lifted her chin. "We've been waiting for you for four days. Everyone got bored, so we decided to blow off a little steam."

She stared at Storng, now poised defiance, and the Silth she had left sitting against the wall fell onto his side. As though a signal, all the others swarmed into the center of the room and started to shout, not only at each other but also at Storng.

Like a change in the wind's direction, Aran's mood shifted, and he wanted out of the room's jungle heat. He left Storng to sort through Silth discipline and returned to the little tropical garden. Though cooler than the room, the garden was at least thirty degrees warmer than the surrounding shipyard and must have been maintained by some lingering enchantment. He had no idea how to do that magic and made a mental note to ask Storng, who most likely had set it up. Of course, with Storng you never knew—maybe he'd taught the young Silth how to do it.

He tried to imagine what the drunken brawl inside would have been like if they knew the magic he did. That would be irresponsible of Storng, but Aran had begun to wonder if responsibility was really a boundary for the old shaman. Teaching magic to Silth other than shamans was dangerous for three reasons. The first was the mischief that could be done. The second was that all Silth magic had to be done without risking exposing them to Humans. The garden was magically maintained but also magically hidden from Human view.

And last, magic was just plain dangerous for the practitioner. It used a tremendous amount of energy—if one of the primary elements of fire, water, or earth, was unavailable to provide the connection to the Earth's energy, it must come from the Silth, as Aran had learned when he tried to save Shra. The same energy maintained the magician's life.

Aran stared out at the unfamiliar landscape. This was not the life he was supposed to have lived.

The night Shra died had worn on, and after she was gone Aran could feel his glamour slipping. She was free from pain. He tried to think about her joy as she became part of everything around him and to send her life energy on into the world with love, but all he could feel was sorrow. When they lost someone close to them, Silth were careful not to be sad, fearing they would detain some part of the deceased's spirit from moving on in the world—it might stay back to comfort them. Convinced that he soon would follow Shra, he allowed himself the full measure of his grief.

Before morning, when the Humans would see him in his true form, giving away the existence of his entire people, he'd have to do something, but right now he didn't have the energy. Her death was his fault. It couldn't be undone. He slumped onto the cage floor.

The activity around him continued as a dull, unobserved buzz. Finally, the camp settled down, with only the light of the guard's flashlight jumping around the tree edges and the occasional bark of camp dogs.

Aran drifted into something not quite sleep, and he heard his own breath become ragged. A key scraped into the cage lock. The cage door creaked open.

"Aren't you a sorry sight!"

From within his stupor, he recognized the deep voice, like lava bubbling up in an old volcano, and his eyes struggled to open. His limbs were too leaden to move.

In the moonlight, he saw a heavy-set Silth perched in the cage opening. His white tattooed face was accented by a green forelock and black beard of hather, with a yellow chest and blue wings spread out to help him balance. As always, Aran's gaze was pulled to the eyes—one pitch black and the other ice white. He focused.

"Storm Rider … go away, Storng," Aran mumbled through parched lips. "I won't be responsible for anyone else getting hurt or killed tonight."

"I have no intention of either. Come on."

Storng yanked him to his feet with little effort. Storng jumped down from the table where the cage had been placed, using his wings to slow their fall. "You weigh too much for me to carry and fly. We have to walk."

"Ummmmm…." Aran's head lolled back, his knees buckled, and he faded into blackness. Tall rows of cages around him. Blackness. Sounds of snoring. Sweep of a flashlight ahead in the trees. Blackness. Unconscious body of a guard dog and its heavy breathing. Blackness. Light playing over them as they rushed into the bushes.

Blackness.

Aran tried to bring himself into the present. His thoughts drug him into the fog of sadness. He picked another memory, a better one, to hold in his mind, to create a barrier to the cloud gathering around him.

He was washing beneath the small waterfall. As water cascaded over his head, a pair of slender arms wrapped themselves around his chest.

He relaxed into Shra's embrace for a moment before turning to hold her close. She pushed him back onto the soft green moss of the rocks and straddled him.

Then another time as she was falling from the rainforest treetops like a giggling rainbow, her dazzling display of colors piercing the shades of green and shadow. With a low-throated squawk, she slowed, opened her wings and tail fan, and landed on a large branch a few feet below him. As she folded her wings behind her bare shoulders, she looked up at him in mock dismay.

"Slower than a sloth," she said, her voice husky and out of breath. "I don't think you want to catch me all that badly."

He laughed as he looked into her almond-shaped eyes, filled with amethyst irises and closer together than those of most Silth. He glanced around, checking the dappled places in the vegetation for possible predators. Satisfied, he tucked his own wings, folded in his tail, gripped the branch with his feet, four toes pointing forward and two facing back, and looked at Shra again.

Smaller than Aran, she had pale, cream-colored skin, contrasting dramatically with the red hather sweeping from her forehead to the back of her head and onto her shoulders. Her nose was lean and her cheekbones high, serving as pedestals for her eyes. Her presence always stunned him, no less than if he had flown into a tree trunk. He liked the way she tasted and smelled, the way she played and how naturally it became more than play.

"Heartless, —you know that's your nickname, so don't deny it— you've stolen so many hearts. I was so sure you'd never steal mine. Now what am I to do?" Before he could answer, she took off, soaring out from the trees.

He followed, emerging from the canopy into the morning sun. "You can't see the sunrise until you clear the treetops" was an old Silth saying, repeated to him by his foster mother when she thought he was too distracted by unimportant things. Once over the trees, he glided several feet above Shra, thrilled to be free of the rainforest. He looked down at her, silhouetted against the green rushing past below them. The red hather of her head continued down to a semicircle of first yellow and then blue feathers covering her wings and tail, with another burst of red in the long tail feathers extending down between her legs. Because of the glamour she cast, a Human below merely saw a scarlet macaw parrot. But to Aran she was the most gorgeous Silth in the world. He flew on, bliss and longing in perfect balance.

Sitting alone in the garden, Aran wondered who he was becoming. Would he be like Storng? When they first met, Aran was a fledging student in the shaman city, and Storng was one of his teachers. While not fat, Storng had a heaviness unusual for Silth. Silth bones are light to allow for flight, but Storng's seemed denser somehow. He was about two hundred years old, only middle-aged, and his nickname was Storm Rider because, unlike most Silth, he loved to ride the winds accompanying approaching storms. Storng was a "Changeling," a Silth who at about mid-life became the other sex. It was not a conscious choice, but simply a biological process that a small percentage of Silth went through. The change had no effect on Storng's career as a shaman. When Aran arrived at Amazonia, Storng had been in ascendance—respected by the other shamans, growing his network of harvesters, and continuing to teach with a fiery glee. Then something happened in the next to last year Aran was there. He never learned what. Storng had been his primary teacher for a year, and suddenly he'd changed. The other shamans distanced themselves from him, he spent more time away from the colony, and he seemed less bold. Not long after Aran slipped away, he heard that Storng left Amazonia as well.

Storng now seemed to be a prosperous colony shaman but more cautious than at Amazonia. Aran had no desire to live like that. He'd take his revenge, and after that he wasn't sure what would happen.

A sound from beyond the garden aroused Aran's attention and he walked to the roof edge. He saw the one-eyed Trow hovering like a malignant humming bird outside the room's tall windows, watching the group inside. He moved to another window for a better angle.

Aran gingerly slipped back into the roof's vegetation. Settling among the thicket of palms, he reflected on the "Tiki Crew," as Storng called them. All different colors of hather, the group had been dressed in Hawaiian prints—three males in doll-sized shorts and Aloha shirts, four females in sarongs. The Tiki Crew was one of several similar troops working for Storng and other shamans in North and South America, but this group was the most productive.

Like all shamans, Storng used his crew to "harvest" the items he specified. They also repurposed some of the harvest spoils from their Human uses. According to Storng, they'd spent the last several months completing his list of articles to harvest and modify before his return. Storng had worked with the Tiki Crew at least once each trip around the sun for the past ten. They must not be as young as they seem. Storng said he helped create their homes, including this one in the warehouse district, where the downstairs was used by a drug-dealing outfit who, because of the spells, ignored their upstairs neighbors.

These Silth worked a seasonal rotation. Part of the year they modified harvested items, filling the balance of their time with eating, sleeping, training, fooling around, and partying. When Storng showed up, they'd harvest for four months, sweeping across from the Florida Panhandle, first east and then south toward Miami. On the trip, they'd take things opportunistically. When they arrived in Miami they'd be paid and given a new list of target items, then they'd make their way back north again.

Aran built a small fire from old leaves and twigs scattered around him. He took out a bag of dried and crushed herbs and carefully selected plants, sprinkling some into the flames. The mix had been prepared during a particular alignment of moon and planets. As the flames turned purple, Aran used a large Harpy feather to waft the smoke into his nostrils. Stilling his thoughts, he listened for his heart to speak while in the trance-like state the herbs induced. Sometime later—he could not have said quite how long—he again became aware of his surroundings. He felt calm and in control, but he was confident that Storng was unaware of how much effort such self-control was taking or the grip his recent trauma still had on his thoughts.

Little sound was coming from within the building. Back inside, he found all except Nadara and Storng cleaning up. Heads down, sullen as juveniles, they picked up, straightened, swept, and washed. Across the room Storng and Nadara were talking, in front of what Aran had learned on the ship was a television. Storng waved him over.

"I told you these things are compromising tech," Storng was saying to Nadara. "They contaminate the crew. You'll all end up tech heads."

"You told us we were allowed entertainment." Nadara's sheepish look suggested she knew that was not quite accurate.

"What I said was … you could play music as long as it was from a record. I gave you a record player."

"But those are hard to find. Plus, the record player has to be wound up again after every few records." She paused. "And all it plays are stupid old records."

"Give me a list and I'll get them for you. They're easier to find these days. But what does any of that have to do with bringing in a television?"

Nadara thought for a moment. "Nothing, I guess. We were just bored."

"Get rid of it. I can't use it, and you can't keep it. Nadara, you're responsible for the Tiki Crew's safety."

Aran caught himself staring at Nadara and forced himself to look at Storng. But his eyes were immediately drawn back to her. No contrivance. In fact, the tattoos and piercings seemed calculated to mitigate her glow, the gravity that pulled him.

He followed the two of them to a stacked pile of cardboard boxes, at least a hundred, each a little more than a cubic foot, and Nadara started through an inventory list, Storng interrupting her occasionally with questions. Feeling useless, Aran was pleased when a short, green-hathered Silth with tattooed red markings below her eyes approached, sweeping up the scraps and litter that covered the floor.

She continued sweeping as she whispered, "Aren't you 'Heartless,' the bard out of the Kawran Colony? You told stories in my colony before I came here. I'm Loana."

"I'm an apprentice shaman now," he replied, trying out the statement for the first time. He liked the way it sounded, but he noticed she flinched at the roughness of his new voice.

Unimpressed by his new title, she asked, "You'll sing for us tonight, won't you? It's been so long since I heard a singer. And you'll tell us stories, won't you? I miss stories."

Before Aran could respond, Storng called everyone over to the now-righted communal table. As the Silth stopped their work, Storng waited at the head of the table, gesturing for Aran to sit at an empty seat to his left. Nadara sat to Storng's right, across from Aran. Each Silth seemed to have a specific seat and weaved around one another to reach it. When Storng clapped his hands together, they stopped their murmured conversations to look expectantly at both of them.

"Introductions are in order. Tiki Crew, this is Aran. Aran, meet the Tiki Crew. Specifically … Don, Marina, Vic, Kirstn, Nick, Loana, and Nadara." He gestured to each, who nodded as his or her name was given. "Nadara is the current Chief, Kirstn the previous one. The crew rotates the job every two years. And the position is elected, subject to my approval."

"Aran is my apprentice," he told them. Seeing the green-hathered Silth who had spoken to Aran begin to squirm, he added, "Yes, Loana. He was the bard—"

"Heartless," she breathed, wilting a little as Storng frowned at the interruption.

"Aran will join you on your harvest. And report to Nadara as we travel. But when I assign him shaman tasks, he answers only to me."

The reporting arrangement was news to Aran. He glanced at Nadara, but she was looking down at her plate. Perhaps, he thought, she was still recovering from Storng's teaching session.

"Will he sing for us? Tell us stories?" Kirstn asked.

"That's up to him," Storng's replied.

Aran's answer was instantaneous. "Sorry, no. I don't do that anymore." The looks of dismay called for further explanation. "My voice has been damaged," was all he said.

"Eat, eat," Storng said after a moment, gesturing toward the food.

The table was set with a mix of Silth-made clay plates and bowls, with cups and cutlery from various Human dolls and with thimbles to supplement the cups. The plates in the center were heaped with cooked vegetables—broccoli, Brussels sprouts, and cabbage—cut into small pieces and similarly cut bananas, oranges, and avocados. A big plate of assorted nuts sat in front of Storng.

Aran surveyed the table as the Tiki Crew lunged for the food. Kirstn was sitting beside him. Storng had said she was the prior crew chief, and Aran watched her lead a couple of her tablemates through a story of her own. Her red-hathered head moved along with her hands as she acted out scenes. Next to her, sat Nick, clearly enjoying her tale between frequent trips to the large beer can they had tapped like a keg. He was the largest of the Tiki males, his striking muscles and green hather and bright purple and white wings stood out.

Marina sat laughing opposite Storng at the other end of the table. Aran guessed she was the youngest of the females, and she was talking animatedly to Vic, the youngest male. She matched Nick in number of trips to the beer tap. Without moving his heavily tattooed arms at all, Vic was in the middle of explaining his theory of why Humans pampered some animals and yet were so cruel to others. As best Aran could pick up from where he was, Vic believed that some Humans only responded to other species when they got some direct benefit from them, but he was having trouble working cats into his theory.

Loana was following Kirstn's story across the table. She leaned forward with hands folded in rapt attention and periodically shouted with delight as the story took some unexpected twist. Don, next to her, would sometimes lean back into her as though reassuring himself of her presence, while he talked with Storng over the top of the still subdued Nadara. Don's booming voice was challenging Storng on some point that Aran was having trouble following, but he knew they were disagreeing from the vigor with which Don was shaking his yellow spiked hather. As the beer flowed, the room volume increased.

His study of the table worked its way to Nadara, who looked up from her plate at him. His breath and pulse quickened. Smiling, appearing very aware of her effect on him, she leaned forward and laid her hand on his. Don and Storng continued their argument over her head, but Aran was only aware of Nadara's eyes. Because Silth could, within limits, look however they wanted, other factors caused individuals to be deeply attracted to one another. Male or female or neither was a choice of projection by each individual, though they could not change their actual physical form beneath the glamour. Because there was no pregnancy, there were few social constraints on sex. In this period of his life, Aran mostly liked and attracted females, though that could change over the course of a very long life.

"How'd you go from storyteller to shaman?" she asked, and he was disappointed when she slid her hand back into her lap.

"I trained to be a shaman for ten trips around the sun before I decided to become a storyteller."

Her eyebrows shot up. He closed his eyes. He knew the question of why he'd stopped his training would follow, and he was unequipped to discuss it. He definitely didn't want to talk about why he'd returned to training.

He sighed and stood up abruptly. Mumbling, "It's been a long day," his tongue seemed disconnected from his brain. He managed a "good night" to the others, nodding to Storng, who'd risen with a quizzical look.

Making his way to the hammocks, he flew up, lay with his back to the room, and thought about Nadara's questions. Why had he left Amazonia? As he neared completion of his studies, he felt confident that the life of a shaman would fail to satisfy him. But the life of a storyteller had been no more satisfying whether drunk or sober. He'd been sure that life with Shra would calm the roiling waters of his spirit. But if he was honest with himself, he still had doubts.

Why had he become a shaman now? To seek revenge. And then what? The life of a shaman had no more appeal to him now than it did ten sun trips ago. He ached for some important calling, something that compelled him, something that invoked passion. But as he searched deep inside, only the beacon of revenge burned in the darkness.

He lay in his hammock, half awake. His sadness was no longer paralyzing, but his anger was the same as it had been when Storng suggested that he return to his shaman training.

Aran and Storng sat atop the crane of a fully loaded container ship. Docked at what Storng said was Puerto Limon, Costa Rica, it was readying to leave with its cargo of green bananas and ripening fruit. Containers stacked eight and sometimes nine high towered more than fifty feet above deck.

After a week of sleeping in a kind of twilight, he'd recovered enough strength to wake up each morning, disappointed that he survived the night. Every morning his first thought was of Shra. Some small gesture—the way she moved her hands when she spoke, how she gave a smile that seemed just a fraction too big and then drew him to it like a bee to a flower. The feel of her embrace, left from a dream he could not remember, faded as his next thought was that she was no longer there. In the second week, he had numbly begun to eat a little and sleep-walk through the empty days.

Three days earlier he had vowed to kill Cowboy, Quaker, and the rest of the poachers.

He watched the activity on the dock and ship's deck below. "I can't stop thinking about her. And I don't want to. I want to hold her in my mind as I kill Humans." His voice was raspy, even harsher than Storng's. The side effect of his near-death use of magical energy had not worn off during his recovery—he would not be a singer any more.

"There are many Humans," Storng said, juggling several seeds without looking at either them or his hands. "And while I know you don't want to hear this right now, many kinds of them exist, just like many types of Silth do. Good and evil, but mostly a mix."

"Silth don't commit evil like Humans."

"Your experience is limited, fledgling. Trust me when I say you're wrong. The only reliably evil creatures are Faeries, and even their evil has varying shades." Storng stopped juggling and cocked his head. "Jaguars kill Silth. Pythons kill Silth. Toucans kill baby Silth. Are they all evil?" When Aran failed to reply, Storng admitted, "Well, the toucans might be." After a pause, he added, "The sun shines equally on the good and the evil."

As the sun beat down on their backs. Aran leaned against a crossbar. The humidity was still high here, but nothing like the stifling, steamy heat deep in the rainforest. For that he was grateful.

"What will you do now?" Storng asked.

He shrugged. "Once again, I'm in the wind."

"You can take up your shaman studies again."

Aran's lips parted in surprise. "You'd teach me again? I thought once someone quit the training they could never return."

"That's just what fledglings are told to keep them serious about the program. No such rule exists. You can't return to Amazonia, and consequently you'll never be on the Shaman Council. But nothing stops you from being a shaman and living in a colony."

"I failed before," Aran said flatly. "Other than trying to save Shra, I haven't used anything that I learned in Amazonia since the day I left. I haven't really thought about it." He hesitated, then, "The first eight trips around the sun after I left were a blur of stories, singing, playing music, and parties—one huge, never-ending party. Then one morning, it wasn't any fun anymore.

"I performed, but there was no meat, no life—just the bones. Then I met Shra. I performed for her."

Storng said, "Time will heal this wound but the scar will always be there. The challenge is how to go on. Training will distract you for a time. Then you can decide where you fly next."

"But a shaman goes among Humans. I only want to hurt them. How can I be a shaman?"

"This problem will resolve itself. You can use the power of the shaman to protect yourself and others, but if you kill Humans, you can no longer be a shaman. We can finish your training on this ship as it travels. Then you'll apprentice with me for a season and after that ... well, there are many paths."

The breeze picked up for a moment, dowsing them with the smells of gasoline and seaweed. Gull cries merged with the sound of forklifts, cranes, and occasional shouts of the men and women loading the ships. The breeze caused the three small harpy eagle feathers in Storng's headband to dance merrily and the many-pocketed baby alpaca cloak he wore to snap and buck.

"How do you know where this ship's going?" Aran asked.

"The knowledge of shamans will be open to you only if you are studying it," Storng rumbled, spreading his arms and wings in a grand gesture.

Aran stared out at the water. "If I agree to this, what I do as a shaman is up to me?"

Storng blew out a long breath. "There are a few restrictions, fledgling. No colony except Kawran can have more than one shaman. You mustn't live next to Human technology. Things like that."

"You said there were no rules, and nobody to enforce them if there were."

"To study you must listen better, monkey brain. There's no rule against taking a student back, and no Silth can stop a shaman from doing so. However, many rules govern shamans, and there are several . . . enforcers. There're those of your sponsoring colony. For some other rules, the shamans band together to enforce them through the Shaman Council. And still others the Faeries will enforce, their ultimate punishment being the shaman's death."

"Great encouragement."

Storng laughed mirthlessly. "This ship leaves in a couple of hours. You coming?"

Aran fingered Shra's bracelet, thinking about what he could do with the powers of a shaman. If using them would allow him to avenge her death, he didn't care about the costs. He hadn't thought about using

*shaman powers since leaving Amazonia, and he realized he'd been
carrying a box he'd been afraid to open. "I don't see why not."*

CHAPTER TWO

Scene 1

FAELEN (TROW)

"Why here?" Faelen lay on his back in the rainforest litter, looking up at the two Trow standing over him. He shifted to escape the stick poking him in the back.

Fod used his good eye to read, "Faelen, disgraced general of the King's army, you are officially exiled from the Land for a period no less than one hundred of the years in this world."

Faelen studied the burn scars mangling much of Fod's face. Otherwise he resembled any other Trow—whip-thin, pale-skinned with long fingers and sharp features. His hair, the color of rotten walnuts, hung to the shoulders of his uniform, and, even standing over Faelen, he smelled of sweat and salt water. Faelen looked down at his own torn and dirty clothes. Probably does not smell as bad as I do. Fod was one of the Trow who had trouble holding his glamour in this world. He could hide his face, particularly his burns, but he could not establish a consistent height and shape. He had given up for the moment and appeared in his unaltered form.

Fod solemnly continued. "You are prohibited from alcohol and the manipulation of species, especially parrots. If you violate this prohibition, your time here will be extended." He folded the paper, slipped it into his uniform pocket, and stepped back.

"Fod, you are a stupid sack of elbows."

Although Fod's expression did not change, his jawline quivered slightly. Faelen looked up at the other Trow. "Why bring me here, Thest? There is neither decent alcohol nor parrots in the Land. Should you not ban me from the Earth rather than to it?"

Thest was tall, lean but muscular, towering over Faelen with ramrod straight posture, he had remained silent and unreadable. His ash-blonde dreadlocks seemed resistant to the breeze blowing across them. Slowly he lowered his gaze and fixed Faelen with shark-like, unblinking grey eyes.

"You have missed the point. Everyone knows you will not be able to conform to the terms of the exile. Your stay here will be permanent." Thest fingered his necklace, a leather thong with a jade stone formed in the Trow symbol for strength. "Specifically, in this region, since the Paerries leading to your current state are located here. The area is also near to one of the remaining portals, making it easy to monitor you. You can move elsewhere should you desire, but I doubt you have that much initiative."

Faelen responded to Fod's chuckle with, "You forest fairy. The trees are smarter than you. A conversation with any mountain burro is more stimulating."

"Kick him, Lord Thest?"

Faelen snorted. "Lord Thest? Lord of what? Did you tell him to call you that? You have no noble rank in the Land, General Thest. Is this an Earth affectation?"

On Thest's quick nod, Fod kicked him, first in the stomach, knocking the wind from him, and then in the ribs.

"The end has come to you for such sharp-tongued ways. You, born to high station in the Land, have squandered your inheritance, wasted your training, alienated your friends and family ….." As Thest went on, Faelen no longer listened—instead, he watched a flock of amazon green parrots sail across the canopy opening.

Thest spotted the parrots and grimaced. "And that will no longer be tolerated. You have fathered half the existing plague of Paerries. Drink and you stay in this world. Inflict more Paerries on us, and worse punishments than exile await you."

"Like having to listen longer to you?"

"I have no time to be your jailer. Your sun will set soon. I must attend to more important things. Fod, come."

Thest flickered like a light with a loose connection and noiselessly disappeared. Fod bared his teeth at Faelen in a version of a smile and kicked him in the face before he too flickered out of view.

Faelen stayed sprawled on the ground. His ribs ached, and he knew his face would as well when he could feel it again. He rolled to his side and vomited on the forest floor. When finished, he slid further from the stench and lay listening as forest sounds re-emerged.

He crawled to a puddle, tore off a piece of his shirt, and wet it. Eyeing his reflection, he dabbed at the blood on his swollen face. The cut would add yet another scar, not that it mattered. At one time his mother had called him handsome, but he doubted she would now. Even before Fod's gentle goodbye, Faelen's eyes were surrounded by dark rings, and his skin had passed beyond Trow pale to fish-belly white. His hair hung in greasy tangles. The high Trow cheeks were sharp enough to cut, the facial evidence of his skeletal frame. *When did I eat last?*

As the light faded and the sounds of the night frogs arose, he pulled a small, cobalt-blue glass bottle from his pocket, propped himself up on one elbow, and took two long pulls, ridding his mouth of the aftertaste of blood and vomit. He slipped the bottle back into his pocket and patted it. Its presence confirmed what Thest had said— they had not bothered to search him because they knew he would keep drinking. He flopped back down in a clear space beneath a huge tree, hands clasped behind his head.

The alcohol dulled the pain, but he had not consumed enough to forget what he had lost. Who he had let down. How he hated himself for his weaknesses, but he hated them more. Them? Who was them? The best anesthetic for self-loathing was alcohol, he thought, reaching back to his pocket.

He would figure out his life tomorrow.

Scene 2

THEST (TROW)

Thest stepped into the entrance garden of his countryside villa on the outskirts of Trembor. The two-story building was vine-covered, the woods enveloping the grounds to its back, and hilly fields spreading out to the front. Thest always found the colors shocking when he returned from Earth. Fields were a vibrant purple, vines an iridescent yellow, and trees black.

Trembor now served as the capital of the Land, the Trow home world. Upon his return from his centuries on Earth, Xafar had sacked the old capital, overthrowing Queen Arianihod and her court, and declared himself King. Trembor also was the location of the two remaining portals to Earth, so Xafar could easily control them from here.

Thest headed through the large open door and down a hallway, emerging in a central courtyard. A fountain burbled in one corner next to a large, stone table covered with loaves of fresh breads, cheeses, cured meats, jams, and chutneys. Fruit was piled in a heap next to smoked fishes and vegetable plates. Demist was eating lunch at a rough-hewn wood table in the nearby shade, three barefoot Humans hovering close by to attend to her needs. She did not look up at the thump of Thest's boots on the stones.

At the fountain, he removed his uniform jacket, shirt, and boots. Trow slaves rushed up to take the items and replace them with a comfortable silk tunic and soft slippers. He carefully went through the ritual of washing his face, hands, and arms with the cool, clear water. No one spoke.

As Thest filled his plate with mounds of food, he glanced at Demist. Even as she ate, essentially alone in her house, she held herself erect, oval face relaxed, every movement fluid, easy, and quick. She was always the same whether on or off the battlefield.

"Your morning?" she asked, with a neutrality giving him no clue as to her mood or what traps the morning would hold.

"A waste of my time, exiling the pervert Faelen and listening to Fod's report on one of the Paerrie shamans. Storng has taken on a new student named Aran. I have had his previous students killed. Most likely I will have to do the same with this one."

As she turned to look at him, thick auburn hair tumbled over her shoulder onto her green gossamer tunic. She favored greens matching her eyes. "You usually know your Paerrie victims' names?"

"I know this one because I have listened to him. He was a singer and storyteller before becoming Storng's student. But something has happened to his voice, and he has been contaminated by Storng."

"Now you will kill him?"

"Most likely. Also, I surveyed the arrangements in the Northeast."

Her brows shot up. "You do not trust that I have the Northeast under control?"

He slowly chewed and swallowed a mouthful before answering. "Of course I do. But I am responsible. So, I must at least check."

"You are taking too long. The Human hold on the Earth has grown tenuous by its own design. It is time. We are ready."

He could tell she was irritated by his inspection of her preparations, but he was in no mood for her criticism. "What do you know of ready?" he spat out. "Your small piece may be, but that one piece will not end the time of Humans. Many prior efforts have failed because of such impatience." He slammed his plate on the table, sloshing food and juices, and sat beside her, shooing away the slaves rushing over to clean up the mess.

"My part is ready," she said, her voice soothing. "But increasingly vulnerable to being discovered. Today I arranged for the military to discover oil and gas around the site. They have locked it down and no longer allow anyone near. I am ready for a new sector. Let me do the Northwest."

She laid her hand on his to calm him, and long nails gently raked his wrist. He pulled his hand away.

"I have the Northwest covered. It is more complicated than the others and takes more time."

"It simply takes harder decisions than you are making," she scoffed. "I am sure because you have so many other important things to do."

He pushed his half-eaten plate aside, spilling more food, and shoved up from his chair. "If this is how you think you get your way, you are mistaken." He stalked from the table, shoving a slave out of his way.

"Stay," she called out, and he hesitated in the doorway. "Sit. I will tell you about how your children are doing."

He did not wish to be alone, and he drew in a breath. One slave was already putting a newly-filled plate and glass at Thest's place. As he rejoined Demist, he ran his hand down her hair and along the curve of her throat before resuming his seat. He marveled a moment at her unscarred, flawless skin. She was a veteran of countless Trow wars that she fought without armor, wearing costumes often distracting her opponents, to their fatal dismay. She was smart, fast and deadly. They had met fighting side by side in one of those battles.

Demist smiled. She told him of the last several weeks on Earth. Despite the warnings of the Trow physicians, she spent every moment she could there. She preferred its wild places to the second-tier social events they attended in the Land, even though she was the one who made them attend. Left to his own choices, Thest would never go. She filled her unused time running with mustangs on the plains, flying with condors high in the Andes, and confronting a bear in the ruins of Chernobyl. She laughed as she told him the stories. The good mood continued as she caught him up on the status of their three children—an older son finishing his many years of schooling now beginning to make his way in Trow society, a daughter, with her mother's competency, who worked far from Trembor, and a young son away at a boarding school.

When her stream of stories finally ran dry, the two overlapping suns of the Land were high in the morning sky. Her smile vanished, and her eyes met Thest's. "If we fail, we will lose all."

"There is no security ... only opportunity."

"You know I hate it when you quote Earth generals."

Scene 3

THEST (SILTH)

A few hours later, Thest walked briskly from his home toward Trembor, through simple, unadorned villas drawing their meager beauty from surrounding parks, grape arbors, and olive trees. All that could be said for the Earth-drawn landscape was that it was preferable to the Land's own stark natural vegetation. As he got closer to the capital, the vegetation was more local, as though it might be an affront to the capital to surround it with plants from a foreign world.

Near the palace, the landscape gave way to the organic curves and spires of city buildings. The palace itself looked like the half-finished work of a madman. The architect had started with a grand vision for the palace but became so protective of it that he ignored the King's suggestions. Some thought Xafar had encased the architect in a wall while keeping him alive, but Thest knew this was not the case. He personally had ushered the architect to his eternal venue.

Dressed in even more formal military clothes than before, he chaffed under the stiffness of the stand-up collar and the heat of the official hat, its cascade of parrot feathers falling to the center of his back. As he entered the enormous entry hall, even he registered the intimidation it had been designed to elicit. Trow guards, wearing uniforms of quilted armor and loosely holding spears of tree roots shined to a high gloss, flanked the hand-carved wood door to the King's chamber at the opposite end.

"Thest," he said as he stopped in front of them. The guards

neither moved nor acknowledged him.

His announcement was simply part of the formalities, as his presence and identification had been known the moment he stepped onto the palace grounds. Runners, typically trustworthy Trow or Human slaves, moved through the tunnels and hidden passageways of the palace, taking information to where it was needed. With neither mechanical technology nor magic to rely upon, solutions in the Land almost always were biologically based. Even passage to Earth, the only place the Trow had magic powers, was courtesy of a fungus that grew in the Land's caverns, turning them into portals to other dimensions.

While he waited, he tried to keep his mind neutral. The doorway and passage to the King's chambers was a living creature that harvested mental energy from those passing through and, as a by-product, read their thoughts. The creature's brain was tethered to Xafar's. Ostensibly for security, the mind-reading passage had saved Xafar from at least two attempts on his life—more typically the King used it to determine the loyalty and confidence of supplicants and functionaries.

Shifting from at-ease to attention, the guards drew their spears tightly to their sides. The spears also were biologically based, with a type of electric eel conscripted into painful service to power them and create an energy blast that could make Thest's eyes explode.

He walked between the guards and kept his mind carefully composed. Just inside the door was a fountain that fed a trough of green water. He completed the ritual of washing his face, arms, and hands, then inspected his uniform to ensure that no part of it was from Earth. One of the many rules during an audience with Xafar was that no trace of Human industrial products would be present. He opened the door to the King's chamber, still keeping his mind blank.

King Xafar turned from the window and laughed. "Thest! You spoil my fun when you know the nature of my doorway and do such a good job hiding your thoughts."

"I have no thoughts to hide, my King."

"It would be an insult to the King to suggest he has a general with no thoughts, so I will assume you put the emphasis on the 'to hide'."

"Of course, Majesty." Thest tipped his head deferentially.

"Such lovely bullshit."

Xafar had been on Earth for several centuries, but much of his slang was from the '40's and '50's, the last years he had spent there. Because the doorway only read thoughts during transit, not once someone was in the room, Thest could allow his mind to temporarily roil at the horror of the King and his chambers.

While most Trow appreciated understated beauty, Xafar reveled in coarseness. His cloak was the tanned skin of Humans, his head shaved, his face tattooed and pierced. His wild eyes, the color of mud, dilated and constricted based on his mood. He wore a necklace of polished bones, the index fingers of his enemies' first-born children.

No jewels, precious metals, crystal, or fine woven clothes were present in the King's chamber. The chandelier was made from the bones of the queen he had defeated, her head grotesquely set in its center. At one end of the room, a simple wooden throne sat on a dais several feet above the floor. At the other was a massive rough-hewn table surrounded by chairs that looked too heavy to move. The rest of the large room was empty.

Four other passages exited the room. One without a door went back into the royal quarters where the Queen and the King's consorts lived. A door led to the gallery of artists. There bards composed songs of the King's battles, painters depicted key scenes from his life, writers told his tales, and sculptors created the many busts that every wise Trow displayed prominently in their home or business. Servants came and went through another door. The last one accessed the working part of the palace—the King's ministers and all the functionaries required to manage a kingdom, the dungeons, and the Room of the Advisors. Thest had been told that the King had over a hundred advisors working night and day to plan for the Land's future and anticipate challenges to Xafar's authority. They ran a network of spies and informers that reached everywhere, but because they themselves were never allowed to leave the palace, Thest feared this room the most.

A scream echoed throughout the chamber, and Thest wondered whether it came from a Human or Trow. When Xafar waved his hand, the scream stopped, replaced by low moans and the quick intakes of air that accompany expectations of pain. Thest had never figured out if the sound effects of the King's chamber were real or feigned, but in either case they were theater with a purpose. *It will be that kind of meeting.*

He brought his thoughts back under control. "You summoned me?"

Xafar studied him briefly, then, "Thest, my one true treasure. I count on you to rid the Earth of Human magic."

Thest nodded his acknowledgment to prelude.

"But even treasure can lose its luster." Xafar looked out the window again. "I want to return to Earth. To fly. Have powers. Hear the sun rise. Smell magnetic storms. I need to travel from mountaintop to sea bottom. To escape the utter monotony that is the Land. I can no longer tolerate Human interference. Because of them, I cannot even touch the Earth's surface without my skin smoldering. They have driven us out and no longer even recall our existence. They think our vermin, our 'rats and cockroaches,' are 'fairies'—the ultimate insult. Are you the general who will rid me of these pests? Are you a warrior Trow, or have I made a mistake and put a flower fairy in charge of my troops?"

"Majesty, I move as quickly as I can. The East is ready. North and South will be ready within a Trow week. The West is underway."

"Underway?" Xafar settled himself on the throne and leaned forward, looking down at Thest with suddenly dilated eyes. The moaning rose in volume, and the aqua-colored room darkened to blackish-green. The meager light from the window disappeared. "Underway. Are we a month away from completion? A year?"

Within the noise of the moans, Thest heard something familiar. He froze, ignoring Xafar and listening with every molecule of his being. There. Faint, but unmistakable—his older son Hepler, softly talking to someone, but not in pain. Is this a trick? A few hours ago, Demist had said Hepler was still at school in Tantar, far to the north.

"A year to finish putting things in place in the West," he managed to say. The shock of having heard Hepler's voice caused him to blurt out, "Provided that there are no … distractions."

"Distractions?" Xafar did not look at him but instead studied a nearby tapestry. "You mean my son Faelen? You find dealing with him beneath you?"

Now twice as loud, the moaning made it difficult for Thest to concentrate. He listened again for Hepler. A quick shout was followed by a scream from nearby, and he suspected it emanated from his predecessor. Thest's promotion had occurred when the prior general failed to return from this sort of meeting. In the space below the high ceiling, red lightning bolts began to shimmer noiselessly. Xafar fingered his grisly necklace, and Thest's mouth went dry at the madness swirling in the King's eyes.

Thest swallowed hard and lied. "No, I did not speak clearly. I meant that dealing with Paerrie affairs distracts me from my bigger undertaking. It would be easier just to wipe them out."

"Of course that is what you meant." Xafar's fingers curled into fists. "First, let me remind you that it is a rare honor to be asked to assist in the King's affairs."

"Certainly, my—"

"Do not interrupt," Xafar snapped, as the moans broke into crying and another scream pierced the room. "Second, let me also advise you that more than lands and title will be forfeit should you fail me," he shouted above the painful din.

Thest's lips parted slightly at the sight of blood flowing from Xafar's hands—in his anger, the King's fingernails had pierced his palms. Xafar seemed oblivious, but Thest was hypnotized by the blood dripping onto the King's floor. He forced himself to meet Xafar's eyes.

"A price must be paid on the Earth," Xafar went on, "for every Paerrie death by Trow hand. The ebb and flow of magics there are already dangerously out of balance, creating pain when we are in a place once beloved to us. The extinction of Paerries caused directly by us could cause the Earth to respond to us as an outside predator. My advisors say this may prompt the release of psychic toxins designed to disrupt organizational ability. We believe Humans have already paid this price for their destruction of species. No, Paerries must be disposed of indirectly, along with the Humans. I have plans I do not share with you. While you were indeed by my side when I took this throne—I took this throne. And I know how to retake the Earth."

"I regret causing you to think I question your wisdom. Just frustration showing."

As Thest lowered his head in a bow of supplication, every sound in the room ceased except for Hepler's voice, sounding normal and oblivious to danger. The room brightened, returning to its original color. Light flowed in through the window, and the lightning vanished. As he wiped his bloody hands on his thighs, the madness drained from Xafar's eyes. Several moments passed and Hepler's voice faded.

Xafar whispered, "Are you my general? Are you my warrior?"
"Yes."

"One Earth year. If in that time you have failed to begin the final stage, another will be general. And you will be FUBAR. You know this term?" he asked without waiting for an answer. "In the meantime, your son has had the good fortune to qualify for training here at the palace with the children of my court. It is a high honor. He will be done in a year. The nature of his graduation will be up to you."

As he left, Thest knew Xafar was listening to his thoughts, and he made sure all centered on his determination to succeed. Most Trow misunderstood the corridor, Xafar once had told him–it was far more important to know what someone was thinking when leaving than entering the room. Not until he was far down the corridor did he allow himself to exhale loudly, lean against a column, and wipe sweaty hands on his tunic. His King was unstable and dangerous. As he recalled an Earth expression— "crazy as a sack of eels."

How would he restrain Demist when she heard about Hepler?

She would lay siege to the palace.

CHAPTER THREE

Scene 1

Brophy (Human)

The four parked Brophy's truck along the dirt road, out of sight of the work area. They made their way through the rainforest to the broken edge where the clearing around the buildings began. They paused, with the big yellow earth-moving machines between the structures and themselves.

In the advance literature, the developer called the new development an "eco-resort." Brophy was sure that label would make up for the old growth trees cut down to create its sprawling grounds. Not washing their guests' towels each day would be of great comfort to the displaced wildlife. The white-lipped peccary had disappeared from Costa Rica, and the harpy eagle and great green macaw were soon to follow. The jaguar and Baird's tapir were hanging on by a thread. Pissed off at death and destruction for recreational purposes, Brophy, Juan, Chilen, and Joss decided to do something about it.

Much discussion, disagreement, and negotiation took place before they finally settled on a plan. Juan had just finished reading and was inspired by The Monkeywrench Gang, a tale of eco-intervention, so he had been eager. Brophy had been the one who talked Joss into it. He was there mostly to impress her. She cared so much about saving the rainforest and its animals. While he cared as well, normally he would have shrugged and gone back to surfing. Now he wondered if he'd made a mistake bringing her. In the truck on the way over, she sounded so conflicted about their intentions.

He slid a look at her, silhouetted in the light from the security poles. She had pulled her honey-brown hair, which normally grazed her shoulders, into a tight ponytail, and the lighting made her pale, freckled skin almost alabaster. Her petite frame—at five feet four inches, the top of her head barely reached his shoulder—moved back into the darkness. She wore a black hoodie and jeans. He'd convinced her to remove the gold hoop earrings, saying they'd catch the light or snag on branches.

She had been the hardest to persuade that they should take this particular course and had insisted they not sabotage the construction equipment. That would have been a lot easier, since it was near the road, but she said it would just hurt the local contractor and his insurance company. If they were going to do something, it needed to impact the developer directly. Brophy knew she was right, but what they'd decided on was a lot harder than putting sand in some gas tanks.

Brophy couldn't figure Joss out. She was passionate about the rainforest—that he knew. She banned liquor and drugs from the biology station where she lived, and when they'd gotten her to go dancing, she drank fruit juice or tonic water and lime. But put her on the dance floor with a salsa tune? Magic. Her energy swept up the room, her laughter infecting all around her. She dressed in baggy, conservative clothing but always with some small, feminine quirk. Like tonight—she was wearing pink and blue fingernail polish, on a "monkey wrench" raid.

When Juan held up a hand, they all froze. *He's acting like we're in a war movie,* Brophy thought, shaking his head. He'd known Juan since high school. Neither had run with the normal cliques of jocks, nerds, goths, or rich kids, and they shared the bond of outsiders. Juan was more socially aware and knew the edgy music, the other outsiders, and the interesting things to do. Juan had family in Costa Rica, so after graduation, he and Brophy headed down to surf, hang out at volcanoes, and smoke weed. Any accomplishments since had been accidental.

Juan had no trouble picking up girls for both of them with his surfer dude good looks. He had jet-black hair straight down to his shoulders, a square chin, and light coffee-colored skin. He was shirtless tonight, showing off the muscles that came to him effortlessly. Brophy was thankful Joss appeared indifferent to Juan's good looks. Maybe her type was Juan's polar opposite, namely him. He ran his hand over his newly-shaven head, realizing she had commented neither on it nor the hipster beard and mustache he'd grown since she saw him last.

He noticed that Chilen was locked on Juan's every move. They'd met Chilen on the surf beach, and he'd attached himself to Juan like a remora to a shark. Chilen rarely talked of his past, and Brophy didn't even know his real name. For tonight, Chilen had blackened his doughy cheeks and was wearing camo, and it definitely was hard to pick him out moving along the forest edge.

As Brophy moved up beside Joss, her perfume caused his brain to seize up. Who wore perfume on a guerilla raid? Not that he cared— he just breathed it in and idled. He still was uncertain as to why she'd agreed to come. Was she bored? Interested in him? Or just exploring who she was?

They'd met at a Vegan Festival, where they shared a picnic table with six other strangers. When she saw "MEAT IS DEATH" tattooed on his forearm, she mused aloud if that meant he'd tattooed death on death. After a few confused moments, he figured it out and answered, "Only a philosophy major would say something like that." As it turned out, she was a psychology major, but the conversation had led to others. While she accepted his invitations, she maintained a friendly distance. He hoped that the night's shared adventure would change their status to "more than friends."

Juan signaled, and Chilen unnecessarily mimicked the signal for them to move forward. They were even with the buildings and ready to send the developer a message that her company, Paradise Found, was unwelcome. Thomasina Rojay had been in the news a lot lately. She raved about how Paradise Found would provide jobs for the locals, her plans to buy crafts and products from the local villages, and how the tourists would pump money into the local economy so kids could stay in the towns where they grew up instead of moving to the city. These were all good things, but every developer promised them, and mostly they never happened or at least not the way described. The jobs were primarily low-paying ones making beds and cooking breakfasts. The local villages didn't make the items tourists wanted to buy, so most of the "crafts" came from factories in the city. The life of hustling for tourists had little appeal for teenagers bound for those jobs in the city.

Even if all Rojay promised was possible, she'd achieve it by taking another chunk out of an already too small habitat, interrupting another set of migration and hunting patterns. The local environmentalists had begged her to redevelop one of the many failed ecolodges already there instead of fragmenting the forest further with a big new road that would inflict new carnage on the region's native wildlife.

Brophy realized he was repeating to himself Joss's arguments for the need to take some type of action. He might not be as clear on the details for "why," but he knew how to make things happen. Before coming to Costa Rica to surf, he'd been living in the States, part of the time in Baltimore where he organized tagging and street art events. He knew how to get a group into place, avoid the police, have contingency plans, and most of all, get the work done. Even when he'd gone to California to earn money harvesting weed, he learned how to complete a job. The growers had a minimum daily harvest. If you got "happy" and failed to meet your quota, you didn't get paid that night.

Back when Rojay's project was up for approval, Juan had debated her on a local television program. He argued that the damage she was causing was unnecessary, and she rebutted that the country couldn't afford to create habitat reserves on all private property, that habitat would only be preserved if owners figured out how to monetize the wildlife. That was what it came down to—the continued existence of wildlife would be allowed only if translated into currency.

The two gasoline containers Brophy was carrying sloshed when he set them down too quickly. Juan gave him the stink eye, and Brophy glared back. Juan and Chilen also carried cans, while Joss had a dozen flares tucked inside a small canvas backpack.

They weaved among the buildings, most covered in fake thatch roofs with porches built from trees that once stood on the property. Although the outer wood was chemically treated to withstand termites and resist fires, inside the buildings were untreated two-by-fours and finishes. The trick was to start the fire inside, where it had ample time to burn before being seen. Pull that off in multiple buildings without using sophisticated timers. Avoid being spotted by the guards. And … get away.

Fortunately, the guards were in their own shack, located near the back of the property. During his prior reconnaissance, Brophy had found that was where they stayed most of the time. Like with all the other resorts, the guards were there to keep stuff from being stolen, and no one had thought to protect against vandalism in the middle of the rainforest.

Each of the guys was responsible for two buildings. Because Joss refused to torch any buildings, her assignment was to distribute the flares and keep lookout for the guards. When Juan had mentioned he might bring along his pistol, she got right up in his face saying, "Then you do this without me." The pistol had stayed behind—or at least Brophy was pretty sure it had.

As he stood outside the first building, Brophy hesitated. He was hoping for a triumphant guerilla mission, the excitement of which would create a bond with Joss, but if things went south, she'd hold him completely responsible. If she'd only come because she liked him, he'd probably screwed everything up.

According to the building plans filed with the regional office, his first building was a dining hall. Once inside, he sloshed one full container of gasoline around the hall and side rooms before moving on to a residential building. He splashed there as far as his gasoline would take him.

Joss appeared beside him, holding his flares. Instead of handing them to him, she put them behind her back, gnawing at her lip. "Brophy, this feels wrong."

"I know," he agreed. "But somebody has to stand up somewhere."

"I'm not sure I think this is 'standing up.'"

"We've talked it to death. And it's too late to back out now." He reached behind her and gently took the flares. "Thanks. You better go."

The plan was for each person to light his first flare, drop it and return to his first building, toss the next flare, and race for the tree line. If no one had seen them, they would head straight to the truck. But if someone was in pursuit, they'd haul butt toward another road a few miles away, then double back to the truck.

Now that everything was about to go down, he felt a shiver of fear. Too committed to worry now, he told himself.

He looked at his watch. It was time. On the way there, they made a big show of stopping to "synchronize their watches" just like in the movies, so all would ignite their fires simultaneously. But he was the only one who actually wore a watch—the rest pulled out cell phones and looked at their screens. Not nearly as cool.

When he lit the flare and tossed it against the gasoline-soaked wall, the whoosh was louder than he expected. The heat punched him hard. He whirled and tore through the doorway for his other building, where he lit another flare and flung it into the room. The ignition noise was even louder, the blaze larger than before. His feet felt rooted to the floor, and he couldn't seem to look away until heat and smoke rushed toward him, forcing him out. His eyes had trouble adjusting to the darkness when he got outside. He paused, blinked rapidly, and saw orange glows already evident in the other buildings.

Rounding the corner of the last building between him and the tree line, he ran straight into a guard. They bounced off one another and both hit the ground hard. Brophy turtled on the ground trying to catch his breath, while the guard landed face down but recovered faster. He pushed to his feet and shakily tried to pull his gun from his holster.

Brophy gasped, thinking I'm toast, but still unable to move. The guard freed the gun from the holster and aimed it at him. And …

crumpled. Chilen was standing behind where the guard had been and grinned as he tossed the two-by-four board on the ground.

"Come on, quit lazing around." Chilen grabbed Brophy's hand and yanked him to his feet.

As they ran, flames shot through the roofs of buildings and shouts multiplied in the compound. Brophy could see his shadow as he crossed the open area between the buildings and the edge of the trees, so he knew he could be seen by the guards. The four bolted for the trees, Brophy sucking in air and trying not to cough as the smoke swirled around them. Chilen was faster and had caught up with Joss well ahead of Brophy.

The shout behind him confirmed what he had feared. "Mira! Allie estan!"

Another shout. "Jose's down. El esta herido!"

Brophy heard a gunshot, and the fallen tree three feet to his right exploded, sending splinters into his right leg. It hurt, but not that much worse than hitting the fire coral on a wave gone wrong. Through the orange-lit smoke, he could just make out the others ahead of him. More shots rang out, and he saw Juan spin and fall, holding his shoulder. His breath coming out in ragged gasps, Brophy kept running. Joss and Chilin picked Juan up and dragged him into the trees.

Brophy cut left so the shots coming after him wouldn't be directed toward the others. He made it to the edge of the jungle just as another bullet hit a tree, embedding more splinters in his face. He heard crashing in the distance and realized the others were aiming for the truck. They must've decided that with Juan wounded, "the run through the forest," as they'd called it in the contingency plan, was no longer an option. Brophy knew the guards would figure out their path and intercept them by heading down the road from the buildings. His friends would never make it.

He stepped back out of the trees into the light cast by the fires and ran along the tree line, trying not to limp. His leg burned like crazy. Surprisingly his face didn't hurt, but every so often he had to use his shirt sleeve to wipe away blood running into his right eye. The guards spotted him, letting loose with even more Spanish curses. The majority of shots seemed to be going wide because none were hitting around him. He kept running as hard as he could, lungs starting to ache, leading the guards away from the rest of them.

At the edge of the clearing, a path led into the forest, and he stumbled onto it. Register the terrain, he told himself. Jump this log. Dodge that branch. Before long he had to stop—the light was too poor for him to safely manage the path, and the wall of darkness intimidated him. He doubled over panting, pulled a small LED flashlight from his pocket, and pushed on, hoping he was far enough ahead to avoid being seen. Maybe the guards were fat, middle-aged, and out of shape. He could hope, anyway. He ran ten miles daily, so he was confident of his ability to move quickly. Although the sprint left him breathless, his pace through the trees was not that difficult, especially now that he could see more clearly. Adrenaline must have kicked in, lessening his leg pain.

Prior to the mission, the group had memorized the main trails to the road. Brophy had a small flash of pride that his planning was paying off. *This one will meet up with a wider trail in a few hundred feet. Then I can really get my speed up.* He hoped the others would figure it out and pick him up at the other road. If not, he was in for a long, dangerous haul. The guards would have called the police, and eventually, even as slow as they seemed to be, they would reach the road. *If I'm still there ... well, maybe I can hide in the trees.*

He stopped thinking and ran harder.

Scene 2

BROPHY (HUMAN)

Chilen let out his odd, gasping belly laugh. "Joss was the one who got it. Juan and I were going, like, where is he? He isn't stupid enough to still be looping around, is he?" He was supporting Juan, who was ashen but smiling broadly, as the group walked up the path to the biology station.

"Well, I'm just glad you did. Spending the night out there wouldn't have been fun." Brophy fingered the dried blood on his cheek as he limped along. "How'd you know, Joss?"

"As soon as I heard the new round of shots, I knew you must have left the trees. The only reason for you to do that would be to get them to focus on you. Lead them away from us. Thanks."

Brophy watched as she started up the steps to the small wooden building. She had spoken little in the car and shown none of the adrenaline-fueled glee he and the others were experiencing. Once inside, she flipped on lights. Chilen and Brophy half-walked, half-dragged Juan into the next room and laid him on the bed, where he promptly passed out.

Joss looked down at Juan. "I'll call Miguel."

"Um, Miguel's a vet," Brophy said doubtfully.

"Call a doctor, and he'll report a bullet wound." She spread a blanket over Juan and chewed on her lip like she always did when stressed. "I'm sure the police will have alerted the hospitals."

"I think Angel's pre-med," Brophy said. "She'll be here soon. I bet she can patch him up."

At the mention of Angel's name, Joss screwed up her face as though she had just found a dead coati in her bed. "Well, let's get him cleaned up at least. I've got cotton balls and peroxide in the bathroom." When Chilen looked pointedly at her hair, her eyes narrowed. "Funny."

Joss returned with the necessary supplies. As she worked on Juan's shoulder, Brophy heard a car followed by footsteps on the gravel walkway and a rap on the front door. He and Chilen went out into the main room to find Angel and a man already inside. Angeles, "Angel" for short, was a tall, dark Latina with sharp features, whose smile didn't quite make it to her eyes. The short, light-skinned man with her had a patch over one eye. He neither spoke nor smiled.

"Hola, que pasa amigos!" Angel said. "Stanley Ryder!"

"Hey, Angel!" Brophy gave her a "bro-hug" with a clap on the back, then turned to the man. "Hey, dude. I go by Brophy. Only my mom and Angel call me Stanley."

When the man clasped Brophy's hand but merely stared, Angel said, "Fred doesn't speak English or Spanish."

Chilen went through the same hug with Angel. "So, what does he speak?"

"I am still trying to figure that out," Angel said, making Brophy and Chilen laugh. "How did the mission go?"

Before Brophy could answer, Joss called out, "It went great. If getting shot while burning up somebody's property was the plan."

Angel took Brophy by both shoulders and held him at arms' length, scanning his injuries. "You look a little beat up, but not that bad."

"No, I'm fine. It's Juan." Brophy hooked his thumb back toward the bedroom.

Angel followed them and looked down impassively at the unconscious Juan. "Bullet still in him?"

"Nope." Joss gestured to the exit wound and rolled Juan to his side, exposing the entry point on his back and all the while refusing to make eye contact with Angel.

Angel pushed past Brophy and Chilen. They heard the front door open and soon she returned with a large, canvas satchel. She ordered everyone from the room and closed the door. Fred remained standing beside the front door like a guard, arms folded across his chest and staring off into space.

Joss led Brophy to the kitchen table and unceremoniously shoved him into a rickety wood chair that squealed its complaint. "So, was this our big statement tonight?" She sat down beside him and dabbed peroxide on his cheek with a cotton ball. "Risking our lives to burn some buildings they'll just re-build? Doesn't feel like much. In fact, I feel slimy."

Although he had thought he was trying not to flinch, he twitched slightly as she worked on his face. The corners of her mouth quirked up, and she blew on his cheek, like a mother caring for her little boy. *How could her breath smell so good after what they'd been through?* His tasted like smoke and forest funkiness, and he pressed his lips firmly together to spare her.

"A thousand small acts," he said from the corner of his mouth. "And if you aren't doing something to fight the plague, then you're responsible for the plague."

She plucked a sliver of wood from his cheek, and he winced. "Don't go all Camus on me. There are lots of ways to fight, and this isn't the right one. If you want to go to the books, I think we violated an Art of War principle. We joined a battle we could not win. This isn't the way to win the war." She removed another smaller splinter and leaned back in her chair. "And I really want to win it."

Brophy smiled, even though it hurt like hell. Intellectual banter. Beautiful girl, washing blood off his face and making him feel warrior-like. Adrenaline still pumping. He felt great ... until she started working on his leg.

A few minutes later, Angel emerged, shut the door behind her, and turned down the music Chilen had cranked up. "He is all fixed up. Should be fine. He woke up briefly and told me what happened. You guys are awesome. And you, Stanley Ryder ... you are the hero of the evening."

Brophy beamed, but Joss was having none of it. "Hero? He kept us from getting caught, but there were no heroes tonight. This was absurd."

"Naw, Joss, it was needed," Angel said calmly. "We have to show them we will act. I agree this mission was small, but Return has bigger plans. Tonight was just a test run to see how you guys would do. Have to admit, I did not expect gunplay." She opened the refrigerator and checked its contents before grabbing a water bottle. "You people do not believe in beer?"

She guzzled half the water and said, "You did great! I want you to come with me to San Jose and meet the rest of the Return chapter. I think Juan's gonna be out of play for a while, but the rest of you should come next week."

"That's cool," Brophy said, and Chilen chimed in, "Excellent!"

Lips pressed tightly together, Joss stared at Juan, glanced at

Brophy, and stalked out the door.

Brophy shrugged at Angel's blank look. "She'll be back. She has to—it's her place. Besides, she's never been a big Return fan. Thinks they're too violent and that 'violence breeds violence.' And that 'you don't fight the dark with more dark.'" He made air quotes as he spoke.

"No worries." Angel downed the rest of her water and picked up the black bag. "Gotta blow. Stanley Ryder, you are officially the new leader of this Return cell. Congrats!" She pumped Brophy's hand with mock formality and left, Fred close on her heels like a dog with his master.

Brophy and Chilen grinned at each other, and Chilen said, "I'm outta here too, Bro."

Alone except for the sleeping Juan, Brophy rummaged around in the kitchen cabinets, hoping to find a bottle of tequila. When he saw the sobriety prayer on the refrigerator, he remembered: no liquor allowed—Joss's Rule Number One. He opened the refrigerator and grabbed a small bottle of guava-pineapple juice.

He thought about the evening. He doubted tonight's actions would have a positive impact, but now he was head of the cell. His primary goal had been to impress Joss, but she was pissed. He really did want to make a difference though, so perhaps his new position would let him do some things the way she wanted and have a real effect. Maybe this is that big wave that surprises you, but once you're on it, you end up doing something radical.

He propped his aching leg on a kitchen chair and raised the glass to the empty room. "And I am king of this quiet earth."

Scene 3

Jim (Human)

Jim climbed out of his blue VW Beetle into the bright sunlight of Yellowstone's Canyon Visitor Education Center parking lot. The center had just reopened for the spring. A patch of snow hugged the base of the monument sign in front, but, according to the young lady at the park entrance, an extended drought meant most of the snow was at higher elevations.

He stretched like a runner and jogged in place a little to warm up. He'd driven almost sixteen hours in the last two days. Coming from San Francisco, he'd crossed California and had hoped to cross Nevada to Winnemucca, but he got a late start and only made it to Reno the first day. That left him the rest of Nevada and all of Idaho before the last bit of Wyoming. His favorite part was the Sierra Nevada Mountains—it was like being born again—and the only scary experience had been encountering big mule deer standing in the road late at night. He'd grown up crossing the long distances of the Australian outback so the trip hadn't been a strain.

With a few hours to kill before his quarry would be in the field, he removed his sunglasses and entered the center. He was interested in volcanos, and his internet search had told him that inside was information about the Yellowstone super volcano's potential impact.

He'd hiked the Aranal volcano in Costa Rica and Hawaii's lava fields, and he'd read books about Tambora's eruption in Indonesia. Ten times more powerful than the famous Krakatoa eruption, Tambora was the equivalent of a hundred hydrogen bombs exploding at once. Dormant for five hundred fifty years, Tambora had given thirty generations of Humans a false sense of security.

When on April 10, 1815, four hundred million tons of sulfur dioxide and water vapor exploded into the air, Tambora killed over one hundred thousand people quickly and another eighty-two thousand more gradually. Refugees from the area created regional conflicts, and "the year without a summer" led to crop failures in Asia, North America and Europe. All from one volcano! The eruption not only disrupted the monsoon cycle, causing the Yangtze Valley to flood, but also produced acid rain in Italy. Cholera, aggravated by starvation, swept from India to Moscow. Cold conditions stimulated the spread of typhus, and food riots broke out in many countries. Some argued that the death toll from Iceland's Laki in June of 1783 had been worse, with climate disruption killing as many as six million people. Jim had studied these as well as Vesuvius, Pelée, Bacobaco, and others.

Inside the center wasn't much warmer than the parking lot. He skipped the plexiglassed explanation of how volcanoes work and went straight to the super volcano display.

His first surprise was that he was standing on the super volcano. The term had been birthed in a 2005 BBC documentary and later adopted by scientists. He read about Toba, a super volcano that erupted seventy-four thousand years ago in what is now Indonesia. It created a six-year winter believed to have driven the first migration of Humans back to the equator during the one thousand years of cold, dry conditions that followed. Another super volcano called Taupo was located in New Zealand. Of the six super volcanos scientists believed they'd identified, three were in the United States, and one lay under

Yellowstone Park.

Jim found it eerie enough to be standing on the park's volcano. When he used the calculator to enter where he lived and determine an eruption's impact, he didn't feel all that much better. If this one erupted, the only difference between being here or in his home city of San Francisco was a quick death versus a slow one.

He left the center, grabbed a granola bar, and munching on it settled back in the car to review his quarry's dossier once more. Around two p.m. he began navigating his way to Hayden Valley. Enough snow lay in the upper areas that the bison and elk herds should be in the valley, visible from the road. He pulled up behind the Park Service truck and parked along the road looking out on the valley. A ranger was bent over a spotting scope mounted on a tripod, and a few more scopes and observers were set up along the road ahead.

He climbed out and scanned the valley. In the distance he could make out a herd of bison, clustered in a ring looking outward. He studied several dark objects grouped around a grassy mound but couldn't quite make out what they were. As Jim rounded the car and walked over, the ranger glanced at him, gave a brief nod, and returned to the scope.

"What'cha watching, mate?" Jim shoved his bare hands into his pockets. Both men wore heavy down coats, but he eyed the ranger's thick gloves enviously.

"Aussie or Kiwi?" the ranger asked without taking his eye from the scope. He had a medium build and straw-colored hair showing beneath his ranger hat, and according to the dossier he was twenty-eight. "I'm Zach." He stuck out his hand.

Jim shook the offered hand. "I come from the Land of Oz. Jim."

Zach nodded. "Watching wolves. Sneaky canines. Entered the valley and played like it was a great big dog park. Made a big show of leaving and then slipped back behind that aspen copse over there. When the elk came back, thinking they were safe, wolves jumped the cow. Wanna see?"

"You bet. Thanks." As Jim peered through the scope, a series of yowls and yelps broke the silence. He looked around. "What's that?"

"Coyotes. Upset 'cause the wolves are taking so long. They're waiting until the wolves get full and move on. The coyotes know just how far away the wolves need to be before the coyotes can eat without being attacked. Wolves'll eat once, then lie down near the kill. They let the food settle awhile. Later they may eat more or move off."

Still looking through the scope, Jim said, "Wolves are leaving." He huffed out a cold breath and grinned. "Wow. A bald eagle just landed on the elk and started eating ... wait, now there's two more."

"Yeah, they'll grab a quick bite before the coyotes run them off."

"So these are the reintroduced wolves?"

"Yep. One was a pup born to one of the original packs. Having the wolves back has made a big difference. Coyote population's gone down, 'cause they compete with the wolves. But the fox population's gone up, since they compete with the coyotes but not the wolves. Elk population has shrunk, and new aspen started growing 'cause the elk are afraid to go in the groves. New aspen growth improved the stream quality and increased the trout. Wolf's an apex predator, sets the stage for everything." Zach chuckled. "Sorry, part of my job. Give that lecture a coupla times a day during tourist season."

Jim blinked his dry eyes a few times. "We've been talking about the great white sharks at home. How they have the same relationship. I hate them. Scared to death of them. But it sounds like they're needed to keep things in balance. You look cold—buy you a coffee?"

Late that evening, as Zach lay snoring on his couch, Jim slipped from the room. All had gone perfectly according to plan. The ranger had invited Jim back to his cabin for a few beers and to talk more about Yellowstone's ecology. Zach had been such an alcohol light-weight there was no need for the roofie Jim brought just in case.

Once inside the office, he flipped on the tiny flashlight attached to his keyring and quickly hit pay dirt—in one corner was a stack of geologic maps. He scooped them up and quietly left through the screened porch. After coasting to the bottom of the hill, he started up the car and let out a triumphant whoop.

Because the summer crowds had not yet descended, few people were in the park, and most had settled in for the night. Traffic would pick up in mid-May and increase steadily to peak when school let out. The cold air felt good—temperatures had dropped considerably during the night—but Jim cranked up the heater to clear the windshield. The dusting of snow early that evening made the landscape magical in the light of a partial moon. He slowed down, weaving among elk standing in the heat radiating off the road or grazing in the open spaces along the side. Worried one or more might be suicidal and bolt for the Bug, he breathed more easily when he left them behind.

He saw signs for the park attractions and thought about the people who'd soon fill the roads—kids, moms, dads, and grandparents. Though he had no idea why the woman wanted the maps, he thought it might be bad for those people. Then he pushed that thought from his mind by considering the substantial amount of money he'd been promised, half of it paid up front.

In Bozeman, the restaurant's lights shone welcoming patches

of brightness into the early morning street, and inside the smell of breakfast and low friendly voices lifted his mood even further. He put the bundle of maps on one side of the booth and sat on the other. After a quick look at the menu, he ordered an omelet, bacon and wheat toast with honey from Tiffany, a perky blonde who looked in her early twenties and called him "Sweetie." The restaurant was a very public place for an exchange, but that was all right since he would be on his way shortly. No one knew him here, and it was unlikely he would ever return. Besides, he liked people around—meeting the woman who had hired him in somewhere like an isolated alley would've creeped him out. She was creepy enough.

Before long, Angel slid into the booth and glanced impassively at the maps beside her. She was in black from head to toe—knit cap, leather jacket, jeans, gloves—and her first word was a brusque "coffee" directed at Tiffany. As she peeled off her cap and gloves and smoothed down her hair, Tiffany returned with coffee, cream, and sweeteners. Before she could get out another "Sweetie," Angel snapped, "That's all." Tiffany's smile faltered, and she hurried away.

Angel asked, "Any problems?

"Nope. Piece o' cake."

Angel glanced at the bundle of maps, not unrolling them any further than necessary to confirm they concerned Yellowstone geology and had the U.S. Interior Department seals. She pulled an envelope from her inside coat pocket and slid it across the table. Jim resisted the urge to look around before picking it up and thumbing through the cash.

"We good?"

"Perfect." Jim tucked the envelope inside his own coat pocket.

"Nature Now thanks you for your assistance."

Clearly dismissed, Jim eyed his uneaten breakfast sadly, but he wasn't about to argue. He twisted around in search of Tiffany and his check.

"I got this." Angel blew on her coffee and took a sip.

Jim shrugged, very aware of the thick wad of cash pressing against his chest, and as he left, he looked at the people he passed. One couple trying to tease their kids out of morning grogginess. A grey-haired man chatting with Tiffany. Other couples and foursomes beginning their days with soft conversations.

Suddenly he felt sleazy. Though he knew none of them, he felt like he might have just sold these people out. As he laid the thick envelope on the seat beside him, he told himself he wasn't really sure Angel had anything bad planned. Probably just working for the oil companies or the gas companies and trying to find some new vault of underground payoffs. Instead of going straight back to San Francisco, he'd visit friends in Denver, where he'd lived until recently. Then, maybe it was time to go back to Sydney for a while. He pushed his thoughts to eating at the Palace Arms in Denver that night with Tom and David.

A coupla bottles of wine would lift his spirits. No, not wine … champagne!

Scene 4

ANGEL (TROW)

As Angel looked out the restaurant window, she saw that the morning had turned from black to grey. She dug into Jim's breakfast and was finishing the last bite of toast when Thest walked up. Dressed like a Human in a heavy coat, jeans, hiking shoes, and a knit cap, he slid in opposite her. His clothes were all black like hers, except for the red cap. His glamour had transformed his lean, muscular, seven-foot Trow frame and long black dreadlocks into a six-foot, grey-haired, soft Human.

"Lord Thest." Angel lowered her head almost imperceptibly, the closest thing to a bow she could manage in a crowded restaurant.

"Just Raymond today, Angel. Problems?"

Angel managed to suppress a laugh. *Raymond? Really?* When they met among Humans, Thest randomly picked Human names, all fitting like a smaller man's coat. "None whatsoever, Lor—I mean, Raymond."

Thest scowled, his unblinking shark eyes fixed on her. "No fingerprints on anything other than that of Humans?"

Having served Thest a long time, Angel was no longer intimidated by him. "A Human encounter and a Human theft. If they catch him, all he has is Nature Now."

"Good, but perhaps too good. How will they trace it afterwards?"

"Following the event, his 'suicide' will be discovered with a note confessing his role. We will leave much Human evidence in the next stage. I recruited him because of his popularity. His death will attract a great deal of attention. We will leave some of the maps at the scene along with Nature Now literature."

Angel sighed and tried to wave Tiffany off, but the waitress walked to the table undeterred and, from her expression, clearly irritated.

With false politeness, Tiffany asked, "What would you like, sir?"

"Nothing. Leave us."

Tiffany glanced at the growing group waiting for tables and with hands on hips huffed out, "Fine. But much longer and there's a rental fee."

Like most Trow, Thest could not read Human body language and was unruffled by the exchange. He had spent a great deal of time on Earth, but not much of it conversing with Humans. Angel had spent more time among them than most Trow, so Tiffany's emotions were obvious, but she was trying Angel's patience.

"Just bring us the check," Angel snapped, and Tiffany left scowling.

"Who will you use?" Thest asked.

"I think Stanley Ryder Brophy, the young male in Costa Rica, will work."

"Not much time to raise him in the organization. Are you sure? We are behind schedule and cannot start again. We cannot afford another mistake. Nor can you."

Angel leaned forward, eyeing Thest intently. "I have made no mistakes. I fixed the mistake of another. That Human boy learned too much of us, and I removed him. There was nothing else to do."

"It set us back months. And I have 'removed' the one who slipped. Let us say, then, that none of us can afford more mistakes.

The sun will soon set, and us with it if we are not successful."

Angel said nothing at first and then understood. "Ahh. You have had a meeting with 'the boss.'"

Thest nodded as he slid from the booth. "Unpleasant."

CHAPTER FOUR

Scene 1

ARAN (SILTH)

Aran and Nadara kept their distance from the blazing campfire as they landed. Spring was becoming summer, with frogs, cicadas, and other insects adding warmer weather choruses to the snaps and crackles of the fire. As dinner cooked and night fell, the four tandem teams returned to camp. Conversations were loud and laughter frequent. Perched on a rock a short distance away, Storng had just finished interviewing Nick and Kirstn, both chuckling as they hurried to join the others.

Today ended the third week of their borrowing campaign. The group had traveled to the eastern section of Florida, where they would spend the bulk of this year. Because they harvested during the winter in western Florida, they never did a summer campaign there. The Silth's initial exuberance over being free of the warehouse dissipated as they settled into the new routine. Still, spirits were high and evenings filled with songs, stories, beer, sweet fruit wine, and laughter.

Storng had held them at the warehouse for the first three weeks reestablishing discipline and packing up what they had already gathered. Each morning there were fewer of the boxes in the warehouse, though Aran wasn't sure how they left or where they went. The day before they left to harvest, he sent them off on a picnic. When they returned to the warehouse, all the boxes and packages were gone.

Despite Storng's saying that Aran's training was finished, they'd spent several hours daily in more training, with Aran coming to the hammocks late each night tired and surly, only to get up, have breakfast, and work with the Tiki Crew through much of the day. Every day included extensive physical exercise, deep meditation, and combat training similar to Human martial arts. It had been centuries since the shamans had been targets of rising Silth princes or generals, but they stayed prepared.

Even when Storng stopped and joined the Tiki Crew for their nightly communal winding-down, Aran continued his practice. He could have found a place far from the nightly sounds of the "Bikini Beachcombers" or the "Bambi Molesters," but he told himself it was good to perform with distractions. If anyone asked him how training was going, he said: Magic is like a muscle—it takes time to grow and be rendered supple enough for usefulness. That usually netted him an odd look and solitude once more.

But he wasn't just training to be a shaman. The rest of the Tiki Crew were experienced harvesters—experts at breaking into houses and businesses, identifying the desired objects, and, most importantly, not getting caught. Aran practiced on the businesses and houses around them, and sometimes Nadara accompanied him to help him learn the harvester tradecraft. He was surprised by how much Storng had left out. Aran learned about picking locks, recognizing and disabling security systems, and avoiding cameras—it was useful to be able to fly but sometimes a struggle to be so small in a world of Human sized equipment. He learned about dogs and cats as well as the working habits of Humans, their sleep habits and interactions with their children, their cars, and many other aspects of their lives.

Nadara teased Aran that his reputation must have been magically induced—he socialized so little he couldn't have legitimately earned the name "Heartless"—but he didn't rise to the bait. He ate with the others. He listened to their stories of prior adventures and learned of the relationships existing among them. He took care not to be sullen but shared little with them. He wasn't actively hiding anything—he knew Silth gossip well enough to know the team would have quizzed Storng on anything they didn't know, and he knew Storng well enough to assume he had told them everything. But he just didn't like talking about himself … or talking much at all right now.

But like emerging from a huge thunderstorm, each day seemed a little brighter, the rain a little lighter. Finding himself enjoying his shaman skills was unexpected. Shaman training was the most extensive education in Silth society, but because Aran remembered pretty much everything after one telling, it came easier to him than to some. What he really enjoyed, however, was Storng's surprised pleasure when he was able to complete a task not only mistake-free, but also with the flair of a showman, like the storyteller he was.

He also liked being around Nadara. She was obviously aware of her effect on him and the other males, moving with an effortless grace, but at the same time using her power gently with charm. She flirted naturally, without manipulation or maliciousness. Flirting seemed to be part of her normal interaction, and the other Silth females appeared unthreatened by it. As she was the only unpaired member of the crew, Aran was teamed with her as they prepared for their borrowing campaign.

While the constant thundering darkness seemed to be moving on and Aran almost guiltily caught himself laughing with the others, sudden storms still devastated him. In the middle of some activity, out of nowhere and like the squalls that stalked the Gulf of Mexico, would come the deep sadness. Memories blotted out whatever had been in his mind. At first the Tiki Crew tried to help, but when it became plain there was nothing they could do, they pretended not to notice.

They had left the warehouse and begun their borrowing campaign. Each day the teams would go out to their assigned areas and forage through the Humans' houses and sheds. They had lists of target items which Storng adjusted according to the search results—enough string, more doll clothes, no more canned fruits, watch for lighters and matches. They spent every day experiencing the tension of potential discovery, an absolutely unacceptable event.

Tonight, Nadara and Aran had been the last to return, and Storng called them to the rock. Nadara stomped over and threw herself down on another rock opposite him, flapping her wings irritably before folding them behind her. As Aran perched on a rock a little further away, she glanced at him, frowning, before giving her attention to Storng.

"Nadara. Aran. You're late. Problem?"

"Things didn't go well," Nadara replied. She never seemed as affected as Aran by Storng's intense gaze and contrasting eyes, the white one now reflecting the fire.

Storng lifted a brow.

"Go on, Aran," she snapped. "You're the storyteller."

So much for letting her do the talking, as he'd intended. He absorbed her deliberate slight in calling him a storyteller, not a shaman, by watching a firefly winking its way over their heads. Many more flitted about, filling the canopy.

The hathered brow over the white eye arched even higher. "Aran?"

"Things began well enough. The first four houses went without incident. We left our harvest bags in the woods and found an open window on the side of the fifth house. The screen was easy to remove. We found lots of swag—doll clothes, foil, razors, and more—and piled it outside the window. We were almost finished when a car drove up. Instead of parking in front like we expected, it pulled beside the house. The window we'd come in was facing the car, so we couldn't escape before they came in. The Humans got out of their car with a young one and a big dog that they chained on the side porch near our window. As they came in, they were arguing about whether or not it was too hot out for the dog. They yelled at the child. Then at each other."

He paused, shaking his head. "Typical Humans. The male came in and slammed the window shut. Said he was 'turning on the air.' When they left the room, we flew over to the window. The dog saw us and began barking like crazy. We were trapped—"

"Monkey scat," Nadara interjected. "We could have gotten out then. All you had to do was conjure the window. I probably could have opened it. Clasp wasn't that hard."

"The dog was loud," Aran argued, "and the Humans were moving around. We could have been seen. Anyway, we were flying from room to room, trying to avoid all three of them as they randomly moved about. We ended up in the kitchen where they'd begun making their dinner, and—"

"And you wouldn't go in the closet."

This time he ignored her. "Nadara had on an egret aspect, while I glamoured as a blue heron. The female adult saw us. Screamed that there were big birds in the house. She grabbed a broom and with the other two started chasing us around. The male had a big stick. The female missed me with the broom and knocked over a skillet of oil she'd been heating, setting the stove and broom on fire. She tried to put out the broom by shaking it and spread the fire to the kitchen curtains. While they were distracted by the flames, we flew to the back of the house. Nadara got the door open, and we hit the sky."

She picked up the narrative. "But before coming here, we circled back to make sure the Humans were safe."

"Nadara wanted to make sure they were safe. I didn't really care," Aran said flatly, drawing back from her angry stare.

"So you left an inexplicable pile of swag outside the window." Storng was quiet a moment. "It probably won't matter given the other distractions. Are you both all right?"

When Aran corrected her quick "yes" with "except for Nadara's burns," she scowled more deeply and countered with, "Just some singed feathers. No real damage."

"Good. Nadara, go get food. Aran, stay."

Storng and Aran sat in silence. In the distance Nadara drew whoops of welcome from the Tiki Crew, and Storng finally spoke. "What happened, Aran?"

"I couldn't make my brain work. No words came. I couldn't decide what elements to use. I didn't want to make a mistake that would cause Nadara to get hurt."

"Yet that's exactly what you did. Your actions must come immediately, without hesitation."

"I don't think I can—"

"Don't think. Just act. The art of instancy—do the right thing in a split second." Storng looked hard at Aran. "You can't cut yourself off from those around you to avoid pain. Or from action to avoid mistakes." He fell silent a moment, then, "Eat. Let the others help you heal."

"But I wasn't hurt."

"That's not what I meant. Also remember, you may not like the Humans, but Nadara and the Tiki Crew are trained to do their work without harming them. Do not cause them to violate their code."

He left Aran to join the Tiki Crew, and another shout went up in unison. "Storng!"

Aran watched the light dance on the trees. As if on some schedule, the fireflies had stopped blinking. He smelled the smoke and food's spices and listened to the crew as they grew more boisterous. Instead of obeying Storng's instructions, he walked off in the opposite direction.

In the weeks before leaving Panama City, he'd made daily trips into the city to study Humans, needing to know his enemy. He sat on roofs, watching them walking the streets and wandering in and out of shops. He brought his hatred for them, planning to fuel it with observations of their evil acts. But what he observed was mundane—the acts of people going about their daily lives, tending their children, promenading and courting, making their livings.

He sneaked into houses and buildings, thinking that evil acts would be done in private. Although he witnessed acts of meanness and real cruelty, he also saw kindness and love. He couldn't connect these latter actions to rainforest destruction or the endless hunting of species to extinction.

Plastic bags floated in the harbor despite signs warning that they harmed marine life. Garbage was washed up on the beaches, and one morning he watched sadly as the last sand dunes for miles were being bulldozed. Every stream had numerous pipes entering it. But as he watched workers occupying construction projects, boats, and manufacturing buildings, he failed to see the evil aura he expected. Consequently, he was confused and frustrated by his inability to find a target for his anger, always simmering inside and threatening to boil over at the slightest provocation.

Then the harvesting began, and he couldn't act against Humans without risking the well-being of his partners. Without focus, he wasn't performing his job well.

I'm neither a good shaman nor a decent harvester. Is this really the path for me? Perhaps I should just go.

Nadara had been kind. This last harvest problem was not the only one Aran had created, just the first that had come to Storng's attention. When he was close to Humans or their habitat, Aran became distracted and anxious. He made mistakes. Until now Nadara had covered for him, even though some mistakes had endangered them both.

Storng had been right—Aran had discovered that not all Humans were evil. But the reason he had become a shaman was to avenge Shra's death. If he no longer had a reason, why was he a shaman? The poachers were still out there and still his ultimate target. But here he was sneaking into houses, instead of finishing off the poachers. Should he leave and go on after them? He sat in a tree, the way he ended most nights, wrestling with his future until he would grow so tired he would fall asleep.

But tonight he shook himself and soared into the tree canopy, finding a spot on a very tall tree where he could see across the canopy top. A full moon shone in a cloudless sky, lighting the treetops in a strange green milkiness. This canopy was relatively lifeless compared to that of the rainforest, where the trees contained many more creatures than on the ground.

He knew there was no going back to storytelling. The Tiki Crew thought he was avoiding it because of his voice or mourning Shra. The latter was part of it—guilt rose up whenever he was having too much fun—but there was more to it. He couldn't find the stories any more. Though they were all still there, and he could recall them at will, part of the storyteller's job was to draw on the right story at the right time. To assess the mood or the needs of the audience. This skill … this vital skill … was gone. Moreover, he really couldn't bear the sound of his damaged voice.

Was he going to matter? Was he even still alive? Would he love again? Would he get someone killed with his sloppiness? *But I've grown stronger. I have the skills of a shaman if I'll use them. If I let Nadara and the others teach me, I can learn this harvest game. I'll be even stronger when I return to the colony and track down the poachers.*

The resolve of a decision finally made filled him, and he remained a few more minutes in the wash of moonlight. With a flap of his wings, he shot out of the treetops and into the night, flying straight up until high above the landscape and able to see for miles in all directions.

Yes, time to get on with it.

Scene 2

ARAN (SILTH)

For the last four weeks, the Tiki Crew had stuck to residential areas. Tonight's target, however, was a Dollar Store. They would all participate, with Storng leading the harvest.

While Storng and the Tiki Crew worked inside the store, Aran would remain on watch outside the back door. Storng had told the others that Aran was the only one who could broadcast the shaman thought communication. By mutual agreement the shamans rarely used this method of communication, since it was picked up by all of them within range, and they believed that disembodied voices heard too often in their heads would result in insanity. Aran wondered if the Humans' constant attachment to cell phones and music headsets proved or disproved the validity of the shaman concern.

He suspected reasons for his assignment other than his ability to communicate. The incident with the fire had irritated Nadara enough that she told the others about his repeated mistakes. His refusal to socialize with the others made them stop trying to coax him into their nightly wind-down sessions. He still slept poorly—his dreams of Shra filled him with longing and remorse. He dreamed of flying with her just out of reach. The flailing of his arms, attempting to touch her once more, sometimes woke him with a shout loud enough to wake the others.

Perversely, as the others pulled further away, Aran felt himself gaining confidence. He watched Nadara as she worked, and he listened carefully at nighttime as the others told stories of the day's adventures. His errors were decreasing in the harvests. He found himself lingering longer at meals. Though he always left when time came for them to sing and tell more traditional stories, now he only moved far enough away to avoid being called upon, still close enough to listen.

If the choice for him to be outside on this harvesting reflected their concern about his abilities, he was fine with that. He'd do the job well and earn their trust.

He watched the others move into position in a pond nearer the parking lot. The security light amplified their many colors as they flew into place. *Rainbow thieves* was the phrase that came to his mind.

As the crew drew closer to the building, Aran caught movement in the corner of his vision. He peered into the bushes about fifty feet away and saw nothing, until the Faerie from the cargo ship stepped out into the open.

"The Faerie," as Aran had come to think of him, was a constant presence. Like now, he made sure Aran knew he was there, without alerting the others. He was always the same one, with the eye patch and facial burns, and Aran could see the blue glow around his glamour. Sometimes during a sighting, like now, he glamoured as a tall, whip-thin Human, while at other times he would appear short and fat, as if someone had blown him up like a balloon. At first Aran had thought there were two, a fat one and a skinny one, but when this one reverted to his Faerie form, the eye patch and scars were always visible.

Without mirth the Faerie smiled, not so much a smile, actually, as the baring of teeth. Not uttering a word—he never did—he stepped back toward the bush and blended in so perfectly Aran could no longer see him.

When this almost daily stalking had begun, Aran found it disconcerting. The constant threat of death it implied added to his moodiness. Because he could neither react nor tell anyone but Storng, it isolated him even further. Storng's only response was to mutter, "Get used to it." But now, following what Aran thought of as his moonlight transformation, he just shrugged it off. If the Faerie wanted to kill him, he would have already done so.

It was on the cargo ship that Aran had first learned his training might carry a death sentence and constant scrutiny from beings he had thought were no longer on Earth.

He fluttered down to the container he and Storng had opened, in the furthest row of the highest stack facing forward. In front was the plateau created by the lower stacks of containers continuing toward the bow. The space could not be observed from the ship's bridge or from below. An electrical cord ran to the back of the container, allowing refrigeration of its contents. The door was difficult even for two Silth to move, and in the end Storng used a spell to assist them. They left the door slightly ajar so they could come and go, taking the fruits inside as needed.

Sliding into the container, Aran gorged on pieces of an anona, some breadfruit and caimitos, as well as part of a banana.

On the afternoon of the sixth day out of the port they were exercising on the containers. Aran's muscles ached and his joints throbbed. Had Storng asked him to snap his fingers, he doubted he could have complied. As usual, Storng seemed barely winded by the endurance exercises or the strength-building ones of tossing heavy bags back and forth.

When they finally sat down, Storng reminded Aran of how important it was for a shaman to be able to clear his or her mind. No spell could be cast, no portent read, no alignment achieved without the ability to block out everything else and settle the mind. Aran was listening to Storng's voice as it seemed to get further and further away ....

"Wake up!" Storng thundered, jolting Aran back to full attention.

As the sun, streaked with orange and descending below the horizon, colored the deck, they squatted before the container, several open vials and their contents spread in front of them.

"I think you remember one or two things."

That was the most charitable comment Storng had made over the course of the week. Mostly he called Aran rude names. He had always been poor at positive reinforcement.

"I thrive in the sunshine of your constant praise."

Storng chuckled. "Ah, yes, there's the attitude."

Ignoring him, Aran said, "These magics are disappointingly small. I expected more. They don't have ... I don't know ... weight." He stood and stretched, extending his wings for a few quick flaps before refolding them. "The 'stay-away' spell you put around us, different carrying, healing, and communication spells, some binding and hiding spells? The magics of a merchant. Maybe not the healing. Chanting, powders, and the orientation of objects are all very mystical but deployed for the benefit of commerce. They don't seem to pull deeply on the power of the Earth elements."

"Ha!" Storng pressed his lips into a thin line of displeasure. "Just as impatient as ever. This is why you flew away from your practice before. It was not 'exciting' enough."

"I won't fly away now. But I know there should be more."

"Shamans are the healers for their communities, dealing with its physical and mental problems. They're the priests and counselors. But

in many ways shamans are merchants." Storng rearranged the vials and packages, providing some order clear only to him. "We go among the Humans, locate useful things, and harvest them for our colonies. The prosperity of a colony often depends on our resourcefulness and ability to distinguish what's useful, what can be formed into usefulness, and what is merely attractive."

"Storng, shamans are not merchants. They steal stuff and gain status in the colony by giving it to the pandemonium. They don't make anything."

"Porcupine poo!" Storng fixed his black eye upon Aran. "When the Humans take honey from the hive, do we consider them thieves? If so, is the bear that preceded them also a thief? When they shear the wool from a sheep, have they robbed it? We are simply harvesting some of the Humans' excess production for our needs. We don't take items that cause harm in their absence. Just as the sheep may have some distress, we may cause a few Humans distress, but they get over it quickly. We don't take so much that they realize it's gone. Most times they think they just misplaced things."

A whoosh of air sounded from the water's surface, beyond their sight, followed by several more. Storng walked to the container edge and looked down. "Porpoises!"

"As for the magics … those you mentioned are the ones you need to be a shaman. I never said they're all the Silth magics. But why do you desire those you don't need? Are you greedy, fledgling? Do you think they may bring you power? Do they excite you?" Suddenly Storng's eyes were fixed on Aran's, enormous and hypnotic.

Aran felt the darkness in himself well up, and he clenched his teeth to lock in the words on the tip of his tongue. He broke eye contact, took a deep breath, and held it a few moments before releasing it and looking back at Storng, who was staring at a point behind Aran's left shoulder. Storng snarled.

Astonished, Aran twisted around but saw nothing. "What are you doing?"

Instead of answering, Storng unfurled his wings and flew up to hover at the edge of the container. He glanced around before staring intently in one direction, his face darkening. After a few moments he settled back beside Aran.

"What?" Aran demanded. "What did you see?"

But Storng just gazed out at the water.

"Why aren't you showing me more powerful magic?"

To Aran's surprise, Storng's gaze dropped to his hands. "You have the elementary understanding of the way magic works in this world. But you still have much to learn."

Aran's cheeks flushed with anger, but he said calmly, "And that is not an answer."

Storng looked sharply toward the top edge of the container, and several long seconds passed before he spoke again. "I—I can't teach you more magic because the Faeries prohibit it. I can't tell you more. It's far too dangerous."

As the ship left the Mexican port of Progresa two days later, Aran kept after Storng to explain. He never doubted he would wear the old Silth down—he'd always been able to get his way in finding out what he needed to know.

More disconcerting than Storng's reticence was Aran's sensation of being watched. His finely-honed predator alarm had activated with the prickling of feathers and slight elevation of heart rate, both signaling *something amiss. He felt like he was being stalked by an unseen jaguar, known only because of unexplained sounds, the lack of sounds from other creatures, or perhaps only a change in air pressure. Try as he might, he couldn't determine the source of his anxiety. Perhaps it was the result of Storng's odd behavior. Had his mentor developed some strange idiosyncrasy, or was there really something on the ship to fear?*

On the first morning back at sea, they watched the now cloudless sky. The plop, plop, plop of water could be heard all around them as rain water, having fallen only a half hour before, ran off the containers. The storm had come suddenly, whipping the ship back and forth like a puma finishing a small animal. And then it was gone almost as quickly. It seemed strange to have a rain storm not be followed by the jubilant cheers of frogs.

As the shock of losing Shra wore down into a dull, daily pain, Aran was aware of other absences. The sun rose without a bird chorus, just as the stars came out without a frog symphony. Because rain was no longer a constant condition, he was more tuned into the drips of water. He went through long portions of each day without speaking other than to recite the words of conjuring in the sub-audible murmur that Storng taught. He thought of the joke that Silth have fifty different words for green, to describe the many variations of rainforest color, but only one word for yellow, the same as the word for banana. Little green existed on the ship.

Determined to get the answers he sought, he tested Storng again. "I can't come up with any reason why there would be more powerful magic that some shamans would possess but not others. Are there different grades of shamans?"

"No. All the males and females serving as shamans are the same—

there are no higher and lower ones. There are different levels of power or authority. Some are apprentices like you, others powerful eyeball-plucking shamans like me, or members of the council. But even they rotate out of the council position after a few years."

"Then why would you keep certain magics secret from me? Do you also not share them with other shamans?"

Aran could tell from Storng's resigned expression he had decided answering was preferable to more days of interrogation.

"Because ..." Storng began and broke off, motioning to Aran to follow him inside the container. He pulled a vial from his cloak and removed a pinch of soil. He muttered as he sprinkled it in front of the door, and it closed with a click, plunging them into darkness. Aran heard a soft scrape, and a small flame sprang from the cylindrical lighter Storng held. As Storng chanted, a ball of flames about the size of a breadfruit floated up to the ceiling.

He shoved the lighter back in his cloak and whispered, "Because the Faeries don't want Silth to become too powerful, they prohibit the teaching of certain Silth magics. Many older shamans know a few of these prohibited magics. It used to be the forbidden magics were quietly taught. My teacher, son-of-a-coati that he was, secretly gathered many of these magic formulas over the years, and he stuffed them into my head. But the Faeries have made it clear—that's where they should stay."

Aran sat quietly thinking about this answer for several minutes and then drove forward with his questions. "First, does what you say mean you've talked to Faeries? I didn't think they were in this world that much. Or that they talked to Silth. Second, what would they do if you taught it anyway?"

"The Faeries never fully left the world. A large faction stayed, but

its members were changed by the rise of Human magic, becoming hard and violent. They sent an army back to the Land and took control. Now they rule the other Faeries by force. They come and go in this world, each with different tolerances and different mental deformities from their time above the ground."

"And ...? Go on."

"The Land, where Faeries come from, was peaceful. The Faeries don't have any powers there. They have powers on Earth, which is why they love to come here."

He removed an avocado from a bin, split it, and tossed a quarter of it to Aran. They sat in the flickering light eating, each lost in his own thoughts. After they were both rested, they pushed the door open a crack, and Storng slipped out. Aran followed him, watching as Storng looked behind the container, flew up, and peeked over the top before shooing Aran back inside.

"Okay, what is that all about? We're in the middle of an ocean, and you're worried about Faerie eavesdroppers?"

Storng's eyes narrowed. "It is most important for you to get this lesson. They're always listening and watching. There's one among the crew, and he's shown himself to me. An act of intimidation. Like peccaries—they follow me without relief. There're plenty of Faeries on Earth." He gave Aran a side-long look. "Surely even you, slow as a sloth, must have wondered how new Silth could be created if the Faeries were all gone."

"I thought—I guess I figured they just visited this world."

"No, many Faeries dwell here. And yes, unhappily I have spoken with them. They've come to me twice and warned me not to teach what I know. They threaten to kill me if I teach you."

Storng moved to a new portion of the container. Bananas and avocados got boring—this section contained pineapples and cashew fruits. Storng pulled out a knife and cut into a pineapple, as if when he was fully occupied Aran could ask him no more questions.

But Aran refused to be dissuaded. "So how do you know they aren't bluffing?"

"They aren't, fledgling."

"I know the colonies fear Faeries. But have you ever known them to kill a Silth?"

"Yes. Listen to me. They. Aren't. Bluffing." Storng slurped away at a piece of quayaba, swiping at his hather from time to time as the juices trickled down his chin.

Aran prodded a mango with his foot. "You want me to force you to tell me more so you wouldn't be responsible for the consequences."

Storng hesitated, then, "The last few years have left you dangerously perceptive. I hope you aren't right, but you could be."

"Why not just go ahead and kill you?"

"Don't give them any ideas."

"Seriously ...."

The ball of light Storng had created suddenly sputtered out.

"Apparently, they still don't want anyone but shamans to know they're active in the world," came Storng's voice from the darkness. "And they fear that several shamans turning up dead would alert the Silth. You're not even supposed to know they're in the world other than as occasional visitors. But I think you have to know so you can be on your guard."

"On my guard?"

"Be careful. You're in danger."

Aran heard Storng mutter a spell, and the door reopened. Before Aran could speak, Storng was out and flying to the higher part of the ship.

"What danger?" Aran yelled after him, thinking it was a good thing they were having this conversation while they were on the ship. He would have hated to chase Storng through the rainforest.

Before he could follow, he heard the sound of footsteps moving across the top of the containers. When Aran peered over the top of theirs, he spotted a squat shape, standing on another container and watching Storng fly. It looked like a short, fat Human with an eye patch, but it had a blue shimmer around it, indicating a glamour. The Faerie turned and looked directly at Aran. His expression did not change, but the glamour faded, and in place of the Human stood a tall, thin Faerie with a heavily scarred face and only one eye.

He started toward Aran, limping quickly across the container. Aran dropped back inside, looking for a hiding place. As he heard steps across the ceiling, he clawed into a pile of limes, throwing them back on top of himself. The door squealed as it was forced open, and he held his breath in the darkness. The steps stopped in front of him, replaced by the sound of a deep chuckle. Aran's lungs began to burn. His mind conjured up the big Faerie standing there waiting for him to move. He burst from the pile with a yell, only to find himself alone in the container. He panted as limes rolled around the container floor.

Once he'd regained control, Aran found Storng in the rigging and settled in beside him. He'd already decided not to mention the Faerie, fearing it might cause Storng to stop answering his questions.

Aran asked, "Who were the Silth killed by Faeries?"

"Two students … . Have I mentioned I'm not very good at keeping secrets?"

"No, it didn't come up. You might have touched on this whole 'marked-for-death' thing before I agreed to resume training."

"You might not have consented to become a shaman. And you must. You'll do great things … or die an extraordinary death. In all honesty, the portents aren't at all clear on which. Anyway, the idea is that if I don't teach you the prohibited magic, they won't kill you."

"How do they know what you teach me?"

Storng shrugged. "That's why there's a Faerie on the ship."

Aran's heart was pounding. He took three deep breaths and asked himself if he was angry with Storng. No, what he was feeling was not anger. It was … excitement. He wasn't upset, just fatalistic. He wanted these powers—they might be the key to gaining his revenge. Yet obtaining them might lead to his death.

"How were your students killed?"

"Not long after I started teaching at Amazonia, one student stood out—Raskaw. She could do exceptional magic. Raskaw was excited and eager to learn. I thought we were being careful, but back then I didn't realize how hard it is to be beyond Faerie scrutiny. A few days after we began, a Faerie with one eye and burns over half his face appeared in my chambers. He tossed her body on the floor—the bodies of Silth killed by magic do not disappear—and said, 'This is your fault. Do not teach these magics again.' Then he disappeared.

"The other shamans were suspicious. Why, they wondered, would a Faerie bother to kill and return a Silth body? What had she done? I'm ashamed to say that I didn't confess my role. In the end, nothing came of it. Many years passed, and I taught without incident. Then about a year before you left, I had another exceptional student. Poloniak. This time I took every precaution I could imagine."

"And still he died," Aran said somberly.

Storng nodded. "Within days his body lay at my feet, and the one-eyed Faerie said there would be no more warnings. The other shamans were alarmed when a second student of mine turned up dead by magic. Ultimately, not long after you left, the Shaman Council met and decreed that I should no longer be a teacher. I never told them what had happened, but they knew enough.

"You're my first student in ten trips around the sun. But I can't teach you all the magic I know. And it's important you understand there are boundaries, for your own survival as well as mine. You're a shaman, and you'll do amazing things. But you must be alive to do so— 'there are no great works done by the dead.'"

Aran rubbed his face with both hands, suddenly tired. "I saw the one-eyed Faerie. He was watching you."

"I know."

"Storng, just teach me how to be the most powerful shaman possible. I'll worry about staying alive."

Settling into a comfortable squat behind the Dollar Store, he folded his tail and wings. He looked closer at the building, an ugly flat-roofed block rectangle with a simple sign in front and its parking lot unredeemed by landscaping. The store sat toward the back of the lot, and a paved area behind it contained a dumpster, enclosed by rotting wooden fencing and two concrete posts to deter delivery trucks from hitting the door. A wide road in front linked the parking lots of other equally unimpressive commercial buildings. At the far end of the rear parking lot, where Aran hid, a storm water pond had become a cattail marsh.

Dense cloud cover obscured the summer moon. As the Tiki

Crew stood in the pond, steamy fog obscuring its surface, they reviewed their roles. Storng was in charge of disabling the alarm, the crew targeting the list of items they sought, and Aran ensuring their escape was uncompromised. Hardest of these tasks was the harvesting. This type of store was one of "The Big Three"—the discount, hardware, and craft stores Paerries depended on for the basic goods of their civilization. Because they drew so heavily on these sources, the Silth had to spread these harvests out to avoid suspicion.

Storng would handle payment tonight. The Silth paid homeowners by leaving shaman-blessed good luck charms to improve the owners' fortunes, but when they borrowed at The Big Three, they left jewels. While the crew believed they were paying for what they took, Storng told Aran he suspected the store managers simply pocketed the jewels. Aran asked "What's a store manager?" "Isn't that wrong?" and "How do you know these things?" Storng answered all the questions except the last one.

Silth craftsman could make many things—they could weave, sew, throw pots, bake ceramics, carve wood, and craft furniture. But they had no manufacturing, so tools, basic elements of goods, and finished goods themselves had to be obtained.

Although they wouldn't take a substantial quantity of any one thing, the list of tonight's items was long, from sponges and Epsom salt to tape and tweezers. While each crew member had his or her target items, Storng would search for the unexpected items. The crew wondered how Storng could be sure the listed items would be in the building, but he was never wrong.

Storng pulled a cardboard box from the dumpster, setting it next to the back door so he couldn't be spotted from the doorway. As the lot cleared of cars, anyone who happened to notice would merely see a large egret—they were common enough birds in these parts—standing beside a big box. Odd, but by no means alarming.

Finally, a young woman emerged through the back door, wearing the Dollar Store uniform of khaki pants and shirt with "Rose" embroidered on the left pocket. She propped open the door with a broken cinder block and started carrying boxes to the dumpster. When done, she grabbed the box Storng had hidden behind and tossed it in the dumpster, but he'd already slipped inside the building. She moved the block aside, and the door closed behind her with a sharp click.

Aran could see the Tiki Crew fidgeting in their positions in the pond. The lights and sign snapped off, plunging the front of the store and most of the parking lot into darkness. Rose and an older woman exited the back and left in their respective cars.

With the back lot empty, Aran joined the crew as they rushed from the marsh to the back door. Storng was to have hidden inside where he could see the code the last employee punched in to arm the alarm and would disable it using the same code. No one spoke. No one moved. A loud pop from inside was followed by Storng opening the door. Aran dragged over the same broken block Rose had used and propped it open. As the crew filed in, Storng shone a small flashlight on the open alarm panel, where a thin stream of smoke winded its way upward.

Storng shrugged in response to their questioning looks. "I saw all the numbers she entered except for the last one. So I used magic. It will probably work." He added, "Humans say 'the best laid plans of mice and men' …."

Aran had no idea what that meant—the mice he knew made

no plans. He followed the others, curious to see what the interior looked like before taking up his position outside. The crew, each one carrying a harvest bag, spread out in the giant room, with its rows of shelves faintly lit by parking lot lights shining through windows. The bags were magically enhanced to hold more and absorb much of their contents' weight. Storng called them "rowling bags," but never explained why.

As the others ran to their assigned portions of the store and started stuffing items in their bags, Storng hurried down an aisle, looking right or left and shoving additional items into his own bag.

"Buuhahaaa," said the grotesque face suddenly appearing in front of Loana. She let out a shout and tried to kick Don, who ran off laughing with mask in one hand and penlight in the other.

A few moments later, Don yelped as Vic pelted him with automatic fire from a Nerf gun. As Don chased Vic, Storng shouted, "Stop that, you pack of peccaries! Work faster!"

Aran's eyes adjusted to the light coming in the windows, and he realized how easily they could be seen from outside. He reluctantly worked his way back out and to the edge of the parking lot.

About thirty minutes after the crew entered, the first police cruiser's flashing blue lights reflected off the trees behind the store. Aran closed his hand around the soil he held and sent his thoughts to Storng. *Big problem. Police.*

He found himself bathed in blue light, and he jerked back into the shadows watching the lights of a second police car pull in front of the store. He nearly squawked as two officers got out of the first car, pulling out flashlights and unsnapping their gun holsters.

The shorter one spoke into his arm mike. "Back door's propped open with something."

Aran thought to Storng, *two Humans advancing on back door,* and heard Storng's response as clearly as if he were whispering in his ear: *Trapped. Can't go out front. Will be seen if they enter. Can you distract?* Aran scanned the ground around him. If he failed yet again … no, the Tiki Crew needed him.

As the officers neared the door, Aran eyed the police car behind them. He flew over and quietly opened the front passenger door. Heaving a sign of relief when no light came on, he closed the door carefully enough for it to catch with only a slight click. He stepped across to the driver's side. While he understood the concept of cars, he had no clue how to make it go. He saw pedals, but his feet couldn't reach them.

He knew the car worked by fire, and he wanted it to move backward, so he mentally reached out to its engine. As he began to chant, he immediately realized this wouldn't work, as there were no flames in the engine. Apparently, it needed fire to begin. He pulled out a lighter, clicked it on, and resumed the chanting as Storng had taught him. Little magic existed within the words—their repetition simply calmed and focused his mind.

Just as the police started in the back door, Aran forced his will into a magic burst and shot it into the steering column. The car lurched backward, its lights flashing on and off, horn blowing and siren wailing. Both policemen whirled around, mouths agape, and bolted for the car. But every time they got close, it leaped again, just out of their reach. The car lurched and stopped three more times across the rear parking lot and behind the other buildings. The engine wasn't going, Aran was simply causing it to work for a few seconds at a time. At

Aran's bidding, it gave a final burst of several dozen feet before slowing to a stop between the police and the storm water pond. The energy had damaged the electrical system of the car so the blue lights spun madly with the siren wailing in alternating patterns of sounds.

Guns drawn, the officers rushed the passenger side of the car. Both shouted, "Out of the car! Hands in the air! Out of the car!"

Aran dove out the driver's side just as one policeman darted forward, threw open the passenger side door, and jumped back. Seeing no one inside, both hurried around the car to the pond's edge, their lights sweeping across its misty surface.

Surely they can hear my heart. As the policemen trained their lights on him, he hoped they saw a large blue heron ambling through the water. He froze, lifted one foot out of the water, and twisted his head slowly to look at them. After sticking his foot back in the water, he forced himself to keep the same pace while wading into the cattails and reeds. He glanced up as the sounds of a flock of birds passed overhead, but it was impossible to tell if it was the Tiki Crew.

He waited among the cattails as the officers circled the pond and searched. When a van brought in two large, floppy-eared dogs, he realized he was really starting to dislike the animals. Both went crazy as they sniffed Aran's path from car to water. But as their handlers circled them around the pond, the frantic barking ceased, and they merely whined in frustration. He listened to the policemen's angry speculation over how someone could have gotten past them.

Light had begun seeping into the morning as the older employee came to check that the back door was locked and she and the officers finally left. Aran landed to the smell of breakfast and the shouts of "Aran!" from the Tiki Crew, all awake awaiting his safe arrival. Nadara took one arm, Loana the other, their skin warm from the fire, and each ran a hand over his chest.

Nadara said playfully, "My hero!" and he rolled his eyes. They pulled him toward the flames where Don, Vic, and Nick were playing a lively reel as Kirstn and Marina danced with abandon. To the others' surprise, Aran laughed and joined in.

Before long, a small silver flask was being passed around, and he found it shoved into his hand. As the sunrise glinted off the metal, he lifted it to his lips. Just one sip would be okay. Just one … to celebrate. But when he saw his face reflected in the silver of Shra's wide bracelet on his arm, he shook his head, passed the flask to Vic, and picked up a cup of water from a nearby stump.

As he turned back to what had become a substantial bonfire, he saw that Nadara had stopped dancing and was eyeing him. He raised his water to her in a silent toast and smiled. She winked, clapped her hands above her head, and rocked her hips to the music, wings spread fully behind her. Loana grabbed her hand, and they skipped around the fire. Aran snatched up the Silth squeeze box beside Vic and played with the rest until the sun was high above the trees.

CHAPTER FIVE

Scene 1

JOSS (HUMAN)

Joss walked among the big cages between the lodge and the rainforest edge. Most housed one or two big scarlet macaws, noisily commenting on her passage, but a few held great green macaws, white-crowned and brown-hooded parrots, and crimson-fronted parakeets. Around the cages, more parrots came and went—some were prior releases, while others just enjoyed the food and company. For Joss, their raucous chatter was a joyful shower of noise.

Calling each bird by name, she tucked food and water into cages. She talked to them about their health, their relationships, and when they'd be released back into the wild. She told them to appreciate the wealthy private donors funding their reintroduction. As she started to say how plentiful they once had been in this part of the country, she stopped herself, not wanting to make them sad. Silly. They won't understand, but still ….

She told them about the nearby colony of green macaws she monitored. She even spoke about the easements she had negotiated with surrounding farmers to protect the parrots, jaguars, and howler monkeys inhabiting the region. Each farmer was paid to leave a corridor of his or her property in trees or underbrush, along the edge of the next property or a stream, and not put out traps or poison on their farms. This provided a way for those animals with a wide range to roam freely;

a side benefit was refuge for songbirds from raptors.

Easements were the recorded, legal documentation of those commitments. If Joss could secure the protection of an entire property, she'd be thrilled, but if she could protect only a corridor of forest along a river or a known wildlife passage, at least that would allow movement between the government-created and private wildlife refuges—the islands of protection.

"But then someone loses a goat or chicken," she said aloud. "And out comes the poison. Easements can be hard to enforce." Joss laughed as Ruby, a scarlet macaw, bobbed her head in complete agreement. Next to her Bocco hopped from foot to foot.

"I think I'm pretty good at this job," she went on, moving her cleaning supplies to the next set of cages and filling food trays. "I help people understand how important preserving you is to the economy. In return I earn a little money. Enough to buy some olives and sunflower seeds. And I get to live in this beautiful lodge. Smack dab in the center of three thousand acres of rainforest awesomeness. Every day I bask in the magic of this world."

The program she ran at the Casa de No Gatos for her patrons was a mix of rehabilitation and captive breeding for wild release. The scarlet macaws were permanent residents, sometimes seriously disabled in accidents and brought here to live as the source of new scarlets. Ruby, for example, was a wild parrot who lost both eyes to a cat before being rescued, while Bocco had been struck by a truck. The center hoped to re-establish the huge flocks of scarlets once inhabiting the region. Most of the other birds were rescued from poachers—this place was just a way station on their journey back into the wild—or they had been donated from homes having outlived their owners or exhibiting behavior making them unwelcome in the home. The center was trying to adapt these, like the newborn scarlets, to life in the wild. Many of the parrots had been Joss's companions since she had arrived four months earlier, not long after the fire.

She still thought about that traumatic night. Working at the biology station had left her feeling like the witness to the slow death of a friend—the continued nibbling away at the rainforest. But that night showed her that, frustrated though she was, violence was not her path. That night had also been a trigger, almost costing her sobriety, even after all these years. It took her a week to find her center and get her act together enough to stay on her path. She increased her exercise to a full hour each day, meditated an extra half hour, and participated in her online AA meetings every night. Her journal showed how close to drinking again she had come.

She quit both Return and her job at the biology station. She'd been packing to return to the States when some friends recruited her for the current job. They had little difficulty in persuading her—it was her dream job in so many ways. She had meaningful work that made a difference and time to do her sobriety support. She read her favorite blogs from Mental Floss and her magazines The Week, People, and even The New Yorker, though the latter mostly for the cartoons. She was also writing music. Still, the isolation, while at first a relief, had begun to wear on her. She hadn't expected to be lonely.

She hoped that Kate would take her up on a visit. The invitation she'd extended probably was not the most compelling. "Leave New Orleans. Come stay with me in the middle of the jungle. There'll be no alcohol in the house, no smoking, no drugs, and I'm on a pretty strict diet." The food could be the deal-breaker for Kate, though both had agreed that chocolate was not subject to restriction.

But it wasn't as if she had no social life. She could go to the nearby village. Most came by river but there was a winding rut road allowing her access to a little soda where she could have her favorite breakfast—black beans and rice seasoned with onion, peppers, and a hefty dose of the local savory condiment "lizard sauce," as well as fried eggs, sour cream, and corn tortillas. Refescoes, a blend of fruit and ice, and coffee were her staples if she came later in the day. Or on a "wild and crazy night," maybe a horchata, made of ground rice and cinnamon. Every couple of weeks, she danced salsa at local bars. Being in bars around liquor was a challenge, but so was too much loneliness. Bars, church, and the parrots were pretty much her only choices for companionship since she'd eschewed the whole tourist sex scene.

She had plenty of friends among the locals and the extensive expat community in the surrounding biology stations. But the distances, lack of roads, and working 24/7 except for an occasional night off, meant she could go for days and not talk to someone in person. Most of the biologists were either older than her twenty-eight years or young interns still in college. She had occasional visits from benefactors and transient travelers, and chatted with family and friends every couple of days, thanks to a voice and video internet app. The lodge's internet was solid and free. But mostly she talked to parrots.

These days, she worked to stop the destruction of the remaining rainforest through letters and meetings and the hard work of rehabbing and raising parrots instead of staffing the biology station. What would be the point, she'd ask friends during an evening dance break, of building a tourist infrastructure if along the way they destroyed the very thing tourists came to see? She worked hard to help tourists understand the rainforest as more than a setting for zip lines and tropical meals.

The public, and even the private, conservation conversations were mostly civil, although tension had risen recently. Two resort owners had been killed in a fire following a local environmental activist's beating—to protest the deaths, several of the larger resorts shut down for two weeks and sent their workers home without pay. The environmental activist community pointed out that the beating, which left the woman unable to walk, followed the disappearance and presumed deaths of three other activists in Costa Rica, five in Brazil, and two in Ecuador. The incidents divided the community. Joss hoped Brophy had not been involved in the local incident.

She closed the cage door. "Well, yes, Jimbo. I like Brophy." Jimbo cocked his head to the side, listening intently. "Just not as much as he wants."

She'd sat beside Brophy at their first Return meeting and enjoyed his "surfer dude meets concerned environmentalist" vibe. She allowed him to talk her into the raid, letting the excitement of actually doing something overcome her boredom. The catastrophe of that night's raid and fires had cooled her feelings for Brophy, though he seemed undaunted. Really, she knew better—the alcohol-fueled misadventures of her youth should have taught her that these things never ended well.

She had to distance herself from drama. Staying sober was hard enough. Harder still was staying sober and trying to make a difference in something small like the extinction of entire species. No, she definitely didn't need Brophy's drama on top of all that.

She smiled when she saw a shaft of sunlight piercing the trees not far from the parrot cages. Putting down her supplies, she crunched over through fallen leaves, and as she tilted her head back, the sun shone warm on her face. She lifted her arms away from her sides, spinning slowly in the light.

Scene 2

Merit (Silth)

"Merit, what're we doing?" a small, blue-hathered Silth asked. "How's she any different from all the others around here?"

With their usual parrot glamours, Merit, the blue, and one other Silth were sitting on a strangler fig tree branch at the clearing's edge.

"I really don't know," Merit said. She wasn't in the mood to explain the procedures they followed.

"She seems to take good care of the parrots, and she lets most of them go."

The blue had directed her comments to a random point in the yellow hather of Merit's forehead. The side of Merit's face didn't move when she spoke. Though unscarred, the muscles had been damaged in the same event that had taken her hand. Merit didn't follow the almost universal custom of the Silth to project perfect features. She'd utilize her parrot glamour, but beneath it, she allowed the world to see her as she really appeared. Used to projected perfection, most Silth avoided looking directly at her face.

As Merit shifted, her Silth-made uniform creaked. The mix of fabrics and leather resulted in a tunic that fit tightly enough not to snag on trees as she flew, but loosely enough for her to fight.

"We're in charge of security for Kawran, and we follow anything potentially a threat to it. This Human— "Joss" I think she's called— spends much of her time in the field, at the parrot gathering place.

While some on the Council fear she might be the advance scout for more rainforest destruction, I think her intent is benign".

Merit liked this Human, although she wondered how Joss could stand to be alone so much. Silth were almost never by themselves, but this Human spent most of her time away from her kind. She appeared self-sufficient and independent, and she seemed to care deeply about the nature of the rainforest, judging from the way she managed the lodge and its surroundings. Merit appreciated the way she talked to the parrots as she checked on and fed them, and she wondered if the conversations were her way of fending off loneliness. Sometimes she talked as though she thought the parrots might answer. Having watched the Human release parrots who'd recovered from their injuries, Merit knew she was not intent on enslaving them. But she couldn't really determine exactly what the woman's intentions were. In the meantime, there was no reason to scare the young blue.

"This is just field study," Merit finally said. "Take good notes on what she does."

Scene 3

FAELEN (TROW)

Faelen lounged at the edge of the same clearing. He could see the heat of the Human female, her parrots, and the hidden Paerries even when they were hidden by the vegetation. He knew why he watched the parrots. Their beauty pulled him to them like a magnet, and watching the others was probably an act of boredom. He slid a look at a small troop of howler monkeys—they were making their way, hooting and growling, from the hillside to the fruit trees near the lodge—but his gaze returned to the parrots.

He was sober occasionally in the blur of days and slept when his body demanded it. When it rained, he bathed. He thought a lot and remembered a few of the sober thoughts. Time dragged. The terms of his exile assured it. The rest of his life … hundreds, potentially thousands, of years.

What was he going to do with this life? Even watching his beloved parrots had lost some of its joy as he realized his stay in this world would be permanent. Except that he would go mad well before then. That happened when Trow spent too long in this world filled with Human technologies.

What will it take to end my sentence? He could stop drinking. Beg his father's forgiveness. Promise to live a useful life in the Land. Unfortunately, he had no skills, at least none that his kind valued, so he would have to rejoin the Trow army. The thought depressed him even more. He was good at killing Trow. Not at art. Or commerce. Just killing. Or rather hunting down rebel Trow and killing them. Good enough to become a general in his father's forces. But that life took its own toll.

The appearance of a truck with TOYOTA in big letters on its front ended Faelen's musings. It lumbered through the ruts leading into the compound and stopped in front of the lodge. A Human male climbed out and went inside.

Angeles, Thest's assassin and spy, got out and leaned against the front of the truck, scanning along the edge of the clearing. Faelen watched as her eyes stopped on the tree where the Paerries sat, and a grin sprang to her face. In the Trow's spectrum of sight, the Paerries were not hidden at all. Angeles's eyes moved further along the tree line, stopping just where Faelen was peering through the trees, and she grinned again. Then she pushed off the truck fender and ambled into the nearby forest.

Faelen could not recall Angeles's actual Trow name, just the one she went by on Earth. He knew Thest used her to eliminate both Human and Trow "problems," individuals who had seen the wrong thing or did not heed a Trow warning. Angeles had spent more time on Earth than any other Trow still alive. Rumor had it that she had a trophy room hidden away, where she kept souvenirs of her Human, Trow, and other Earth species kills. But several decades ago she had been removed from the Earth, told by Trow physicians that she could tolerate no more exposure, so Faelen was surprised to see her here.

As the Paerries shot out of the tree, Faelen stepped back, a quick spell rendering him invisible to Angeles, and melted into the brush. Angeles is back, pretending to be a Human. Xafar's big plan to retake the Earth must be underway. Faelen had been absent from the palace long enough that he had no idea it had actually begun. This changed everything.

Suddenly his future was much less predictable.

Scene 4

Joss (Human)

Finished with her parrot chores, Joss was inside the lodge when she heard the truck. From the sound of the engine, she knew it was Brophy, but she really hoped Angel wasn't with him. Something about the woman—a little craziness deep in her eyes, a hardness to her personality, a tendency now and then to be clueless as to others' emotions—wigged Joss out to the point of fear. At times it almost seemed Angel had brainwashed Brophy.

The door opened and Brophy called out, "Joss?"

She was in the public part of the lodge so technically knocking was unnecessary, bur still the familiarity of his walking right in uninvited caused her to growl under her breath. *Well, at least I know he's not a vampire.* He was alone.

"Hi, Brophy. How's it going?"

"It would go better if you'd come work with us," he told her, walking up too close to her before taking two steps back.

She said nothing—they'd covered this ground several times before.

He glanced around at the room, bigger than any in the biology station where they'd retreated after their eco-resort raid.

"Pretty Spartan."

The walls of the public rooms were free of decoration except for a few black-framed parrot photographs and a big map hanging behind an old, steel monolith of a desk. Three metal file cabinets, rusty along the edges, sat against the wall below the map. Near the desk, a low table with four folding chairs was littered with maps and legal documents for conservation easements and passage agreements. Field gear and transportation cages for the parrots as well as their food and veterinary supplies took up much of the room, in a way she knew looked haphazard to Brophy but worked for her.

"I came to say good-bye. I'm gonna be on the road a few weeks, so I won't be able to check on you."

"Don't really need checking on, but nice thought. And you're going ...?" She knew better than to ask, but the question just slipped out.

"Ehhh, can't really say."

"Doesn't matter." She turned away and shuffled some papers on her desk.

His words tumbled out. "You should come with us. Everyone misses you. There's lots to do and I ... we need you."

She suspected he'd rehearsed more elegant words, but no matter. She had no interest in or sympathy for him or another effort to recruit her back to Return. She sighed. "Not my world any more. I have plenty to do here."

"With these parrots? The easement and passages stuff? Small potatoes. You have to think bigger. The world needs you ... to step up. These tiny steps you're taking won't stop the bulldozers. Anyway, this ..." he swept his arm toward her desk, "Won't matter when the temperature changes this habitat."

"Stop," she snapped. "Spare me the lecture. I won't use violence to confront violence. I agree we have to do more. I'm studying Martin Luther King and Gandhi, trying to figure out what a truly non-violent but committed movement would look like. I just know your way won't work."

The result of their raid was, as she predicted, only delay, and the eco-lodge they burned had opened seven months behind schedule. Juan left the country to avoid explaining his injury and fearing that if the police got DNA from the blood he left behind, they might trace it to him. News coverage had been extensive, and he felt exposed.

Worst of all, somehow Joss's biggest benefactor, Doug Waits, had heard she might have been involved in the arson. A gruff but humorous man, Doug loved the rainforest and visited Costa Rica every chance he got. A biology professor in a small Tennessee college, he'd come into a substantial inheritance late in life. He was allergic to controversy, and when rumors of her possible involvement began circulating, he said he could no longer support her at the biology station. To her relief, he'd given her a good recommendation when her new sponsors called him.

"Joss, there's no neutrality. If you don't fight it, then you're part of it. King, Gandhi, Mandela were successful because there was a real threat of violence in the alternative. No ANC ... no desire for the peaceful alternative."

She sighed. "You think people chose massive change through peaceful means only because of fear, instead of the inspiration that these men and those who stood beside them brought. I think you're wrong. Read Paul Hawken's *Blessed Unrest*. We have the biggest social movement in humanity's entire history at work. Brophy, you confuse nonviolence with collaboration. Always have. I fight every day. But I'm not going to hurt people." She stopped, realizing that she had let herself be drawn into an argument she didn't want to have and that she was chewing on her bottom lip. Stupid habit.

He huffed out a breath. When he walked over to the table of maps, she resisted a sudden urge to sweep them all up so he wouldn't see her work. But then she realized he wasn't looking at the maps.

"I agree with you," he said quietly, much to her surprise. "That's why we're focusing on property. And doing our best to avoid hurting anyone. Hurting people just turns public sentiment against you."

"So you didn't kill those two resort owners?"

"What? Of course not!" His mouth dropped open and he shook his head. "I'm not saying their company didn't deserve it." He rubbed his face with his hands and then ran them back over his smooth head. "Nor that someone I know didn't do the work to find out they were the ones who beat Maria. But hell, no, I didn't do it."

You sound a little too proud that I'd think you might have, she almost blurted out. "You just painted the targets on their backs."

"Someone else decided they should answer for their crimes."

"I know it's supposed to be a secret and all that, but I heard through the grapevine you now head up Return's entire Costa Rica chapter, not just a cell."

"You're right. It is supposed to be secret." He paused, and she could tell he was waging an inner war as to what he should divulge. Finally, "I have a leadership position, but no one person leads Return. People come, people go. People act on their own. Leadership is based on action."

"Return is responsible for farmers not talking to me. For my inability to get donations from the business community."

"Are you saying that's my fault?"

She sighed again, knowing she wasn't getting through and unsure what she even wanted from him. "I'm saying that when you exercise the kind of force you're using, you generate a backlash making it harder to achieve our goals. And it is your fault you're not taking this in a better direction. Finding other alternatives to terrorism. The world has lost both its tolerance of terrorism and its ability to hear why anyone would turn to it."

Brophy flinched and began to say something, but stopped. After a pause, "I came here to talk about us. To ask you to come with me. But if you insist on talking about the cause, let's discuss the reality of a world in which humanity is a plague, a virus across the landscape. Its sprawling cities, its voracious agriculture and its destruction of forests. Its willingness to destroy everything else for its own ends. So many species lost every year, forever. Soon there'll be nothing left but the big machine for supporting Humans and the animals that feed and entertain them."

He studied her map's brightly colored stickers, indicating the farmer arrangements she had made. Suddenly he spun on his heel to face her. "This is not something that can be addressed by saving a few parrots! Negotiating one last passage for a few species that won't be allowed to survive because they don't further Human interests? That's fiddling while Rome burns!"

He rushed back to her, standing almost nose to nose, with fingers repeatedly fisting and releasing. "Everything that Humans touch withers. In computers they'd be the virus that destroys the system. In the real world they're the virus destroying the host. And don't offer me platitudes about love, or art, or even the innocence of a child. All I see are the self-serving actions of a species that believes it's entitled to destroy the Earth for its needs and desires."

She had taken a step back to put distance between them.

Mouth dry, she started to speak, but he put up his hand.

"I'm not here to fight with you. It was a mistake for me to come at all. Take care of yourself, Joss." When he opened the front door, it smacked into the wall behind him and bounced halfway back.

From the doorway, she watched him glance inside his truck before calling out, "Angel! Time to go."

So scary Angel is here after all. Joss winced as the woman materialized from the forest and loped toward the truck. With a jack-o-lantern grin directed at Joss, she slid behind the wheel, while Brophy took the passenger side. As Joss watched the truck bounce down the road and disappear into a shadow, Brophy never looked back.

She shut the door, and a tiny shiver skittered up her spine. Both Brophy's words and his demeanor had frightened her, the latter for the first time. Whatever Return is up to, it's really, really bad.

CHAPTER SIX

Scene 1

ARAN (SILTH)

Aran coughed as a gust of wind sent tendrils of smoke swirling his way. The crew had built a fire every night they could, and when they first started their journey, the flames were inviting on chilly nights. In the warmth of summer, the fire had become communal, with everyone sitting at least twenty feet away from the heat. Except tonight—Storng was close, looking across the flames as he spoke, embers glowing at his feet.

Although Aran steadfastly refused to tell any of the stories for which he was trained, he had come to enjoy the evening ritual of hearing others' accounts of the day's adventures and their version of stories.

Storng was retelling the story of the schism between Faeries and Silth and why both hid from Humans. When he faced one direction, the fire reflected in his white eye, changing to darkness when he turned the other way. Aran knew the story well—he had told it himself numerous times. Woven in was the story of the different magics of the three species, as well as the basic magic of the world. Storng was using a "call and response" form of storytelling, by starting the tale, asking another Silth to continue it awhile, and then taking over again. He told them it was a test, to see if they "knew as much about magic as a coatimundi."

Storng began with, "When Earth was young, and the plants and animals were emerging, Earth's magic brought balance to this new world, folding wind, fire, water, and soil in with this new life. As the rain fell and a stream was born, it came into balance with the land through which it flowed and the lakes and oceans it fed. Banks formed, covered with grass to hold the dirt in place and filter the water. Stones slowed the water so it wouldn't wash away the banks. The water gave life to the grass and trees at its edge. All was in balance. It was this balance that was the magic, not the creation of the things themselves or even their function. Science, as the Humans call it, or religion explains these functional aspects of life—but it's the balancing force that is Earth's magic.

"As plants reproduced, certain insects learned ways around their defenses so they could eat while not destroying the plants, and their relationship continued for ages. Certain bird species learned to eat some of these bugs but not all, so the birds prospered. Other birds ate these species of birds. And they prospered. Bacteria learned to thrive while making their animal hosts healthier.

"A magic exists in the world, running through all the living things, that constantly realigns them with Earth's systems. In this magic, the waste product of one species always becomes ..." he trailed off, pointed to Nadara.

She said, "Becomes the food for another." Vic sniggered, his grin instantly wiped away when Storng turned his dark eye upon him, and Nadara continued. "There are always checks and balances keeping one species from overwhelming the others. Even though the climate and context conditions are constantly changing, there is a return to balance in each successive circumstance.

"That was not the only magic," she went on, gesturing with sweeping arm movements. "When something disrupted the relationships—a drought or a flood came, or some disease took out one of the creatures in this chain of beneficial dependencies—the Earth system would adjust, returning to a stable state. Another species would adapt to take their place. A whole series of adjustments might occur, restoring harmony. This was magic. This balancing force shared among all things animate or inanimate is called 'Earth magic.' Then Humans came into the world. Although infused with Earth magic, they developed another magic, stronger in some ways because it was easy to use whether by an individual or collectively. It got even stronger when they combined it with tools. That magic broke the world."

"No," Storng interjected. "That magic allowed them to bend the Earth to their will." He picked up the story again. "Humans have their own magic. One in which their will and the things they pray for, focus upon, believe in, become reality. This is true whether their belief is explicitly aimed at creating the reality or unconscious. One manifestation of this magic was—" He gestured to Don.

"Their creation of technology." Don's voice boomed even when he tried to speak softly, like now. "In the same way Faeries or Silth might develop spells or other devices to direct their magic, the Humans create technologies that change the world. Other creatures are able to shape the world. Termites construct mounds, birds build nests, oysters form shells, but whatever they do is enveloped by the Earth magic and integrated into the systems and relationships around them. Each is food or shelter for something other than the creature that builds it. But by force of will, Humans have the ability to force the world into objects of their desire, whether or not these changes can be absorbed by the Earth. Animals had made tools, but from the 'Human magic' technology flowed, and the changes by Humans came quickly. They created things to level whole forests, pull minerals from the Earth, and grow crops, whether or not the soil supported them. They turned these into factories, dwellings, cities and farms—products. They bent the systems of air, fire, water, and soil to their desires, forming them into—"

"The things Humans imagine." Storng took up the story thread again. "This magic overwhelms the Earth magic and bends it to the Human will. But sometimes the Earth magic causes unexpected distortions of the results. It struggles to absorb the Human magic and at times succeeds. The Earth might take eons folding a species of bee into balance with the flowers it fed on while pollinating and the bear who raided its hive. Humans create a chemical that wipes out the bee in just a few years. In all of this, Humans are mostly unaware of magic's role in their society. They think of the world as operated through a tension between religion, science, and their free will as individuals. They tell stories of magic to their children without understanding it."

Storng swept his eyes across them. As he turned his back to the fire, it shifted with a low rustling sound and sent ember fireflies sailing above them. "Now a third magic exists as well. Faerie magic. No one is quite sure when it arrived. The Faeries came from beneath the ground, a place they call the 'Land' but we call 'Faerie.' They claim they were on the Earth before Humans. Although they have no magic in their own world, on Earth they have 'Faerie magic.' Theirs is just as disruptive as Human magic because it is the application of will to the world, regardless of the fabric torn by the action. The Faeries themselves, however, found peace in the flow of Earth magic. They came from their world, full of violence and the application of will against will, and in the embrace of Earth magic they calmed and found happiness.

"But the Faeries were allergic to the Human magic and the electrical technologies it wrought. As the world filled with Human magic and electricity, the Faeries were pushed further and further into the wild places or the small Human villages. The Faeries grew weaker and missed their opportunity to remove Humans from the world, something certainly within their power."

Storng stopped and looked over at Aran. Everyone sat completely still as the fire crackled, and Aran continued the lesson in his raspy voice.

"Into this quiet struggle, another race was born. The Silth, the children of Faerie fathers and parrot mothers. Their offspring, part Faerie, part parrot, are harvested by the Silth colonies, taken from their mothers when they are young, and raised with other Silth. Silth themselves cannot reproduce, so they have no children of their own. Silth use weak forms of two magics—Earth magic and a diminished version of Faerie magic. As Human populations rose, parrot and Silth habitats declined. Faeries started abandoning the world, so the Silth population tumbled. Rejected by the Faeries and fearing Humans, Silth make their way in the world apart from either.

"Silth can cast glamours. Their unhatched eggs can support glamours over villages as well. But while they can do a few magics, they have neither Human nor Faerie strength. They inherited some of the Faerie allergy to Human magic. While it causes the Silth no harm to stay on Earth—after all, their mothers, the parrots, were of the Earth—they can be harmed, and their personalities bent and misshapen, by prolonged exposure to technology. Which is why Silth do not manufacture or copy technologies they observe."

Storng took back over and finished the story the group had grown up hearing. What he said was mostly true. Aran now knew what was known only to the shamans—the rest of the story. He'd learned that the Silth have more power than most realize, and that the Faeries kill any utilizing this additional power. They use the shamans and the Silth religious leaders to suppress any efforts at developing this power. The shamans are allowed this knowledge to understand the importance of keeping the secrets ... for Silth survival.

He had asked Storng why, if the Faeries considered the Silth a threat, they chose not to wipe them out. According to Storng, the Faeries had never answered this question directly. While the Faeries did commit the occasional execution of a Silth or an entire colony of them, the Silth didn't know what stayed their hand against mass extermination of them or the Humans. Over the years Silth had formulated many theories. One led to the emergence of a fast-growing religion, New Faerie, with which Aran was quite familiar, as its leader was his brother Casius. Throughout the colonies, its adherents, or "Newfies," worshipped all things Faerie. Many aspired to be Faeries themselves, a physical impossibility. They believed that Faeries had rejected the Silth because they were unworthy and had made mistakes. They would not discuss their parrot lineage, and they were convinced that if they could be strong and atone for their mistakes, the Faeries would accept them and bestow upon them full Faerie powers.

Aran's eyes grew heavy as Storng launched into another familiar story, this one a funny tale of ancient times. Before long he was asleep, the red glow of firelight playing on the backs of his eyelids. He found himself in the dream again, flying above Shra, as always looking down on her with the ocean of green below her. But unlike any of the previous dreams, this time she dipped down into the trees. As she landed and he swooped down beside her, she was laughing. She reached for his face—

Applause, whoops, and shouts woke him with a start. Storng was smiling and acknowledging the Tiki Crew's salute to his tale. Aran faced a round of solicitations for the day's story, and he declined the role of storyteller, pointing to his throat and giving a sad shake of the head.

Feigning reluctance, Nadara stood up to relate the day's activities, circling to each crew member as she spoke. Aran watched her graceful movements. The way she tilted her head to the side when interrupted by questions. The easy way she laughed. The fluid sweep of her arms as she gestured and the way she sometimes undulated her upper body to make a point. Like every other, this day had been filled with minor dramas and adventures, all of which she exaggerated to great effect. She had gentle fun at some of the crew's expense, and, as always, she told the stories well.

Aran had been waiting for her to address the incident on his mind much of the day, and sure enough, "One of our targets today was medical supplies. As you know, sometimes we take from veterinary clinics and other times from doctors' offices or hospitals. Today four of us were borrowing from a doctor's office not open for patients, but with staff in parts of the building. Rather than wait for the staff to leave, we decided to go ahead."

She acknowledged Storng's frown with a slight tip of the head. "We were excited to find more target supplies than expected and removed a reasonable portion, although only a small fraction of the hoard. But as Don, the last of us, was leaving, he overheard the nurse in the office talking about how difficult it had been to gather these supplies. How excited they were to be traveling with them to help a place called Guyana, a country back near our homes. They spoke of how badly people there needed these supplies. That children would live because they received this medicine. After Don told us what he heard, the group discussed it, and we decided to return the supplies. We were almost caught returning swag!"

All the crew chuckled and Nadara continued the story, but Aran knew the decision to return the medical supplies had not come lightly. Normally they did not take a risk to put things back. Loana had argued that the amount they had taken would not make a difference. But Don won the group over with an argument that grew from Silth superstition—if their borrowing caused harm to even one person, bad consequences for the Silth would result.

While Aran was proud of his Silth partners, he had to admit that he also was impressed with the Humans. Storng had been right in saying it was difficult to hate an entire species. But day by day, Aran felt the circle of his hatred narrow, like a spotlight, always tightening, releasing some from its glare, but growing in intensity. When he thought about the poachers who had killed Shra, all traces of good feeling evaporated. They had the capacity for good and evil, and they chose evil.

Aran made his way to his hammock high in a nearby tree.

As they flew up the slope, the rainforest turned to cloud forest. Shra dropped into the canopy, heading for the ruins of Tranack, an old Silth colony. He tensed as he dropped back into the forest's fingers of light and dangerous shadow. Here, trees contained platforms in front of holes and treehouses, as far back as they could see. A much larger structure, built in the center, was still intact but had become part of the forest, like most of the buildings wrapped with vines and covered in green, red, and yellow plants fighting for purchase. The lashings holding together walls and roofs of many of the structures had given way, causing them to collapse like crushed gourds. Limbs punctured floors, and hollow entrances were crisscrossed with cobwebs. No Silth had lived here in four or five lives.

Shra landed on a limb that gave her a view of the whole colony, sighing as she went through the awkward motion of moving her wings out of the way. "Sometimes wings are such a pain." Her yellow sarong gently hugged the curves of her hips—like most jungle-dwelling Silth, she avoided both loose and too tight clothing for easier movement through the trees.

Aran looked out at the old structures, whose arrangement was still the common design for Silth communities. "Back in the strong time, this was a thriving place, with lots of shamans and legions of hunters, warriors, makers and artists. The troupes of singers, unlike me, never had to travel to other villages. Silth did nothing but play instruments in the gatherings."

"If you hadn't flown to other villages, you never would've met me." She winked, sending warmth spreading through his face.

"They told stories for days at their festivals," he went on. "Using big drums and the shared pipes that take twenty Silth each to operate, while a hundred Silth played the whistles, flutes, lyres, and small drums. Human shamans even joined in—that was before the Spaniards came." He shifted on the branch to look at her. "I met you one pass around the sun ago. And it took three months before you'd spend a moment alone with me."

"Ha. Your reputation preceded you. Hundreds of broken hearts. Week-long drinking parties."

He rolled his eyes. "Hundreds? Week-long?"

"That was what your friends said. Others put both numbers much higher. I had no interest in being another Heartless trophy. That's still true. I'm not sure what we're doing."

She flapped her wings a couple of times, sped off toward the central building, and dove inside its open door. He crouched a moment longer on the branch, and then he joined her inside the large room. The floor was littered with hulls, fruit pits, and guano, evidence that birds and monkeys had spent time there. In the center was a square wooden box roughly Aran's size with no top. Inside a large, white egg-shaped object twice the size of his head lay on a mat of woven brown grasses.

He wrinkled his nose. "Awk, smells like monkeys in here." He walked to the window and leaned out.

The lower forest where their day had begun was its usual hot and muggy, and the rainy season, which would bring a constant drizzle broken by torrents, had not yet begun. Here in the cloud forest, it was cooler but almost always shrouded in clouds, with light mist from time to time. Aran noticed that the birds were finally relenting in their exuberant welcome of a sun they could not see, as the mid-morning clouds had already arrived. Their diminishing chorus was being augmented by the rising voices of bugs and frogs, as well as the bass of larger creatures thumping through the underbrush. Even so, the cloud forest was not as noisy as the rainforest.

"I hate the forest," Aran said softly.

Shra rolled her eyes. "You do? Pretty funny coming from a creature who is supposed to live in one."

He eyed the trees wrapping themselves around others, what the Humans fittingly called "strangler" figs. Every unmoving thing had *something else growing on it—moss, ferns, brightly-colored bromeliads and orchids. Trees had long, sharp thorns or poisons, as did the ants, frogs, snakes, and spiders living among them. And it had toucans. Plus, monkeys. Nothing worse than toucans and monkeys … except perhaps pumas, jaguars, snakes, and crocodiles. Even the pigs would happily eat the two of them. And he was always wet. He wore leather when he could, but his typical clothes, cotton shorts and a tunic, were usually heavy with moisture. Amidst the noise around him, there was the steady drip, drip, drip of the morning's light rain as it worked through the undergrowth to the ground.*

He gave a heavy sigh. "I think I'm supposed to live in the sky. Or maybe a meadow. Not where I can't risk walking on the ground because something will eat me or sit too long in one place because something will squeeze the life out of me or put my hand down without looking because something will sting me."

She put a hand on his arm. "Oh, is it so hard here? I had a great morning. More fun than I'd have thought possible."

He kissed her briefly once and then again, this time longer.

"I can't imagine a day without you," he said. "Not a single day. I know how to do three things—tell stories, play music, and build instruments. I'll stay with you in Kawran, build instruments, and raise clutch rescues." While many Silth relationships were exclusive, few were lifelong, so his commitment bordered on the extravagant.

He could see doubt swim through her eyes, and she paused a respectful moment before answering. "I know you say this from your heart, but the jaguar doesn't change his spots. You live for the dance, not the quiet. You've never lived the life you now say you want." She wagged her finger. "You say the words I want to hear, but I don't want to build a cage for you."

He laughed. "I've stayed in Kawran longer now than anywhere else I've lived since leaving my mother's side. Except for Amazonia, the shaman school. For the last ten trips around the sun, I've taught others the stories of our past, our dreams, and our way." He picked up her hand. "If life with you is a cage, I happily rush in and slam the door behind me."

Scene 2

ARAN (SILTH)

The next morning Aran was up with the sun. The Silth worked six days a week because Storng believed their attention to safety would decline without rest. Today was Aran's day off and happened to be a Saturday, the hardest day for harvesting as so many Humans had unpredictable schedules that day.

The morning had its typical noisy start as the Silth loudly extolled its beauty, called out insults to one another, and punctuated their conversations with more squawks and whistles than at any other time of day. Aran ate breakfast with the others and engaged in energetic conversations before they departed to tackle their assigned tasks.

What should I do with myself today? He settled on visiting a Human enclave to watch its activity. The other Tiki Crew members spent their day off with at least one their team mates, but he had no desire for company today. Just as well—Nadara was going to a nearby spring to picnic with Vic and Marina, and the rest were working.

His current glamour was a large, beautiful crane, indigenous to the area. He sat on a huge live oak where long strands of Spanish moss swayed in the gentle breeze. Beside it, a wide trail was flanked by palmetto underbrush. An extensive forest, what the Humans called a "nature preserve," surrounded this area and the nearby cluster of small wood and steel buildings that was connected to the trail. Storng had told him this place was called "The Refuge," where Humans who were broken, emotionally and mentally, went to heal. They came with every addiction imaginable—alcohol, drugs, under- or overeating, sex—and tried to overcome the trauma feeding the addiction as well as find release from their habits' deadly grips. Fascinating, the idea that Humans, like Silth, could be broken in that way.

Over the last several decades, as the stress of increased Human presence and habitat loss wore them down, the number of "broken" Silth had risen. Some shamans argued it was the absence of any big, meaningful projects. Communities no longer undertook the types of infrastructure projects that once brought them together. They didn't build new houses or found new colonies. The ministers of New Faerie insisted it was the decay of their moral core. Whatever the cause, many Silth had lives that revolved around some addiction.

Dozing in the sun, he waited for the Humans to begin their day. He was startled into full alert by the stirring of wing-flapped air. As Storng landed beside him—he was in crane glamour as well—Aran suppressed a groan. He spent less time with the elder shaman now, but when Storng sought him out like this, training inevitably ensued. The last time Storng had found him on his free day, one of the many religious festival days the Silth celebrated, Aran had ended up spending the day making an elaborate colored sand representation of the sky, Earth, and the underworld, bound together with the elements of fire, earth, air, and water. Shamans used these drawings, made with whatever media was available—if not colored sand, then crayons and bits of colored chalk—to meditate, focus more elaborate healing spells, and lead the festival celebrations.

In no hurry for more work, Aran barely roused from his morning stupor. *He always finds me—how? More magic he hasn't shown me.*

Storng settled himself on the branch, leaning forward with his elbows on his knees. After several minutes of silence, he said, "One of the events that changed my life occurred at this very place." He sucked in a deep breath, blew it out, and continued in his deep, gruff voice. "I was here a little later in the day, maybe even on this very branch, when a string of five horses with riders came down the path. Just as they did every morning about that time. The riders were of various ages, males and females, chatting softly as they rode. One of the horses stopped. The girl riding it, maybe eighteen or nineteen years old, climbed off to adjust the saddle straps.

"'I'll be right along, Ellen,' she called out. The older woman leading the riders smiled indulgently and nudged her horse on, calling back over her shoulder, 'Five minutes, Jocelyn. No more.'"

This is so much better than training, Aran thought, now fully alert. A monarch butterfly landed on the branch between them and stayed, as though interested in the story as well. He wondered if the butterfly saw them as cranes or Silth. Either way it seemed unconcerned by their presence.

"I watched her fiddle with the saddle straps until the other horses and riders had moved on. First, she patted the horse and told him, 'Good boy, Doyle.' Then she left him and walked over to one of several shafts of light piercing the canopy. Spotlighted by the sun, she lifted her arms, closed her eyes, and tipped back her head with her face to the sky. She slowly turned, stopping at the end of each quarter of the rotation. I didn't know if she was saluting the sun or the forest, or if she was hearing something I did not. But what drew me in that morning was her smile. One of ultimate pleasure, a deep happiness I found difficult to even imagine. As Jocelyn did her 'ceremony,' Doyle stayed close, munching grass."

Storng's eyes had gone soft and unfocused while he looked out over the clearing, as though he could see her again. "I was in a state where I couldn't imagine such bliss. Had just lost another student to the Faerie. Had left Amazonia and the life of a teacher to become a village shaman. Couldn't figure out how to move much of the harvest back to the colony. And I was sad more often than happy. I suppose all that had drawn me to this girl's few moments of true joy.

"Like some gentle timer had sounded, she opened her eyes, and her arms fell to her sides. Still smiling, she returned to her horse. As she grabbed the reins dragging the ground, he whinnied, reared, and took off at a full gallop. It all happened so fast she didn't drop the reins. He yanked her off her feet, and her head smacked on a large stump. And the very surprised snake on the other side struck her on the right cheek."

Aran realized he was holding his breath. He let it out and asked, "What did you do?"

"I leaped down and landed on the stump." He pointed. "That one. It's still there. I grabbed the snake, rattles going fast and furious, and flung it as far as I could into the grass. Her eyes were glazing over. Her cheek was swelling from the snakebite, her forehead bleeding from hitting the stump. She didn't seem to see me. So there I was, trying to figure out what to do. At some point when she failed to show up, the horse group would circle back for her. Though it was pretty obvious she'd hit her head, would they recognize the cheek injury as a snakebite? At the time I knew little about snakes in this part of the world, except for rattlesnakes, which I'd heard were poisonous. We deal with plenty of poisonous snakes in our part of the world, so I knew Humans die from such bites."

"And you had to decide if you should help a Human."

Storng nodded. "She moaned in pain. I reasoned out loud. 'If I don't do something, she may die. If I do something, the others may return and see me. And whatever that 'something' is—I hadn't figured that out yet—I've never done it before with a Human and may kill her. No ... it's too risky.'"

Aran understood Storng's conflict and wondered what he himself would do in such a case. Given his general feelings about Humans these days, even softened as they were, he doubted he'd take the risk.

"I was about to leave, but I looked at her again. Her skin was grey. She looked younger than I'd thought seeing her from a distance. And vulnerable. I brushed her hair away from her face, all the while thinking 'I'm a fool.' I scraped up dirt and held it against her. With one hand on her head where a goose-egg of a knot was rising, the other on her cheek over the snakebite, I did the recitation I've shown you."

Storng, like Aran, was able to communicate with all animals. Only one in a hundred Silth had this ability, and most of them became shamans.

"To keep her calm, I suppose. Did she answer?"

Storng shook his head. "She'd quit moving at all, a bad sign, and was barely breathing. I heard someone in the distance shouting her name. I concentrated, and I felt her pain flow into me. It quickly dissipated. The poison also entered me, causing me to stagger and breaking my contact with her. Her eyes flew open and grew the size of avocados. She let out a scream when she saw me, or rather, a great grey bird towering over her. Sluggish from the poison, I could barely fly, but approaching hoof beats spurred me on. I made it back to this tree and just leaned against the trunk, with the world spinning like I was drunk.

"Ellen, the woman leading the riders, jumped off her horse, and rushed over, asking Jocelyn if she'd been thrown. Jocelyn said, 'I'd climbed off … a rattler spooked him … I fell, hit my head.' She put her hand to her cheek, which I could just make out was no longer swollen. 'I think the snake bit me,' she said. Ellen checked Jocelyn's head, said it was a 'small bump.' Looked at her cheek, told her if the snake really had bitten her—she couldn't see any fang marks—it must not have been poisonous. She said, 'Let's get you to Nurse Rached.' I didn't know what that meant, but Jocelyn started laughing. That's when I knew she was okay."

"Wow," was all Aran could manage. Storng's story was the first time he'd heard of a modern Silth purposefully interacting with a Human. Such contact was strictly prohibited, one of the first lessons a young Silth learned. There were countless stories of bad consequences of such interactions. Bad for both the Silth involved and the Human.

"I was pretty proud of myself," Storng admitted, "and the dizziness had cleared at that point. As they were riding away, I did a crane happy dance on the limb. Not smart, I know. Jocelyn's head snapped up and she looked right at me. Twisted around, kept staring until my tree was out of view." He fell silent and eyed the butterfly, which fluttered up and away into the higher part of the tree.

"Why do I get the feeling there's more to this?"

Storng shifted a little on the branch before answering. "The next day I went back. Instead of landing on my usual limb, I settled back further in the trees, well away from the trail. I told myself I just wanted to check on Jocelyn, to see if she was well enough to show up. But I was also very nervous. What had she seen? Heard? Remembered?

I'd never revealed myself to a Human. A Silth can be banished for this. But honestly, I was more concerned about what it might do to Jocelyn. Since she was at The Refuge, she was clearly in a fragile state of mind for whatever reason. I might have made it worse.

"Before long, I heard the clomping of hooves on the path, and I was pleased to see her among the riders who appeared. Other than a small bruise on her forehead, her face looked fine, as though nothing had happened. When they got to the clearing, she stopped her horse, and Ellen asked if she was all right. The girl spoke so softly I couldn't hear her, but whatever excuse she gave, Ellen seemed to accept it. She rode on, called over her shoulder, 'Five minutes.' Jocelyn walked over to her usual sunbeam. But instead of performing her normal ritual, she slowly rotated, looking up into every tree as she went."

"Looking for you."

"If I'd had any doubt, it vanished when she spoke. 'I think you're out there. You're not a normal bird. I heard you talk. And I know you saved me.' I just sat there, not moving, with no clue as to what to do. She kept on talking. 'I know I hit my head. I know a rattler bit my cheek—I heard it. And today? There's almost no sign of either one, because of you. You helped me.' But I just stayed where I was, thinking should I or shouldn't I? And then she decided it for me by saying, 'I just want to thank you. Please show yourself so that—so I'll know I'm not crazy.' She stopped turning and lowered her head, looking very small surrounded by these enormous oak trees."

"And you couldn't let her think that. Risk a setback in her healing."

He gave another nod. "I flew to my usual branch, and the sound of my wings drew her attention. A smile even more brilliant than her previous ones lit up her face, and words tumbled out in a torrent. 'Thank you so much for saving me because I know you did and that I was really hurt when I fell and the rattler got me and you did something to me and I know you can talk and thank you so, so much.' Her cheeks were flushed, and when she stopped talking she held her breath. And still ... I said nothing.

"I remember what she said. Almost word for word, even though I didn't understand every bit of it. She pleaded, 'Please say something. Say anything so that I'll know that I'm not losing my mind.' As I fidgeted on the branch, her smile dimmed a little. 'At least come here so I can touch you and I know I'm not dreaming this,' was what she told me. I didn't move.

"'Look, here's the deal,' she went on. 'I'm an alcoholic, and I'm here in rehab. I'm not going to say anything to anyone about you. I haven't said anything to anyone about you. They wouldn't believe me—they'd just think it was DT's or my meds were off. Or worse they'd think that I had figured out a way to get liquor. So I'm not going to say anything. But here's what's more important. I knew that you were out here somewhere, and even more than saving me from the snakebite, you've done something else.' Then she looked down at the ground and started tracing a circle with the toe of her boot in the sandy patch in front of her. 'Some bad things have happened to me. Some bad people have happened to me ... and I've made some bad choices, and I've tried to self-medicate with alcohol. That's made things a lot worse and caused me to hurt other people I never wanted to.'

"She kept on. 'I'm working my way through all that, but sometimes I wonder what for. And I think maybe there is magic in the world. So I stop in this place, because it feels like a special, magical place. I stand in the sun and try to project all of my gratitude into the trees, the moss, the frogs and everything else here. And I didn't know whether it was making any difference, but then all of a sudden there you were, and you saved me. And you talk. And if you would just speak one more time, I'd know that there really is magic in the world. It would help me so much.'

"Though I knew I should leave, I found myself flying down to her. When I landed, she carefully put out her hand, and I resisted the urge to pull away. As she stroked my side, warmth spread from where she touched all the way through my body. And I blurted out, 'There is magic in the world.' Her jaw dropped, and her face just … what's the right word? … glowed from the secret I'd shared. I heard the others calling her and took off, not touching down until I was at least a mile away."

Aran had to ask. "How did you feel about what you'd done?"

"Surprisingly good. I expected guilt, but there wasn't any. I should have worried about Faerie retribution, but I didn't. All I could think was that I gave that poor girl … hope."

Abruptly Storng took off, and Aran watched him become a tiny speck in the sky before disappearing. Storng didn't actually tell me how it changed his life. But he was pretty sure that the old Silth had just revealed to him his biggest secret yet. He thought about Jocelyn's emotional scars. And his own. He wondered what had happened to her after Storng's visit.

The morning wore on, and he remained in the tree. After more reflection, he decided maybe life isn't about getting rid of scars. They are impossible to avoid and make us who we are. If one lived life, truly lived a life instead of just passively occupying it, there were going to be scars. What matters is how we carry them. Who we decide to be. The lessons they teach. Peace washed over him, something he didn't remember feeling.

As he flew off to rejoin the Tiki Crew, he wondered—what kind of magic did Storng practice today?

Scene 3

STORNG (SILTH)

There's nothing quite like a roomful of rowdy Silth. Seated on top of a tiki totem pole, Storng grinned at his success in bringing the Tiki Crew out for some fun. It was almost impossible to imagine not having fun in this room, with its carved wooden tiki gods, animatronic parrots, palm fronds, hula-skirted Humans, and exotic music.

The evening in Orlando had begun inside Trader Sam's Enchanted Tiki Bar at Disney World's Polynesian Hotel. Storng and Aran disabled security, this time without attracting the police, and used magic to obscure both noise and light during their after-hours occupation. The Tiki Crew reveled in the bar's multi-hued lights, fake windows looking out at beach scenes, and playlists of favorite tiki music. The colored-light ice cubes enchanted them. Around four a.m., though, they'd grown nostalgic for the Old Tiki Room in the Magic Kingdom, so they were closing out their evening there. Before long the sun would be up, and they'd need to move along before employees became suspicious.

Storng listened to a heated argument over the best tiki bars in the world. Amusing, given that before tonight, as best he knew, none of the crew had been further across the threshold of a tiki bar than on the pages of Tiki Magazine. Each participant, except Aran, held a shot glass full of some colorful combination of rum and fruit juice. Two hands were necessary to raise the glass, the equivalent of a bucket of Mai Tai for a Human.

"It's the Mai-Kai in Fort Lauderdale. We could go there now!"

"All the good ones are on the West Coast, dude. Smuggler's Cove in San Fran, Tiki-Ti in LA."

Storng had led them down through Florida. In a few days, they'd reach Miami where he and Aran would depart, taking their haul back to the colony. The crew would rest through the short winter in the Florida Keys in another building Storng had prepared. He would leave them a list of items to adapt. Because the next couple of days would be busy dealing with logistics, it was party time tonight.

Having gotten into the spirit of the event, Don was engaged in lively, alcohol-inspired conversation with "Fritz," an animatronic parrot. "You know, you're not very deep," Don said fuzzily, his dark skin glowing purple in the room's black lights. "You keep saying the same things over and over and over."

To Storng's surprise, Aran had not slipped away as the others grew distracted by their drinks. Instead, he sat cross-legged in the middle of a Silth clutch, regaling them with stories in his gravelly voice. Not the formal stories of his craft, Storng knew—those must be told standing up. The group was chuckling and shouting their approval, so these had to be tales told for entertainment.

Nadara was in that group. Though Storng had suspected she and Aran might become a pair, so far they had not. *For that, Aran is a fool.* Nadara was enchanting, strong, and even-tempered. She was a natural leader, and she had a graceful allure. From the way Nadara hung on Aran's words, it seemed she might at least entertain his advances. Then Storng saw her eyes meet Aran's, and both held the gaze a beat too long.

Ahhh, Storng thought. *When it's too late to form any strong bond or make any lasting commitment. Tonight is when it happens. Perhaps Aran hasn't changed all that much.*

The music they were playing, mostly instrumental exotica, reminded Storng of nights in the Silth colonies and villages. Depending on village size, anywhere from twenty to two hundred Silth gathered around a fire, everyone with an instrument. They included a wide range of drum sizes and a similar assortment of flutes, from small pan pipes that mimicked the sounds of birds to the big ones that sounded like storm winds in the jungle. Some were stringed instruments and others resembled bagpipes, requiring several Silth to operate. Together the instruments might be used to tell the story of a calm night interrupted by a terrible storm or simply to echo the heartbeat of the dancers who would invariably gather around the fire. Storng enjoyed those events, but like tonight he favored a reserved distance from the sounds, physical pulsing of music, and odors of fruit alcohol, cooking food, and pheromones of excited Silth.

Some trigger in the storytelling—Storng missed it— precipitated a fight between Nick and Kirstn, pulling his thoughts back into the room. Limbs flailing, they wrestled across the floor, knocking over tables and chairs. The others, all but Aran, joined in. Storng watched them tussling but also laughing and joking. This was simply one version of Silth dancing.

After letting the mayhem continue awhile, Storng shouted, "Stop!" Each crew member froze in mid-roll or mid-swing, always responsive to his commands. "Clean up. Off to bed." They began straightening the furniture, grumbling "Awww, Mom" and the like. As they filed out the door and flew to the nearby rooftop where they would sleep, they were grinning and slapping each other's backs.

Storng found the mundane, good-natured cleanup relaxing. The journey down to Florida had been stressful. The logistics stress of daily plans. The movement of the harvest. Small, periodic crises. But worst was the part of which the crew had no inkling—the one-eyed Faerie had followed them the entire trip. While he remained unseen by the others, he made no effort to hide from him or Aran. His brazenness made Storng nervous, even though he knew this was the Faerie's intention. At least it was mere intimidation. If the Faeries had wanted them dead, he and Aran would already be dead.

Then there had been the portents. Shamans were trained to read the world around them for signs of the future. Storng wasn't very good at the practice and had to admit his skepticism for its value. He believed that one tended to see things that matched your mood. But each of the last five mornings had opened with a red sky. A vial of potion had shattered in his hand even though it struck nothing. A dead owl lay at the base of the tree when he awoke this morning. These foretold challenging times.

The last back to camp, Storng lifted a brow at the sight of Aran alone in his hammock. Aran rolled over and responded to his stare with an arched eyebrow.

"All is well, Aran?"

"A fine evening," came the sleepy reply.

Still not ready for bed, Storng lay back and gazed at the stars. He grinned, knowing he had learned this from Aran, who often left what he called the forest floor "stifle" for the tree canopy "clarity." He found it impossible to shake his …. He tried to put a name on it. Fear? No, he wasn't afraid.

He simply had the sense that time was running out for him, or at the very least for a way of life he valued immensely.

CHAPTER SEVEN

Scene 1

THEST (TROW)

"Faster. It must proceed faster." Thest felt the heat rising in his face. He threw the last of the under-ripe banana he had been eating on the floor.

The officer who had just finished giving his report remained silent, eyes downcast, and another officer started. In the room where Thest and the five officers were gathered drapes hung in shreds. Broken plates littered the floor. Brochures of local attractions were strewn everywhere. The words WELCOME TO THE ARENAL ECOLODGE were carved into the rustic wooden sign hanging askew over the door frame.

Thest drummed his fingers on the large, low table. "I already know the details. Quammel, finish this meeting and get everyone back on schedule or face the consequences." He shoved up, stalked off, and snapped "Come on" to Fod, standing at his post beside the door.

Outside, the evidence of destruction continued. Vandals had ripped the wires from the walls and carried off any metal they could find. Anything of value had been removed, and the resulting debris shared the grounds with plastic bags and bits of cloth of unidentifiable origin. In the yard around the lodge, scattered ornamental plants and palm trees still held on, but the forest had begun to reclaim the place.

Thest looked up. Almost directly above them, the volcano Arenal sent threads of smoke into the sky. Through the greyness of the overcast afternoon, he could see tiny flickers of red from the volcano's continuous eruption.

"Give me a moment," he told Fod, who crossed his arms and stood impassively facing back the way they had come.

Thest walked to the bank of a small, aqua-colored creek. Depending on one's perspective, he thought, the location was either descending into ruin or becoming more beautiful as the vines, rot, and new growth took it back. Watching shore birds as they waded through reeds settled his breathing and allowed his rage to pass. In a nearby tree, a songbird protested his presence.

Sensing Angeles and Fod approaching, he kept his back to them. "This world has been wearing me down. Eroding me like this creek erodes its banks. First, I am told to rid this place of Humans. Restore this world as the glorious playground of the Trow. A noble cause. But … 'do not accomplish such destruction directly,' he says. So I introduce diseases. These should become epidemics. I start wars. Peace reasserts itself. Contaminate water. But nothing seems to stick."

He kicked a rock, and it hit the water with a loud plop. "Each time, the direction of what I have put in motion changes. The Earth itself seems to work against me. When I have finally figured out a way to overcome this impediment, I become Faelen's jailer. Forced to monitor him, report on his course. I would kill him. He is an irritant, irrelevant to our world or this world. But he is Xafar's son, so I am not allowed. No, I must waste my efforts tracking a drunk, no threat to anyone who does not have to listen to him."

When neither Angeles nor Fod responded, Thest knew it was

because they already had heard this … this rant, he admitted to himself. He also knew they were awaiting instructions.

"I would destroy the seeds of his dalliance as well, but Xafar will not allow it. He has me spread my forces even more, following shamans. He is convinced that if the Silth sense we are proceeding against them, they will panic and reveal themselves to the Humans. How could they do that if we wiped them all out at once? We could do it … we will do it. But Xafar fears the consequences of this as well."

As Thest curled his fingers into fists, two green amazon parrots darted out of the trees and into the sky just above them. Both arms shot up, and blue light arced from his fingertips, turning the birds' feathers to flames. They twisted and turned in agony as they plummeted to the ground. He immediately regretted his action—an emotional outburst would neither inspire anyone nor do much to salve his anger. Furthermore, he liked parrots, just as he liked all the Earth's creatures … except Humans and Paerries, of course. The parrots are not the problem, and tantrums make one appear weak, he told himself sternly. As he thought about it, he realized he did not even hate the Humans.

"Xafar has the cause and effect all wrong. We do not need to wipe out Humans. Their technologies are the problem. We could gather up the Humans tomorrow and take away their technology. We might have to destroy a few cities, but the rest would give up easily. Much of the Earth has little technology. We could purge their machines and wrestle the Humans into reservations."

Nods of approval from Angeles and Fod. "I have nothing against Humans. They are simply bright monkeys whom we have allowed to become pests. But the King wants them gone, so gone they shall be. The Silth, though … they are an abomination. They should not have been created, and I shall end them. And with them, I shall end Faelen as well. The practice of creating new magical creatures in this world was banned centuries ago in Earth time. The Trow who persisted in such crimes have all been eliminated. Except for Faelen. And his royal blood has protected him too long."

Scene 2

FAELEN (TROW)

As Thest and his cronies retreated, Faelen stepped from the trees where he had been listening and hurried to the fallen parrots. Their bright plumage was burned black, and they writhed as blue flames played around their bodies. He squatted, frowning as he extended a finger. At his touch the flames were extinguished, and each bird stilled.

He stroked them for several moments, struggling not to shout from fury and frustration. Finally, he grew calmer, releasing his face from its snarl and his body from its tightness for battle. He gathered some underbrush and covered the bodies, though as burned as they were, he doubted predators would be interested.

Moving further away, he sank to the ground and eyed the lodge. A long while later, he stood, squared his shoulders, and said in a hushed voice, "You think you go forth to slaughter lambs … I will give you dragons to fight."

Scene 3

Aran (Silth)

Aran could sense the hurricane as it bore down on Miami. Although Nadara said it was early in the season for hurricanes, the change in air pressure, disruption of magnetic lines, and the heaviness in their normally bird-light bones warned the Silth that a huge storm was moving their way.

Despite fearful looks and protests, Storng insisted they proceed. "I am Storm Rider," he reminded them.

Nadara drove them forward over the cleared grazing lands that had once been part of the Everglades, getting far more back-squawk than usual. When she scolded Don and Loana for flying too slowly, Aran watched Don make a rude gesture behind Nadara's back.

Loana griped, "This is crazy. We could wait here, be safe. Why's Storng in such a rush?" Don shrugged and shook his head, then both zoomed off after Nadara.

In his self-assigned role as the last in the crew, Aran made sure no one was left behind. He too was confused by Storng's reasoning. Not only was he insisting they proceed into the face of the hurricane, but he also had told Aran that the two of them would be taking a boat back to the colony. The first suggested Storng was in a hurry, but the second belied that. As he brought up the rear, Aran believed he'd solved part of the contradiction. Not knowing what the hurricane's path would be when it hit land, Storng believed that being out in the open of the pastures or even in the swamps was unsafe. Hurricanes were significant to Silth as the harbingers of bad times. They killed entire colonies and destroyed food sources in the areas they hit. The light bodies of Silth were easily pushed around by even a modest wind, and for them rain felt like being pelted by golf balls would for a Human. Part of the tension in the Tiki Crew arose from their general dread of the impending weather, and part was the physical disorientation Silth suffered in the vicinity of hurricanes. Storng said it had to do with the impact of the storm's static electricity on the Earth's magnetic fields, one of the many things he said that left the others scratching their heads in confusion.

Aran believed that Storng wanted them on safer ground, but why didn't he just say so? As for the boat ride, he guessed Storng had some last set of lessons for him before they returned to the colony. In his previous work in Amazonia, Aran learned the extensive shaman teachings, and over the past several months, Storng had taught him more shaman magic, both conventional and some small bit of the prohibited. But he knew Storng was holding back many teachings, hoping the compromise would save Aran's life as well as his own. Aran had watched Storng pause repeatedly as some spell occurred to him and then reluctantly choose not to show it to him. He had given up wheedling him, since it clearly pained Storng to hold anything back.

The wind picked up, and black clouds filled the sky, rolling and bubbling in the same direction the crew was flying. An evil brew, he thought uneasily. He spotted Kirstn, crouched in a palm tree and staring fearfully at the sky. She spread her red, green-fringed wings over her like a Human umbrella, even though the rain had not yet begun. Aran landed and sat beside her, as her eyes darted back and forth over the clouds.

"Watching for Harpies?" he asked. "Smart. All this open ground. Nothing but fields, swamp and a few scraggly trees. But I don't think they would dare take on a group of Silth. Probably best we stick together, though. Don't get too spread out."

Her eyes swung his way before being pulled back to the sky as though by a tether. When she remained silent, he calmly went on, "I actually like these fields and even the swamps better than the rainforest. Fewer things to kill you. Better mix of open and cover. Just clouds. Ugly, but not as ugly as Harpies." She gave a tiny, tremulous smile and lowered her wings a fraction. "Not even as ugly as Nick," he said, picking on Kirstn's frequent mate. "Where is he?"

She nodded in the direction of the other crew members. Then she shook herself from head to toe and folded her wings. When she faced Aran, he expected her to speak, but instead she gave him a rib-cracking hug before taking off after the rest.

Aran watched her fly off, bemused by the burst of affection. When Storng landed next to him, booming "could have been a Harpy," he almost lost his footing on the branch.

"Move everyone faster—it's almost here," Storng said, checking the clouds.

As Storng flew off, Aran eyed the clouds as well and raised his wings, stopping as he realized he was copying Kirstn's pose. Just as he caught up with the rest, the rain started, a gentle sprinkle that rapidly turned into a downpour, each drop a bruising punch. Wind whooshed up from behind, shoving him forward like a monster pushing him into its mouth. He struggled against it, gasping for air.

Houses appeared, sprinkled here and there, as fields and swamps gave way to the western edge of Miami. Then they were over what looked like some abandoned effort at development, with roads installed and a few houses half-built but now overwhelmed by vines, brambles and vegetation, testimony to the swamp's efforts to reclaim the land. They soon found themselves in neighborhoods of houses and apartments with a few commercial areas. The rain pounded them, and the wind threatened to push them into the sides of buildings when they flew lower. Aran's wings ached from resisting the wind, and he had trouble keeping the others in sight. After losing sight of them for several minutes, his pulse slowed again as he finally spotted Kirstn ahead of him, but the rain obscured the others. *I hope she can see someone else,* he thought, trying to blink water from his eyes. When she descended toward an old metal commercial building adjoined by a trailer park, he followed her under a canopy into a long unused loading dock.

A previous visitor had wrenched open the dock doors. The sound of the wind and rain striking his ears was replaced by a cacophony of Silth whistles, clicks, and voices and rain pounding on the metal roof. Each time the wind shifted, the meal sheets of the building shook and rumbled, but the building appeared to be holding together.

"How are you?" Nadara asked, bumping him with her shoulder.

"Great! Invigorated! Let's do it again. And you? All accounted for?"

"Yes, although Storng took off as soon as he pointed to this place. As usual."

She instructed the others to gather wood and build a fire on the concrete floor. The good-natured back-squawk she got showed that the Tiki Crew was much calmer now that they had shelter. Within an hour, all were dry and warm. As couples drifted off to dark parts of the warehouse, Nadara and Aran sat at the loading dock door watching the storm.

Though it was mid-afternoon, the world was dark as night. Wind roared, and rain smacked into the loading bay concrete like wet bullets. The hurricane bucked and shrieked and changed directions, a furious animal affronted by the presence of other creatures.

When Aran looked out across the trailer park, he saw little evidence of Humans. He assumed they had fled before the storm and were somewhere safe. Since he saw no sign of light or electricity, it was difficult to tell if anyone had stayed behind. Perhaps the power was out. Other than trees, no living thing was obvious among the frenzy of movement by inanimate objects. The trees were surrendering limbs, and the wind had begun to carry large pieces of wood, parts of buildings, and anything that had not been tied down. Even though the loading dock was set within a concrete alcove, the flying debris made him increasingly uncomfortable.

He was about to suggest they move further back into the warehouse when Nadara stiffened and said, "What's that sound?"

He listened. He heard the pounding of rain as it struck the concrete and the metal roof … the crash of water flooding from gutters beside the dock … the rumble of the building as it shook in the wind. Then … a different sound—a distant low din like the sound at the base of a high waterfall.

"Son of a toucan! Maelstrom!'" Nadara rushed back into the warehouse and yelled for the others.

Aran had never experienced a maelstrom, but he knew what it was. The storm within the storm. The focused destruction from wind suddenly arriving and demolishing everything in its path. There was no flying through it. No running from it. This building had little hope of withstanding it. Humans called these "tornados," and these storms often hid within hurricanes.

We are so going to die.

He whirled, looking around wildly. Only the floor was concrete. In the floor about twenty feet from him was a big square hole. From the way it lined up with a ramp from the street level outside, he guessed the Humans worked underneath trucks there. He ran over and looked down into the five-foot hole, containing about three feet of oily, stagnant water with trash floating on the surface.

"Over here," he shouted, and Nadara was the first to reach him. When she saw the nasty pool, she winced and frantically checked, as Aran had, for another option. She was no more successful than he had been.

"Everyone grab a piece of wood," she yelled, pointing to the pile next to the fire. "Bring it here. Vic, put the fire out. Hurry."

The roar was louder, a predator hunting their hiding spot. Aran grabbed two chunks of wood from the pile, tossed one to Nadara, and rushed to the ramp leading into the hole. After pausing and, just like Aran and Nadara, casting about for more pleasant alternatives, each of the others reluctantly followed. He clenched his teeth as he stepped into the cold, oily water. As he continued forward, it rose to his shoulders, and he used the piece of wood to float.

Quiet profanities sprang from the others as they waded into the murk. The laggards sped up as the building started to shimmy. Nadara was last down the ramp as the sound of metal tearing and roaring filled their ears. Darkness shrouded them, and they heard the building give way. One of the walls fell down on top of the hole with an enormous crash, and the pounding shook the concrete, sloshing the water around them. Aran could form no thoughts during the onslaught. As his brain absorbed the sensory overload, all he could think of was "Go on, go on" and keep clinging to the wood, shivering. The attack subsided, and he could hear the beast lumbering toward the mobile homes next to the building. He could just make out the screams of Humans below its bass roar. He had been wrong—the trailer park was occupied—and he felt pity for the Humans as he imagined their trailers being tossed like small prey.

Fighting fatigue, he swam toward the ramp. His feet touched the floor, and he slipped and slid his way up the incline, almost falling several times. When he reached the top of the ramp, he bumped into the sheets of metal blocking it and pushed with his shoulder. The metal sheets refused to budge. He heard more sloshing of water as the others joined him. In the ten minutes they spent in the noisy shuffling of metal, the maelstrom had moved on. When they emerged from the hole, what remained of the building was strangely silent. They could see grey sky through the gaping holes in the roof, and over half of the walls were gone, though the steel girders that formed the framework remained.

Nadara was panting. "We're exposed here ... have to move on."

"How will Storng find us?" Vic asked.

"The rally point. Remember? He said if we got separated, we'd meet there."

Vic gave a quick nod and aimed for an open part of the building, the remaining crew close behind. They took off into the light rain and breeze signaling the trailing edge of the hurricane.

As he readied himself to fly, Aran heard shouts from the trailer park side of the building. Still somewhat dazed, he'd forgotten the

Human screams he'd heard earlier. He allowed himself one peek, but as he did, he realized he was looking at where the trailer park used to be. While one or two trailers were still recognizable, the rest had been reduced to jagged pieces of metal and piles of rain-soaked belongings. Survivors wandered through the rubble, calling out names of missing relatives or pets, while others pawed through their soaked belongings. Still more sat stunned on odd pieces of concrete, once steps into homes no longer there. Aran was astonished by how many Humans had chosen to remain. Their televisions and radios would have warned them of the oncoming hurricane. *Idiots.*

Shouts came from a knot of people digging through a pile of twisted metal. Aran saw one of the men bend over and pull out first one child, then another, and finally a third. A crying woman rushed over to embrace a little girl, while the man grabbed the two boys and hugged them fiercely. The rest of the search group trotted over to where a man and woman were yelling into the debris. Aran felt a surprising sympathy for the Humans, but there wasn't anything he could do.

As he turned to follow the Tiki Crew, he heard an odd, faint sound. He eyed a pile of trailer park debris near him. There was the sound again. He heard a whispered plea for help, audible to Silth ears but not to the Humans, most too far away or making too much noise as they moved metal and searched for survivors. The closest Human was at least fifty yards away from the pile, and she knelt beside a small body, rocking and crying, oblivious to anything else. The moaned whisper came again— "Help me"—softer than before. Even Aran wouldn't have heard it now if he hadn't been listening for it.

Using the ruined landscape to hide his approach, he went over to the pile of rubble. Through the debris he saw a grey-haired Human male, his legs tangled in cords and pipes and a large metal beam across his chest. Other wreckage was helping to hold the beam on him. He was barely breathing as the heavy weight forced the air from his chest. As their eyes met, the man's widened, his head lolled to the side, and he lost consciousness.

Aran glanced around, ducked into the debris, and by crouching made his way to the Human's side. He untangled the debris from the man's feet and pulled on the rest that was pressing down on the beam. The metal pile over him shifted ominously. He studied it, deciding it seemed likely to fall in upon them both. The only way to free the Human would be to push up on the beam. He found a solid piece of metal about two feet long, slid it over, and tried to lever the beam. When it barely moved, he repositioned and tried again. The beam moved more, but not enough. When Aran gave up and let it back down, the old man moaned but did not awaken.

Magic. I have to use magic. He could temporarily obtain more strength by drawing on the pools of water that had collected nearby, but for this much power he would have to drop his glamour. If a Human looked into the rubble, they would see a Silth, and a glowing one at that. He was uncertain of what he would look like to Human eyes, but to Silth, a shaman glowed an iridescent white when performing significant magic.

What he was considering was beyond risky—it was taboo. It was one thing to be seen as a talking bird, trouble enough for him if caught by any of the other Silth, quite another to be among Humans and drop his glamour. Even Storng had not gone this far. He listened. He heard no one near, so he returned to the beam.

Aran stuck his back toes into a nearby pool of water. As he spoke the focusing words that Storng had taught, the blue heron glamour he had been using faded. He kept speaking the words and began to glow white. He slowly lifted the beam, and the debris holding it down grumbled and shifted. Once he'd raised it about two feet, he used his foot to shove a piece of metal into place beneath it and set it down gently. If he slipped or if the metal failed to hold, the old man would be crushed. The ground dented slightly, but the beam stayed suspended above the Human.

He released it, saw the Human staring at him in awe, and froze. After what seemed an eternity, the old man's eyelids drooped, and he passed out again. Aran scuttled down to the Human's feet and dragged him out toward the opening. He stopped halfway.

Monkey scat! How am I going to get anyone's attention? Judging by the man's grayish skin and labored breathing, he was fading fast and wouldn't survive the wait for someone to find him. The old man had seen him, so perhaps Aran should just let him slip away, let nature take its course. He restored his glamour.

He moved behind a refrigerator lying on its side and shouted in what he hoped sounded like a Human voice. "Help me! Help me!" He peered back around, but no one had heard. Again, he ducked back. "Help me, I'm dying!" This time, one of the men digging through rubble was looking in his direction, having stopped in mid-motion while moving a large slab of concrete. After one more "Help me!" uttered even louder, the man tossed the concrete aside and tapped another worker on the shoulder. The two ran toward Aran, jumping over and weaving through the destruction in their path.

With long heron strides, Aran hurried away, keeping the refrigerator between him and the oncoming men. When it was too far behind him to serve as adequate cover, he slowed and wandered around peering into puddles, a confused bird who had just survived a hurricane and was searching for food. But curiosity got the better of him, and he hopped onto an overturned trailer.

He watched the men climb down and shout to the others when they spotted the old man. As they pulled him out, the old man regained consciousness, and Aran heard him telling them, "An angel. I was rescued by … by an angel. It was beautiful …. It pulled me out." The rescuers exchanged pitying glances, but the old man's head dropped back, and he lost consciousness again.

When Aran returned to the ruins of the metal building, Nadara was standing just inside with narrowed eyes. With a sinking feeling in the pit of his stomach, he wondered what she had seen. But before she could speak, Storng landed beside them.

"Stop dawdling, you two. Time to go."

Nadara gave Aran a long, searching look before Storng said sternly, "Fledgling, past time to go," and she took off.

Aran twisted around and spotted the two rescuers carrying the old man, getting ready to load him into a pickup truck bed. As he turned back, he saw Storng eyeing him intently. Aran flapped his wings to follow Nadara, but instead he dropped to the ground. As the adrenaline cleared his system, he was almost overwhelmed by exhaustion. Son of a toucan! He knew from practice that the use of magic was like the use of any muscle—there was a price. He thought he'd used enough of the elements, this time water, to reduce the impact, but he'd never felt so heavy.

Storng called from the doorway, "Magic is a harsh merchant, and there's no avoiding payment. I'll hold the others at the rally point.

Join us when you can." He soared into the air.

Coati spit! He knows!

Aran crawled back to the cover of the building waiting for his strength to return. The injunction against showing yourself to Humans was one of the most important rules taught to young Silth. Violating it would get one banished. Why'd he taken the risk for the life of a Human? Would the old man have risked his life for Aran? Was Aran influenced by Storng's story of the girl at The Refuge? Of course he was. It had to have been Storng's intent, so this must have been a test. Had he passed it, or failed?

His strength returned after a short while. Once he caught up with the crew, who had obviously cut their speed for him to do so, they flew through the city to the ocean front and followed it to Port Miami. The sprawling complex was quiet, recovering from the hurricane, and it appeared the area had been spared the full brunt of the storm. The giant cranes for unloading cargo were stationery, trains sat idle, and no Humans moved on the cargo ships. Only the four cruise ships sitting nose to tail along one long pier showed any activity. On them lights blazed brightly, and music and laughter trickled out into the harbor.

The Silth landed on the white roof of one cargo shed. Aran said his goodbyes, hugging each of the Tiki Crew in turn. Each embrace was warm and enthusiastic until he came to Nadara. She barely responded and mumbled her goodbye. Then as he pulled away, she grabbed him in a full body hug, so intense he could barely breathe, and kissed his cheek. She released him, but before she could step away, he caught her in a strong embrace and kissed her lightly on the lips. They pulled apart awkwardly while the others pretended not to have noticed. When Storng landed, the farewells continued, the older shaman basking in the affectionate attention.

As the Tiki Crew became tiny specks in the sky, Aran felt a rush of sadness. Possibly the crew would work with him as their shaman one day ... or he might never see them again. But they'd never again have the relationship they'd shared over the last few months.

Aran himself had changed. He was stronger and surer of his use of magic, more confident of his ability to be a shaman. He could go several days without thinking of Shra, though she often visited his dreams. And Nadara. He found himself ... distracted by her. It was not like the old days, in which he would feel compelled to pursue her, but he was very aware of her presence. And absence. He looked up at the empty sky—he'd miss her.

Storng gave Aran a cuff on the shoulder. "We have a lot to do. Catalog and pack the harvest, arrange its transport and our own, and during all that still finish your lessons."

"You mean finish the lessons when we're back on the ship?"

"Some there. But also now, about how all this is done."

"All what?" Aran wondered if his exhaustion was causing his thoughts to be fuzzy.

"Moving the harvest. Figuring out which ship goes where. Making all the necessary arrangements. But before any of that, some food and sleep."

Food. Sleep. Aran's body responded with a stomach growl and huge yawn. He gathered up the shred of energy he had left and followed Storng, a hundred questions filling his mind.

Scene 4

ARAN (SILTH)

After a meal and several hours' sleep Aran almost felt functional again. He sat cross-legged on a bench in a dusty warehouse corner, eating nuts and fruit while listening to Storng describe the harvest moving process. The wall behind them was concrete. They were far from doors, windows, or other places where someone could hide to overhear them.

"Most shamans can only move as much as they can carry," Storng told him. "Even if they use their crew as porters and use rowling bags, what they can move is limited. Silth are stronger than Humans, but they're small and can't carry a lot of Human stuff. But our colony has prospered, and I've personally done well, because I found another way of transporting things. Dangerous, but it works." Storng paused and closed his eyes. "It's one of my most important secrets and advantages, one I've never told a student." Storng took a long drink and sat quietly for a moment. "It also involves a prohibited magic. Beyond prohibited. If the Faeries find out you have knowledge of this, they'll kill you, and me as well."

"I understand."

Storng chewed on a bite of orange. Finally, "You know that the rowling bags you used in harvesting were magically enhanced. As they hold more, their weight doesn't increase. Nothing special there, as many shamans have them, but they have a very limited volume. Whenever we had a good day, you put all our harvest items in boxes and left them with me. I made you all leave and used a spell allowing me to send those boxes to Faerie, the Land, the home of the Faerie. So long as I don't fly over open water, I can retrieve them into this world."

Aran crunched on a cashew and pondered this revelation a long while before asking, "And if you flew over open water …?

"The connection would be severed, as I know from experience. I suppose I could go to the Land to retrieve the lost swag. The spell I use is an old one said to be that given to Tanton to rescue his wife from the Land. But other than in your stories, no Silth has ever returned alive from there. I'm not eager to try." Storng grabbed another nut from the pile. "Anything attached to dry land is okay for me to cross. As long as I followed bridges and I was cautious, I was able to make it here. The swamps were a challenge, one reason why I didn't fly with the rest of you. I had to pick my path most carefully. You might wonder why water severs the connection, but I don't know the answer. Even the Silth shamans don't research magic much. We just do it."

"Does a boat work?"

"No, that's where the next set of prohibited interactions occurs. Ones with which you're already familiar."

"And that would be?"

"To cross the ocean with our substantial harvest, we must pull it back from the Land, repack it into shipping containers, and arrange its passage. We have to set up all the steps. Drop-off of the containers, their loading and transport to the ship, passage on the ship and through customs, transport from the port, and unloading without arousing the suspicions of others."

"Impossible."

"Possible." Storng trained his white eye upon Aran. "And amusing that while you believe I can transport materials in and out of this world, you doubt my logistics prowess."

"I simply doubt your ability to do this without interacting with Humans." At Storng's hint of a smile, Aran thought, so what am I missing? And then he knew. "You do interact with Humans. That's the prohibition you violate every time you harvest. A Silth prohibition. One you also know I violated today."

Despite the care he had taken in choosing their location, Storng glanced around and lowered his voice. "Never out loud. We live in a world in which almost everything is heard." He spent the next hour showing Aran the method for sending things into the Land. When finished, he said, "But you only retrieve what you've sent. Before you ask, I don't know where the boxes go once in the Land, but they always return unmolested. With never any sign they're seen while there."

"How do you know they actually end up in the Land?"

"Because that's where I send them. The spell works in this world as well. That's how I learned it from my teacher. He used to store things in remote areas of the Earth. You must be able to imagine the area in vivid-dream detail. One story about the Land describes the vast empty areas, and that's what I imagine. The first time you do the spell, it's quite involved, but after the connection is created, it's relatively simply to move things back and forth. And I also know that's where it goes because once when the items returned, a box had accidentally squashed a small flower fairy. I found it stuck to the bottom."

He pulled out two small leather bags and a lighter from his cloak pocket. Removing dirt from one bag, he created a little mound in front of him. From the other bag, he shook out twigs, which he stacked on the mound and lit. Aran watched, fascinated, as Storng chanted the focusing spell, all the while using broad sweeps of his arms. Aran's mouth fell open as all the boxes and bags from the last Tiki Crew harvest materialized before them.

Storng studied the small mountain of materials with satisfaction before climbing partway up to a large brown box. He dug around inside, scrambling back down pulling a book behind him with one hand and holding a cellphone in the other. He grinned as he pushed them toward Aran. "These are the sources of my most powerful magic."

Aran's lips parted in surprise. "A book and a phone?"

"Yes, a phone. And books in general. The books help me figure out how to do things. Like how to operate the phone. Which allows me to communicate with Humans without risk. This phone—they call it a 'Smart Phone.' It gives me access to all sorts of important information—ship schedules, likely cargos, and locations of certain types of buildings. That's how I know where to forage as we move through towns, or how I knew when a ship should arrive in Panama City. The phone is how I'll arrange for a container delivery here so we can load this stuff into it. How we'll arrange for shipment back to the colony." He rubbed his hands together gleefully. "I'd love to use a tablet computer. I wouldn't need the books. But that might be too much technology."

"But books!" Storng went on, almost dancing. "Books give so much more than information. Look in the box." He gestured back up the pile to the box where he'd gotten the book.

Aran climbed the hill of treasures and peered into the box. Storng climbed behind him. Books of all shapes and sizes were crammed inside, ranging from simple "do-it-yourself" manuals to fancy ones with world art pictures. He pulled out one entitled Grimm's Fairytales.

"You don't have your harvesters get these, so you must collect them yourself."

"That's correct." Storng read a few lines aloud before saying, "The shamans have been instructed to keep these from ordinary Silth. They make the priests of New Faerie uncomfortable because they call into question much of their teachings and breed too much familiarity with Human ways. But even the shamans, who are allowed to handle books, rarely use them for practical information, since interaction with Humans is prohibited. These gems give me insights into Humans and their world, plus what they know of Faeries and even us, which is almost nothing. Over the next week as we head home, I'll teach you about the different books and how phones work."

"But how do you pay for things? Surely the containers, service for the phone, those sorts of things must cost money. Human money."

"I'll show you how to open a bank account. That allows you to send and receive Human money. Everything can be done using the phone and an occasional ATM machine."

"Hold on—how will I learn to read the books?" Aran asked.

"You already know how. Just as you already speak every language Humans speak. Just like the ability to speak to animals. It's part of your magic. You've been reading signs and labels as we traveled the last several months."

Aran thought about it. "Yes, I guess I have. But I assumed that only worked with small things."

"No, part of Silth magic is that a few of us can speak and understand every Human or animal language, written or spoken. Most Silth with this skill never realize it because we avoid Human contact. We'll talk more about all this. But for now I want you to watch as I make the arrangements to return to the colony. And remember, you cannot talk about this to anyone—"

"Because it's a prohibited magic and the Faeries will kill me," Aran finished.

"Not just that. This is taboo. Unaccepted in the world of Silth because it risks exposing our people. What you did today at the trailer park isn't allowed. Nor is this method of transporting harvest items. Silth don't kill their own, but they might clip your wings and banish you to live out your days without flight, walking in the forest. It would be a short life." He began poking at the small phone.

Aran watched, amazed Storng knew just what to press to help move them toward home.

CHAPTER EIGHT

Scene 1

ARAN (SILTH)

This ship, different from the last, had several cargo containers on the deck—they included the four large cargo containers needed to move their harvest—but much of its load was below deck, and the hold was mostly filled with pallets, each containing four huge rolls of brown paper. These had been loaded by forklifts, which delivered the rolls onto elevators that lowered so the next layer could be stacked. Storng had shifted one of the pallets back on the elevator, and the driver never realized he had created a space for the Silth.

Aran spent ten mostly sleepless days immersed in information and exploration. Though fascinated by the books, he was simultaneously drawn to and repelled by the phone. The device was technology, and Storng carefully regulated their time with it. Aran was nervous each time he held it and checked himself for signs of psychosis after each session. As forbidden fruit, however, it drew him in and opened a world Aran had never imagined. He could learn about anything, as if he'd grown a new brain with infinite knowledge. This small piece of Human technology felt more magical than much of what he'd been taught in Amazonia. And almost every Human had one. Aran had seen them bent over or attached to them by wires or the little devices they wore on their ears.

Storng told him story after story of his interactions with Humans, what he'd learned about them, what to be careful with, how to get things done. Even though deep in the ship's hold, paper stacked tightly all around them, all discussions were still whispered. So this is the prohibited knowledge? It's not about Faeries—it's about Humans.

Aran meted out questions as they went along. How had Storng kept the Faeries from learning than he used the Land as a repository? Storng said it appeared that they assumed the swag was just going somewhere else on Earth. If the Faeries knew that Storng interacted with Humans, did the Silth also know? Storng told him no, that the Faerie spies had learned it, but they had no incentive even to hint to the Silth that these interactions were possible.

They discussed Aran's plans to tour the colonies surrounding Kawran and select the one he'd serve as shaman. They debated if Kawran, the colony Storng currently served, was large enough to support more than one shaman, as had been done in the old days, but they decided it was better if Aran found his own colony or village near Kawran. Storng also did business with several of them. Aran had no desire to stay in Kawran, surrounded by the places he and Shra had shared.

Over and over, Storng emphasized the steps that Aran must take to hide his activity from both Faeries and Silth. Though the admonishments grew tedious, Aran knew Storng didn't want a third student to die like the others.

Aran supported the sentiment. He no longer awoke disappointed to see a new day. Each one was exciting as he immersed himself in the complications of dealing with Humans and in the books that showed him the best and worst of them. He found that not only could he read, he could read quickly, absorbing a page in just a second. Over the next few days, he devoured books, not just the practical, but books of poetry, history, art, psychology, methodology. Every subject fascinated him. In a book on religion, he could see the similarities between the old religion of the shamans and that of the Incas. In an ecology book, he learned that Humans were aware of what they were doing to the habitats of Earth's other occupants yet seemed helpless to stop themselves.

Each night he'd lie awake trying to process all he had learned. A new kind of restlessness was growing in him, and he was eager to try out his knowledge.

Scene 2

FOD (TROW)

Fod reported Storng's arrival in Port Miami and yet again worked as one of the ship's crew. He hated this monitor-and-menace task, being seen enough to remind Storng and Aran of the threat hanging over them and eavesdropping on their conversations. The task was simple. *Because Thest thinks I am simple-minded. But I am not.*

He had received his scars and lost his eye saving Thest's life in the Trow war that brought Xafar to power. Thest and others acted as if the same trauma had also damaged his brain. Fod did not think so. He still had complex thoughts—he just kept them to himself. He no longer liked to speak any more than the minimal amount necessary. So Thest assigned him to support Angeles and follow Storng.

Fod believed he should just kill Storng and Aran—he had plenty of opportunities. And support Angeles? She was a self-centered puff of a spy. Not military. Fod did not trust her, so he thought of his assignment as keeping an eye on Angeles to protect Thest.

He pushed the dark thoughts away. He was frustrated that he had failed even this easy assignment, yielding ten days of aggravating Human work but no Silth information. Though he knew where the two were, he was unable to get close to their hiding place while maintaining Human form. Even with his enhanced hearing, he could not make out anything they said. As the ship neared Costa Rica, he knew they were likely to emerge before it began unloading. So he watched and waited.

Finally, on the day they pulled into port, two parrots flew up from the hold onto a crane, and their blue glow told Fod who they really were. He strained to listen to their chatter, heard nothing of value, and smacked his fist into a cargo container, leaving a small dent.

Thest would not be pleased.

Scene 3

ARAN (SILTH)

Aran listened with admiration as Storng arranged for the containers to clear customs, then be loaded onto trucks and driven to a remote clearing. Storng reminded him that shamans had the ability to move Silth eggs without them turning to stone, and he had one he would place at the site. That, along with stay-away spells, would protect the harvest from Human discovery. No Silth would disturb it for fear of shaman retribution.

Storng outlined the mix of strategies to spread out the materials, identifying what he would bring to the colony, which things he could use to barter with other colonies, and what he would keep. "Aran, one reason we harvested duplicates of so many items is because half this harvest is yours. You need to decide what you'll do with it."

Aran was stunned. By Silth standards, he had just become wealthy, something he'd never considered as a possibility. Of course, it was his job to give that wealth away to the colonies he served.

The other Silth must have realized Storng was accessing larger amounts of materials than most shamans, but Aran thought they passed it off as a by-product of his powerful shaman magic. Few shamans left Amazonia after teaching there as long as Storng. Those who did tended to be powerful. Storng warned him to be careful of the other shamans—they would be suspicious of the scale of Aran's operation so early in his career and knew what magics he was allowed to access.

Aran found the strategy and logistics in the undertaking almost overwhelming. To have it succeed, Storng must have anticipated most of these decisions months ago when he made the lists of target harvest items. Given that Aran had decided at the last minute to be Storng's apprentice, arrangements had to have been adjusted during the harvest and Aran's training. He was awed and intimidated by the skill.

They arrived at the clearing before the Silth meeting them there. Though it had been daylight for several hours, light was only now trickling over the trees, and direct sunlight had yet to reach the materials. Storng moved his portion of the harvest to a hiding place separate from Aran's, who practiced sending a portion of the materials to the Land and retrieving them in the clearing. Boxes were piled twenty times the height of a Silth in the opening in the rainforest meadow, big ones on the bottom.

Aran was reacquainting himself with the constant noise and motion of the forest. A troop of howler monkeys growled out its warning to other troops from nearby trees, and big blue butterflies fluttered around the clearing, one landing briefly on a box before moving to the next. Already high, the humidity was making his hather annoyingly heavy. He had dreaded returning to the rainforest darkness and nervousness he had experienced all his life. Months of sneaking around Humans, and it's the rainforest that makes me tense.

But as he thought about it, he realized he wasn't tense. He was happy to be back in the rainforest with its familiar sounds and smells. While it had its dangers, he knew them well, unlike those he'd experienced over the last six months. He stopped to savor the way the morning was gathering moisture, preparing to rain by afternoon. Briefly he counted the different bird calls he heard, giving up at fifteen.

Saying their goodbyes, Aran grasped Storng wrist to wrist. But

Storng pulled him into an embrace and thumped him on the back. "Be well and be careful."

"You too, Storng. Thank you for everything."

"We'll see if you thank me in a year. You haven't quite finished your time of apprenticeship, so you can't commit to a village or colony for three more moon cycles. I'll check in with you." As he started to turn away, he paused and without looking at Aran added, "Remember I told you the portents suggest that your future is to do great things. I don't think just being a merchant or a 'thief,' as you put it, is the greatness foretold."

Storng flew up through the trees toward the colony to deliver his portion of the harvest. Aran watched him go before shaking off his thoughts and moving to his boxes to mark and inventory them. The sun, well over the treetops, was turning the dew to steam.

When the bush rustled and crunched, he went rigid, poised to take flight. But a group of Silth emerged on foot, and he relaxed. In front was Merit, tallest of them, in her leather battle dress, heavily armed and more muscled than the others. She mostly looked as he remembered her. The yellow hather above her eyes shifted first to red as it crept up her forehead and then to blue on her head, turning green as it spread down her neck and shoulders and onto solid green wings. Her eyes were orange, with white rings and black irises. But now her unsmiling face was made all the more severe by lack of movement on the left side, where the corner of her mouth also turned down. Instead of a left hand there was a piece of wood, shaped into a useful tool and held in place by straps. Merit was one of the few Silth who didn't project a personal appearance glamour. Most Silth went through their lives with no one seeing how they really looked. This reflected neither vanity nor a cultural mating demand, but simply centuries of practice. Over time the art of such projections had become the ability to add some small imperfection that highlighted the otherwise perfect beauty that each Silth choose to wear. A few Silth, however, could not maintain secondary glamour, and another very few, eschewed the practice entirely. Merit choose not to hide her scars and losses.

She and nine others filed into the clearing, rolling several empty wooden carts, and then five more Silth appeared from the surrounding forest, guarding the flanks. Silth were always at their most exposed when on foot, and when dragging noisy carts the danger was particularly high. All were stony-faced as they reached the clearing.

Merit was "battle leader" for the western colony called Fortress, and Aran had met her in the season he spent storytelling there. She hadn't yet risen to her current leadership position. When he was at Fortress, they'd become close—until Shra, he hadn't been closer to anyone. During the course of his travels, he'd heard about both her new role and her injuries. Many spoke in awe of her rise within the colony, despite her youth and the loss of her hand.

Today she was standing in front of him, and he had no idea why. She surveyed the pile of materials and glanced back at the tiny Silth carts. Suddenly she looked up and gave a quick, harsh screech. Aran turned to follow her gaze, and a rush of air almost knocked him over, as a full-grown harpy eagle landed beside her and bowed its head to accept a quick stroke. Aran took a step back. It was twice as tall as Merit, its rear talons almost the length of a Silth arm. The troop surrounding them beamed with pride at their fearsome mascot.

In most colonies, the role of a battle leader, if they even had one any more, was important only during some crisis or threat of attack from a puma or jaguar new to the territory. Fortress, however, made its living primarily from hiring out its soldiers to other colonies. Long gone were the days when the Silth of the region fought among themselves, as their numbers were too small and the external threats too many. Some philosophers even argued that their fundamental nature had changed over the centuries, and now they were predisposed to peace. But if a colony had something needing protection, was menaced by a predator, or had some dangerous mission requiring movement among the Humans or on the forest floor, Fortress supplied the necessary protection. Other colonies paid them an annual tax just to respond when the colony was in need.

Merit, roughly Aran's age, led many of Fortress's excursions. Officially Fortress had a governing council, like all the colonies, but in the business of fighting or protection, she was in charge. He had no idea what she'd done to secure this position—Fortress's internal rites and customs were very secret—but he knew it had been hard.

"This is a stupid place to stop. Very exposed. Very unsafe."

Aran's smile faded. "Greetings to you too, Dawn Guardian. And to your companion." He tipped his head toward the harpy eagle towering over him.

"Start loading this stuff into the carts at once," she instructed one of the closest Silth. "Set up a detail inside the tree line. As soon as a cart's loaded, move it into the trees. The tents can go in the clearing. Set up perimeter guards on all sides. Watch the sky and the ground."

"I have an egg in place here. As well as stay-away spells. This swag isn't threatened where it is. I'm surprised I rate such a prestigious escort." As Aran spoke, he searched in vain for a hint of friendliness in her expression.

"I'm here at your brother's direction. He instructed us to escort you on your tour of the surrounding villages." She said "tour" with disdain. "A lot of expense to move a storyteller around. And a ridiculous level of danger."

"Ahhh." He recognized several layers to this conversation, at least one having to do with the way he and Merit had parted. Sometimes he wondered at his denseness. He glanced around to see if the others were far enough away not to overhear—with Silth it was hard to tell.

"I'm a shaman. I am not 'touring' as a storyteller—I'm bargaining a harvest. I'll choose a colony in the next few weeks. And I'll pay your wages, not my brother. I can take care of myself, but I could definitely use help in moving the harvest." When she folded her arms across her chest, he lowered his voice and added, "Merit, I'm very sorry about the way I left you. I acknowledge I was immature and callous. All I can tell you is I'm a different person standing before you."

Her cold stare did not thaw in the slightest, and she pointed a finger at him. "You say you're a shaman. We shall see. As far as I'm concerned, your 'harvest' is just a dowry to get some colony to take you. When Fortress is hired, it stays hired by its employer." She chopped her hand downward. "The incident with Shra shows you cannot protect yourself. As to our past, it's … irrelevant. You say a different person stands before me. 'The eyes believe themselves; the ears believe others.' I see only Aran. If you're someone else, you're merely a stranger." As she moved away to issue new orders to those loading the carts, the eagle flew up to a large branch at the edge of the clearing.

The comment regarding Shra had stung as intended, but Aran wasn't upset. He knew he deserved Merit's anger. He also was aware that this assignment, even coming from his brother, was beneath her station, so she must have chosen to do it. He wondered why. It seemed a long way to come to simply express her ire.

He would have to move the egg and recast the spells, but that was easier than arguing. He continued his inventory, marking each of the boxes being loaded into the carts. As he worked, he realized Merit might be right. Perhaps he was a "stranger," even to himself, since he couldn't predict his own emotions. He liked a forest he had hated all his life. He failed to take the bait when Merit tried to pick a fight. When had these changes occurred? Why hadn't he been aware of them as they happened? What else was different?

Scene 4

MERIT (SILTH)

Merit was furious. It was unlike her not to keep her emotions and words in check, and her soldiers mustn't see how out of control she'd become. She'd told herself that she'd proceed without feelings, simply doing a job. Earning compensation for her colony and favor with Casius, Aran's brother and a rising force among the Silth of all the colonies.

She set her hammock high in the trees above the camp, before flying back down to supervise setting up the encampment, still thinking about Casius. She remembered Aran telling her once that the "Newfies" his brother led, in hoping to appease the Faeries and receive their powers, were crazy as a box of hungry coatis.

As high priest of New Faerie, Casius had amassed great physical and karmatic wealth. In the complex economy of the Silth, karmatic wealth accrued when one was a positive social force and did things benefitting others. Or, in its cruder form, when one did favors causing others to "owe" that individual. It was a rough measure of the likelihood that others would defer to one or provide favors in return. Casius also had a place on the council of the Kawran Colony, the largest Silth colony and Aran's last base of operations.

Casius was everything Aran was not. Merit didn't share New Faerie's beliefs, but she knew how to curry favor. She was aware that Aran's relationship with his brother was complex. He was cordial with Casius but rebelled against his help whenever it occurred. Something had happened when they were young that caused some distance between them, unusual for Silth raised in the same family.

Casius had many resources. Aran, however, wasn't wealthy—any compensation he ever received for his singing and storytelling had been spent on Silth females or drinking with friends. Or given away. If anything, he'd amassed karmatic debt. He was a cad. And … he'd hurt her. He'd always ignored the rules, leading to chaos and ruin, and now he'd added magic to the mix. Merit didn't trust magic in the hands of responsible shamans, but she considered it immensely dangerous in Aran's.

So why had she sought to come on this journey? She tried to pass it off as necessary to win praise from Casius, but in truth as long as the job was done well, she'd get the credit whether or not she came. So why had she? Casius asked for her personally—had he hoped to irritate Aran while protecting him? She'd moved another assignment to take this one. Why? To see if Aran was the same, she admitted to herself. She'd planned to observe from some distance, to be cool, separate, and aloof. Instead she was angry and showing far more of her emotion than she intended. So, step back, she told herself.

She studied Aran as he dealt with the boxes. He looked different, more muscular and slightly heavier than before. He acted differently, by not rising to the bait of her attack. The old Aran would have done a wounded bird routine and tried to elicit sympathy for the hurt she inflicted. The old Aran would have flirted with her.

Her good hand involuntarily rose to the side of her face, its damage and the missing hand gifts from a harpy eagle that had developed a taste for Silth. Neither injury had happened when she and Aran passed time together. Maybe he just felt sorry about her new appearance, something she couldn't stand were it true. She spun and dressed down a surprised Silth warrior for a minor infraction.

Her harpy eagle Stalbon circled lazily in the sky, searching for prey. Merit had killed the eagle that scarred her face, only to find a fledgling in its nest. She had raised the bird and taught it to fight. And not to eat Silth.

Again, she slid a look at Aran, who was ignoring the young female Silth warrior beside him. When she finally tapped him on the shoulder and said something Merit couldn't hear, he listened with a neutral smile, gave her what seemed the shortest of answers, and returned to work. The old Aran would have been chatting with her, work forgotten. Maybe something had changed. Was it losing Shra? Becoming a shaman?

She hated this whole line of thinking and stamped back to the center of the clearing. "Move faster! The poachers are close."

Aran's face contorted. "What did you say?"

"Let me say it a different way so maybe you'll understand this time. The. Poachers. Are. Not. Far. Away. The same ones who captured you before." She nodded toward the eastern rising sun. "That way. But don't worry—we'll protect you."

Merit swung around to reprimand yet another Silth, and when she turned back, Aran was gone. She searched among the boxes, growing increasingly concerned. Then she realized she'd misjudged his earlier expression. Not fear—anger. He'd gone after the poachers.

She called to one of her squad, put him in charge of the operation, and sped off toward where the poachers had been seen last. Two of her squad followed without the need for orders. Flying in the mid-canopy, she stopped every few hundred yards and strained to listen. Before long she heard the sounds of a morning camp—pots and other metal pieces clanking together, men calling to one another, and vehicle engines starting and idling.

She landed in a tree about fifty feet from the camp. Stacked under an open-sided tent, almost a hundred cages were crammed with parrots, toucans, and other birds. She surprised herself with the sound of her own growl. Still she saw no sign of Aran. She worked her way around the perimeter of the campsite, scanning the treetops. About halfway around the camp, she spotted him, crouched on a strangler fig branch wrapped around a larger tree. Laden with fruit, it had attracted a wide variety of birds, screeching and squawking as they fluttered from branch to branch.

As she dropped down next to him, he didn't take his eyes off the Humans. She sat and watched with him. Neither spoke.

Finally, "Do you know why I became a shaman?" When she didn't respond, he answered anyway. "So I could become powerful enough to kill these men."

She thought about Shra and the anguish Aran must've felt upon her death. Weighing his statement in her own code, she replied, "I wouldn't blame you. But you mustn't do anything to attract outside attention here. It would hurt the colonies. What do you intend to do?"

"If the poachers all died, who would follow up? They're here illegally, and no one knows where they are. The forest would quickly take the camp. And … I could do it in a way that Humans would take the blame." As he spoke, Aran twisted the large silver bracelet on his wrist.

Merit realized she had no idea if he had the power to accomplish what he described. "I wouldn't blame you. And I long for the birds to be free. But if you do this, you won't be able to be a shaman. A shaman can't kill Humans. Even bad ones." While she was familiar with that part of the shaman code, she also knew that citing rules to Aran rarely had any effect.

Suddenly he dropped backward from the tree and glided to the edge of the camp. She watched as he crept into the tent full of cages and unhooked the doors, leaving them shut. He moved to the trucks lined up nearby, but she couldn't see what he was doing. She looked back over her shoulder, and in response to her unspoken question, both squad members shrugged and shook their heads.

Aran disappeared for several minutes, long enough that she was considering moving to a different vantage point or going in after him, but he reemerged. He ducked behind the tents, pausing at each before heading back into the trees. When he landed beside her, the odor was so strong that she leaned away and wrinkled her nose.

"What's that smell?"

"Gasoline. They use it to power the vehicles."

They continued to watch the Humans moving around the campsite. One, a tall, heavy-set man with graying hair, emerged from a tent, set up a card table, and spread out a big map. Aran said under his breath, "Quaker." The Human called out to the others, who gathered around him, jostling each other and murmuring. Merit thought they must be preparing for their daily attack on the area wildlife.

As a latecomer in a big cowboy hat joined the tightly-packed circle, Aran pulled out a lighter and clicked its flame to life with his left hand. He brought his right arm up along his chest, swept it forward, and pointed toward the vehicles, all the while muttering words Merit could barely hear, much less understand. She followed the line of his pointing. Nothing happened. She tilted her head, confused, but Aran didn't look distressed. While the men listened to Quaker's instructions, small birds chirped and chattered in the trees. The caged birds gave periodic whistles and distress calls.

Aran leaned forward expectantly.

Wisps of smoke wafted up from between the parked trucks, and then flames shot up from each vehicle. When the men finally noticed, they just stood there gaping. With a sudden whoosh, one truck exploded, leaping up from its back wheels to slam back down, burning furiously along with its empty cages and equipment. Each of the other trucks did the same, sending a series of booms echoing through the campsite and giving Quaker back his voice. He let out a yell of fury, and he and the others raced toward the vehicles. But the heat was so intense they were forced back.

Aran tucked away the lighter, grabbed a pinch of soil from another pocket, and swept his hand forward again. The doors to all the occupied cages swung open with loud bangs. The birds scrambled for the openings, bumping into each other on their way out and sending feathers flying. The men didn't see, their attention centered on the burning trucks, and the roar of the flames masked the sound of the birds' excited squawks. Quaker swung around, spied them, and again roared in frustration. Cowboy ran toward the cages but tripped on a root, sprawling face-down on the ground.

But Aran wasn't done yet. He dropped the soil, retrieved the lighter, clicked it and swept his arm forward. Flames licked up the sides of first one tent and then another, until the whole camp was ablaze. One of the men pointed at the tents and yelled. They grabbed water and sand and threw it at the flames. The men backed away from the searing heat, waving their arms and screaming obscenities. Although most had disappeared, a few birds remained, perched in trees or fluttering in the air a safe distance away, as if taunting them.

Merit shifted from one foot to the other, trying to contain her glee. The product of what must have been weeks of hard work was gone, safely returned to the rainforest or on their way home to the cloud forest. Without their trucks and cages, starting over for the poachers would be difficult, if not impossible. Even getting home would be a challenge. How in the world had Aran done all this?

"So ... are you finished?"

Watching impassively, he nodded. "They'll think other Humans did this, the ones who try to protect the birds. The good news is they won't come back. There's no risk to the colony or the Silth."

"If they're smart, they'll consider changing professions," she said. She paused, then asked, "Didn't you became a shaman so you could kill these men?"

"That was why I became a shaman," he answered, his eyes locked on hers. Then he arched a brow. "But it isn't who I became." He took off without a backward glance.

The trees, always damp from the humidity, extinguished any sparks that blew into the forest. Merit realized her reason for being there, to guard Aran from the poachers, had been decidedly removed. Furthermore, he'd proven what he'd claimed—he was a shaman with little need for a guard. She smiled slightly, something she rarely did around other Silth, having seen the result in the mirror. While one side of her face had normal movement, the damaged muscles on the other allowed none. She knew the lop-sided effect of a smile was unnerving for those around her.

Her tension melted away. As the confusion and chaos below

continued, she couldn't help but chuckle. Perhaps not all of Aran's chaos was bad.

Scene 5

ARAN (SILTH)

That evening, Aran dreamed about Shra, both of them in the cage, with her in his arms.

She lifted her hand, and winced as she turned his face to hers. "Tell me ... a story. Distract me ... please."

Aran made his living traveling among the colonies and villages telling stories—storytellers were paid to entertain in the evenings after last meal. But they also served to amuse during the work of Silth who grew the crops, wove bolts of rough cloth, made pots and plates, or carved the intricate figures used in their religious ceremonies.

"Now?" He was barely able to choke out the word.

She shifted, gasped, and blew out a breath. "Tell me ... my favorite. The one about ...Tanton and Galslip."

He shook his head, hands fisted in frustration and swallowed hard. After a few moments, he leaned forward and whispered in her ear.

"Long ago, in the time before Humans' technology drove out the Faeries, when animals and Silth covered the Earth and we all spoke the same language, there lived a Silth chief named Tanton. His wife Galslip was the most radiant, graceful beauty who ever walked the Earth. When she entered the forest, every animal and Silth went silent in admiration. Under Galslip's spell, not only would Tanton do anything for her, but he also extended this love to all creatures. He became beloved and his kingdom prospered."

Shra lay still, eyes closed, and Aran glanced around before continuing. "Faeries sometimes took Silth as slaves like they did Humans. Taken with her beauty, the Faerie called Wanip whisked Galslip beneath the Earth to his world. Tanton was consumed by grief. All animals and Silth grew hostile to the Faeries and prepared for war.

"The Faerie king had ruled for many centuries. Like most Faeries he was not kind, but he was wise and did not desire the needless bloodshed he could foresee. He had little love for Humans or Silth, but he enjoyed the beauty and grace of the forest creatures.

"He summoned Wanip and asked him to return Galslip to Tanton. When Wanip refused to part with his beautiful slave, the king had his men escort Tanton to Faerie, the land beneath the Earth. Tanton came willingly, seeking a way to free Galslip, even though he knew that few who enter Faerie return. When the king generously offered Tanton any of his own beautiful Silth slaves, Tanton carefully declined. The king told Tanton he could not order Wanip, a powerful Faery elder, to part with his property. But, said the Faerie king, while Silth life is but a few hundred years, time itself is long. When the very old Wanip died, the king could arrange for Tanton and Galslip to spend eternity together.

"Tanton had dealt with the Faeries enough to know that every promise they made contained a trick. It was simply their nature. Tanton quickly saw the trick here. Faeries do not die of natural causes. Unless Wanip died in a war or an accident, he would outlive Tanton and Galslip, and they would never be together in this world. Tanton believed that the Faeries have no power in the next world and no power over death—as far as he was concerned, the promise was empty. Tanton had a trick of his own, however, so he agreed to the bargain, in exchange promising not to make war on the Faeries. To celebrate the pact, the king staged a great party, where the Faeries ate and drank well into the

night. *Tanton made a show of participating, but he knew better than to consume Faerie food or drink, lest all memories be wiped from his mind and doom him to eternity in Faerie. When the Faeries fell asleep, Tanton killed Wanip and escaped with Galslip.*"

Aran paused to watch Shra, breathing deeply and steadily. He hoped she'd fallen asleep, but after a moment she murmured, "Don't stop."

He checked again to make sure they weren't attracting attention. "The king was outraged. He couldn't let this insult to his hospitality go unanswered, nor could he allow a Silth to get the better of the Faeries. But he had agreed to a magical pact that Tanton and Galslip would spend all of eternity together after Wanip's death. He sent his army and killed Tanton, Galslip, and all the thousands of Silth of their kingdom. Earth was called 'earth' then and not 'water' because there were no oceans, just land with many lakes fed by streams. When Tanton and Galslip were killed, a mighty earthquake occurred. The lands of the Earth broke into pieces. All the world trembled as the spirit of Tanton, with his love for Galslip, filled the spaces between the broken lands, becoming the vast oceans of the world. Galslip became sand and lay down next to the ocean, within the caress of its waves and its periodic embrace as the waters rise to cover the beach."*

"And Galslip ... and Tanton ... lie next to each other ... to this day," she finished in a voice he could barely hear.

Aran awoke, wondering what Shra would have thought about his response to the poachers. Would she be disappointed he hadn't killed them? He didn't think so. But like an itch that couldn't be scratched, Aran found that the fact that Human behavior was no different today than it had been yesterday left him unsatisfied. It took a long time for him to fall back asleep.

CHAPTER NINE

Scene 1

ANGEL (TROW)

Angeles was bored. Humans bored her—they would talk endlessly about things and end up doing nothing. At the moment, she was suffering through Stanley Ryder, Juan, Chilen, two women, and a man discussing the massive climate change intervention program the Chinese had just announced. She imagined creative ways to kill each of them—she had ended many Humans, Paerries, and Trow, taking pride in her creativity in their deaths.

According to the back and forth among the group, "geo-engineering" was the name for Humans' large-scale interventions in natural systems, in this case trying to avoid the impacts of global warming and climate disruption. To address the adverse consequences of their technology, the Humans proposed to use even bigger applications of it, such as putting metals in the ocean to stimulate plankton, which would absorb the carbon causing global warming, or creating massive reflective areas in the desert to reduce heat. Putting salt water in the clouds to increase their reflectivity and reduce the sun's heating of the atmosphere had also been proposed.

In spite of the tedium, Angeles continued following the conversation so she could report back to Thest. The general might not care, but then again, he might enjoy hearing anything reflecting poorly on the Humans. With Thest, one never knew what he would consider important.

Stanley Ryder, who everyone else called Brophy, was saying, "—people just want some magic techno-bullet allowing them to proceed without changing their behavior."

Once the furor over the eco-lodge attack died down, Juan had returned to Costa Rica. Being wounded for the cause had increased his popularity with Retreat's other members. A meeting did not pass without Juan telling his significantly embellished story and some fresh face accompanying him home.

"It's not just the Chinese." This from one of the women. She gestured to the magazine in her hand. "Listen to this quotation from a guy in the U.K.'s 'Stratospheric Particle Injection for Climate Engineering' project. 'Full-scale deployment of climate engineering technologies will be the clearest indication that we have failed in our role as planet stewards, but there is a point at which not deploying some technologies would be unethical.'"

Juan scoffed. "Typical— 'Hi, we're 'SPICE' and part of the group that screwed things up, but trust us, this time we're here to help.' You know this isn't going to end well. There are always unintended consequences. And geo-engineering may be the Human undertaking that'll kill us all."

Angeles forced herself to listen as they went on about the many large-scale, well-intentioned Human projects with unintended side effects—lead in gasoline, freon in refrigerants, connecting this waterway to that sea, draining that marsh, removing wolves, or spraying DDT. Humans were idiots. But her job was to get these guys to do something about it, not talk it to death. Perhaps if she stuck her pen through Juan's eye and into his brain, they would stop talking.

She looked over at Stanley Ryder who seemed even more frustrated. He drummed his fingers randomly on his walking stick, covered with meaningless runes.

"Well, what're we going to do about it?" he asked the room.

"What are we going to do about the British?" Juan shook his head. "What can we do? We're far away from them."

"Yeah, Chilen's right," said another newbie whose name Angeles was never told or had forgotten. "The U.K., unlike Costa Rica, has a big freaking army, and I don't think we're gonna take on China or Russia."

Stanley Ryder rolled his eyes. He pushed up and headed out the door.

Angeles looked at the others, shrugged, and followed. She found Stanley Ryder sitting in a porch chair, rocking furiously.

"Walk with me."

The rocking stopped. "What—in the dark?"

"I got a light." She pulled out a small LED flashlight, pointed it toward the front yard, and illuminated a wide area with the powerful beam. "Besides, we will walk on the road, and there is plenty of moonlight." She knew Stanley Ryder had grown up in Minneapolis, and while the fool loved nature in the abstract and in the daylight, he was afraid of it when darkness fell.

He studied the landscape a moment, got up, and stepped off the porch, Angeles close on his heels. Away from the building's lights, moonlight shone on the road, and she switched off the flashlight. Stanley Ryder walked with his hands jammed in his jeans.

"What if a group was actually doing something?"

"What?"

She stayed quiet a few more steps, then, "What if I said there is a group doing something? Something big but very dangerous. Would you have the cajones to do it?"

He gave a heavy sigh. "I'm friggin' tired of the 'big' yet useless move to attract media attention. I don't think the world's gonna wake up. Look at the U.S.—woke up and then went back to sleep. Hell, I'm not even sure it would matter now. The game's done. Humans are done. And they're going to drag everything else down with them."

Perfect. That fatalism would work to her advantage. "Some people believe there is another way. A way that would be hard. Hard to accomplish. Hard on lots of Humans, and lots of other species. But in the end, it would rebalance the system, allow everything to flourish. Sort of a … 'reboot,' if you will."

He huffed out a breath. "I don't believe any such thing exists. Even if it did, it's definitely not within the ability of any small group of people to implement it. And I'd have to be convinced it didn't have the same problems as geo-engineering, another big undertaking with unintended consequences." He was quiet for a moment, then added, "But that being said … if there was a realistic solution, you couldn't stop me from participating."

"Even if you might not live though it?"

He chuckled. "Ya know, that's one of the things slowing down environmental martyrs. Most are atheists who don't believe they have anything waiting for them on 'the other side.' We aren't very keen to complete the circle of life and become one with the Earth. You need to find a Christian … or at least a pagan." When he received neither a laugh nor smile, he said, "Yeah, Angel, I got the balls to see something through to the end. But this is just bullshit, 'cause I don't think any such plan could be realistic."

They trudged along the dark road in silence, Angeles giving Stanley Ryder time to mull things over. Every jungle sound ceased when the two approached and resumed when they moved further down the road.

"I need to clear it with some people," she said, as if she was doing him a favor. "But if they okay it, I will show you the plan. These are very serious, committed people. Hard to say no to. If you cannot find a flaw in the plan, they will expect you to proceed with them. Do not start down this path unless you are ready to follow it a hundred percent."

As he walked beside her, brow furrowed in thought, she decided it best not to push. Before long they reached the big paved road leading into town.

She said, "I am going. But I will be back in touch in the next three days."

"Going? We're in the middle of the freaking jungle."

"I have a ride meeting me a couple of miles down. When you get back to the cabin, do not tell the others about this conversation. They are not ready. They are little children playing pranks on the adults and whining because the war goes on around them, but they are not allowed access to the guns." She handed him the flashlight to use going back and stared at him until she got an uncomfortable nod in return.

As she walked away, she was confident Stanley Ryder would agree to be involved. She mulled over the theatrics of waiting three days. Yes, it was the right tactic. Anything faster would seem like it was not a deep organization. Humans knew it took time for large groups to process a decision, but in truth, the decision was already made.

Stanley Ryder was their target for the project. While she still had to inform Thest, Angeles had known for a while that she would win over the Human—it was simply a question of waiting for the right time. Tonight had been it. In three days she would close the deal.

Angeles's tongue flicked into the night air, tasting the fear that followed like a cloud around her. Trow eyesight showed her the small animals scurrying away in the darkness.

She stepped into the forest, flickered, and vanished.

Scene 2

ANGEL (TROW)

Angeles reappeared in Hell. While the name of the location amused Thest, she considered it another manifestation of the general's increasingly loose grasp on reality that he arranged to meet here.

Hell was no power location—the Trow gained no energy here. Not like the mounds in Ireland, Angor Wat, or even the pyramids, all built by Humans on old doorways of power. Power from yet another world besides Earth or the Land. It was not even like where they used to meet, the volcano in Costa Rica, which had connection to the power of the Earth. No, Hell was simply a tourist spot in what the Humans called Grand Cayman, not far from its capital.

Angeles stood on the wooden deck overlooking the rock formation that had prompted the place's name. The deck was at the rear of a restaurant, unused at this time of night. She drummed her fingers on a railing as the moonlight shone on a field of jagged black limestone and dolomite rocks, formed in rough stalagmites across a couple of acres.

The only buildings were the closed post office and gift shops with the sign: "Welcome to Hell." Tourists had their families pose with the plywood cutout of the devil—his face was a hole for them to stick theirs in—and afterward they would purchase hot sauce, hats, and postcards to send from "Hell." Angeles thought about how hard the typical Human family worked for the money allowing this experience, trying to weigh it against the fact that they seemed to have fun. They laughed and joked with one another, their great experience made even more perfect by souvenir hats.

She did not understand that aspect of Humans, one of many that confused her. Although the Trow understood Human language, emotions were tricky. Understanding Human actions, or even what Humans referred to as "body language," was difficult for most Trow. The Trow had serious levels of emotion, but unlike Humans they did not weave them into their body language and actions. One could not read a Trow's emotions—for her work among Humans, she had to practice showing them. She knew that when Humans encounter someone who does not display emotions, they become wary and less inclined to interact.

She studied the devil cutout again. The devil story had been inspired by early Human contact with the Trow, causing Humans to create tales of gods and magical beings like fairies, elves, and trolls. Human disappearances led to stories of them being lured away by ghosts and supernatural beings. These days such disappearances produced stories of predators, Human traffickers, and serial killers.

Thest's sudden appearance at her elbow interrupted her moonlight reflections. While she had worn her usual jeans and black t-shirt, Thest's "disguise" for the meeting was an Aloha shirt and a baseball cap bearing a Caribbean bar logo.

Looking around, the general said, "I know, but I just love this place."

She was used to Thest's uncanny ability to discern thoughts. Especially in the absence of body language. Trow could not read minds, but Thest came as close to it as she could imagine. It was one of the ways he kept those around him loyal—they believed he would sense a betrayal as soon as it appeared in their minds. She believed it as well.

First, she filled Thest in on Stanley Ryder. Then she outlined the steps for graduating the Human from Retreat to the next level of the organization "Nature Now," which she had nurtured into being over the last several years. Because of the threats it had made and the actions for which it had taken credit, it had made the FBI's list of terrorist organizations operating from the United States.

"Good, Angeles. The other groups are ready. Everything else is in place. This is the last piece of the puzzle. You must keep him and the rest of Nature Now thinking they are the only active cell. That it all depends on them." Angeles did not respond—she knew the plan well—but Thest seemed to sense her impatience. "The campaign is going well now. We have made up for lost time. Xafar is pleased."

"I find a 'pleased Xafar' hard to imagine, what Humans call an oxymoron. Like a 'jumbo shrimp'."

"Jumbo what?" But he did not give her an opportunity to explain. "Well, as pleased as Xafar ever gets, meaning no one dies today." He paused, gazing out at the rough landscape, and made a sweeping gesture with his arm. "All of this will be yours one day."

She slanted a look at him but kept her face composed. Trow did not really attempt it often, but one consequence of Thest's long Earth exposure was that he tried humor. Despite her limited experience with the effort, she was fairly certain he failed.

"This area and what the Humans call Central America," Thest went on. "The Trow who come here to live will serve you. And in this world, you will answer only to Xafar."

Fod materialized in front of them. "Greetings to you both."

As Fod brought Thest up to date on his own mission, Angeles's mind wandered back to Stanley Ryder and what needed to happen next. Fod said something about "not really seeing anything," and Thest's response of "kill him anyway" pulled her back to their conversation. She listened with interest.

Fod looked puzzled. "Perhaps I have misstated something, my Lord. I did not mean to convey that I think the young shaman Aran is any threat whatsoever. Though I did not observe them on the return ship, I saw them almost daily from the time they left here until they boarded the ship. And I have watched Aran since he returned. He appears to have been trained in the most conventional way. I would take pleasure in ridding myself of the job of monitoring him and the older shaman, but I do not see a reason."

Thest scoffed, "Old Storng does not change his ways. He has merely learned to hide his conversations and training from you. I'm sure he has told the young shaman Aran far too much and sworn him to secrecy. This is not the time to take risks. Kill him in a way that causes the Paerries to banish Storng. When Storng is not so much in their thoughts, we will quietly end him as well."

"As you wish." Fod bowed and vanished.

Thest turned to Angeles, frowning. "The time for whimsy is gone for now. Perhaps it will return later. We will not meet here again until the world is free of Humans."

Angeles found herself alone again and lingered, looking at the black rocks and their moon-generated shadows. There was little enough whimsy now, and it was often a cloak for the madness that grew in the Trow living in this world. She missed true whimsy, which in a military campaign was like a 'happy Xafar,' another oxymoron.

All this will be mine. What does that even mean? Would she

really be Queen of Central America? Able to determine the life and death of any creatures remaining there? Harvest its precious metals and stones? Judge the affairs of the Trow who settled there and tax them as she desired? If so, putting up with the Humans at Nature Now would almost be worth it.

Though they gave lip service to the characterization of Humans as a scourge, they really sought the same simple outcome as other Human organizations, a happy future for their kind. Unlike Angeles, they did not really see Humans as an invasive species that should be exterminated from the system.

A family of two parents and three children emerged beside the closed stores. As they rushed to the devil cutout for pictures, she imagined them bursting into flames and savored the sensation of pure pleasure.

Perhaps my notion of whimsy is different from others'.

Scene 3

Brophy (Human)

"Lots of folks don't recall the violence in the civil rights movement," Jack said. "They remember Martin Luther King, but not so much Malcolm X, Stokely Carmichael, or Huey Newton, who more explicitly said that violence would be the only answer if wrongs weren't righted. They recall the freedom riders and occupation of lunch counters, yet forget the riots and Black Panthers. Because the cause was right."

Morris answered, "Yeah, but they kept hunting the folks who killed people in their protests over the Vietnam War for a long time after they stopped chasing folks for property damage. After they decided the cause was right."

Brophy listened to them argue, struck by the physical differences between them. Jack was a tall, thin, Nordic-sort-of-looking guy, while Morris was a stocky, short African-American with a neat beard and bald head. Inside a small Boston townhouse, the three were sitting with five others, while Angeles and another woman were finishing the bombs on a side table. Most of the room's occupants were college students or bright dropouts in tech jobs. Brophy felt a little out of their league. The crude tattoos on his forearms— "Greenpeace" on one and "Meat is Death" on the other—seemed to clash with the polished presence of the others. The danger of being in the room with the bombs, combined with a conversation bouncing all over a history both real and imagined, seemed surreal, close to an out-of-body experience.

He suddenly missed the jungle.

"Well, we aren't trying to kill anyone tonight." Jack eyed the rest of the group, shifting restlessly at the mention of deaths. "We're just talking about Morris's concern that we might accidently hurt someone. But we've timed it so nobody should be there. And in the end, they shouldn't be working for these guys anyway."

Morris chuffed. "Man, you need to read more. That's what they always say. Turns out the guy who dies is some poor black man who took the janitor's night shift. Works three jobs to put his only child through college. Doesn't even know what they do in the place."

Jack said with exaggerated patience, "That's why we're timing this for 4:30 in the am. Cleanup crew's gone. Only person there is the guard, and he'll be at a station far from the lab. We'll leave evidence that this hit was carried out by carbon deniers, worried about the consequences of the geo-engineering interventions being developed in this lab."

"No one's going to believe deniers could actually string together the thoughts necessary to be worried about interventions," chimed in a woman in the circle. "Tanya," Brophy thought her name was. The others laughed. Brophy was making a quarter disappear and reappear on the table beside the bombs.

"They're the ones we should be going after," another woman said. "Not folks trying to come up with a solution, however misguided."

After a moment of silence, Jack argued, "We don't need to go after them. Nature's already proved them wrong. Even if elected folks won't acknowledge it. But they've cost us so much time and given so many people excuses to postpone action. We should erect statues to them so their names will be scorned for the rest of time. Statues covered in pigeon poop, up to their knees in rising water, saying 'these are the people who brought us to this.'"

Brophy remembered the similar conversation back in Costa Rica. At least here in Boston, this one was leading to action.

Jack was on a roll. "But it's the scientists and engineers who'll destroy the Earth. The Earth will survive the carbon like it has before. It may kill off the Humans and a lot of other creatures before it rights itself, but it'll survive the carbon. It's the interventions that are purely Human vanity. It's these guys that are going to turn the Earth into Mars. And it's up to us to stop them. Because nobody else will."

Angel called from across the room, "Ready."

"Ok," Jack said. "Let's go over the plan one more time."

Everyone, including Brophy, leaned forward. It was important, he thought. The right thing to do. Worth the risks. He was thrilled to finally be doing something to address the big picture, not just trying to stop some rich people trying to build something where they shouldn't. The big, big picture.

He looked at the intent faces around him and at Angel, who winked at him. He knew he was in the right place, at the right time, with the right people, and with the right weapons.

CHAPTER TEN

Scene 1

ARAN (SILTH)

Aran felt good, better than he had in a long time. He soared above the canopy, enjoying the late afternoon sun on his back, the wind sliding by, and the moist, earthy forest smells. They were in a "dry" season, which meant it rained a little less often. The change of pace was welcome.

He'd spent the last several weeks in almost constant contact with different Silth villages and colonies. Having just arrived the night before with three Silth helping carry his swag, he'd spent a busy day working in yet another new colony. He stayed several days in each place, getting to know them, letting them get to know him. He gave out a few gifts, sold a few conveniences, but held back the bulk of his harvest. He thought of it as his dowry. What colony or village would he marry?

Each colony had to work past who they knew him as before. Its residents would demand songs and stories—that was how they'd always known him, how they'd welcomed him in the past, sought him out, and enjoyed his presence. They always expected him to move on to the next spot.

He told them stories, but not initially. First, he established himself as shaman. He addressed any sick or wounded in the colony, just as Storng had taught. He met with their council, learned what was broken or missing, and negotiated a price to fix or furnish it. Storng had taught him to negotiate these prices for services, even though he could have provided them for free and lived off the sale of his swag. But long ago the shamans learned that the colonies did not have the appropriate appreciation for what they got for free. Still, the harvesters, even though paid, didn't do their jobs to line the pockets of shamans— they worked for the good of the colonies. The shamans put most of their profits back into the colony, supporting art, music, and health.

Only after the Silth and their colony were in good working order did he consent to tell stories. Even then, they were the traditional, more somber ones, not the rollicking fun tales with which he had once entertained. As his mood improved, his sense of humor returned, but he needed to maintain some gravitas. He joined them in the communal music sessions but didn't sing, which he missed. His voice had never recovered, and its gravelly quality didn't lend itself to song. But each colony accepted the change readily enough. Though there were other singer/story tellers, maybe not as popular as he'd been, few shamans traveled beyond Amazonia. He had always felt valuable to the colonies as a bard, but not especially useful. Now that the poachers were no longer the center of his focus, he wasn't sure where his life was going, but it was good to feel useful.

He could go several days, a week, maybe, without thinking of Shra. The sadness still came, sweeping in and disappearing as suddenly as it had arrived. But these episodes were far less frequent. He tried not to feel guilty about the change.

He continued flying along the river's edge. Far from where Humans usually ventured, he was surprised to hear a shout from below. He circled back to investigate and landed on a tree branch. Someone was lying on his side near the river bank, his leg twisted and the foot caught in the roots of a tree. Propped on one elbow, the figure was waving a bottle and yelling at an enormous crocodile creeping out of the water.

"Go away, you great foolish beast! Haa! Get out of here!" He threw the nearly empty bottle at the crocodile and fell onto his back, eyes closed.

With a jolt, Aran realized the figure was not a Human, but a Faerie, surrounded by a faint blue glow. He coasted down to the apparently unconscious figure and faced the crocodile. While a few animals like monkeys could tell a Silth was not the bird he appeared to be, many could not. He wasn't sure about crocodiles.

Dropping his bird glamour, he said quietly, "You don't want to eat him, cousin. He would be very bad for you. He'd hurt your insides."

The crocodile stopped its advance, apparently surprised both by the sudden appearance of the un-glamoured Silth and his somewhat limited understanding of what Aran was saying. He knew the crocodile, while smart in its own way, didn't use language like Silth but instead got "a sense of things." And the sense Aran was projecting was "no good to eat."

This guy must be really hungry, he thought, as it ignored the "no good to eat" signal and crept forward again. A little louder, "You don't want to tangle with me, cousin. I am very dangerous."

He pulled out his lighter, clicked it, and swept his arm forward, sending fire billowing out toward the crocodile. Without pausing, the creature redirected in a wide, leisurely loop back toward the river.

Aran focused his attention on the fallen Faerie, who was conscious again and up on one elbow. Bleary-eyed, he grinned at Aran and collapsed, out cold. Aran freed the Faerie's foot from the roots. Worried the crocodile would change its mind, he dragged the Faerie, almost five times his size, further from the river. He was panting by the time he had moved the dead weight into a small clearing.

The smell of alcohol was strong on the Faerie's breath. Aran propped him, head lolling to one side, against the buttress roots of an enormous corcovado tree, and started a fire nearby. He gathered leaves and roots, added water from the river, and crushed them into a paste. He forced it past the Faerie's lips, drawing drunken half-coherent curses.

"Stop struggling. This will sober you up."

The Faerie's resistance ceased. He stared at Aran through one rheumy eye and spat paste into Aran's face. His head again tipped to the side, and he began to snore. Shaking his head, Aran washed his face in the river, keeping careful watch for the crocodile. He found a nearby fruit tree and ate his dinner squatting near the small fire he built.

A Faerie. He had captured a Faerie. Maybe. He didn't really know how to capture a Faerie. And his was a snoring, snorting, foul-smelling enigma.

Faeries were much less impressive in person than the stories led him to expect. Mostly he looked like a once handsome Human, at least six feet seven with almond-shaped eyes, except that his ears and nose were more pointed and cheekbones more prominent. He was achingly thin and dirty from his greasy hair to the bottoms of the light boots he wore, and his pale, fish-belly-colored skin looked unnatural on any living creature. His face was deep yellow-purple around a healing bruise, and patches of dried blood and vomit were crusted on his tunic. His fingernails were long and dirty, and what Aran had seen of his eyes was pale blue, jaundiced, and bloodshot. Aran could not hazard a guess what color the clothes originally had been, but they'd aged into a dirty grey.

If this really was a Faerie, it had certainly fallen on hard times.

Should I just leave? Even a hungover Faerie was probably dangerous. He could leave him here, his conscience clear having saved him from the immediate danger of the crocodile. But something made him stay. Perhaps empathy, for he had awakened several times after drunken days in a similar state. Or perhaps it was the challenge of capturing a Faerie. Whatever the reason, he tried to recall the old stories that told how to complete such a capture.

Near midnight the Faerie woke up enough to lift his head and ask, "What are you doing, little one?" The potion Aran had given him had sped sobriety, though not as quickly as it worked on a drunken Silth, and the slurring of his speech was no longer present.

"I've captured you and you must obey me," was Aran's immediate response.

"Really?" The Faerie chuckled. "Is that what they taught you in Paerrie School?" For the Trow, "Paerrie" was a derogatory term for the Silth, but it had been around so long that Silth sometimes used it themselves. Similarly, Aran knew that Faeries did not call themselves "Faeries," but he didn't know what word they used.

"Well, yes. If you save a Faerie's life, he must obey you. You earn his undying service."

The Faerie smiled darkly and eyed the sparks from the fire floating into the air. "Sadly, you've been misled. Faeries cannot feel gratitude. The only thing you would earn is death." His chin dropped to his chest, and the earlier snores seemed a mere warm-up to those he currently produced.

Aran reflected on what the Faerie had said. By morning the creature would be completely sober and probably rested. He'd expected the paste to sober him up and restore him immediately, but apparently it was not as effective on Faeries as it was on Silth. If the Faerie was telling the truth, he very well could begin the day by killing Aran. Of course, that was what a Faerie would say to try to escape being captured. Should he just snuff out the fire and leave him to the rainforest's mercy? He listened to the noises, including enough thumps and bumps to suggest a cougar or pigs or another creature happy to eat someone on the ground. He added more wood to the fire.

The Faerie was mumbling, mostly indistinct sentences, but occasionally some coherent series of words would emerge. He seemed to dream of some confrontation, given the way he jerked and the angry tone of his intermittent shouts. Aran kept his distance so as not to smell either the Faerie or his breath.

Suddenly the Faerie shouted in his sleep, "Do you know who I am? Do you? I am Faelen, son of Xafar. You do not treat me like this …" and his voice trailed off.

Another story told to young Silth was that if one had a Faerie's name, one controlled it. But what if that was a myth as well? Aran pondered these things and waited for the Faerie to rouse. Finally, the sky brightened, and the birds started their salutes to the morning.

"Faelen, son of Xafar, wake up." When the peacefully sleeping Faerie did not stir, Aran tried again, more forcefully. "Wake up, smelly croc-bait!"

Faelen's eyes flew open and then narrowed. He appeared to be concentrating, playing back the events of the evening before. "Thank you," were his first words. "Thank you for the bit with the crocodile."

He was quiet a moment, then slyly, "How is it you know my name?"

Ignoring the question, Aran tried to look more confident than he felt. "I have called you by your name, and you are bound to serve me."

"You are big on this 'serving you' thing. Not enough maids in Paerrieville?"

"I'm not sure that the 'bit with the crocodile' doesn't count for something more than just 'thanks,'" Aran added a little less forcefully.

A smile split Faelen's face. "You do not know squat about Faeries, do you?" When Aran said nothing, Faelen asked, "If by chance I were to serve you, what is it you desire so badly?"

"I want you to teach me Faerie powers."

"That would simply make you dead." He looked puzzled. "Did I tell you that earlier? Seems like … no matter." He went on with mock formality, "Why do you wish these powers, o' tiny lord of the rainforest?"

"My friend and teacher is hunted by Faeries. And I wish to protect him."

"An answer not likely to be true. For if they hunted him, he would be dead by now. Who is he, and why do you think he is hunted?"

Aran took it as a hopeful sign that Faelen had said "if they hunted him," suggesting he was not one of the hunters. He paused, unwilling to give the Faerie too much knowledge. "He is a shaman. I don't know why they hunt him."

"Ahh … a lie. He must be Storng, making you most likely his newest student. So, student, you are already dead. He killed you the moment he began teaching you. You know why they hunt him. And you know it is more likely you who they will hunt next."

Aran found disconcerting the quick insight of the creature who only hours before could not defend himself from a crocodile. "Faelen, son of Xafar—"

"Faelen. The rest is just for show."

"Faelen, will you honor your duty to serve me?"

"Why would I want to spend time with a Paerrie under a death sentence?" Faelen cocked his head to one side. "What is your name? How much do you know already? How much is there to teach?"

"Well, since I don't know how much there is to learn, I can't really answer that question. But I know some. And my name is …" Aran trailed off, worried that giving his name would give the Faerie too much power. "My name is Casius."

"Another lie. We are quickly establishing that you are not very truthful. Tell me, Aran, are all Paerries such poor liars?"

Aran flinched at his name, suddenly unsure as to who had captured whom. If he told Faelen what he knew, maybe he would be embracing a death sentence that had not yet been handed down. Still, the certainty with which Faelen had identified him as Storng's doomed student suggested it was a given he was already marked for death.

As Aran outlined his training, Faelen neither moved nor interrupted. When Aran had finished, Faelen stood and stretched, all the while saying nothing as he looked out into the rainforest. Despite the day's bright beginning, clouds were gathering and a light mist forming.

Faelen sat down cross-legged in front of Aran. "You have told me enough for me to know that both you and Storng are effectively dead. Storng knew better than to teach you these things. Reckless beyond belief. Had he had not already caused the deaths of his other students, perhaps I could understand it. Many holes exist in your knowledge, and the level is that of a small child in the Land, back when there were such. For example, all individuals have more than one name—formal names, common ones everyone uses, special title names, and secret names only they know. If someone could be controlled by having his name repeated by another, you could not introduce yourself to anyone. You could not call out to him across the room because he would not have told you his name. Only the secret name gives control. 'Faelen' is my common name. You have no control over me."

Without warning, Faelen flung his arm up and pointed his index finger at Aran. Thick madeira vines whipped out from the tree nearest him, encircling his entire body so tightly that struggling was impossible. "I am exiled here in this world. Turning you over to the Trow would buy me passage back to the pleasures of my own world." He glanced up as two blue parrots flew out of a tree close by and disappeared into the misty sky. "This would be true whether you were dead or alive." Faelen flicked his finger and the vines fell away. "To your great, good fortune, however, I hate the Trow, and the Land holds no pleasures for me. For a small price, I will teach you what you desire. And because you are already dead, I will not have done you any harm."

So they called themselves "Trow." "And that price would be?" Aran asked, rubbing the shoulder a vine had pinched.

"I am tired of having to sneak into Human settlements for my … elixir. Bring me a bottle nightly and I will teach you."

A surprisingly small price, Aran thought, and one he should accept quickly before Faelen changed his mind. "Agreed." He produced a miniature bottle of rum from his cloak—thankfully he was carrying it for use in his negotiations—and presented it to Faelen. "I'll bring you a bigger one tonight. Where shall we meet?"

"Here is as good as anywhere. And this is your first lesson. When a Trow accepts something from you, he or she is honor-bound to the deal you have struck. Just not always in the way you may think."

"Is that a warning or a threat?"

"Exactly." Faelen vanished with a flicker and slight pop, the air rushing into the place where he'd once stood.

Scene 2

ARAN (SILTH)

That night Aran showed up with the required bottle, one of several in the harvest share Storng had given him. Although functional, Silth liquor was not as flavorful as that of Humans. Consequently, a good bottle of Human liquor, whether rum, scotch, or tequila, made excellent barter.

Aran was pleased to find Faelen waiting at the same spot as before, having bathed and changed clothes. The Faerie appeared healthy with no sign of a hangover, and Aran attributed Faelen's renewed vigor to the potion Aran had administered. Probably best not to mention that.

Faelen greeted him with, "You are probably being watched, certainly by Trow and perhaps Paerries as well. I checked and you were not followed. But in the future, you should assume there will be an effort to do so, at the least. And I expect them to kill you soon."

Aran ruefully noted Faelen didn't say "try to kill you."

"The first thing you must do is learn a spell to tell if you are being tracked by Paerries. I will also show you a spell to avoid the Trow's ability to remotely track you. You will use this every time you come to see me. The first time I detect you are being followed by either Trow or Paerrie, you will never see me again."

Unlike the Silth, Faeries spoke no words to perform their magic. Faelen taught Aran a complex series of gestures, which when performed with a single powerful image held in the mind would not only result in the desired magic, but afterward would repeat the magic by simply summoning the image. He taught him how to detect the nearby presence of Silth or Faeries and block the latter from tracking or seeing him with anything other than normal sight.

As the sky brightened, he said, "Not bad for a night's work. You learn quickly. I can see why Storng believes you have potential. It should take us about three weeks to cover what is needed."

"Three weeks? Every night?"

"Three weeks. Every night."

Because they had worked together and Faelen didn't kill him, Aran's mood had lifted. He reflected upon all he'd learned that night, and his answer was obvious. "Of course."

Each evening they followed the same routine. Aran grew exhausted—when finished with Faelen, he caught a little sleep in the morning before his day began—but he found he was addicted to the learning. Faelen taught him amazing things. How to fight Faeries. How to track others. How to cast Human glamours and even Faerie glamours. Some nights he would tell Aran about the Land and its occupants. Each day's dawning caught Aran by surprise because the time passed so quickly.

The same couldn't be said of the days. Aran grew distracted from interviewing with the colonies for a potential position. He still visited each, fixing what required it, whether broken Silth or device. But he ceased telling stories, and he started selling and distributing more of the harvest he carried. Staying interested in seemingly mundane things was difficult knowing each day might be his last.

Merit noticed, and he eluded the guards she sent to tail him as he slipped away at night. When she decided to follow him herself, he also escaped her. She sent her harpy eagle to follow him, but the bird's limited night vision was no match for Aran's evasions.

Finally, she confronted him. "Aran, you're completely worn out. The darkness below your eyes could pass for night. You're squandering your 'dowry' like you don't expect to see another sunrise. Where are you sneaking off to each night?"

He tried to make light of his evening disappearances, but she persisted. He left unchallenged her speculation that he was sneaking into colonies to spend time with Silth females. But the accusation appeared half-hearted—he suspected that had been the first thing she checked. She was making it increasingly difficult to leave each night, but all he needed was one brief unobserved moment, and he could render himself undetectable to Faerie and Silth alike. She grew angrier by the day.

After two weeks of harassment, Aran had had enough. "You chose to work for my brother, not for me. So I have no reason to share my whereabouts with you. You protect the caravan as it moves in the day. You're neither my jailor nor my guard at night. As you have seen, I can take care of myself."

For the next week she barely spoke to him, but she did stop trying to follow him. He couldn't confide in her because he knew two things for certain. One was that if he told her what he was doing, she'd try to protect him from the dangers of interacting with a Faerie. The other was that Faelen would detect her and leave as he had threatened. Aran was learning so much, and it was too important for his and perhaps Storng's survival to end his learning prematurely. Consequently, he endured Merit's ire, hoping he could make peace with her later.

On the last night of the third week, Aran showed up, the usual bottle tucked into a rowling bag, to find Faelen sound asleep beneath a strangler vine. The nearby fire was something new—on all other nights, they had worked in the glow of moonlight or with blue Faerie light on overcast nights.

"Old Faerie," Aran said softly. "Hey, old Faerie, wake up."

Faelen opened one eye. "As Faeries go, I'm really fairly young."

"Which means what—you're only as old as the dirt of this forest?"

Without getting up, Faelen took the bottle, surprising Aran by unscrewing the top and taking a big swig. On previous nights, Faelen had arrived sober and never drank until the very end of the session. When Faelen thrust the rum bottle, a pint and, thus, almost Silth-sized, into Aran's hands, Aran tipped it slightly toward Faelen as a toast, spilled out a drop or two, and handed it back, ignoring the Faerie's quizzical look.

"An indulgence," Faelen said, gesturing toward the bottle. "This is the last night we will work together. I have a lot to say, so there will be no practice tonight. Just talking." He picked up a loaf of bread warming on a nearby rock, broke off a piece, and handed it to Aran. "Among Russian Humans is a saying—'you are not serious about drinking unless you eat something as well'."

"And we are serious about drinking tonight?"

"I am. I think you are not."

"Liquor and I don't agree. Or perhaps it is better to say we agree all too well. Causing days, weeks, and even months to disappear in our friendship. So … I broke it off."

Faelen eyed him before lifting the bottle to his lips, dribbling a little rum down his chin but making no attempt to wipe it off. "I will tell you something about me, something about you, and some things about this world. Finally, there will be one more payment required. First me. I am the son of the current Trow King. I too have a problem with alcohol." He waved the bottle at Aran. "Perhaps the two things are related—I do not know. Alcohol, in part, got me exiled to this world. As I have told you, this world is not currently a healthy place for the Trow, so it is considered a punishment to be exiled here. But the two things I love are here in this world. One is obviously Human alcohol—for some reason only mead can be made in the Land. The other is parrots, and they are another reason I am banished.

"You have grown up with the knowledge that you Paerries come into this world as a cross between parrots and Trow. I am part of the reason Paerries exist. I am captivated by the beauty of parrots. They are the second most beautiful thing in this world." Although Aran thought he was effectively masking his feelings, Faelen smiled knowingly. "You are thinking about me making love with parrots. You are trying to imagine how that happens, while simultaneously being repelled by the notion."

Aran's jaw dropped, and Faelen smirked. "Mind-reading is unnecessary when your thoughts are so plainly displayed on your face." He had been vague about whether or not Faeries could read minds.

Faelen poked at the fire with a large stick. "Maybe you are even more disturbed by the possibility that I could be your father. All of this disturbs the Trow as well, but not for the reason you think. When the Trow have deep affection for something in this world, they cannot help but bestow some of their magic on it. This has been true for as long as we have been coming here. The Humans have enjoyed the benefits of this relationship as we fell in love with their music, or their math, or even some individual amongst them. Think of it like this. When a Human sculptor looks at a block of marble, he knows that inside it is a beautiful sculpture. With the addition of his skills and affection, this sculpture can be released from the rock. When released, do we think of that statue as simply a piece of the original rock? Or do we think of it as something greater than that?

"It is considered a high honor in the Land to have helped to create something beautiful in this world. I happen to think that the most beautiful thing in this world is you Paerries. No coupling with parrots is involved in the creation of Paerries, just proximity, a lust for beauty, and a little bioengineering. One of the many ironies of being in this world is that we bring to it beauty, and it kills us.

"The Trow are masters of bioengineering. In the Land we have neither electrical technology nor magic. But we can manipulate living things into weapons, tools, and appliances. When we came to this world, we found that we could create whole new races of creatures, and Paerries were one of those races."

He looked at the ground. "Perhaps I suffer a father's pride. But when the attention and science of Trow like me is turned to the beauty of parrots, they birth Paerries. And you astonish me. Like a Human artist who creates a painting or sculpture more powerful than herself, or the Paerrie singer who writes the ballad that goes on long after she is gone, I am amazed by you." He picked up the bottle and took a few sips before continuing. "But the Trow fear you Paerries."

"Fear us?" Aran said, astonished. "Why? We're simply weak impressions of Faeries."

"Weak? When in the last three weeks have we encountered a spell or a magic you did not instantly master? Do you know that what I have taught you in three weeks takes the typical Trow years to learn?

And is what I have taught you the limit of your abilities? Not at all. You have the ability to understand all languages and a range of Earth magics for restoring balance, both gifts from your Earth-born mothers. The Trow fear that Paerries may be more powerful than they. It is why they forbid the teaching of Trow magic to you. You might block them from their desire to retake this world from the Humans." Faelen paused a moment before adding, "Humans were also created by the Trow."

Aran gaped, and Faelen laughed. "The Trow have tried many experiments over their millennia of Earth occupancy. Some have been successful—the platypus, for example. Some were really bad ideas, like mountain-squids, a cross between mountains lions and humboldt squids intended to create useful pets but which wiped out almost all life on the planet. But two creations have caused us the most trouble— Paerries, for the reasons I told you, and Humans. We tried several different versions, and most were uninteresting, but one was fascinating and allowed to grow a substantial population. Unfortunately, the Trow miscalculated their ability to rapidly populate and create technology. And we never thought about Humans accessing magic. So now the Trow want to rid the Earth of Humans." Faelen went on to describe what little he knew of Xafar's plans to deal with the Humans.

Aran grew increasingly animated and asked many questions, most of which Faelen couldn't answer.

The logs shifted, sending sparks flying into the air. Aran was so overwhelmed that his mind could no longer form questions. Each time one would begin, a new set of realizations would tumble out, and he'd understand what some other aspect of Silth history really meant.

As he drained the last of the rum, Faelen was listing slightly.

He removed a vodka bottle from a bag leaning against the tree. Aran had suspected the bottle he brought each night was more ritual than necessity.

After an extended silence, Faelen continued. "You have ventured where no Paerrie has before and will die for it. The question is whether you will impart any of this knowledge to the other Paerries. The bigger question is what they will do with it. It could destroy them as they fight among themselves. The Trow could destroy them if they are not ready when they come to wipe them out. It could pervert them into something ugly as they lose the innocence that is part of their beauty. I do not know how the story will end, and I rather doubt I will see it. As soon as the Trow realize what I have done, I will be killed, King's son or not."

"Why?"

"Which 'why'? There are lots of 'whys.'"

"Why risk your life? Why me? Why choose the Paerries instead of your people the Trow?"

"Too many 'whys.'" Faelen gazed into the fire with eyes growing increasingly unfocused. "I have one more fee to request in return for my teachings."

"What? Name it."

"I want a story. I love Paerrie stories."

"I don't want to tell the old stories. You hear how my voice sounds, and for some reason no stories come to my mind anymore."

"I want a specific story, and you will remember it. You told me of the loss of your Shra to Humans, and that as she died you told her a story. I want to hear it."

"Ahhh, I do know that one." Aran began to tell the story of the doomed Silth lovers. He thought it would hurt, but instead it seemed to lay in place his mission. He would honor Shra by fighting the Faeries. The notion barely formed, but it was there.

They talked about inconsequential things as Faelen faded even further. Finally, and with difficulty he pushed himself up, staggering back to the tree where Aran had talked to him that first night. He settled into the roots and rolled over with his back to Aran.

"Aran, maybe I will see you again one day," he mumbled. "Probably ... not. Did you ever wonder ... if it was really an accident that we met? Or how it was ... that even a drunken Trow ... could not dispatch a ... crocodile?"

Aran waited, but Faelen said nothing more. After throwing a couple more logs on the fire, Aran rested his hand on the Faerie's shoulder until he heard soft snores. He had wondered about the incident with the crocodile, so Faelen's questions came as no great surprise.

"Goodbye, smelly croc-bait. It wouldn't be so bad if you were my father."

Scene 3

QWERT (SILTH)

Qwert practiced silently opening drawers. Even though no one else was in the cabin, she was determined to polish her technique. The current drawer, however, stuck before relenting with a loud screech. Because she was small, even for a Silth, she had to either reach down from the dresser top or else move a chair over to reach the higher drawers. You can't open a drawer from the top without making noise. Well, something new learned.

She had selected the glamour of a green parrot, a natural choice given her mostly green hather and the yellow highlights above her eyes. If a Human came in, they could comprehend a parrot on their dresser, but they would have trouble believing one had dragged a chair across the floor to rifle through the drawers. So ... she clearly had no choice but to work from the dresser top. As she shoved the offending drawer back in, she winced as it screeched even louder than before and fought the desire to take flight. She stopped, shook the tingling from her arms, and rolled her neck to regain focus. To her relief, the next drawer down slid open quietly.

Technically this was not work—it was practice. She was strictly forbidden from taking anything from the house. The rule applied to all houses within easy reach of the Silth colonies. Otherwise these houses would have been picked clean in successive harvests, and the search would have begun for the thieves. She felt a tiny twinge of guilt knowing she wasn't even supposed to practice here. Houses for such use were designated, carefully monitored by trainers, and safe for honing harvesting skills. But she enjoyed the rush from working in the unsanctioned ones. She believed it was better, more realistic training for the test as well, particularly in dealing with nervousness.

Soon she and nine other Silth would be escorted to a nearby Human city suburb and given a deadline for collecting a list of items. The task was much like the scavenger hunts they'd done as fledglings. Silth successful in retrieving all items in the allotted time would get the chance to become harvesters. When Qwert was little and heard Aran Storyteller's campfire stories about harvesters' lives, she'd been captivated by the notion of travel to exciting places, frequent danger, and the unsung hero status of providing for the colonies.

Again she worked the upper drawers—the top one made such an aggravating noise every time—and jumped to the floor to do the lower ones. She had reconnoitered the cabin before deciding to practice there. Its sole male occupant was gone most of the time, no dog or cat was in residence as either was a deal-breaker, it was isolated, and with the graveled drive an approaching car would easily be heard.

As though summoned by Qwert's thought, a car crunched down the drive. She flew to the window, gaped at the Toyota Cruiser, and rushed to the back door. When she saw the heavy locks, she realized her error—she had forgotten to develop an exit strategy the moment she entered the house. Her instructor's words popped into her head, "Always make an exit plan as soon as you arrive. No matter how fast you think you'll leave, you must know instantly what to do if the primary exit is blocked."

Two car doors slammed, and she frantically looked around. The cabin consisted of only three rooms, one being the bathroom and way too small for an effective hiding place. That left the bedroom or the main room, the latter comprised of a tiny kitchen, small eating area, and sitting area with a couch and a couple of chairs. The front door would open into that room. She saw no obvious hiding places there either. As the door lock rattled—fortunately she'd followed protocol and relocked it after entering—she dashed back into the bedroom. Her heartbeat thundering in her ears, she studied the spare furnishings as she heard voices and footsteps inside. Not many hiding places here either. Under the bed? In a clothes hamper? There—the freestanding wardrobe closet next to the room's only window. She opened the door as slowly as possible to avoid squeaks and squeezed beneath the clothing hanging inside. She stood trembling in the dark, furious at her fear. Listening for the sound of a dog's claws, she heard none. In fact, she realized she could hear nothing that far back in the closet.

When she put her eye to the crack in the door, she saw the shadows of two Humans bringing groceries into the kitchen. She heard them making lunch and discussing people they had encountered at the grocery store. Chairs scraped against the floor, and she knew they must be eating. As they talked, she moved from half-listening to full attention when she heard something that sounded like "people dying is all part of the plan."

She risked opening the door just a fraction more and saw the two seated at the table, wolfing down sandwiches as if they had not eaten in years. Looking closer, her throat closed and she swayed, almost tumbling out of the closet. One of them was casting a glamour of a tall Human woman—but she was surrounded by a blue aura. She was a Faerie!

Because the Faerie was hiding in the glamour, Qwert assumed that the Human didn't know he was keeping company with one. That might help her. The Faerie wouldn't be able to do anything overtly Faerie, such as hitting her with the blue lightning bolts Aran had described in his stories. She calmed down and concentrated on their conversation.

"We have talked about this before, Stanley Ryder," the Faerie said. "You have to break some eggs to make an omelet. We cannot save the world without significantly reducing the Human population. It is not enough to slow its growth or wait for it to level out. It is already at unsustainable numbers, and everyone wants their slice of the middle-class pie, including meat for dinner, a car, and a big house. The Human population will eventually crash, whether by food shortage, disease, lack of water, or war. But in the meantime, they are going to take everything else out with them. This will be the course of the future. It is up to us to change it."

Qwert strained to hear but there was only silence. The Human— the Faerie had called him Stanley Ryder—finally said, "We've talked about a few strategic deaths before. People who'd made choices endangering Humanity. Intervention scientists. Climate disruption-denying politicians. I get that this is a war to save the planet, but I'm not on board with the death part. What you're talking about is massive. Men, women, and children who are doing nothing but living their lives. And to save the other species? It'll kill off most of them as well. Angel, there has to be another way!"

Angel? A Faerie named Angel? Of course—she was using a Human name to further her deception.

"There is not another way. You know it. You have seen the figures. Everyone is talking about how we should stop worrying because the Human population is going to top out. But look at the consequence of prosperity. As everyone prospers economically, yes, they stop having so many babies. Problem is, everyone uses five times the resources the Earth has. We will industrialize the last of the rainforest and the last of Africa. We will fight wars for the last of the fresh water and rare metals."

Stanley Ryder said, "Or we'll develop energy sources so cheap that we create abundant water through desalinization. We'll recognize that the rainforest and the plains of Africa are vital for our future and protect them. We're developing genetically-engineered crops that can grow in the desert. So—"

"How can you fear the large-scale intervention in the climate and not recognize that the same reasoning applies to genetically engineered crops? We will not do it safely. There will be unintended consequences for us and for the Earth. And protect Africa? Have you seen the project the Japanese are trying to build in Kenya? It blocks the last migration route of the elephants living in the major parks. Have you seen the resources the Chinese have bought in Africa? Africa will be the new China. Cheap labor, cheap energy, and boundless nearby resources. Africa's gone. Humans are locusts, consuming the planet. As individuals they are innocent, but as a species they will not stop until they run out of stuff to consume."

Qwert watched as they cleared away their lunch dishes, and they moved out of sight. The discussion continued in the kitchen, but she couldn't make out the words. Even though her heart thumped against her ribs like a fly in a jar, she tiptoed out of the wardrobe and over to the doorway.

She heard Stanley Ryder clearly. "Even if I do buy into this … if I agree to become one of the biggest mass murderers in the history of mankind … how do you know it'll work?"

"We have had people running scenarios a couple of years now. And we know what the results will be and just how effective. Yes, there will be massive impacts on all species but none lost. With the dramatic reduction in the Human population, the other species will have sufficient habitat to rebound fast. Think about the area around Chernobyl. You have heard about how fast species expanded in this area after the reactor failure drove out the Humans. Bears, wolves, everything came back. Imagine that for the whole Earth. There will still be Humans. But it will be a few hundred thousand years before they can again endanger the Earth. Maybe they will have learned their lesson by then."

Not believing what she was hearing, Qwert sagged against the door frame, and it gave a slight creak. She drew back in panic. The Human was talking and she doubted he had heard but given Faeries' acute hearing Angel probably would have. Qwert knew Angel couldn't see her from where she sat but suspected she soon would find an excuse to enter the bedroom. If Angel could get out of the Human's sight, she would scan for Qwert and know she was there.

Qwert hurried to the open window and lifted the curtain. A screen blocked bugs and other creatures from entering the house and her from leaving, at least if she followed the protocol of leaving no trace.

She heard movement in the other room as Angel said, "I think it's in the bedroom. I'll look for it."

Qwert frantically searched her pockets. The window frame was deep enough that the curtain would hide her for a minute more. She pulled out a one-sided razor blade and slashed the nylon mesh, making the cut just long enough for her to squeeze out. She heard the closet door being thrown open and the sound of Angel rummaging through its contents.

Slipping through the screen, she flew as fast as she could and ducked into the nearest dense bushes. She looked back at the cabin to see the curtain being pulled back and Angel eyeing the slashed screen. As Angel searched the edges of the rainforest, Qwert withdrew further into the bushes. She knew little about Faerie abilities, just what the old stories said. She took off from the other side, remaining in the undergrowth and hoping to make it beyond Angel's scanning senses.

As soon as she had enough trees between her and the cabin, she flew up and out of the canopy, hardly able to breathe and with no idea what to do. She imagined Angel finding some excuse to separate from the Human and come after her. Could she track her?

After a few minutes, she spotted a clearing with a group of Silth, several carts, and a campsite with temporary Silth buildings. She swooped down to the clearing and landed in front of the central structure.

A male Silth was seated at a Silth-sized table in front of the make-shift tent structure, its roof covered with branches with leaves woven through. Through the front tent flap, Qwert spotted stacked boxes and a small table covered with odds and ends of a harvest. The Silth's blue hather was accented with shaman tattoos, so crisp they had to be recent. But he looked familiar to her, not as a shaman, but as something else she could not quite recall. She rushed to him but could not find the air to form words. He leaped up, grabbed another chair, and gestured for her to sit. She collapsed gratefully and tried to calm her breathing as he poured water into a wooden cup.

He handed her the cup and said gently, "I am Aran Shaman. Tell me, how can I help you, fledgling? When you can speak, that is."

She almost burst into tears, finally recognizing him as the

storyteller from her childhood. Her reason for wanting to be a harvester. And just the Silth she needed.

Her story spilled out between gasps ....

Scene 4

Aran (Silth)

Aran had begun the day as he had each one since finishing his training with Faelen, sorting through the swag and choosing the items best for the village he was to visit. Most were small clans clustered around a matriarch who'd adopted and raised successive generations of Silth rescued from their mothers' nests. The children in turn brought mates and adoptees of their own into the village.

Aran's negotiations typically were with the matriarch, or with her and her council. On the first day of his visit, he would bring standard swag items and on subsequent visits ones purchased or given in response to the village needs. Most went into the village storehouse, to be distributed later.

Somewhere in the middle of readying the day's delivery, he'd gotten distracted by his thoughts and wound up sitting by the morning campfire, cup in hand with work half done. This happened frequently, and he thought of it as "the attack of the meditation." The sun was high in the morning when he came to himself again. As usual, two themes occupied his thoughts. One was straightforward enough—how could he find out Xafar's plan and stop the Faeries from retaking the Earth? With so little information, there wasn't much to think about. He was considering how to trap the Faerie he now knew as "Fod." He had not seen Fod for several weeks. When he had been working with Faelen he used the spell to prevent tracking all the time. Since then he had been experimenting. He would drop the spell for a short time, usually just before he was relocating, and then turn it back on when he moved. It seemed to be confusing Fod enough that he had not found Aran. Or perhaps he was simply harassing Storng instead.

The other subject was more complex. He realized he was the only Silth in the world who had this extraordinary level of Faerie power. He was marked for death because of the level of teaching Storng supposedly had done, although Storng had not really instructed him in many things that worried the Faeries. The dangerous teachings violated Silth edicts against Human contact, not Faerie prohibitions. Though the Faeries were ignorant of the extent of his training from Faelen, according to Faelen they would still seek to kill him, simply because he was Storng's student. If they succeeded, no other Silth would learn what Faelen had taught him. But if Aran tried to pass the Faerie magics on to his fellow Silth, they themselves would likely banish him.

A riot of feathers and gasping suddenly ended his morning's reflections. She said her name was Qwert, and the story she told struck Aran like a lightning bolt. Was this a lead on the Faerie plot? Why else would a Faerie be hiding among Humans? But what exactly were the two talking about doing?

When Qwert finished telling him what she knew, Aran said, "The Kawran Council's in session. We'll take this information to them—now. Grab some food while I get ready."

The camp was mostly in the trees, with hammocks strung in the branches above most predators' heights, the clearing a rally point for unpacking the boxes and directing their delivery to the different villages. As the group awoke and prepared for each day, there was plenty of activity among the trees and much less in the clearing, since distribution began after the Merit's exercises. She said, "My troops are soldiers first and then pack animals. I don't want them losing their edge.

Being prepared for all circumstances is what ensures certain victory."

He had made peace with her, making it clear he was no longer leaving camp at night, listening to her suggestions on how to plan the days, and even encouraging her input on negotiations. Though he had to pretend interest, she had excellent negotiation skills and seemed to care about the outcome. If nothing else, she cared about the villagers who received the swag. Even during peace, her attitude toward Aran was at best ambiguous. Most of the time she was professionally distant, but occasionally she would show some sign of interest, and when she caught herself, she quickly veered into some hostile statement. Her behavior was almost as confusing as his feelings toward her.

Aran left Qwert at the table eating pieces of fruit and vegetables and downing nuts as fast as her small hands could break them into bite-sized pieces. He searched for Merit, by her hammock, located deeper in the jungle than the others, and at the breakfast and exercise areas. One of her squad said she'd taken out a morning patrol and wasn't expected back until mid-morning. Aran told her captain that he was going to Kawran. He declined the offer of an escort.

As he walked back into the clearing, Qwert looked lost sitting by herself among the containers.

"Ready, little one?"

"Absolutely." She grabbed a small nut and crammed it into her mouth before joining him.

He took off toward the colony, Qwert close behind. Although they carried news of imminent danger, he was exhilarated by the cool morning air, the wet scent rising from the recent rain, and the chatter of birds. Frogs, excited by the rain, almost drowned them out. In the distance, he heard howler monkeys. It was his favorite time of day to fly.

Qwert came up beside him, and he had her describe again what she'd seen and heard. Is this the first evidence of the Faerie plan to retake the Earth? He gave her a side-long look. Or just the over-active imagination of a fledgling? But because of Faelen, he knew her story was true.

"Qwert, you had an early start to be in that house before dawn."

"I watched the place yesterday and knew no one was there. 'A good harvester gets up before the sun and by mid-morn his work is done,' my teacher said."

He laughed. "In my experience, a good harvester is dragged out of bed, typically hung-over, and relies on everyone being gone to do her work. Many Humans don't leave for work until eight-thirty or so. You work on houses midday, businesses at night and in the early hours before they open."

"You know about harvesting? I mean, more than just the stories?"

But Aran was no longer listening. Before their flight he had utilized Faelen's spell for detection of Faeries, as he automatically did before any movement. When he practiced the spell with Faelen, he was immediately aware of the Faerie's presence, but he had never actually experienced detecting one other than Faelen. What he felt now was different—a disorienting awareness of Faerie presence, like being spun suddenly and violently.

He had just enough time to summon a shield when the air around him lit up blue with Faerie bolts. All his practice had been on erecting a shield for only himself, and his assumption was an attack would be directed at him. Qwert went rigid as the blue energy surrounded her. Eyes wide and wings still extended, she began a slow tumble into the forest canopy below. He streaked after her as she bounced through the branches in the trees.

Another bolt came, this time directed at him, but his shield blocked it. He reached the canopy top and dropped onto a branch to check the sky.

Three Faeries hovered above, looking down through the trees. One he recognized as the one-eyed Faerie Fod—Faelen said he worked directly for Thest—but he had never seen the other two. All three had stopping firing and were floating in the sky near one another. He couldn't hear what they were saying, but he assumed they were trying to detect him in the canopy. Because he'd used the spell for avoiding detection, they'd quickly figure out that he was using Faerie powers.

He flew down through the branches and landed beside Qwert's still body. Even though he knew he was wasting his time, he checked for breath. None. He stroked her hather and smoothed away the look of shock etched on her face. He should leave—if he stayed below the canopy, the Faeries would have no ability to detect which way he went. He needed to get Qwert's news to the colony, and he was aware that time was of the essence. But he couldn't move.

He cradled Qwert's head in his lap. The Faeries' confusion wouldn't last—eventually they would come below the treetops and spot him. But all he could think was, "I've failed again." The words looped continuously through his brain, numbing him to inertia.

Faerie bolts struck the ground and sizzled around him, but he stayed where he was. He was dimly aware of the Faeries' strategy, create covering fire before coming beneath the canopy. Next, he heard Merit's battle whoop above the trees, and the attack on him ceased. The sounds of an airborne struggle filtered down.

He launched up into the trees. As he looked through the treetops, he realized what he was seeing was no "battle." Merit, her eagle, and her two squad members were harassing the Faeries but hardly seemed to be a threat—although they were firing their arrows, they merely bounced off the Faeries' shields. The arrows were tipped with poison from the frogs but were tiny relative to the size of the Faeries. It was like watching small birds harass a falcon. When the Faeries dropped their shields and fired their blue bolts of energy, the Silth were forced to dodge and swoop to avoid the deadly fire. They were outmatched and wouldn't last long, but Merit charged as though invincible. She stopped a quick moment to whistle Stalbon away from the fight, probably because the eagle had no defense against the Faerie bolts.

Fod focused his attention on her and Aran heard him shout something indistinguishable to the other two Faeries. They turned to Merit, ignoring the other two Silth, and Aran's realized the three were going to attack her simultaneously. She would be killed. Without thought his arm swung out, projecting the protective shield around her just as all three Faeries dropped their shields and fired. Even with Aran's shield in place, the force of the combined blast knocked her from the air, sending her spinning head over feet toward the treetops. Just before she would have struck the canopy, she rallied, righting herself and returning to the attack.

Demonstrating how well Merit had trained them, the other two Silth had not paused in their fight, striking each of Fod's companions with arrows while their shields were down. The wounded Faeries flickered and disappeared. Fod, his face twisted in anger, vanished an instant later.

Aran sucked in deep breaths and returned to Qwert's body, dropping to his knees. Cautiously the three Silth dropped below the canopy, spreading out as though preparing for the fight to resume.

"I wasn't sure if we'd find Faeries or Silth here," Merit said as she landed next to him. When Aran didn't look up or respond, she went on. "We need to go. They may be back with reinforcements." She gestured to one of her squad members who stepped forward, gently gathering the small figure into his arms.

Merit instructed the other warrior, "Go back to the caravan. Move it. Hide it. Put it in the old ruins. Then catch up."

Dropping to the ground, she laid her hand on Aran's arm. His chin dropped to his chest, and tears flooded his eyes.

In the distance, there was the rumble of thunder, and Merit eyed the darkening sky. "We need to go—it's not safe here."

CHAPTER ELEVEN

Scene 1

ARAN (SILTH)

Aran and Merit waited before the Kawran Council platform. During his days as a storyteller, he often had performed there and should have felt comfortable today. But something was wrong.

They stood in a large rectangular depression surrounded by trees. The depression created acoustics transporting any sound, even a whisper, at the center, its entire length. At the head of the rectangle stood a huge tree embraced by an equally large strangler tree. Over the years, the strangler's limbs had been carefully formed into a series of balconies sometimes supporting buildings, mostly administrative, and sometimes framing doorways directly into the tree. The largest balcony faced the public square. Most days the square was an open-air market containing items gathered from the forest or harvested from Humans. But when issues of importance arose, the council convened on the balcony above the square to discuss, debate, and decree.

Trees surrounded the commons, each holding dozens of Silth homes in cut tree holes or rooms perched on branches or balconies. The colony residents would gather around the commons, on the ground and along the branches and balconies, to listen to stories, music, and the occasional council pronouncements.

Aran hadn't been surprised that their request to meet with the council was immediately granted. Although Merit's position in the Fortress Colony assured her a position on the council, she was still several years away from minimum membership age. Nonetheless, she was highly regarded. Aran was a shaman, and while a new one, that position accorded stature as well. Moreover, Aran had insisted they were bearing urgent news of which the council should be aware.

What was unexpected was being summoned to the square instead of the administrative rooms, where day-to-day business was conducted. Why would their report be given in the presence of the colony residents and not just to the council? Why risk panicking the colony residents? A breach of protocol … and mildly worrisome.

The council ran the Kawran Colony, the largest Silth colony in this part of the world. When colonies spread across the continent, it had been the capital of a Silth Empire. Mayan priests regularly came to stand in the commons, bringing gifts to honor the Silth, followed by the priests of the Aztecs and Incas, the last exceptions to the general Silth avoidance of Humans. In return, the Silth played for them and gave them gifts including the best their remarkable crafters could produce, as well as jewels and metals harvested from places still inaccessible to Humans. The exchanges sometimes went on for days. But after the Spaniards arrived, the Silth withdrew from even this limited Human contact as their world dissolved.

Silth governance was complex. Each colony had its own council, and as the population declined, each individual colony asserted more control over its own affairs. Consequently, most Silth argued that the Kawran Council was just a colony council with delusions of grandeur.

The council chose its eleven members—there was no public election. Certain positions were reserved by tradition. One was always a shaman, whomever the shamans selected to represent their order. In earlier times the Silth religious leader served on the council, but the old religions had waned and now it was the head of New Faerie— Aran's brother Casius. Usually the leader of the warrior clan would hold a position, but that was Merit, who was too young. The rest of the council was drawn from leaders in the colony and nearby villages, those identified as popular and perceived as wise.

The council's rulings were supposed to bind the Silth, but even then, it was more complex than simply issuing an edict. If the Silth disagreed with the decision, they ignored it. No police or enforcement arm existed—something either made sense and the community enforced it, or not. Consequently, the council either led from behind after determining the will of the Silth or used this platform to make its case to the public.

Merit had not taken time to clean up, so she used the drizzling rain to dab at the dust and flecks of dried blood from minor wounds that covered her face, and the grit that dulled her usually shiny leather. She still held the bow in the clamp that attached where her hand had been. The clamp was held by leather straps so that when she held her bow arm straight, the bow was ready to use.

Flanked by the two squad members who had fought beside her, Merit seemed aware Aran was looking at her. When she turned her face toward him, he didn't flinch or turn away. She was fierce and beautiful. And she was angry. She'd told Aran that not only was she furious at the Faeries, but she was also upset with him for leaving the camp without an escort. He argued that it wouldn't have changed anything, but she wasn't convinced.

On the way there, he'd filled her in on what Qwert overheard.

He told her how the Faeries attacked Qwert, apparently tracking her after the Faerie calling herself "Angel" detected her presence in the cabin. He deflected Merit's questions about his ability to shield them from the Faerie bolts, vaguely alluding to shaman powers. He knew she had worked alongside enough shamans to doubt this was a normal shaman power. Though plainly suspicious, she grudgingly expressed gratitude. But Aran recognized that both the need for protection at all and it having come from him contributed to her anger. She stopped cleaning and paced like a caged jaguar.

The council filed onto the platform and took their places on a semi-circle of stools facing the commons, Casius, unsmiling as always, directly in the middle. In the Silth world, "brother" or "sister" meant the individuals were raised by the same adoptive Silth mother, not that they had come from the same parrot mother. Mostly the Silth tried to obscure the origin nest so there would be less lineage friction. Aran and Casius knew, however, that they came from the same nest, as well as being raised in the same household. After too much fruit liquor, their father once told them they were the products of a rare occurrence—two Silth fledglings born to a parrot mother. Aran had been removed early because the nest monitor didn't believe Aran would survive Casius's aggressiveness in feeding.

Aran and his brother rarely spoke. Their beliefs were deeply different. Aran followed the ancient religion of the Silth, utilized by the shamans in their daily practices. His brother's version of New Faerie held no place for these beliefs.

He recognized the old shaman at the far left—Anuli was her name. He'd never paid attention to the names or backgrounds of the others. The entire council looked grim, more so than seemed warranted having heard little of the news Aran and Merit brought. But that was probably because of Qwert's death. When the council held a meeting in the square, attendance wasn't mandatory, and unless it was a slow day, the porches and trees often held few Silth. Today these spaces contained far more than usual. Aran would have liked to think the increased numbers were due to his renown as a storyteller or Merit's as a fighter, but somehow, he doubted it. As his unease grew, Merit glanced at him with lifted brows.

The elderly female Silth at the right end of the row leaned forward, layers of jewelry clattering as she moved. The gold stood out against her hather, still a bright blue glamour in spite of her years. "I am Tellick, today's speaker for the council. Aran Storyteller and Merit Warrior Leader, you have been summoned before the council to explain certain events in which you have been involved."

"I am Aran Shaman, and we requested this meeting with the council to bring you important news."

The crowd murmured disapprovingly. Aran suspected this wasn't only from shock at the painful raspiness of his voice, but also disapproval of his beginning by correcting a council member and speaking before he was invited to do so. But what he had to tell them was too important to be delayed by the normal council games. He believed, like most Silth, that the council spent most of its time like a Human's dog, chasing its tail. He'd also spent the last several weeks negotiating with village elders and councils throughout the region. He knew from experience that in the first few moments of an exchange, the parties established their relative positions. Frustration turned to anger as he struggled to appear calm, and he wondered why they were making this more difficult.

Tellick's eyes narrowed, and the corners of her mouth turned downward in the deepest of frowns. She pursed her lips and glared at him for a moment, as though trying to will away his rudeness. "What then, Aran Shaman"—she stretched the word shaman out derisively—"do you have to tell us?"

Earlier Aran had watched Qwert's body being carried into the square and placed on pillows nearby. He assumed the several Silth crying quietly nearby were family members. Although he wanted to tell them how brave she'd been, he was ashamed he hadn't been able to protect her and instead kept his distance. But now he looked at Qwert again, took a deep breath, and relayed what she'd overheard. He described her escape and subsequent death as the Faeries tracked her down, the crowd leaning in to better hear as he talked. For years he'd told them stories that amused or taught them, but he believed that this one would fill them with fear. When he finished, the council tipped their heads toward the center of their semicircle and spoke in low, inaudible tones.

Finally, Tellick addressed Aran. "Qwert was young. Full of energy. Full of life, but also full of fantasies. She most likely misunderstood what was being said and expanded the half-understood tale into a full fantasy. We do not believe in a serious plot to destroy most life on the planet, because there's no way such a thing could be done. And we certainly don't believe a Human and a Faerie would be discussing it in a forest cabin. What you describe is the stuff of a dear little one's imagination." Tellick looked at Qwert's body and shook her head sadly.

Aran glared at Tellick, shocked by the dismissal of Qwert's story, but it took only a moment for him to realize why. Because the council didn't have the benefit of Faelen's knowledge, it was relying on hundreds of years of predictable Silth and Faerie behaviors to draw conclusions.

"If what you say is true," he answered, "why would the Faeries come after her?" He couldn't say why he believed Qwert's story. It would be unwise to tell them a Faerie, with whom he'd spent weeks training and learning information that could get them killed, had said such a plot was underway.

Tellick's face hardened. "That is indeed the question. And the reason you were summoned. We don't believe the Faeries came after my little dear one. They came after you, Aran Shaman."

"Why would you think that?"

"We'll come to that, but first I'd like to know more about this aerial battle." Tellick turned her attention to Merit. "You are Merit, Warrior Leader, Dawn Defender, and you have a reputation as a superior fighter. But the depth of your talent must have been hidden from the world." She paused and took a sip from the wooden cup beside her. "Because in the entire recited history of Silth, this council does not recall a time when Silth warriors—matched with an equal number of Faerie warriors—has won a battle. Your tactics must be exceptional. But you say you didn't witness the beginning of the attack?"

Merit took a step away from Aran. "No, Council Member. We came along after the battle was begun. The Faerie were firing bolts into the trees below."

"So, we have only Aran Shaman's impression that the attackers fired upon Qwert when they appeared?"

"Yes." Merit paused, then added, "The testimony of a shaman."

"Hmmmm, yes." Tellick sounded unimpressed. "Then you and

these two of your squad engaged the Faeries?"

"That is correct."

"And mere bows and short swords drove off Faerie bolts?"

"Perhaps the attackers had already done what they came for, Council Member, having killed Qwert. They must drop their shields when they fire, and they were firing down into the trees. We wounded at least one, maybe two when their shields were down."

"And I can assume your squad's version of the events would match your own?" Tellick eyed the two warriors flanking Merit. But instead of addressing either, she gave a command. "Restum, approach the council."

A young Silth male stepped out from the crowd. He wore a gatherer's uniform with its many pockets. Gatherers brought back fruits and nuts from the rainforest around the colony. His red hather was peaked into a longer brush down the middle of his head, his face heavily tattooed.

"Is what they describe correct?"

"Yes, Council Member. As I was gathering nearby, I heard shouts and came to the top of the trees. I saw the warriors arrive as the Faeries were firing down into the jungle. Although I didn't see the shaman or cousin Qwert, I did witness the warriors wound the Faeries. They were very brave."

"Undoubtedly. Was there anything unusual when the Faerie fired back at them?"

"No, Council Member, not so I could tell. I've never seen a battle before, so I don't know what is usual. The Faeries shot and the Paerrie warriors dodged and weaved. It would've been beautiful had it not been so scary. And then all the Faeries directed their fire at one

Paerrie, Dawn Guardian I believe, but cannot be sure with it being far away. The air lit up blue around her, and she fell from the sky. The Faeries all disappeared. The warriors were so brave and—."

"Enough, Restum. Thank you. You may step aside. Merit, do the warriors of the Fortress Colony have a new defense against Faerie magic? You survived a direct attack by three Faeries. Before you answer"—Tellick tipped her head toward the shaman at the opposite end—"Anuli has discussed the matter with your shaman. He said you do not."

Merit's face darkened. "The citizens of the Fortress Colony do not discuss our weaponry. Nor would our shaman."

"I will confess some subterfuge was involved in obtaining the answer," Anuli admitted. "But I knew of no such power among the shamans. So I inquired as to whether he and the Fortress Colony had been developing dangerous weapons." She stared pointedly at Aran.

Aran returned the look. "If the shamans have no such defense and Fortress has no such defensive weapon, is it not more likely that no such weapon exists among the Silth? Are you suggesting I have access to and used Faerie magic?"

Anuli seemed surprised by the directness of the question and made no reply. In an instant, an unexpected stillness deep within Aran replaced his anger at the public attack. He recognized the story the council wanted to tell before they even began, and he was determined to make it difficult. But he didn't see any way to win this public confrontation.

"But that couldn't be, could it, my brother?" Aran looked at Casius, who had displayed no sign he even knew Aran, much less was related to him. "If I had access to Faerie magic, it would mean that this could be achieved without the grace and permission of the Faeries. New Faerie and its struggle for acceptance by the Faerie Host would be a sad waste of time."

Casius scowled. "No one accuses you of having access to Faerie magic." Although Tellick eyed him sharply, he went on with the same soft tone of condescension. "You are correct that someone in your state of consciousness could never achieve alignment with the Faerie Host. But you've been trained by a shaman reckless with his past teachings. We believe he's been reckless again and has given you dark powers the Faeries struggle to help us avoid. Surely his mistake has caused you to be before us today, responsible for the death of yet another Silth female. Her blood, my brother, is not on your hands as much as it is on Storng's."

Aran flinched as though slapped. "So, am I to understand this is where the council is heading? The Silth are advised of a plot that may alter our world, as well as that of Humans and all the other creatures here. And we're told that the source of this plot is the Faeries. Yet this council hints at punishing me for successfully defending against an unprovoked Faerie attack. Even if your theme was true, that Storng has given me these incredible powers, you cannot believe that you should punish me instead of such discipline coming from the Shaman Council. Or more implausibly," he said slightly louder, sweeping his hand up and toward the platform, "believe that someone with the power to defeat Faeries would submit to any sanctions you decree."

At Aran's gesture, every council member except Casius shrank back, and even Merit looked worried until Aran's arm dropped to his side. "Casius, you disgrace yourselves and our people," he said bitterly. "You enable our slavery to the Faeries. We are their bastard children, and yet you desperately, tragically seek their affection and acceptance."

An elder council member to Anuli's right bolted to his feet with astonishing speed. "Enough! This council will not be addressed with such disrespect. Blasphemy has no place before us. This is no story. No fictional account, Storyteller Shaman. We are responsible for the safety of the Silth. Storng made a mistake in training you, costing a life and now threatening this colony. If the Faeries came for you in the sky, they will track you here. They may kill any in contact with your dark magic." He turned to Tellick. "I call for the banishment of Aran, shaman of no place."

Ignoring the dark mutterings of the crowd and a shout of "What evidence?" Tellick addressed the entire council. "Your response?" To either side of her, every council member except Casius and Anuli affirmed the banishment with one quick nod of the head.

Casius said, "Brother, I tried to save you from this. I sent Merit to watch you. To monitor you for me. To keep you from doing something stupid." Merit's jaw dropped, and she gave Aran a slight shake of her head. "But you leave me no choice," he went on, his words dripping with disdain. "I don't know where you get your blasphemous views, but you endanger all good Silth. I support the banishment."

At the end of the row, Anuli looked at Aran with a pained expression. "I have always believed Storng would bring ruin to us all. I feel you are reckless in manner and action, just as he is. Perhaps more so. But you're correct—this is a matter for the Shaman Council. We discipline our own. Therefore, I oppose the banishment and recommend that Aran Shaman be sent before the Shaman Council."

Tellick's brows drew together in obvious displeasure. "We govern by consensus. Because we do not have it on this matter, we must meet until we develop a consensus on what action to take." The noise from the crowd grew louder.

When Aran stepped forward and raised his hand again for their attention, Tellick looked down at him. "Have care—we have no more patience for what you say."

He struggled to hold on to the stillness inside. To ignore the question of Merit's loyalty, his brother's baiting, the body lying nearby, and Tellick's disrespect. Focus on changing their course of action. They must address the Faerie plot. No one could convince them but him, and since he was likely to be dead soon by Faerie hand, he must act quickly to set them in motion.

"I know how this process works. You'll go to your chamber by yourselves, not to work on the right way to proceed, but to find leverage to make a shaman change her position and support the banishment. What can you give her or threaten to take that will shift her? This seems a waste of time. I am a shaman. I am also a storyteller. If tonight you allow me to tell the colony one last story, I will accept banishment."

His words drew gasps and a burst of quiet chatter from the crowd, abruptly ended with Tellick's angry "Enough!"

Aran cycled through different emotions. Each time he looked at the small form lying on the pillows, he felt crushing guilt in not being able to save her. Anger at the council's arrogance replaced the guilt, and he realized he could simply take control. One blast and Tellick would be gone. Faelen's warning that the Silth could destroy themselves with these powers rang in his mind. His emotions shifted yet again, sliding into resignation. Perhaps they were right about the danger he posed to the colony.

As the council members leaned in to discuss his proposal,

the crowd's whispering resumed. Merit shifted and laid her hand on Aran's shoulder. He knew the message she was conveying—without hers and the colony's protection, he was unlikely to survive. For the typical sociable Silth, such a lonely death would be the worst. More importantly, though, her touch in plain view of Casius, the rest of the council, and the colony told Aran what he needed to know. She hadn't been disloyal.

The council members stopped talking and straightened in their chairs. Anuli's look of relief was clear evidence of their verdict. Tellick rose, hands in fists and white-knuckled at her sides.

"Aran Shaman, the Kawran Council accepts your proposal, provided your story contains no blasphemy. You have the remainder of the afternoon to get your affairs in order. This night you may tell your last story, after which you shall accept your banishment without incident."

Her pompous pronouncement of "this meeting is ended" had Aran suppressing an urge to laugh. He took Merit by the upper arm and whispered urgently in her ear as he led her from the square.

Scene 2

ARAN (SILTH)

He stood calm and confident in the center of the commons, a tall bonfire burning beside him. The sun had dipped low behind the trees in the west, leaving deep shadows where the firelight did not reach. Torches on the balconies and porches flickered on the crowd.

Aran thought the entire colony had attended the earlier council meeting—no, make that council attack—but tonight Silth filled every space on the ground around the open commons and balconies. More had gathered in trees and on roofs. Word must have gone out to surrounding villages to bring so many Silth to one place. Even in the growing darkness, bright Silth body colors gave the gathering a festive look, but the crowd was somber. The talking and laughing usually preceding a storytelling was absent. The chamber door opened, and the council members filed out to take their seats, some still wearing their anger from earlier, while others merely looked curious. Casius was expressionless.

Aran circled the fire, scanning the crowd. After one full circle, he smiled, spread his arms, and opened his wings to reflect the fire that lit him in red and orange hues. He halted, turned, and with his back to the fire flapped his wings, causing the flames to leap and briefly change to dark blue. His smile widened as the crowd murmured its appreciation for the trick.

His ragged voice was low, forcing the crowd to stop shuffling and move closer to hear him. "I am Aran Shaman. But I was once a storyteller, and I am here to tell you one last story. All my previous ones have been true. Well, perhaps it would be more accurate to say there has been truth in all my stories, including this one.

"As you know from many tellings, handsome Faeries fathered the Silth with our radiant mothers, the parrots. We Silth are born in beauty out of this encounter. But you may not recall that parrots haven't been the only ones transformed by the Faeries. Some Faeries were drawn to the grace and the power of our enemies—the harpy eagles." He gave a patting motion with his hands to hush the hisses before continuing.

"From the harpy eagle mothers came the Harpies. Powerful beings. All bird-shaped, beautiful women with huge, clawed talons. Like Silth, they produce no offspring of their own. In the time when flights of Silth would darken the sky for almost the entire day, legions of Harpies also existed. This story is from that time.

"The Harpies were not raised in villages like the Silth. They were feral, kicked out of their mother's nest soon after birth. They had no common language. Drawn together by their shared hatred of all living things, they roosted in the high places of the mountains. Although they barely knew of their magic, the one thing they did know is that they had the evil power to contaminate anything with the stab of their claws. They would foul water sources, forcing the parrots to travel long distances from their nests and leaving their fledglings vulnerable. When the parrots were away, the Harpies would swoop in and steal young Silth to feed to their leader—Mapowra." That drew more hisses from the crowd.

He continued his slow, crouching circle around the fire. "Mapowra was three times the size of any Silth, and her putrid breath could cause entire forests to rot." He smiled at the giggles of the small Silth. "Like all the other Harpies, she was beautiful and poisonous. But while most of the Harpies would eat anything, living or dead, Mapowra only ate young Silth stolen from their nests or grabbed from the forest floor.

"She despised the Silth colonies because they took and protected the youngsters, raising them in Silth villages. When Mapowra's minions came to collect her food, the Silth guards posted around parrot roosts sounded the alarm. So she decided to destroy the local Silth colony. She crept into the colony and with her talon deeply pierced the egg shielding it. Contaminated instantly, it began to radiate evil. Within moments, the colony's Silth grew angry and suspicious, turning on one another. Fights broke out. Blood was shed. Hiding in the shadows, one small Silth named Klickaw had seen Mapowra contaminate the egg. He tried to tell the colony's advisors, but they refused to listen, accusing him of fabricating the tale for attention."

He faced the fire and spoke across its flames. "A warrioress named Kalias arrived at the village and witnessed the evil the Silth were inflicting upon one another. She knew something was wrong—Silth did not behave in such a manner. When she heard that Klickaw had tried to tell the advisors what happened, she sought him out. He didn't want to repeat his story to her and, given the treatment he'd received from the adults, he wasn't even sure he believed it any more. But Kalias drew it from him with patience and bribes of nectar candies. As soon as she heard him, she knew in her heart what he said was true. She implored the entire colony to raise a group, to strike down Mapowra, but none would join her. When she sought out the council and told them the egg must be removed, they laughed, saying that the colony's safety lay in the egg. Then, because they too were affected by the evil egg, they accused Kalias of seeking to undermine their authority. No one believed her."

The crowd was silent, enrapt faces reflected in the flickering flames, orange once again. Although Aran knew the council members would be chafing at the story he had picked, it was a traditional one that all knew, so no one could accuse him of directly pleading his case. He was careful not to look at them at any time during his presentation.

"Then Kalias stole the village's egg," he went on. "She followed complex magical procedures to move it—she had assisted in the construction of other villages. One wrong move, however, and the egg would turn to stone, leaving the colony exposed. Even as it was, the removal would expose the colony to the risk of discovery. She hoped to return it by the following evening, so they would be vulnerable for one day at the most—still a big risk.

"She flew with the egg toward the mountain kingdom of the Harpies. As she ascended, holding it close to her chest, two Harpies guarding the passage confronted her. She held up the egg and announced, 'Mapowra has requested this egg, and I bring it to her. She will be very angry if you cause me to drop it.'

"While the Harpies couldn't speak, they could sense the general meaning of words, enough to make them fly ahead to alert Mapowra. She was smart … for a Harpy." The crowd chuckled and guffawed. "She knew this was the egg she had contaminated, and she was certain the Silth hoped to break its spell by bringing it to her court. So she decided to kill Kalias."

He paced around the fire, illustrating each portion of the story with pronounced arm gestures, leg movements, and facial expressions. Though his voice was still a harsh rasp, it was strong and his words distinct. The Silth leaned forward, quiet as could be.

"Mapowra swooped down from her high perch, and Kalias listened carefully. When she heard the air part before the great eagle creature, she waited, knowing Mapowra would try to drive her talon into Kalias's back. Just as Mapowra was about to strike, giving her great cry of 'eeeeoa,' Kalias spun around. Mapowra drove her talon into the already contaminated egg Kalias had clutched to her chest. Poison from the egg flowed back into Mapowra, and she shrieked from the agonizing pain. As Kalias watched, Mapowra's beautiful features withered, her breasts sagged and her muscles wasted, and she transformed into a hag. When she saw how her hideousness repelled even the Harpy guards who'd followed her, she flew away from the mountain.

"Relieved of the poison, the egg sealed its puncture and resumed its normal beneficial glow. When Kalias returned it to its nest in the center of the colony, Klickaw was there watching. After replacing the egg, Kalias put her finger to her lips, so he knew to keep her secret, and she left with the colony none the wiser. For months the Silth marveled over the strange weather that had made them act so oddly. Mapowra was not seen again. The colony never knew it had been saved from a danger it didn't even know existed."

Aran lowered his gaze and folded his wings, the traditional way to end a dramatic story. Just as the wings folded, the fire turned blue and leapt into the night sky before falling back to its true form.

The Silth pounded on the ground and their wood structures to show their appreciation, the clamor echoing through the square. Aran finally looked up at the council's balcony. Tellick stood glaring at him in the torch light as the council members filed back into the black doorway behind her.

Scene 3

ARAN (SILTH)

After leaving the square, Aran found a quiet place near the colony to wait. He needed to focus on his next moves and to summon courage, because he was afraid. He'd told the story to remind the colony, to wake them to the danger they faced.

He couldn't push back too much on the council, since banishment usually was accompanied by clipped wings, a true death sentence. Because no shaman had ever been banished, there was no precedent, but he suspected the council feared what he might do if they did try to clip his wings. They were right—he wouldn't allow it—but a direct fight would force Merit to make even harder choices than he was requesting now.

He studied the fireflies moving in the canopy, and he listened to the comforting night noises of the rainforest. He couldn't imagine a world without the rainforest, or Silth, or even Humans. Perhaps toucans. And monkeys. *I can definitely imagine a world without monkeys.*

He thought back to his conversation with Merit that afternoon.

"Aran," she had said, "I agreed to come guard you, nothing more. I was never a spy."

"I know. It's my brother's attempt to get at me. You may or may not even like me—I'm never quite sure—but I know you well enough to believe you wouldn't be his spy."

"Why would he say that?"

"I think he's jealous because he believes Storng has given me powers that Casius has sought all his life. Faerie-like powers. Casius and his New Faerie followers think that they're the ones who should receive such gifts."

She looked him directly in the eyes. "Did he? Did Storng give you Faerie-like powers?"

"He gave me some skills prohibited by the Silth and some that would trouble the Faerie if they knew about them. But not many. The council is wrong to blame Storng for that. No Faerie-like powers came from him." He was acutely aware of the tightness wrapping his chest as he confessed, "I got those directly from a Faerie."

He went on to tell her about Faelen and training with him. He also said that Faelen's warning followed by the Faerie attack convinced him Qwert was correct in what she reported.

Merit kicked him hard in the shin. "You could have told me!"

"Ow." He bent over to rub his leg. "Sure. And you would've let me go each night to meet with a Faerie who was filling my head with knowledge. Knowledge likely to get me and others killed. You wouldn't have followed me, right?" As she glared at him, he said, "So the council is right. I am a danger to everyone here. But they're wrong about the danger from the Faerie plan. I knew there was nothing I could say to convince them of the danger of the plan without them being distracted by the danger I represent."

"You have a plan?" When he told her, she responded with, "That's a really stupid plan. And you will die."

"Perhaps." He gave her instructions on what to do with his swag if he was killed and suggestions as to how she might find Faelen.

She sighed. "Yet again, your refusal to follow rules has led to your troubles, and you've endangered others as well as yourself."

"I think you have lost the jaguar in the kaleidoscope of butterflies," Aran said softly and without defensiveness. "The Faerie plot to end our world would exist whether or not I learned Faerie powers. We'd merely be unaware of it. And even if we were aware, we'd have no hope of stopping it. If I can get the colony to understand that the plot is real, and I can enable you to get taught by Faelen, there would at least be hope."

Merit shook herself and rolled her shoulders, eyeing him as though trying to see something inside him. "Do you have anything of value on you?"

Perplexed, he asked, "Is this a robbery?" When she didn't smile, he said, "A small bag of jewels and gold."

"Give it to me."

Aran shrugged, removed the bag from his cloak, and handed it to her.

"I've finished my work for your brother. You have just hired Fortress Colony to help you protect Kawran. Fortress does not take sides in internal Silth politics. And we certainly do not follow scofflaw shamans in their quest for self-destruction." She chopped her hand down to cut off his protest. "But when we're hired to defend against a credible threat, we'll do whatever is necessary to defeat the danger." With that, she flew away.

Merit's right, he thought, sitting in an avocado tree following the evening's storytelling. *It is a stupid plan, and I'll probably die. But it's the best I've got.* In the distance, shouting indicated that the crowd hadn't dispersed, but he couldn't make out the words. The Faeries would be looking for him. He thought about his brother's betrayal. They'd never been that close, and their paths into adulthood had taken them even further apart. The council Aran could pass off as doing their best given limited information. But Casius ....

Slowly, piece by piece, he dissected the day's events, including Qwert's death. If only he had wrapped the shield around both of them. But months of waiting for the Faeries to come after him and the constant practice of summoning a shield only for himself led him to the automatic response. He leaned back against the tree trunk and went into the deep meditation practiced by the shamans.

He must have sat there for several hours, he realized later. The square was quiet, the rainforest noisy. The fireflies had disappeared, leaving a uniform darkness beneath the trees. He felt more focused, ready to take on whatever happened next. He'd head toward the old colony, where he and Shra had played, and spend the night there. His part of the harvest, what remained of it, was there.

He flew to a path along the river, a well-worn animal trail followed by all who came to quench their thirst. Because of the adjoining river, it was covered by fewer trees, and enough moonlight found its way through to make it an easy route. He half-hoped a jaguar or cougar would attack—it'd be a welcome distraction. As the black river burbled beside him, he made no effort to mask the sound of his passage. Noises parted around him like a curtain, ceasing as he neared and resuming as he made his way further along. He'd covered a couple of miles when he realized the curtain had vanished. Birds, frogs, and night insects made no sounds at all, and even the river seemed hushed.

His hather prickled ... and he knew.

A voice boomed through the darkness. "Aran, bastard Paerrie, pretender to Trow powers! Show yourself or your colony will die."

Aran landed and stood stock-still. The voice seemed to emanate beyond the meager light across the river, which though deep was fairly narrow. He peered through the darkness, trying to spot the source of the words.

"I know you are there," the voice continued. "I can hear you. I knew the Paerries would throw you out into the forest as soon as they were afraid. Even had I not been warned, I could have guessed. It is what they always do. They are cowards. Show yourself."

Warned? Who would warn the Faeries? And why is this one demanding for me to show myself? Then he remembered he still had spells in place preventing the Faerie from finding him. Combined with the darkness, they kept them from knowing where he was, but it also was why they knew it was him. They would have been able to "see" anyone else moving along this path.

"Mongrel, show yourself. I know where your precious colony is, and I will kill a third of it tonight. If you do not surrender, I will kill another third in the morning. And the last of it tomorrow night."

In the shadows across the river, Aran spotted a faint bluish glow, and though he couldn't be sure, he thought he saw three figures. The voice—he assumed it was Thest's given what Faelen had told him—went on to describe where the colony was, the number of Silth there, the location of nearby parrot roosts, and graphic details of how they'd be destroyed.

The faces in the colony swam before Aran's eyes. No, they had not risen to his defense. Yes, through their silence they'd allowed his banishment. But they didn't deserve to die, nor could he be the cause of it.

"Show yourself," Thest shouted, "or their blood will be on you. Produce a light so I can find you."

As Aran picked up a branch, he thought about Storng and Faelen and the trust they'd put in him. He drew in and blew out three deep breaths, pushing back his fear and anger to substitute a sense of control and resolution. He wouldn't sacrifice the colony, but he also wouldn't go down without a fight.

As Thest kept goading and threatening, Aran lit the branch, held it high above his head, and shouted, "Here, Thest. I'm here!"

"Ahh, so you are," Thest said, the torch light reflecting off him and the two Faeries flanking him. "Years ago, I heard your music and storytelling. You should have remained a bard. This world needs more music. Instead, you let Storng recruit you into his deadly agenda, and I heard of you once more. Today I heard your name a third time as Fod recognized you with the fugitive. But after today, I will not hear of you again. And as you die, do so knowing I am still going to destroy Storng, your colony, and everyone who may have seen your forbidden actions."

Sweeping his arm upward, his hand directed toward Aran, Thest smiled. But the smile faded, replaced by shock, and his arm fell limply to his side. Realizing the Faerie was staring into the rainforest behind him, Aran took the chance—never turn your back on your enemy! —and spun around.

Light after light was appearing, first a dozen, then twenty, fifty, and hundreds. Aran gaped—all were torches lifted high above Silth heads. All at once the Silth swarmed, the effect as though the forest was host to an army of demented fireflies. As the lights danced and whirled closer, he recognized several of the colony's Silth members.

Aran knew Thest would still be able to find him as the only light born by someone he couldn't locate with his Faerie sight. The Silth didn't realize the extent of the Faeries' power of sight or Aran's ability to avoid it. He drew closer to the nearest Silth, mimicking his path a few steps before extinguishing his torch.

Thest roared from the other side of the river, and the three Faeries fired into the trees, aiming at the lights. Aran heard a horrific scream as one of the Silth was hit. He rushed down to the river's edge and threw up a shield. He had never tried to do one so large—he couldn't possibly cover all the moving torches.

"Fly! Scatter!" As he shouted, he saw many Silth flying up into the canopy, using the trees for cover. He yelled to those closest to him, "Get behind the shield! Put out the lights!"

The bolts Thest and the other Faeries were shooting struck the shield, and Aran assumed the others were gathering behind it. Over his shoulder, he made out dozens of Silth, faces taut with fear. Just as many of them were looking at him, wide-eyed with wonder, as at the Faerie bolts bouncing off the shield and lighting up the night. Most carried the poison arrows and spears the Silth used to fight off predators.

One of the male Silth near the front lifted his bow and fired toward the inside of Aran's shield. Instead of ricocheting off like the Faerie bolts coming across the river, the arrow sailed out through the shield, lodging itself in the Faerie's shoulder on Thest's right. Instantly dozens of arrows sailed toward the Faeries, striking both of the ones who flanked Thest.

As soon as Thest put up his own shield, Aran recognized the change in the balance. When one is casting a Faerie shield, you cannot fire a bolt without lowering or moving the shield, he remembered Faelen saying. They had practiced moving back and forth between casting the shield and firing the bolts. Since Faerie bolts were unable to go through it in either direction, they couldn't be fired from behind a shield. Aran realized, though, that while they are effective at blocking an arrow or spear coming from the outside, unlike the Faerie bolts, arrows or spears could be fired from behind one. Thest had to keep his raised in order to avoid the arrows, and he couldn't fire with the raised shield. The Silth would also know where Thest was because the shield could be seen in the darkness.

Just as Aran started to believe they could survive the fight, five more Faeries flew down into the light of the Faerie shield. They must have been watching for Aran in the sky and heard the battle sounds. They paused, and two of the now six Faeries moved out in each direction to flank Aran's shield. He knew he couldn't expand the shield, and eventually they'd achieve an angle allowing them to fire around it at the Silth behind him. He'd never fired a bolt before except in practice, and he was afraid to drop the shield even for a moment to try.

Suddenly the shields of the two Faeries moving to his right lit up as gunshots rang out. In the light of their shields, Aran spied Merit and her squad attacking the two from the air, firing Human pistols harvested from poachers and by shamans over the years. Each pistol took two Silth to maneuver, one to hold it and the other to fire, but the warriors' accuracy was evidence of their long practice. The bullets fared no better than the spears in piercing the Faerie shields, but the speed of their attack and constant motion of the flying Silth stopped the progress of the Faeries in flanking Aran on that side.

From the other side came Storng's unmistakable gruff shout and the higher pitched voice of the Kawran Council's Anuli. The two shamans engaged the two Faeries moving in that direction, throwing fire, water and wind in rapid succession. They held the left flank. But the assault on Aran's shield resumed. As Thest held up a shield, the other Faerie would duck out and fire at Aran before dropping back behind the shield as the arrows sought them. Aran was weakening—he'd never held a shield this big or this long during practice. His heart sank as three more Faeries appeared near Thest.

Thest moved closer to the river's edge. He and the four Faeries floated out over the water, keeping two shields in place as the others leaned in and out to shoot around them. Silth arrows rained down on them but failed to stop the advance. Under the barrage of Faerie bolts, Aran's shield flickered and vanished. Just as the light of the shield disappeared, a blue bolt struck him in the shoulder. He spun and collapsed, clutching his bloody and burned shoulder. Thest advanced toward him. Now unprotected, Silth scattered in every direction as blue bolts flashed, fired by the four Faeries accompanying Thest.

A figure appeared on the shore between Aran and the advancing group of Faeries. Holding a blue Faerie shield much smaller than the others, he agilely deflected several of their bolts heading straight for Aran. The shield disappeared, and he fired once left, once right, each time hitting a flanking Faerie whose shield was facing the other way.

One of the Faeries next to Thest shouted, "It is General Faelen!"

Thest snarled, "Faelen, you fool. Traitor!"

Grinning, Faelen lifted his arm and fired five times in rapid succession into the river beneath Thest and the other Faeries. As steam and boiling water geysered up behind Thest's shield, the Faeries howled in pain and all of them, including Thest, disappeared. The remaining Faeries holding each of the flanks looked over at the empty middle of their line, flickered, and vanished as well.

Faelen started toward Aran, but he stopped short and called

out, "Humans coming."

He ducked into the dense part of the forest. The Silth pulled back into the trees as two bright points of light appeared along the path, moving rapidly toward the river's edge.

Aran tried to push himself up with his good arm. A massive wave of dizziness washed over him, and he fell backward again. As he hit the ground, his wounded shoulder twisted, creating a jolt of pain so intense he almost cried out.

The darkness smothered him and he lost consciousness.

Scene 4

Joss (Human)

For the last ten minutes, Joss and Kate had been running down the path, their flashlight beams bouncing in the darkness. Each time Joss paused to climb over roots or cross a fallen rotten tree, she heard Kate's heavy breathing behind her. She slowed a little so her friend could catch up.

Kate panted, "Are you sure this is a good idea? Racing through the rainforest at night?"

"Those were parrot screams. I'm sure of it." The sounds had not been from far away, maybe beside the river flowing near the compound where Joss lived. But there wasn't a direct path from the compound to this part of the river.

"Right, and something was after them. Do we really want to meet it in the dark? I don't think we can outrun a jaguar." After a pause with no answer, Kate gave a knowing chuckle. "Right, you just have to outrun me. Not too hard right now."

Joss laughed. "Almost everything we should be afraid of will run from us."

"Almost?" was Kate's reply, up an octave from her usual voice, but Joss kept up the pace. "Almost?"

"Well, a cougar won't necessarily run. A jaguar would unless on a kill. Snakes don't run. At least not the fer-de-lance. Nor do crocodiles, usually. But otherwise it's fine. Oh yeah, and pigs. We don't want to mess with the pigs. They'll hunt us down and eat us."

"How far back to the cabin is it?"

"Come on, I won't let anything happen to you."

"Pigs," Kate muttered. "My obituary will read 'she was eaten by pigs.' The sad thing is, there'll be people in New Orleans saying 'uh-huh, that's what I always thought would happen to her.'"

They burst into the clearing beside the river, and Joss swept her flashlight beam around the area. "I thought I heard gunshots. Maybe poachers will run from us. Maybe not." She pushed on before the drop-jawed Kate could say anything.

"There. Movement over there." Joss had seen several somethings skitter away from another something and swung her light that way. "Heyaaa! Get on! Get on!"

Not really knowing what she was shooing away, Joss trotted over and gasped. On the ground lay a large blue macaw with closed eyes, its feathers torn and blood oozing from its right side. She crouched, gently running her hands over the bird to determine if anything was broken and if it was alive. Its head moved slightly as she probed, and she saw the faintest rise and fall of its chest. She breathed a sigh of relief and looked over at her friend.

Kate was frantically probing the darkness with her light, shining it in one direction, and then—clearly convinced something was sneaking up on them from the other direction—flipping around to shine it that way, spinning again and again.

"You know," she huffed, "when I said I wanted to come hang out with you? So not what I had in mind." She mumbled under her breath, "Left a nice, safe shop in New Orleans to hang out in the rainforest. In the middle of the night. To be eaten by—"

"Kate, have you always muttered this much and I've just

forgotten? It's gonna be okay. Looks like this poor thing's alive but badly hurt. We heard so much noise there must have been more parrots. Stand next to it while I check."

"All right. I'll stand here guarding the dinner of whatever's out there. Comforted in the knowledge you promised you wouldn't let anything happen to me. In the rainforest. In the middle of the night. With no weapons."

Joss gave Kate a reassuring pat on the arm. As she searched the clearing she found strange scorch marks, broken tree limbs, and other signs that a major struggle had taken place. She found some blood, but absent were feathers or other parrot bodies. Maybe her flashlight was just missing them—it was hard to know in the dark—but she thought not. As she neared the trees, she had the creepiest feeling she was being watched. Despite her earlier bravado, her breath hitched, and she decided her search had been good enough.

She made her way back to Kate. "Something big happened here. Can't tell what, though. Maybe it was poachers. When it's daylight, I'll come back and look around more."

"Don't think it's a good idea to tangle with poachers out here in the dark."

"You're right. Let's go." When Joss picked up the parrot and cradled it like a baby, it still failed to stir or open its eyes. "You lead, I have my hands full."

Kate glanced around uncertainly. "Happy to. Uh, where's the path?" When Joss tilted her head in the correct direction, Kate took off like the dreaded jaguar was in pursuit.

The same ground they'd covered in ten minutes took almost an hour going back. Getting over roots and fallen trees was much trickier with Joss carrying the parrot. Kate even volunteered to take a turn, for all her bluster taking it tenderly and without squeamishness. Streaks of daylight were appearing as they reached the cabin.

"See, Kate, you survived the adventure safe and sound. Why don't you get some sleep while I work on this fellow?"

Kate let out a loud yawn. "No argument from me."

Joss watched Kate make a beeline for the bedroom and laughed to herself. They'd become fast friends in college and stayed in touch. Kate had accepted Joss's invitation to visit, leaving her younger brother in charge of the strange little French Quarter shop that sold both real and fanciful animal skeletons, scorpions preserved in resin, crystals and New Age paraphernalia, and anything else that captured Kate's interest. The shop did well with the odd assortment of tourists visiting the city. Kate looked the part of the proprietor, with her purple-tipped black hair, nose stud, and tattoos of an all-seeing eye on her upper arm and a thorny rose on her ankle. The extra pounds she had put on since college showed her fondness for Café du Monde beignets and New Orleans cuisine.

Kate referred to herself as an "indigo," someone who could read people's auras to discern their moods, and insisted she had dreams foretelling the future. As she carried the parrot into the infirmary, Joss wondered if Kate had seen this evening coming, but clearly from her friend's behavior she hadn't. She'd described Costa Rica to Kate as mostly boring but a place where Joss could do something meaningful and stay sober. A week later she had Kate tearing through the night to rescue an injured bird.

Joss laid the parrot carefully on the metal treatment table. "It's okay, little buddy. I'll have you fixed up in no time." She pulled out the instruments necessary to treat his wounds, saying, "I wonder what attacked you. Whatever it was, it got you pretty bad."

With all she needed laid out on a tray, she doused gauze with alcohol and dabbed at the wound, trying remove bloody dirt and debris. When the parrot squirmed and squawked softly, Joss stopped and tossed the gauze back on the tray.

"Well, okay. Looks like a sedative's needed. Don't like doing it—it's always a little dangerous—but I can't have you moving. I may need to set that wing. And no question you're in pain. I can't even tell what your injuries are. It's like you were burned and shot. Must be something nasty the poachers dreamed up." She shook her head. She had to be wrong—why would poachers damage their targets?

She took out a tiny syringe, jabbed the needle into a medicine bottle, and injected the bird with the contents. Her mouth went dry. Almost instantly, the bird had transformed into a different creature—a winged, little … person.

"No, let me go!" He struggled to get up, sheer panic on his face.

Joss stumbled back from the table and let out a small strangled cry of disbelief. She clamped her hand over her mouth. *This. Isn't. Possible.*

The creature managed to prop on one elbow, but his chest heaved spasmodically. He collapsed, once more tried to sit up, and fell back, his face showing total defeat. As the drug took greater effect, his eyes glazed over and closed. His struggles ceased and his breathing slowed, settling into a steady rhythm.

Joss crept closer, almost doubting her sanity. He was perfectly formed in his dimensions, with stunning feathers on his wings and where a Human would have hair. What is it? He … what is he? *He talked. I heard him, understood him. But he was a parrot. Am I dreaming? No—I know I'm awake. I fell in the forest and hit my head on something.*

Even as her mind raced, her instincts kept her hands moving, feeling for broken bones as well as cleaning and bandaging the wounds. Once again she had the creepy sensation of being watched. She glanced out in the hallway and then up at the room's only window, a small rectangle almost six feet off the floor.

Two parrots were peeking inside. Only she knew they weren't parrots.

And somehow she could sense ... they knew she knew.

Scene 5

STORNG (SILTH)

"Storng, what do we do?"

"About?" Before Merit could answer, Storng said, "First we have the problem of the Faeries trying to kill Aran. They'll now destroy the entire colony because it has seen the power Aran has. A second problem."

Storng and Merit had watched Joss work on Aran, witnessed her response when he changed form, and seen her spot them at the window. They kept looking through the glass as she put away her supplies and laid Aran carefully on the camp cot in the corner.

"Aran's plan had been for me to bring a few of the colony elders out to follow him along the river. He hoped the Faeries would confront him and reveal their intentions to cause so much death. By witnessing this, the elders would believe him and take the necessary steps."

"A foolish plan, certain to end in his death," Storng said.

Merit winced. "He knew it was a big risk. I don't think he anticipated quite so much force would be there, or that the Faeries would use the threat against him of killing the colony. I decided a different approach would be better. Which is why I reached out to you and brought most of the colony."

"Now they have indeed heard Thest's intentions and know he will kill them. We should be able to get them to move to safety." He nodded as though they had solved their first problem. "The fact that they're trying to kill him means they're likely trying to kill me as well. We have a wounded

Aran, whom we must retrieve before the Faeries come looking for him. And some strange Faerie fought on our side in this recent skirmish, but we know nothing of his intent or history. Another problem in and of itself."

"He's Faelen, a Faerie outcast who's been secretly teaching Aran Faerie magic." Merit paused as Storng raised his eyebrow hather. "Aran hoped Faelen would teach other Silth as well. He also told me how, if anything happened to him, I might be able to contact Faelen. But I have no idea how he ended up in the battle."

Storng thought a moment. "There is also the question of how Thest knew Aran would be banished tonight. He said he'd been warned. By whom? Did Aran do it to set up the confrontation?"

"I doubt it, because I don't think Aran knew how to contact Thest. He just assumed they'd be hunting for him, and that if he was obvious enough, they'd find him. But don't we have a more immediate concern? This Human has seen Aran's true form. She knows what we are."

"The least of our problems, Merit. Humans have seen us many times over the generations. Most convince themselves that it was their imagination. Obviously, she won't, as she is working on Aran too directly. But who can she tell? Who would believe her? As long as we get Aran out of there, she has no way to prove her story." Storng peered intently through the window again and murmured, "There is something familiar about her. I know her from somewhere. He stared a moment longer and then smiled, "Oh, yes, of course. 'The river of life has a surprise around every bend.'"

Just then, a second Human walked into the room, and Merit watched her mouth drop open. "What the—what the hell is that?"

Storng sighed heavily. "Maybe this is a bit of a problem."

CHAPTER TWELVE

Scene 1

THEST (TROW)

Thest strode down the long hall toward Xafar's chambers. He had bandages across the left side of his body, his arm was so burned it required a sling, and the skin on his face was blistered. Despite his injuries, he never slowed, cape billowing behind him and face hardened. He ignored the sentries' salutes. Brushing past the attendants outside, he slammed his good shoulder against the chamber doors, and they burst open.

He saw a table, long enough for at least a dozen Trow, its surface barely visible from the array of dishes it bore. Most of the silver serving platters were covered, but those open held a vast assortment of meats and breads. Seated at the head of the table, Xafar looked up at Thest with such intensity that he faltered and stopped short. Xafar shooed away the guards who had pursued Thest and gestured for him to sit at the empty place setting beside him.

Thest started to speak, but Xafar's eyes narrowed, cutting him off. As he sat, servants instantly rushed to him and filled his plate. He stared at it angrily, but plainly Xafar was determined to continue his meal, so Thest began eating as well. Hampered by his inability to use his left hand for cutting, he picked up his meat and tore it off with his teeth. Not very mannerly, but effective nonetheless. He realized he was hungry and could not remember when he had eaten last.

They ate without conversing, as any time Thest would try to speak Xafar would silence him with another look. It occurred to Thest that because of the doorway, Xafar already knew what was on his mind. The room filled with the sound of scraping plates, chewing, and the crunch of crusty bread. The servants cleared the plates when empty and refilled the wine glasses, elaborate silver pieces embossed with hunt scenes.

Propping his elbows on the table, Xafar leaned forward. "Your lieutenants briefed me. The key aspects appear to be that you tried to kill Aran, the rogue shaman. You were repelled by a force including much of a Paerrie colony, two elder shamans—one of these Storng—warriors from another colony, and last but not least my son Faelen. In this fight the shaman Aran displayed, and the others witnessed, a level of power no Paerrie has shown before. We can only conclude that his training by Storng has now been supplemented by Faelen's. Is this a fair summary?"

"Yes, my lord, and I—"

"I know. You want to kill them all."

Thest's fists shook with the intensity of his hatred, and he shoved them under the table so Xafar would not see. "Indeed."

"But first you need my authority to put a Trow not under your command to death. And to kill my son and not be killed by me, you need my blessing."

"The act of treason in training a Paerrie is great. I do not recall any comparable crime that has not been punished by death. I know he is a prince and your only son—but he goes too far."

"Careful, you do not put bounds on the act of the sovereign

or his heir," Xafar said calmly. "But you are correct—he does go too far. I do not know if it is because of his habits or his temperament, but no matter." Xafar looked off into a distant corner of the room for a moment before he continued, "The queen carries another child. The physicians say it is a boy and that he will be born in a week. On the safe event of his birth, you may kill Faelen. Not until then."

"And what of the Paerries?"

"Aran and the two shamans must be ended quickly before they can process and share what happened. But I do not want to destroy a colony, as it could set off a war. There are still too many Humans for us to risk that. We will exterminate the last of the Paerries later, and without Faelen they will be no threat. Proceed with your mission. If you complete your tasks, this incident will not matter. Do not be distracted from your tasks."

"But they have seen the Trow defeated by Paerries, which will spread through their stories. A Paerrie wielded a power never before seen. They are still afraid of Aran and of our reaction to him, but soon they will wonder if this means they can stand against us. If we strike fast, we take out the colony while the warriors from the other colony are still there. We cauterize this wound. I am almost ready with the other project. Even if there was a war, it quickly would be rendered irrelevant."

"I do not want you or your forces distracted. We are staking all on your tasks."

As Thest weighed his options, Xafar watched him with an almost amused look, despite having just authorized him to kill his son.

"I understand. I propose that my mate Demist lead the force to eradicate the colony and the shamans. She has proven herself countless times in battle and led troops many times on your behalf. She has been a part of my work and will take care not to do anything to interfere with it. She has completed her portion of the mission."

After taking another sip of wine, Xafar said, "I approve this action. But your choices are upon you. If she fails, you fail. You have already been unsuccessful in dealing with this Aran affair. If you were not so critical to the Trow recapture of Earth, you would have sealed your death. If you—living on borrowed time, I remind you—are willing to stake yours and your son's fates on Demist, so be it. Let her destroy the shamans, the colony and the warriors."

Thest could not let it go. "And ... Faelen?"

"As I said, in one week upon the successful birth of a new heir, you may kill Faelen. You. This is not a task that may be delegated, nor shall it ever be mentioned here in the Land. I would prefer that the Trow not think much about the death of my family members. It might foster troublesome ideas. If any of this hinders your completion of your true mission, you will be replaced. Your estates will be forfeited. Your son will die, and over the years you will decide that he was the lucky one. We are done."

Scene 2

Joss (Human)

Joss decided not to tell Kate about the parrots in the window, as her friend had almost been tipped over the edge already. The sight of the small figure on the cot, unconscious again, had set off a stream of gibberish that Joss patiently waited out. Once Kate pulled herself together, she bent and touched him gingerly.

Kate swallowed hard. "Wow. He's real. He looks like something I would have created and sold in the shop. What is he? Where'd he come from?"

More questions from Kate, many of which were Joss's as well, flowed on for several minutes. When Joss just shook her head in response to each, Kate gave up and stood staring in wonder. Luckily, she didn't look up at the window, where the parrots still could be seen. After a brief internal debate, Joss also chose not to mention this was probably not her first encounter with one of these creatures. She gathered him up and moved him onto a more comfortable daybed across the room. He didn't stir.

She looked at him and tried to speak loudly enough for the parrot watchers, or whatever they really were, to hear. "I'm going to town to get more antibiotics—he'll need them to recover. Please don't leave. I won't hurt you or tell anyone about you." She glanced up at the window where one parrot was bobbing its head up and down, which she hoped meant it was acceptable to use Human antibiotics on the creature.

"Why are you talking so loud?" Kate demanded. "You think he's hard of hearing? Why do you believe he'd understand you? And why won't you tell anyone?"

"We can talk about it in the car. Trust me. It'll be all right." She gently led Kate from the room, adding, "You trusted me last night, and you weren't eaten by pigs."

Scene 3

MERIT (SILTH)

Merit watched the Humans drive away. She and Storng slipped into the cabin through the door, left slightly ajar, and flew to the bed. Under other circumstances she'd have stayed close to the door, listening for the Humans to return. But given what Joss had said and done for their benefit, she knew they had plenty of time.

When Aran awoke and let out a groan, Storng said softly, "Aran, can you hear us?"

"Need to go … colony in danger."

"You can't leave yet," Storng said firmly. "You're injured too badly and need the medicine the Humans will bring. We could treat you, but you'll be on your feet faster if they take care of you. Merit and I will help the colony move."

"Faeries will … will track the colony."

"We'll try to mask its presence. Maybe we'll spread out."

"No." Aran motioned at the old shaman to lean closer, and Storng listened intently as Aran whispered in his ear.

Merit strained to hear, unsure as to whether Aran was giving instructions in the event of his death or giving Storng insight into the amazing power she'd seen in the recent battle. A power that might mean death for all of them. Still, if she was honest with herself, she wanted that power. Fighting Faeries with guns, arrows, and spears no longer seemed enough. She was struggling with her emotions, so far from any touchstone of familiarity. Showing themselves to Humans, battling Faeries, able to use Faerie magic—it was like someone had stuck a beehive into her mind. Aran and chaos go hand in hand.

Storng straightened, frowning, and met Merit's eyes a moment before telling Aran, "I'll take care of it. But they'll likely come for you. As soon as you get the medicine and can move, you need to go. This location is too close to where they left you. I don't think the Faeries will do anything in front of Humans, but something is changing. They grow bolder."

"The entire colony may die because of me."

"No, Aran. It's my fault—once again I pushed too far. I never should have taught you."

"Ha! I might be dead, and you might be dead, but the colony would be fine if this was simply about your teachings. Seeing that Silth…. have the power of Faeries is what put the colony at risk."

"I think we can all agree that you are both irresponsible sons-of-toucans and that you share the blame for all awfulness in this situation," Merit interjected impatiently. "The question is what's next?"

"Tell me about your Faerie teacher—Merit says his name is Faelen—who fought on our side. How do you know him?"

"Faelen's the son of the Faerie king, Xafar. Used to be a general. The—the father of … many Silth." Aran paused and closed his eyes, and for a moment Merit thought he had lost consciousness again. "Water," he said weakly. She found a thimble of water the Human had left beside the bed and gave him a drink.

Aran went on, his voice a little stronger. "As punishment, Faelen was banished to this world. Together we confirmed that, with the proper instruction, Silth can perform Faerie magics. He's taught me many of them."

"The secret that Faeries kill shamans to guard. Whenever we get too close to it, deaths occur."

"I can only die once and working with you pretty much assured that I'd be hunted. Now I have the power to hide and fight. We must share this with all of the Silth. It's our only hope."

"The Faeries will declare war on us, Aran. The only reason they haven't because they fear it will expose us all to the Humans."

Aran grimaced as he shifted slightly. "War is coming anyway. Faelen says the Faeries are increasingly in this world because they are getting ready to take it from the Humans. The plot Qwert overheard must be related to this. It's the beginning of the end of the Humans. After the Faeries clear away the Humans, next they'll remove the Silth. We'll have no hope of survival if we don't prepare."

"Then you must leave quickly, as soon as you've received treatment and are strong enough to fly. You must be a high target for the Faerie. So is everyone who's seen your power." Storng looked at Merit. "We must talk with the council, then spread the word to the other colonies."

As Storng flew toward the door, he called back over his shoulder, "I'm going to check outside and make sure no one has come for you yet."

Merit gazed deeply into Aran's eyes trying to judge the nature of his heart, and he stared back at her uncertainly. When she began to unfurl her wings, readying to follow Storng, Aran pulled her close, wincing with the effort.

"I can show you how to fight the Faeries, Merit. Right now. If they kill me, no other Paerrie knows. But if you gain this knowledge, you, everyone you teach, and everyone who knows you have this power will be under a death sentence."

She gave him her lop-sided smile. "Have you ever thought about what my 'job' is? I wake up each day facing a good possibility of death."

As he taught her the basics of the Faerie blast and shield, he could only describe and demonstrate without lifting his arms much from his chest. He explained that a Faerie bolt was normally several times more powerful than that of a Silth and the shield much stronger. For a short time, a Silth could match that power, as he had at the river, but it came at a high price. Beyond his wounds, he was drained of almost all energy, she realized. As he continued his instructions, the last of his strength ebbed away, and his head lolled to one side. Her breath hitched, and she breathed a sigh of relief when she realized he was still breathing.

Though she doubted he could hear, she said, "I know enough, shaman. I'm off to show my squad how to fight Faeries. And I'll be back to help you show the Faeries that they've grabbed hold of a porcupine."

Scene 4

ARAN (SILTH)

Aran awoke to the sound of a car, and the dim light told him many hours had passed. He struggled to stay conscious but failed.

Sometime later he jolted awake to find the Human female sitting beside him. As she applied salve to his wounds and administered a shot in his uninjured shoulder, she kept trying to talk to him. She said her name was "Joss," but he was unable to focus on the words that followed or keep his eyes open. Once more he sank beneath the surface of wakefulness.

The next day, each time he fuzzily came to, the light cast through the window had moved further across the wall, and the reflections on the ceiling had migrated. The following day was more of the same. Finally, on the third day after the river battle, he awoke with his head clearer and no light shining through the open window. He listened to bird and tree frog songs which, when added to early evening insect sounds, told him the sun recently had gone down. He heard Joss talking to someone in the next room, and he pushed himself up with his uninjured arm. He was pleased when he found himself able to get to his feet and keep standing despite a few seconds of dizziness. He rotated his injured shoulder and lifted his arm partway in the air. While it hurt, he realized he was regaining strength quickly, and he gave a mental thanks to Joss and her medicines. He felt certain he'd soon be able to fly.

He heard the sound of wheels on rocks, and Joss rushed in. She scooped him up and carried him into a small bedroom he suspected was hers. Laying him on the bed, she whispered, "Stay put and quiet," and shut the door behind her. It took Aran a moment to recover from the sudden loss of control in being carried.

He heard a male call out, "Joss? You here?" and "Come on in, Brophy" was her faint reply.

He looked around the room curiously. An empty olive jar was on the floor beside the bed. On the nightstand lay several books and journals, and an electronic photo frame was cycling through pictures of Joss and others that Aran assumed were family and friends. A small desk was littered with papers and more pills than he had ever seen in any Human's possession. Drawings labeled "New Yorker" covered one of two bulletin boards, and three small posters were pinned to it. The first said, "If ignorance is bliss, why aren't more people happy?" and the one below it read, "Fall three times, get up three times." The largest of the three was titled "Serenity Prayer." The second bulletin board had the words "Dream Board" at the top—it was filled with pictures of dogs, parrots, and other animals, as well as one of a handsome young man and a boat.

The quiet murmuring between Joss and this Brophy—even with his Silth hearing, he was unable to make out any words—had Aran sliding into a comfortable state of near sleep. He vaguely heard her say with obvious distaste, "Oh, and you brought Angel," and he jolted wide awake.

"Buenas noches, Ms. Jocelyn," came the reply from a woman. "Stanley Ryder, we need to go."

Stanley Ryder. Angel—Angeles. Stanley Ryder was the name Qwert overheard, and Angel must be Angeles, who Faelen had warned was the Faerie spy. A Human and a Faerie—this was the team Qwert heard discussing an attack on the Humans.

Launching himself off of bed, Aran ignored the sharp shoulder pain as he flew across the room to the door handle and cracked the door just slightly. He dropped down to the floor and peeked out. Standing in the doorway opposite him was a Human female, out of sight of the others. When she spotted him, her eyes widened, and she put her finger to her lips. He pulled back in, his heart jumping around in his chest like a frog in a bag, his legs barely holding him up. That must be Kate. He had heard Joss say her name. As he leaned against the wall, he resisted the urge to slide to the floor. *This Faerie has to be hunting me!*

He looked back into the room. Joss was talking with the young Human male she called "Brophy", but whom Angel referred to as "Stanley Ryder". She gnawed on her lower lip as she listened. Her agitation seemed obvious to Aran and probably any other Silth, but Stanley Ryder seemed oblivious. Aran checked again and confirmed he was indeed Human, not Faerie, but he wasn't able to see Angel.

"Something huge is about to happen," Stanley Ryder was saying urgently. "You need to come with me."

Joss scoffed. "That's what guys always say."

"Come on, Joss. I'm serious."

"And so that 'something huge' is going to affect me way out here?"

Stanley Brophy said in an exasperated tone, "Definitely. I can't tell you what. But I guarantee it'll reach you."

"Stanley Ryder, you should not tell her anything."

"I'm not, Angel. Wait outside. I'll be right out."

Angel stepped into Aran's line of sight—she was a Faerie. *I'm going to die. Oh, monkey scat, I'm going to die!*

Angel angled her head toward the hall. Holding his breath, Aran pulled back, fearing the Faerie might detect and confront him. Instead he heard footsteps and the door to outside open and close. He relaxed a little and was able to think more clearly. He leaned back into the hall. *What's a Faerie doing with a Human?* The "something huge" must have to do with the Faerie plot to retake the Earth. Kate was still listening from her doorway.

Stanley Ryder was telling Joss, "—to trust me. You'll be in danger if you aren't prepared. If you won't come with me, at least stock up on weapons and supplies as though a long time will pass before you get more. A really long time. Please come with me."

"Where are you going that'll be safer than here? And what exactly are you doing that's so dangerous? You won't hurt anyone, will you?"

Ignoring her questions, Stanley Ryder glanced at his watch. "Look, I gotta go. I had a bad feeling you might not come, so I brought you some things." He pointed to three large boxes beside the door— apparently Angel had carried them in—and took a couple of steps as though to leave. Joss grabbed his arm, and Aran drew back again as she pleaded with the Human to tell her what was going on.

Angel was not hunting him—she was proceeding with the Faerie plan. Angel had caused Qwert's death, and Aran found himself engulfed by the same lust for vengeance he'd felt toward the poachers who killed Shra. In Qwert's case, however, the death was murder, not an accident.

He squeezed out of Joss's bedroom window, sucking in a breath when he scraped his injured shoulder. As he slid around the outside of the lodge, he saw the big Toyota Land Cruiser in front, with all of its doors wide open. Angel was sprawled in the back seat, booted shoes caked with dirt and sticking out the door nearest Aran. A salsa tune blared from the car's radio.

Aran flew through the back-loading door and hid behind some of the suitcases, the music masking any noise he might have made. He had barely settled in when he felt an elbow dig into his ribs, and Merit settled in beside him. She gave him a "don't even think about it" look. When he pointed to where Angel lay and mouthed the word "Faerie," she switched to a "you're stating the obvious" expression.

The cabin door banged shut, and boots crunched on the gravel. The Human slammed the truck's rear door and passenger door on the driver side. The car shimmied as he climbed behind the wheel. Aran and Merit remained still, holding their breaths.

Angel pulled herself out of the back seat and spoke over the loud music, clearly amused. "I can tell by your face she did not listen. I told you it was a waste of time."

Scene 5

STORNG (SILTH)

Storng worked his way behind several canisters on top of the refrigerator, and from his vantage point, he watched the two women. While Kate consumed her breakfast of fruit and bread as if famished, Joss tore through the rooms.

She called out from the bedroom, "I wouldn't have thought he was strong enough to leave yet." And with a worried note, "I hope the antibiotics were enough."

Kate responded between bites. "Stop looking. He isn't here. I saw him up and around when Brophy was here. Seemed pretty agitated. Maybe Brophy was the one who attacked him out in the forest. And why is he 'Brophy' to you and 'Stanley Ryder' to that scary Angel chick?"

Disappearing into another room, Joss gave no answer, and Kate chuckled as she spread fig preserves on a bread slice. "Anyway, we seem to be parrot-man-free."

Storng had traded his parrot glamour for that of a Silth of extreme age. Though he considered his normal glamour youthful given his actual age, he transformed himself to appear quite ancient, with a waist-length white beard and wrinkles from head to toe. He amused himself by choosing the very moment Kate made her "parrot-man-free" remark to land on the table and arrange himself cross-legged.

Her half-eaten bread landed on the table jelly-side down, and she went slack-jawed. Then, "Jos-s-s-s!"

Storng arranged his face into a somber but non-threatening

mask. Time to solve at least one problem.

Standing in the doorway, Joss eyed him a moment and gave a weak smile. "No, it's really fine. No big deal. Drop right on in." To his surprise, she veered into the kitchen and started piling dishes into the sink with a series of clanks and clinks. "A parade of fairy-tale creatures passes through here daily. It's nothing really."

"Good morning, Joss." He had to speak loudly over the din, and he modulated his voice to reflect his apparent age, counting on the Humans' respect for the elderly to help him. "You've been busy this morning. Thank you for helping my friend. Very kind of you."

Joss spun and leaned back against the kitchen counter. "Will he—is he all right?"

"I don't know. He left in the vehicle with your friend—Brophy, is it? He is apparently concerned about what Brophy has planned. Do you know what it is?"

Joss walked over and gave Kate's shoulder a squeeze. Her friend, much paler than usual, had managed to pick up her bread and was trying to wipe sticky fig preserves off the table with her paper napkin. The napkin was shredding, leaving tiny bits of paper stuck to the table, but she kept working at it while sneaking side-long looks at Storng.

Joss collapsed onto a chair. "First, I can't believe I'm having this conversation with some sort of being—I don't know what you are—sitting on my table. Are you and your friend aliens? And second, I can't believe that when you talk, I can understand what you're saying. Third, Brophy's not really my friend, though he wants to be, and more. I don't know why I told you that."

She gave herself a light pat on each cheek.

"Fourth, I have no clue what it is he's up to. And finally, do you guys frequently interfere in the actions of Humans?"

He laughed and eyed Joss thoughtfully. She was bright and kind, and he trusted her. He contemplated Kate—still silently watching him, she'd picked up a banana with a slightly trembling hand and was eating again. While he knew this one meant no harm, he didn't trust her in the same way.

"You and I have met before, Joss. More than ten years ago, in Florida."

She jumped up from the table so violently that her chair tipped backward and hit the floor with a loud crack. Her hands flapped like agitated butterflies. "Oh. My. God. That was you? I wasn't even sure it really happened. After a while, even though I wanted to believe it, I convinced myself I'd imagined it. Then when I saw your friend, I thought 'maybe it was one of these'."

Kate found her voice, her eyes wildly moving from Joss to Storng. "Wha—what? What are you talking about?"

"I told you the story, Kate. The magic talking bird when I was at The Refuge."

'Holy mother of god. I always thought that was just DT's. It was him?"

"Apparently."

The corners of his lips quirked upward. "I'm not an alien, but rather of a race of beings older than Humans. We are the Silth—children of parrots and Faeries. Some of us can talk and speak any language Humans do." He kept talking as Joss flipped her chair back upright and sat down. "More precisely, I always speak the same way, yet Humans hear it in their native language. We never interfere in the actions of Humans unless they threaten us directly. That's why I'm unsure of what my friend

Aran is doing. But I think it has to do with one of the women—the one called Angel—not actually being a Human. She's a Faerie."

"Angel ... is a ... Faerie?" Joss repeated, paling a little, and Kate coughed and sputtered as she choked on her banana.

He gave them time to recover. He hoped that assistance would not be needed for Kate's choking, but when she dissolved in giggles, he decided her airway was clear and he could continue. "Angel is from a very old race of beings from another world. She is in fact an alien. Humans have referred to her people by many names through the course of their history, but in more recent times mostly as 'Faeries'."

"They also used to live on this world," he went on, "but Human technology caused them psychological harm. It turned them from good to bad. They returned to their home world and took over leadership of their people. They've worked for many years to return to this world and retake it from Humans and Silth. Now they are up to something new, and your 'not-really-a-friend' is part of it. Although I don't think he knows he is working with Faeries."

"Angel is a Faerie? A ... bad Faerie?"

"Yes, Kate," he said patiently, masking his frustration over her slowness in comprehension. Hoping Joss was processing faster, he said to her, "Are you going to tell anyone about Aran and the Silth?"

She sighed. "Like anyone would believe me. But no, I won't tell anyone if it will endanger you."

"It would, far more than you can imagine." Storng locked eyes with Joss's and passed one hand in front of her face, clutching a closed vial of water in his pocket with the other. "Do you promise?"

"Yes, of course."

He waved his hand again. "Then I have bound you to your

promise. You will not be able to speak of this to anyone."

The spell only worked when the subject truly was committed to the action, in effect allowing them to be bound to it. He turned his attention back to Kate—she had finished eating and seemed to have drifted off into a slack-jawed state of shock.

"You Kate, I'm afraid, cannot be trusted with this knowledge. I am sorry."

Leaping to his feet, he saw both exchange looks of alarm. He crossed the table and passed his hand in front of Kate's wide-eyed face while reciting the beginning of a spell. Her expression softened, and she stared blankly ahead in a trance-like state.

Joss gasped. "What are you doing to her?"

He ignored her. Kate allowed him to take her hand, sprinkle some of the water from the vial onto her palm and rub it gently. Then he stepped back and restored his parrot glamour. Her eyes cleared, and her brow furrowed in confusion.

"Um, Joss ... why is there a parrot on the table?"

Joss opened her mouth, but nothing came out. Her lips closed so quickly Storng heard her teeth clunk together, and she looked at him incredulously. His spell would prevent her from explaining that moments before the bird had been a small, elderly winged man. He watched as she realized it and thought through an allowed answer to the question.

Finally, she shrugged. "He's just a parrot I'm working to rehab. Must have gotten out."

CHAPTER THIRTEEN

Scene 1

ARAN (SILTH)

As the Cruiser bounced down the rutted road, Aran had trouble concentrating. Perhaps it was a side effect from the drugs Joss had given him, amplified by the pummeling from the crates and boxes packed around them. Merit was pressed against him, and although she'd shown no sign of affection, maybe his body remembered when her proximity had been more intimate. An odd time for amorous thoughts, he thought.

Whatever the reason, he had difficulty following the thread of the conversation between Angel and Stanley Ryder. He knew they were talking about a big event, but he had no idea what, only able to catch fragments of conversation.

From Angel, "There's no more discussion of whether. We're talking about how. You're in too deep for whether."

The vehicle had picked up speed. Increased road noise and the radio music allowed Aran to hear only snippets of Stanley Ryder's response, including "history's biggest mass murderer" and "bigger than Hitler, Stalin, Attila, combined." Aran shifted and squirmed, his back to Merit, leaning his head as far as possible to catch more of the discussion.

Stanley Ryder snapped, "I'm turning this off. It's giving me a headache." With the music off, Aran could now hear clearly. "I'd feel better if I knew that she was safe. Normal life will be disrupted. Food'll get scarce pretty quickly. Foragers will be aggressive. People won't be able to live outside of protected areas. And even there, the chaos in the manufacture and delivery of drugs and food will be deadly."

"I told you we will get the local organization to take her in as soon as we start. She will be fine. Funny guy. Like you said, we are about to become mass murderers. The most notorious in the history of mankind. Causing the deaths of millions of Humans, a large portion likely to be children. And you are hung up on Joss."

"I'm not that thrilled about being a mass murderer, but we love who we know—the others are just statistics to me. They don't really exist now, and their disappearance is a non-event. Necessary for the survival of the other species that Humans refuse to acknowledge share this planet with them, but necessary for the survival of Humans as well. Angel, intellectually I know what we're doing is necessary for the survival of future Humans. Besides, we're simply accelerating their inevitable self-destruction. We won't wipe out humanity—we'll simply scale it back a few thousand years to make room for the rest of nature. And people will still have their technologies … but the scale will be different."

"Preaching to the choir. I am just saying you have got to get her out of your mind. Focus on what you have got to do. There is no room for mistakes. No one has ever pulled off something like this."

A few miles passed in silence before Stanley Ryder spoke again. "Okay, Angel, let's go through it again. I'll fly back to the States tonight. Nuke's already there, team's taking it out to Yellowstone."

Angel picked up the thread. "It will be in the town outside the park. Your job is to take it into Yellowstone. Drop it in the hole and park it over the weakness. That is where detonation will have maximum effect, set off the super volcano. Secure and set the timer. Then drive like hell to be out of range when the bomb goes off in two hours."

"Can I get out of range in that amount of time?"

"You will be beyond the nuke's range, plus protected by the hills. However, you will still be in range of the resulting eruption. So drive hard. Do not let cops catch you. And do not stop for anything until you reach the coast. Make your way up the coastline to the compound. Join the others."

"How far will the volcano impact?"

"Being a super volcano, it will affect the entire northern hemisphere. Shut down the U.S., Canada and Mexico, greatly diminish China and Europe. Darkness will cover much of the north for at least a year. Planes will not fly or growing seasons occur. Ash will fall in all the major cities in North America. Every engine and heating or cooling system needing air will clog and stop. We expect the volcanic eruption to continue at least five months. South America will be impacted as well, particularly in the northern cities."

"So the Human population scales back, but more importantly the technologies spewing carbon into the world shut down. But won't the volcano pump as much carbon into the atmosphere? Won't other species be affected adversely?"

"We have been through this, Stanley Ryder. I showed you the charts on the carbon. Yes, the volcano will push a lot of carbon into the atmosphere. That will be offset by the almost complete shutdown of North America's cars and factories and the slowdown of everywhere else. The temperatures will drop because not as much sunlight gets through. Yes, other species will be severely impacted. But they will survive and later thrive as they return to habitats Humans have stolen from them. Let us go back over the details of how you are getting the device into Yellowstone. I want to make sure you are on top of it. We get no second chances."

Aran leaned back from his strained position and could tell from Merit's eyes she'd heard as well. He wondered about Angel's involvement, though—it made no sense. From Storng's and Faelen's history lessons, he knew the Faerie wanted to return to this world. But how would this event help that? Why was Angel helping? Just general Faerie mischief? Or was the true impact of the event bigger than Angel described and thus setting up the Faeries' return? Of course it was.

"You must get word to Storng," Aran whispered to Merit. "It must be a Faerie plot to—."

He broke off, realizing all conversation in the front had ceased. When Aran peeked between the boxes, Angel was looking straight at him, hand raised for silence.

"Stop the truck, Stanley Ryder! Now!"

The truck screeched to a halt. Merit pushed through the suitcases to the back door. She grabbed the handle and flew out of the truck just as Angel rounded the side. Aran watched in horror as Angel grabbed for her and missed by inches. As Merit soared into the sky —Angel lifted her arm. But before she could blast Merit, Stanley Ryder walked up from the other side of the truck, and Angel's arm fell limply to her side.

Aran shrank back into the luggage. That was too close … too familiar. His mind was not replaying Merit's successful escape, but rather Shra's unsuccessful one.

"What was that?" Stanley Ryder asked.

"Freaking parrot somehow got in the back."

"Pretty wild. I better take a look." Stanley Ryder started moving items aside to check. Jostled by shoved boxes, Aran stayed low and used a vague glamour that effectively camouflaged him until Stanley Ryder finally announced "All clear" and slammed the door.

"I'll be right back. Need a bio-break." Angel's feet crunched on the clay and the sound grew fainter.

Aran knew Angel was entering the forest to alert the other Faeries and send them after Merit, but there was nothing he could do. Before long, Angel returned and paused behind the truck, but he had in place the cloaking spell that prevented Faerie detection and knew she would not sense him. Suddenly he remembered Thest had anticipated his being cloaked, and the general had to have told Angel of this ability. Would it cause her to search the back more carefully?

To Aran's relief, Angel climbed back in the front seat. "Okay, a little excitement! Rock and roll."

Aran settled slightly, exhausted. In spite of his throbbing shoulder, within seconds he was dreaming he was high above the forest canopy. Below him were Shra's beautiful colors streaking along with the green of the rainforest below. He felt himself relaxing, drifting. Suddenly, an eagle flashed past Aran and grabbed Shra with its enormous talons. Both tumbled head over feet into the canopy. He jerked awake. When the truck failed to slow, he was grateful that the road noise had masked his warning shout.

Scene 2

Merit (Silth)

Merit flew over populated areas, hoping to hamper the Faeries' ability to attack. She was confident they'd come for her—Faerie "Angel" would've found some way of alerting them of Merit's knowledge, and no doubt they'd have a way of locating her. She had to survive to tell Storng and warn the colony. How were they going to get to Silth everywhere? Could they stop this?

She tried to focus and shift her mind to tactics. She was good at them. Apparently Aran had told Storng how to cloak from Faerie sight, since when he returned to the colony he was teaching it to all the members. She wished she had stayed to learn the technique, but she'd been intent on teaching her troop how to use the Faerie shield and bolt. Now she could form a shield and fire a bolt, but she was good at neither. A Faerie warrior could easily defeat her. She needed her troops, but she hadn't had time to redirect them from their stations outside the lodge.

She concentrated on her surroundings and dropped closer to the ground. In this part of the country, "populated areas" was a relative term, and though there were always some houses within sight, many stretches existed with mostly trees or fields. In one of these spaces the Faeries struck.

They came from the perfect blue sky above, in the form of Harpy eagles. They were not glamoured just to look like eagles—they had actually become eagles, something Faeries but not Silth could do. Whether from intuition or some slight shift in the pressure, Merit sensed them just before they were upon her. She dodged frantically to her right, avoiding the talons of the first one but colliding with the wings of the second. She bounced off and fell twenty yards before regaining her orientation and diving for the trees.

Unlike regular Harpies, the Faeries wouldn't give up just because she entered the canopy, and sure enough she heard big wings flapping behind her. Once freed of the possibility of Human eyes, Merit was sure they'd revert to Faerie form and blast her. She'd have to lose them. But how could she, hampered by the sparse canopy years of farming had left in this area and the Faeries' ability to sense her presence? She continued her plummet toward the treetops.

"No," she mouthed, as a Faerie suddenly appeared, positioning himself at the top of the tree for which she was aiming. She tried to break to stop and form a shield, but her momentum propelled her toward him. He lifted his arm, and she knew she was done for as she saw the blue bolt leave his fingertips. But it sailed over her and slammed into the eagle closest to her, sending it plummeting into the trees below.

Holy jaguar scat! The bolt miss had to have been on purpose. She recalculated and flew behind the Faerie. She hoped it was Faelen, the same Faerie who'd previously come to their aid.

The other eagle pulled up behind her, transforming into a Faerie, and he shielded just before being struck by a second blue bolt. This Faerie hovered, while the one in the treetop continued holding his arm forward ready to fire. After a few moments of the standoff, the sky Faerie flickered and blinked out of sight.

The treetop Faerie grabbed Merit's hand, and she saw the world blur and twist away. A new scene came into focus. She looked around frantically before realizing they were at the abandoned colony treehouses in the cloud forest.

The Faerie released her hand. "You are Merit, friend and protector of Aran. I am Faelen, Aran's teacher."

Even though she had wondered if it might be Faelen, the confirmation left Merit speechless. She had never spoken to a Faerie before and simply gaped at him.

He held her gaze a moment. "I am not quite sure what he sees in you. Perhaps your quick mind and witty repartee."

His gibe broke the spell and restored her speech. "You're Faelen, who has condemned Aran and probably our whole colony to death. But you're also the one who appeared and saved us in the fight by the river. Thank you for your timely intervention, yet again."

He seemed to hold himself a little taller. "Why were they attacking you?" After she told him what she and Aran had learned, he nodded. "I knew something was going on. Xafar will not rest until the Trow have retaken this world. Where were you going with this knowledge?"

"To alert the colony and Storng. But I've no idea what we can do. I think we'll be attacked, but we must also do something about the bomb in that faraway place."

Just then a flock parrots flew over them, their shrill calls bouncing around in the empty colony. Faelen flew out the treehouse window. Merit paused a moment, marveling again that Faeries flew without wings, before she flapped hers and followed him up into the treetop. She watched with him as the flock headed on and two more appeared nearby.

"They are so beautiful." He gazed at Merit, tilting his head. "You Silth inherit their beauty. Both in form and spirit. You are blissfully unaware that you are the most beautiful creatures on Earth."

He looked first at her distorted mouth and then at her makeshift hand. "The injuries you bear are those of triumph and bravery. Only adding to and not detracting from your beauty."

Though she thought of herself as immune to such things, the pride and praise he expressed caused her to blush, and she blurted out, "Are you Aran's father?"

He grinned. "The world may be on the brink of collapse, but everyone still wants answers to the father questions."

"Or we could just watch parrots."

"I do not know if I am Aran's father. Or yours, for that matter. The magic leaves no DNA, and since there is not actually a coupling, there is no way to test. I am not the only Trow to produce Paerries. And you seem to assume that only male Trow produce Paerries. It is an act of magic, not procreation."

As the parrots landed in a tree close by, he added, "The tension of desire to be a part of something and the physical impossibility is a heavy burden. And sadly I am not that strong."

Where the bottle in his hand came from, an unlabeled flask full of clear liquor, she had no idea. *I should go. There's so little time. But he just saved my life.* He offered her the bottle, and she took just a sip, but it was enough to cause the world to warp a little.

She grimaced and handed it back. "What is that?"

"Escape. From the world. From what comes next. From it all. The Humans refer to it as 'moonshine.' Moonshine ... a beautiful name for an ugly liquid. Drinking changes nothing. It does not alter the fact that the Trow will soon hunt me down and kill me. And it does not change the fate of Paerries." After he took another long pull on the bottle, it disappeared. "But first let us try a few things that might change outcomes. You saw that Aran can fight like the Trow, with shield and bolt?"

"Yes. Well, I've seen the shield. Not so much of the bolt. He told me this is something you taught him. He explained the mechanism to me, but I'm less familiar with magic than he is, so it doesn't come naturally. I couldn't remember how to do it when the harpy-faced Faeries attacked just now."

"Do you wish to complete your learning? I suspect with your existing fighting skills you will be a quick study, despite the lack of magical experience. That is good, as I do not think your colony has much time."

Her mouth was dry, her hands clasped tightly together. "I'd happily accept a death sentence for a tool to help save the colony. Will … will you stand beside us?"

"No," he said flatly. "This is your fight. I have my own. But I will do my best to make it fairer."

Scene 3

THEST (TROW)

As he stood beside the lake, Thest twisted the stone on the chain he wore around his neck. Normally hidden in his tunic, it emerged when he was nervous. He watched the lightning's almost constant flashes across the water, thousands of strikes every hour. The Humans called this "Lake Maracaibo" and its lightning "Catatumbo," meaning "the everlasting storm." He turned his face up into the heavy rain, allowing the water to cascade down his cheeks. *This world! This world is filled with so much beauty!*

His wounds were largely healed, but his mind refused to still. He fingered the rough turquoise, a gift from his father on his first excursion into this world. His father, who with his mother had backed the queen, failed to survive the Trow wars that had propelled Thest's career.

The lightning flashed, and the booms of thunder collided like the marks of war among giants. A nearby strike stabbing into the lake brought his mind back to the present. *Never confuse faith that you will prevail in the end with the discipline to confront the most brutal facts of your current reality.*

The last two weeks had brought everything into place. A new prince had been born, freeing Thest to finish Faelen. He and Demist had set up the plan for her attack on the colony. Because Faelen had been protecting it, they postponed the attack in case they needed to dispatch him as part of the battle. She and her squad launched their attack several hours ago. The other pieces around the world were in place and ready to go, except for two.

They could not find Faelen, which was a surprise but not too much of a concern. He would turn up as soon as he was drunk, which happened almost daily. But they also could not find Aran, which was worrisome. Fod had searched everywhere, and none of their spies could tell them where he was. Fod had confirmed that the other Paerrie, the battle Paerrie, was back at the colony. Thest was unaccustomed to failure. Once Faelen was removed from the picture, however, there would be no more surprises. An attack on the colony would end the warrior Paerrie and Storng and draw Aran out from hiding.

Demist had been prepared if Faelen tried to defend the colony. She was to contact Thest since only he was allowed to kill Faelen. *So what is going on with her? She should be finished by now.*

Like the Paerries, the Trow could communicate over long distances without the aid of technology, but it would be heard by every Trow on the Earth. Because they could jump through space on Earth, they usually found it easier to talk to someone face-to-face. Today he had expected, yet not received, word of Demist's success in destroying the Paerries' Kawran Colony. He took the risk of projecting to her.

"Demist?"

No answer, but that did not necessarily mean anything. She could be in the middle of a battle or just postponing the good news of a victory. Asking her where she was would be foolish and alert Faelen to her proximity. It was past time, however, and she could always send a quick messenger, but she had not.

Did his worry represent affection for her or concern regarding the mission? Concern for his son? He once had deep affection for her when they were younger, but their stay in Earth's contamination changed them both. Now he loved the memory of her, but her actual presence more often irritated than soothed. But she was reliable, resourceful, and bold. And because their son's life was at risk, highly motivated. She was a more than competent general—something must be wrong.

"Fod," he called to his ever-present aide, sitting nearby in darkness but illuminated every few seconds by the lightning. In several strides, Fod was at Thest's side and awaiting instructions.

"Continue the search for Faelen," Thest told him. "He is not supposed to be able to hide from us."

"Not when he is drinking. As you know, if he stops the liquor, he can mask like any other Trow."

"Find him! He is never far from his beloved parrots. Come find me when he is located."

Thest flickered away, reappearing at the edge of the apparently unoccupied Paerrie colony. Recent blast marks scorched several structures, signaling a fight, but he saw no bodies. The Trow disappeared when they died of non-magical causes, as did Paerries. So if the Trow were struck by arrows or bullets, their bodies would be gone. But if they were felled by magic bolt, their bodies would remain. No bodies.

Two of his guards appeared beside him. The three walked the empty paths among the Paerrie trees. Mostly, the Paerrie dwellings were too small for them to go in, but they were also too small to hide a Trow body. One of the guards peeked into a window, but he said he saw nothing. There. There on the edge of the colony Thest saw a foot sticking out of a bush. Slowly, heads swiveling, the three inched toward the body.

It was the first of a line of Trow bodies, laid out respectfully behind the row of bushes in what had been gardens. Over half had wounds that looked like they had come without warning, mostly on the backs and sides. Ambushed. The rest appeared to have died in a face-to-face fight. Their bodies were proof they had died from magic, not bullets. But there was something different about them. He stared a moment before realizing what it was—when a Trow died from a Trow bolt, the wound was large, but these bodies had dozens of smaller wounds.

He was long past shock at the sight of bodies—as a veteran of the Trow wars, he had seen many, including those of friends and family. He recalled standing over the bodies of his parents. Still, as he walked down the silent row, he was filled with dread. This was undoubtably Demist's force. As he continued down the row of bodies, he came upon what he had feared.

Demist had dozens of wounds and must have put up a fierce struggle. He knelt beside her and stared at her beautiful face, relaxed in death. He felt that place where Trow emotions live—diminished, scarred, and shriveled from exposure to technology for so long. That place ached. He reached for the talisman that always hung from her neck and fingered it gently as his vision blurred. He lifted it off her and slipped it into his pocket.

He pushed up, studied the arrangement of the bodies, and searched for messages intended or accidental. They had been moved here from the different places they would have fallen, away from the elements and hidden from the carrion eaters. No trophies taken. No disrespect. Not of Trow doing, not by Faelen's hand, as he would have left them where they fell.

These Trow have been bested by Paerrie warriors.

Replacing his sadness was a rising tide of anger, not at the Paerries, which as far as he was concerned would be akin to being angry at vermin. They were what they were, and they would be dealt with soon enough. Only one Trow would have been so bold, so stupid, so reckless as to arm vermin. Faelen.

A low moan came from the line of bodies, and the guards rushed forward. A young Trow male was struggling to stand, but he collapsed back onto the ground. Thest knelt beside him.

"What happened?" As he asked, he studied the young soldier's wounds—he had a poisoned arrow protruding from his arm and would not be alive long. "What happened?" he repeated, shaking him hard.

The warrior coughed, blood speckling his chin and Thest's face. "We surrounded the colony at dawn. They had ... guards posted but most were just waking up. A troop of howler monkeys ... was moving nearby. Must have seen us, starting barking. Suddenly the— the Paerries were gone." He coughed again, and blood flowed more freely down his chin. "You could ... tell they were still there. But we c-could no longer ... sense them. Paerrie guards started shouting. All the Paerries fled to their ... to their ... buildings. Demist ... she sent part of us in ... on the ground ... and the rest ... by air. More of them came from the sky." His eyes closed, his head fell to the side. He gave one final gasp before he stopped breathing and flickered from the world.

Thest could fill in the rest of the story himself. The ones on the ground were surprised by an attack with Trow bolts fired by the Paerries and perhaps these poisoned arrows as well. The Trow in the air had fought longer but would have eventually lost when additional

Paerrie forces attacked from above. Demist must have already been dead or she would have called for support. With no order to withdraw, the force would have fought to their last member. They were all dead. And it was Faelen's doing.

He felt his blood rise, and his fury suddenly had focus. He could sense where Faelen was, and he knew Fod could as well—it was like a beam of light suddenly shown with Faelen at its center. The traitor seemed to be announcing his presence.

Wanting to be the one to kill him, required to be according to Xafar's order, Thest blinked away. He reappeared at the base of a tall, broad-canopied tree, where Fod stood flanked by four Trow. Thest's two guards also appeared.

Above them Faelen was lying on a branch and singing. Thest recognized it as an old love song on its surface, sung about the love of a young Trow for another, but widely understood as a metaphor for the Trow's love of Earth. He looked at Fod and lifted a brow.

"He just appeared. And he makes no effort to conceal," The sound of singing echoed throughout the forest. "What of Demist?"

"Dead," he said flatly. "The entire raiding party was dead. Because of the treachery of this one. Perhaps he was even directly involved. If only I had more time, I would love to stretch his death out over a century."

Thest and the party floated up and surrounded Faelen. He seemed unsurprised by their arrival, and he continued his ballad while watching birds, they did no seem to be parrots, on a nearby tree. Thest followed his gaze and this time chose not to destroy the birds. Instead he flicked his fingers and sent a wave through the air, causing them to fly up swirling and screeching as a few feathers floated down behind them.

Faelen stopped singing. "That was completely unnecessary. Did it make you feel better?" His speech was slurred, and he raised the mostly empty bottle to his lips to drink deeply.

"You have dishonored your father," Thest railed. "Betrayed your race. Accomplished nothing. You think you have done something, but your action is only an inconvenience. We will wipe out the Paerries. Perhaps the parrots as well, so there can be no more Paerries. And you will die a whimpering death, as you deserve."

"'You will die a whimpering death,'" Faelen said, mocking Thest solemnly. "Blah, blah, blah. How do you stand to listen to yourself?" Most of the slurring vanished as he continued. "I will die. Of that I am certain." He paused as though having forgotten what he would say next and then remembering went on. "But as for the rest, you are wrong. I have changed the world. In more ways than you can imagine. You will curse my name the rest of your short life." He threw back his head and laughed.

Thest fired point-blank into Faelen's chest and blasted him from the tree. Faelen bounced off branch after branch and crashed in a crumpled heap at the base of the tree. His face clear of emotion, Thest looked down at the body.

"Leave him out in the open," he ordered the others. "Let the birds and the ants carry him into this world. His spirit will never find its way back to the Land. And he will never trouble me again."

After speaking briefly with Thest's guards, Fod asked, "What about the colony? No one can find its residents. Apparently Faelen not only taught them how to fight, he also taught them how to hide."

"Forget them for now. We must stay focused on the plan." He

remembered his son and Xafar's hold over him. "We are too close to get distracted now. Without this one, they have no idea what to do with what they have learned. We will deal with them later. I hope the shamans Aran and Storng survive, and their warrior-wench as well. I will take them to the Land as a gift for the king. Their screams will fill his halls for generations."

Scene 4

Aran (Silth)

When Aran climbed into the truck, he'd assumed that the Faerie Angel and the Human Stanley Ryder were on their way to initiate their catastrophe. Much later that day, he realized he was wrong.

Stanley Ryder seemed to be on a tour of "farewell stops" that went on day after day. He was saying goodbye to many friends, while hinting broadly that they should be prepared for "something big." Angel seemed fine with it, busying herself with phone calls and whispered instructions to someone apparently far away.

Aran followed from the air when the pair switched locations. Using his best harvesting skills, he tailed them into the houses and apartments they visited, where he watched Stanley Ryder give away his belongings and bid farewell to friends. The delay gave Aran a chance to rest and heal. But he was always afraid to leave them, not sure if he could find them again if they suddenly changed locations. He needed work on tracking others. Faelen had taught him how to disappear in one place and reappear in another, but Aran continued to have difficulty visualizing his destinations, even the return to where he left Stanley Ryder.

He'd had two weeks but he still had no clue how he'd stop the two,. They discussed no more details of their plan. He didn't have the phone Storng had given him—it was back with his belongings. He couldn't unlock other phones, much less determine how to make a call or to whom. One unlocked phone asked if he needed to make an emergency call, and he answered "yes."

"911. What is your emergency?" the Human female had said in a Spanish monotone.

"There's a big bomb in a building. They're going to use it to start a volcano."

"What is the building's address?"

"What's an address?"

"Where is the building, sir?"

He thought, then said, "Near Yellowstone." The voice did not indicate whether or not she knew Yellowstone's location.

The monotone continued. "Is anyone in immediate danger?"

"They say it's 'nuclear' and people will be hurt for hundreds of miles."

"Who has the bomb, sir?"

"A Human named Stanley Ryder and a bunch of Faeries."

A pause, then sharply, "Please identify yourself."

He had set the phone back on the kitchen table where he had found it. Before long, several police cars took away the Human male who lived there. Nothing useful seemed to happen.

Two days later, Aran heard Angel admonish someone on the phone. "Don't talk about that—Homeland hears everything. They'll stop the plane."

Aran found a quiet place among the trees and spoke aloud, "Oh mighty Homeland, hearer of all things, stop these evil ones before they reach the nuclear device!" Once again, nothing useful seemed to happen.

He hoped Storng was having better luck. In desperation, he set fire to the roof of the building where Angel and Stanley Ryder were staying, hoping to destroy something critical to the success of their plan. But Angel extinguished the flames before the fire department even arrived. Each day Aran failed.

The pause also gave Aran time to think. Why was he, a small forest creature, trying to interfere in the affairs of Humans and Faeries? The true target of the Faerie attack was the Humans. What did Aran care whether the Faeries culled back the overgrown Human population? The Faeries had created them—did that give them some responsibility for the Humans' damage to the Earth? Like Humans had with cows? But the Faeries had created the Silth as well, and Aran didn't feel that gave them the right to exterminate them. Moreover, the Faerie plan would cause the deaths of many creatures besides the Humans and potentially the deaths of the Silth themselves. In many ways the Humans were irrelevant—Aran was fighting for life on Earth. He knew that Shra, for this reason, would approve of his fight.

Finally, Stanley Ryder and Angel started packing suitcases and boxes and putting them in the hall. Aran chose a case with a mesh expansion to allow him air and the ability to hear what was happening. After partially emptying it, he stuffed the clothes he'd removed into the garbage. He climbed inside, worried that the case might be opened to add some last-minute item, but they loaded it in the truck and drove off.

Angel was updating the Human on their project's progress. "The transit team has already moved the device to Bozeman, Montana, where it should be easy to move it into the park. The preparation team has gotten the site ready. They have been working on a 'deep' archaeological dig inside the park for almost a year. The hole they have dug is much deeper than the Park Service realizes, and the device will be placed inside it to be detonated. The crust is very thin there, and the hole will help direct the blast to activate the super volcano."

Stanley Ryder was quiet as they drove on. Peering through the mesh of his suitcase, Aran could see Angel looking pensively at her companion.

"You going chicken on me? You do remember we are doing this for the Earth. This will save her."

"No, I'm fine." But Aran thought Stanley Ryder didn't sound particularly convincing.

They drove in silence and before long reached a small airport. After the gate slid open, they drove out on the tarmac and stopped, getting out to speak to a man inspecting a little plane. Two young men started moving the boxes and suitcases, including Aran's, from truck to plane. He felt no trepidation—after dealing with poachers, maelstroms, and Faeries, flying on a plane seemed like no big deal. The Humans and Angel got in, and the plane shuddered as it started up. The noise didn't prevent him from falling into a deep sleep, from which he awoke later, disoriented, as the wheels bounced on the runway and the plane taxied to a stop. After a few minutes, he heard voices, and the boxes and suitcases around him shifted as they were pulled out.

He looked through the mesh at another small airport, this one treeless with heat rising in waves from the black tarmac, and he had the sensation of moisture being sucked from his body as he was loaded into a blue van. Even though his shoulder had been healing well, each jolt had him pressing his lips tightly to keep from groaning. Before long he was moved again, this time to a nondescript white and brown warehouse-looking building.

Inside the huge room, his suitcase was added to a large pile of other suitcases and containers beside a green cargo van, rear doors open. In the center of a table was a complex device he assumed was the nuclear bomb, surrounded by six or seven people performing different tasks. No, not all "people," since at least half the group consisted of Faeries. And although he knew what a bomb was, he remained unclear as to what "nuclear" meant. The only meaning conveyed to him when Stanley Ryder mentioned it was "really big, really bad."

Dirt-encrusted equipment—picks, shovels, buckets, and scaffolding—was scattered around the room, and crates bearing the words "ARTIFACTS" and "THIS END UP" were stacked nearby. He had no idea what artifacts were. As he listened to the group interact, he could tell that, like Stanley Ryder, the other Humans were unaware that they were surrounded by Faeries. They were too casual, treating them like Human colleagues.

As a tall young man started toward the boxes and suitcases that included Aran's, another called out, "Sam! Eight or nine. Enough to stack up at the back door and behind the driver's seat."

Several others joined in as Sam pulled boxes and cases from the pile. Aran could see them loading the van, and he grew increasingly nervous when his suitcase remained unchosen. The movement of boxes stopped as all hands gathered around the now crated bomb, and Angel and Stanley Ryder helped lift it into the van. The group returned to shove more boxes in between the bomb crate and the van doors. Aran winced as his suitcase tumbled through the air, and he sank further into it as it was tucked into the last available space inside the van.

With a low rumble, the van moved out of the warehouse and idled in the parking lot. Aran shifted to listen through the suitcase's mesh. They were waiting for other cars to join theirs. "There's the third car. Let's go." The van took off.

Angel was saying, "—paperwork with the Park Service is done. When we arrive, they will confirm everyone's picture ID's. Give us approval to head to the site. To them we are a team of archaeologists arriving with more equipment. They are used to us coming and going. Once there, we will see a shack. The hole is in there. One of the biggest logistical challenges was getting it deep enough while hiding the dirt generated."

Stanley Ryder snorted. "The team smuggled a nuke into town, and the dirt from digging a hole was 'one of the bigger logistical challenges'?"

"Yeah, it is all relative, I guess. But it was a lot more dirt than from digging up old bones. Anyway, we will get to the site, drop the bomb into the hole tonight while the rest of the team gets far away. You set the timer—it is on a machine near the hole—for two hours. Bolt like a bat out-of-hell. Remember, two hours' fast driving will take you beyond the direct blast zone. About a hundred miles away if all goes right, but still in the area affected by volcanic ash fall. You will have an oxygen mask, so it will just be a question of whether or not the car's air filters fill up too fast."

"What about the people without masks?" When Angel did not respond, Stanley Ryder asked, "How far do the effects of the volcano go?"

Angel gave a heavy sigh, clearly exasperated. "Man, you know the answers to these questions. You are asking the same ones over and over. Many people will die. The disruption of technologies, power production, and food delivery will cause others to die. Diseases not seen in the U.S. for decades will reappear. I know this is hard, but in return the Earth will live again."

"Why can't you start the timer?"

"Because four of us are gonna 'replenish' the group's funds. We have got jewelry stores, banks, and other high-value targets to hit on our way out of town. We hit them fast, and we do not worry about cameras and security because those places will be destroyed in a few hours. The police will have more important things to do. But we need about six hours' head start. Gives us time to rob the places, but not enough time for them to upload info to the FBI."

Aran was having trouble breathing and put his face against the mesh. His feet were going numb. Was what he was feeling due to his confinement in the case, or from overhearing this Faerie's casual dismissal of so many lives? *I'd welcome a world with fewer Humans, but not achieved this way.*

When Stanley Ryder said nothing, Angel went on. "You can not get cold feet now. The world is counting on you. You said you could do this."

"I know I said it before, but I'm still having trouble getting past the kids. And I know I said they're just statistics, but they don't deserve to die painfully, which they will. Their parents may have earned it. Their society definitely did. But as individuals they're just trying to get by. They have … hopes and dreams."

"Stop. You are freaking yourself out. This is not about earning or deserving it, or any of that stuff. It is about the same reasons they choose to kill the coyotes and the bears, or thin the elk herd. It is a practical need to allow the other species to thrive and is for their own good. Without thinning back, the species of man will overwhelm its resources and take itself out as well as much of the rest of the world. Hard, but necessary."

The van stopped in a parking lot next to the park's administrative building. "Paperwork should only take a minute," Angel said as they got out.

Aran thought furiously. How could others not be aware of this? Could he tell someone … someone who would not be distracted by the creature bearing the news? Who does one call when Faeries are about to destroy the world? Maybe he could talk to Stanley Ryder and try to talk him out of it. He seemed to be the weakest link in the chain and having second thoughts. Perhaps if he showed himself to the Human, the shock would be enough to disrupt things. But when? When Stanley Ryder was alone, of course. If Aran appeared while Angel or any other Faeries were there, they'd merely kill him and proceed with their plan.

He knew nothing about disarming a bomb. While, thanks to Storng and Faelen, he was now stronger than the Faeries would expect, he had little hope of overcoming that many. Yes, the weak link was definitely Stanley Ryder. He had to find a way to get him alone.

Once they returned, Stanley Ryder had no sooner slammed his door than he announced, "I can't do this. It's not that I can't imagine it. I'd be okay living in a world where someone had done this. But not me. Not me."

"Too late to back out now, amigo. Turn left here."

The van bounced down a rutted path, tossing Aran back and forth in the case. He gritted his teeth, both in pain and frustration, while the two continued to argue. The Human grew increasingly adamant that he wouldn't be the one detonating the bomb.

Once more they rolled to a stop, and Angel said, "Well, here is the thing. All the check-in process here, as well as the entrance security video, is uploaded to the cloud. So later on, when they are trying to determine who did this, I will forever be an enigma to them. But they will know exactly who you are. And that you had a lead role in setting this whole—"

"There won't be anything to know if we don't do this."

"No, you miss my point. You have mostly served your usefulness. I do not need you conscious for anything else."

Zzzzzzt. The odd, dull buzz was followed a moment later by rustling and the door opening. A male voice shouted, "There you guys are!"

"Yeah, it was tense getting in," Angel called out. "Stanley Ryder's catching a little shuteye, so keep it down as you unload."

"Geez, he must be pretty frosty to be able to sleep at a time like this."

"No fear, dude. No fear."

Aran cut through the mesh of the bag and slid past the bomb, feeling queasy just being in its proximity. He squeezed past another crate and into the space between the driver and passenger seats, just as the rear doors opened.

Another male asked, "Whatda we do with these suitcases?"

"Just throw them on the ground," was Angel's answer.

Stanley Ryder was unconscious, breathing but slumped in the driver's seat in what looked like an uncomfortable sleeping position. Aran tried shaking, pinching, and hammering hard on the Human's arm, but he got no response. The buzzing he'd heard must have been Angel stunning Stanley Ryder, and Aran had no idea how long the Human would be out. He hadn't even known there was a stun version of the Faerie bolt.

The big bomb crate scraped as the team extracted it. From

the window Aran watched them move it beside the shed that must be housing the deep hole. Through the shed door, he could see someone at the controls of a machine, and he assumed it was the remote-control Angel had described. He watched helplessly as the team removed the bomb from the crate and carried it into the shed.

As a group of ten or so assembled outside the shed, Aran used the hand crank on the door to lower the window slightly and listen. All the Faeries were busy with tasks—the group that was gathering was comprised of only Humans. After lining up in front of a Faerie-operated video camera, each person read a short statement giving his or her reasons for participating in the event. Although several were nervous and shaking, none wore masks, seemingly unconcerned that the video would make them wanted individuals. When the last statement was read, the group waited, murmuring among themselves, as the cameraman fiddled with the camera. His thumbs-up and "it's all been uploaded to the cloud, so we're good to go" was followed by cheers, backslaps, and hugs.

A pretty weak way for the world to end, Aran thought.

Angel waved the Humans toward a grey cargo van. "Okay, everybody in."

While the team filled up the vehicle, Angel spoke with the driver and occupants, too quietly for Aran to hear. After a few minutes of conversation, a female Faerie emerged from the front passenger seat, and she had no sooner shut the door when the grey van pulled away. She and Angel hurried back to the green van, and Aran scrambled into the back, feeling utterly exposed. Although boxes still separated the back from the front, between them was an empty, open space where the bomb crate had been.

As she opened the driver door, Angel was explaining, "The Humans will be knocked out and the van left in the radius where they will all be killed. But there will still be enough DNA to identify them. It will look like they waited too late to run, got caught in the blast."

"And him?" the female Faerie asked, grunting under the load of helping Angel pull Stanley Ryder from the cab.

"The video feed will show him sitting at the controls right until the explosion. We just have to position him so he looks conscious and functioning." They carried the Human's limp body toward the shed, leaving the driver door open. Aran slipped out and hid on one side of the shed.

The female Faerie came back out and scanned the site. "Everything looks good," she shouted back over her shoulder. "I will drive off in one of the cars so it will also be seen leaving." After she left, the remaining Faeries disappeared, leaving only Aran, Angel, and the unconscious Stanley Ryder.

The thought of fighting Angel intimidated Aran. Though he'd defended himself against Faeries, he'd never attacked one. And there was something just fundamentally scary about her. He considered looking in the window but was afraid she'd spot him. He was glamoured as an amazon green parrot, which he knew might be conspicuously out of place here in the American west, but he didn't know an appropriate indigenous bird.

Creeping around to the front door, he looked through the space where the hinges separated the door from the wall. Angel was arranging Stanley Ryder at the control panel. She stepped back to look through the camera and readjusted him a little.

Inhaling deeply, Aran was just about to slip inside when he

saw Stanley Ryder stirring. Adjusting the tripod height, Angel had her back to the Human and didn't seem aware that he was conscious. The Human looked around, clearly confused, and his eyes narrowed as he recognized Angel's back. He slid his hand noiselessly to the wrench lying on the panel, lurched off the stool, and staggered toward her.

She whirled around and gave an ugly laugh. "Did you grow a pair all of a sudden? Oh, wait. That was a sneak-up-behind-move. Not that brave. What now?"

As Stanley Ryder swung the wrench, Angel easily dodged the blow aimed for her head and chuckled. The Human stalked the Faerie, and the Faerie played with the Human. When they rotated so that Angel's back was to the door, Aran stepped into the doorway and raised his arm, marshaling his energy for a killing bolt. But whether because of some small sound or just a change in the draft, she sensed his presence. She leaned away from the bolt, which burned a small hole through the side of the building.

"What the hell!" Stanley Ryder shouted, looking from the doorway to the wall. "A parrot?"

Angel's face was twisted in fury, and she turned her back on Stanley Ryder. Aran got his shield up just as she fired at him.

"Damn!" Although he had just seen his former friend shoot blue lightning from her palm, Stanley Ryder swung the wrench again. Angel held up a hand, and the tool froze a few inches from her head. With an almost casual flick of the Faerie's fingers, Stanley Ryder slammed against the wall and slumped to the clay floor.

With one hand, Angel fired bolt after bolt into Aran's shield, using the other to fling anything not nailed down—tools, rocks, half-empty soda cans—at him. The constant barrage from the advancing Faerie was too much. Aran couldn't find an opening to return fire. Finally, with Angel standing almost directly over him firing point-blank, Aran's shield flickered out.

As Aran dropped his glamour to conserve what little energy he had left, Angel changed her aspect as well. She was suddenly taller, more muscular—a fierce-looking Faerie in leather battledress. Her black hair formed a Mohawk on top of her head and continued as dreadlocks down her back. Sharper than Faelen's, her features were dominated by a twisted smile never making it to her black eyes.

Towering over Aran, Angel lifted her hand as though to administer the final blast, but instead she picked up a roll of duct tape from the table. She pulled out a short strip and slapped it on Aran's heaving chest. When she released the tape, it continued on its own with amazing speed and wrapped around him, first up to secure his arms and mouth and then down to pull his legs tightly together, causing him to fall. When the winding stopped, only his eyes and the top of his head showed above his mummy-esque body. Unable to speak or move, he lay staring at Angel. She gave him a kick to make certain he was fully secured.

Angel turned back to the controls, saying jovially, "The end of the Paerries is near. Their end, and that of the Human virus infecting this land. The return of the Trow to this world as its rightful rulers is at hand. In five Earth years, we will return and finish our work." She smirked at Aran, who was wriggling in vain trying to loosen the tape. "Your friend, the traitor Faelen, is dead at Thest's hand, his body rotting in the forest. If your colony is not already gone, it soon will be. In some ways I would like to leave you alive, just to enjoy thinking about how you would suffer in your diminished world."

Aran stopped squirming, trying to decide if the Faerie was bluffing. As though reading his mind, Angel said, "Your colony may have evaded the first assault, but it is only a matter of time. I was not there for Faelen's end, Fod was. He told me Faelen died whimpering. Begging for mercy. Recanting. But die he did, as the worst of cowards." As she spoke, she faltered a little, as if Aran might know she was lying. Indeed, he was thinking with complete certainty Faelen was no coward.

She resumed her work. "First order of business—retrieving and erasing the last few minutes of recording." She moved to the camera. "Images were automatically uploaded to the cloud, so they have to be destroyed."

He didn't completely understand everything she said, especially about the "cloud" which had been mentioned before. It certainly must be a special cloud, he thought. But he did get that the Faerie was eliminating and manipulating evidence.

She gave a flick of her hand, and another roll of duct tape floated to her. As before, she pulled out a small piece, this time flinging it toward Brophy, awake and trying to push himself up. The tape left him, like Aran, unable to speak or move.

"And you, my dear Stanley Ryder, will be remembered through the rest of the short existence of mankind as the one who helped kill the race. The murderer of women and children." Angel struck a pose over the Human, ramrod straight with hands on hips as if to emphasize how alien she was. "But for the Trow … well, I was going to say you are the one who saved the Earth from its dominance by the Human species. But you failed at that and have become just a tool. You can take comfort knowing we will be much better stewards of the Earth."

She eyed the confused expression on Stanley Ryder's face. "Oh, of course. You have no idea what is going on, do you? Well, I am what you Humans call a 'Faerie,' though we call ourselves the Trow. We are from another world, another dimension—no one is quite sure what the relationship of the worlds is. We used to rule this world but were driven out by Humans, our own creation, who were completely unaware of us as more than myth."

She tipped his head toward Aran. "And him? He is a Paerrie, the half-breed scum of the forest. Lesser creatures. Bastards created by the Trow artist-bioengineers by crossing parrots with Trow." As though the Human had actually spoken in response to this revelation, Angel shook her head sadly. "I know, it is quite disgusting, is it not? Well, we are going to fix it all."

Aran tried not to think of Faelen—it wasn't the time. But he could not help the tears that welled up and trickled down his taped cheeks. He knew he couldn't free himself. Theoretically he knew how to blink to another place, but how could he pin down the destination? By the time he got the tape removed wherever he ended up, it would be too late. He could call Storng and the other shamans, but he hadn't yet taught them how to transport like Faeries, so they couldn't possibly get here in time.

Angel said, "Zero hour will be 1:00. It is now 10:45. There is nothing left for you to do but die."

Angel was right—Aran could think of absolutely nothing. Despair overwhelmed him. He'd lost, let everyone down. Silth. Humans. The other Earth creatures.

He closed his eyes, accepting the inevitable and sliding into a meditative trance. Into his mind swam an image of Storng coaching him through the use of magic in fighting. He heard him saying, as clearly as if the old Silth were actually there, "There may come a time when you think you've lost a struggle and spent everything inside you. Relax. Calm yourself, and you will find your hidden reservoir."

He settled deeper in the trance. His consciousness spread out like a puddle and flowed through Stanley Ryder's bound body. He could feel the tension of the Human's muscles and the pounding of his heartbeat. Below the shack where Angel stood, Aran's mind spread through the roots, drawing nutrients out of the soil from the big tree outside. He gained awareness of Angel's body. The flow of her blood. Beat of her heart. Breaths she took. He had done this exercise many times with Storng, but never as anything more than a relaxation technique.

He tried to stop Angel's heart, but she just continued manipulating dials. He moved his focus back to the roots, sensing the dirt and moisture around them, but when he tried to move them, they resisted. Again, he heard Storng's voice. It is not the nature of roots to move suddenly. Earth magic is a slow thing. Water creates great canyons over centuries. Roots break the face of mountains over centuries.

He wiggled the fingers of his right hand, secured by the tape but pressing against one of his pants pockets. Scraping at the fabric, he worked his fingers inside, grasped the vial of dirt, and pried off the top with his thumb. He spilled the dirt into his pocket and dug his fingers into it. What he was attempting was new territory for him. He had influenced sentient beings before—he had warned a puma or crocodile or even Humans with stay-away spells—but never a living thing without coherent thought. Unlike Angel, Aran did not know how to manipulate inanimate objects, so he could not cause the wrench to fly through the air and smash into Angel's face. But he had a different idea. He did not draw on Faerie magic, since he had exhausted his store of it as his shield flickered out of existence. Instead he reached far deeper, into the Earth magic that was his legacy from his parrot mother. He relaxed and reached out to the tree.

As he concentrated, he felt the roots respond, gathering energy from the trees around them and the living creatures in the soil, grass, and bushes. The roots moved slightly. He concentrated harder and spoke the focusing words softly into the tape so Angel did not hear. More energy poured in from everything touching the ground. He felt the worms and bugs die as their energy was drained. An ache in his forehead became a sharp pain right behind his eyes. The clay floor buckled and shimmied.

Angel gaped at the floor, her right arm flew up, and she pointed at Aran. But before she could fire, a giant tree root tore through the clay at her feet, encircling and yanking her up toward the ceiling. Before Angel could blink away, Aran spread his consciousness from the root and took control of the Faerie's heart. This time, he stopped it.

Her eyes widened just before she went completely limp. The pain behind his eyes was so intense he could not sustain his concentration. The root relaxed, and Angel hit the floor with a thud. After resting a few moments, Aran let his consciousness flow once again into the root. Sweat poured off him, and he clenched his teeth against the pain. He drew the root toward him and manipulated two of its smaller subroots, forcing them to rip tape from the top half of his body until he could work his arm free. As the smell of the root's fresh dirt filled his nostrils, he released the tree, and the big root toppled to the ground. He stripped off the rest of the tape himself and rushed to Stanley Ryder, who came to as Aran tugged at his tape.

"What are you and what was she and oh-my-god did you turn off the timer?"

"Son of a toucan!" Aran flew over to the controls. The numbers were decreasing, but the rest of the apparatus made no sense, so he flew back and frantically yanked on the rest of Stanley Ryder's tape. "I have no idea how to stop a timer."

Finally free, the Human jumped to the controls. "In the movies, there's always an off button." He flipped a switch and grinned. "Done. Plenty of time to spare."

As it dealt with the adrenaline dump, Aran's body trembled, and the pain behind his eyes remained sharp and disorienting.

He looked at Stanley Ryder, now slumped on the floor with his back against the detonator. But he seemed in good enough shape to hear the answers to his questions. "Like she told you, Angel was a Faerie. An alien creature. I am a Silth, created by these aliens from what you call a parrot. Born on this Earth and wed to it. The Trow, Angel's race, also created Humans. Angel and her kind were driven from this world by the rise of man's technology and control over the planet. They want it back. So the plan was to wipe out Humans and Silth. Retake the world."

The Human's flushed face was returning to normal. He carefully rolled onto all fours and pushed himself up to standing. "But why'd she need me?"

Aran's trembling had lessened, the pain more tolerable. Flying up onto the table to be closer to Stanley Ryder's height, Aran thought a moment before concluding, "Apparently she wanted Human evidence at the scene, so no one would suspect anything and search for another explanation. I don't know why they cared. There must be a timing issue. They must need Humans to believe for some period of time that other Humans caused the cataclysm."

"What happens now? Can't the Faeries—Geez, I can't believe I'm saying that—just return and start the timer again?"

"Yes. Which is why it's crucial to get Human authorities here to take over the situation."

"Well, I know how to do that." Stanley Ryder pulled out his phone and typed in a couple of characters. But then he stopped, and his eyes panned the room.

"Something wrong?"

"Other than I was attacked by a Faerie, and I'm talking to some kind of parrot-man? What could be wrong? By the way, what's your name?"

"Aran."

"Okay, Aran. I'm just trying to figure out what the cops will see. And how I'll explain it. And I really don't want to be here when they come."

Aran knew it wasn't up to him to worry about Human justice for Stanley Ryder. He had mixed feelings about this man, without a doubt responsible for what almost took place, willing for it to happen even though unable to carry it out in the end. But in his favor, he did help fight against Angel.

"They'll figure out you were here from all the evidence Angel has left," Aran pointed out.

"That's okay. If this gets lots of news coverage, they'll have to think about the issues Nature Now has raised. They'll know how strongly we feel about this. Maybe it'll be good. Whether that means I live as a fugitive or go to jail, it doesn't much matter. Uh ... you know you're bleeding, right?"

Aran looked down at his shoulder. Blood seeped from the wound—it must have reopened in the struggle—and he felt a little dizzy.

"No, dude, from your eyes."

Aran touched his eyes and stared at the bright red blood staining his fingers. "I'm fine," he insisted. But he felt himself fading. "How do we get the authorities here?"

"Oh, yeah. I'll call 911 and tell them what's up. Then I'm going to scat in that car out there."

"My calling 911 once didn't work out so well."

The Human lifted a brow. "Well, I know they'll come with lots of firepower. And hard questions I don't want to try to answer. Wanna come?"

"No, I'm going to stay. Make sure everything is covered when the authorities get here."

"Okayyy …." The Human looked at him skeptically. "How's that work?"

When Aran ignored the question, Stanley Ryder shrugged and finished punching in the numbers. "Yeah, there's a big bomb at the archaeology site in Yellowstone Park. I think it's a nuke. The site is #137. Someone's been killed. And they may be back to set off the bomb any minute now. Hurry."

After pushing the "End" button, he set the phone on the table and pulled another from Angel's pocket. "They can track the GPS in mine, so they'll know it really is at Yellowstone." Aran had no idea what a GPS was but clearly something good. "I may get a little use out of her phone before they start looking for it."

He grinned. "Goodbye, talking-fighting-parrot-man. I don't begin to understand what happened today but thank you. I wouldn't be alive if not for you, and neither would a lot of others. This is so not the day I thought it would be."

As Aran listened to the Human drive away, he was getting woozier. He needed to find a place to hide and monitor things until the Humans had secured the place. He glanced at Angel's body, thinking something was not quite right—had it moved slightly from where it had been before? But he was too dizzy to stand there and figure out what was different.

Just as he reached the door, its frame exploded, skewering his face and arm with bits of wood. He whirled around. To his horror, a shaky Angel was on her feet, one hand pointing toward him. With the other, she flipped the cover off the switch Stanley Ryder had turned off and restarted the timer.

The bolt Aran fired went wide. When he fired again, the bolt was weak, and Angel had already put up her shield so she easily blocked it. Aran staggered toward her, his strength almost gone and the Faerie magic not yet recharged. As Angel dropped her shield and fired, Aran ducked behind a big wooden crate, which exploded when hit, blowing him backward into a pile of shovels and picks.

Angel screamed, "No, no, no!" and Aran shook his head trying to clear it, Angel slowly coming back into focus.

Lips parted in disbelief, teeth bared, Angel was transfixed by a blue hologram-like image of Faelen, who pointed at her, threw his head back, and dissolved in laughter. As the soundless image repeated in a continuous loop, she kept clicking the switch on and off. But each time, Faelen's laughing face appeared and, given her reaction, the timer was refusing to start. Taking advantage of her distraction—Aran used every last bit of his energy to blast a blue bolt into the Faerie's head. She jerked, twisted, and slid into an unmoving heap on the floor.

Is she really dead this time? He realized what was wrong before. When he believed he had killed Angel earlier, he didn't expect there to be a body. Now that he thought about it, though, Qwert's body had remained when she was killed by the Faeries. Death by magic must be different than other forms of death. As he mulled that over, he prepared to send Angel's body to the Land using the same spell he and Storng used to transfer harvested items there. It wouldn't do for Humans to find a dead Faerie here. Once Aran crossed water, the body would never be able to be summoned back to Earth.

He could barely raise his arms to his cloak pockets to remove the items he needed. He pulled the last reserves of stored energy from Shra's bracelet and his pendant, hardly able to hold his eyes open to complete the spell.

Just as Angel's body disappeared, Aran heard sirens in the distance, and he staggered outside. He fluttered awkwardly onto a branch of the tree that had saved his life, startled to find that, while still green, all of its leaves were withered and drooping. He managed to glamour as a great horned owl, which he could hold if he didn't move, and settled down to monitor what was happening. He hoped this kind of owl was indigenous. He thought about Faelen. He didn't really understand why the Faerie had taken up the fight against his own kind, but he was infinitely grateful he had. He had no idea what Faelen had done to the bomb, but he must've gotten access to it in the warehouse several days earlier and set the timer to freeze moments before detonation.

Lights and sounds poured into the darkening clearing. The responders had arrived quicker than Aran expected, and he wondered if Stanley Ryder had gotten away. Cars raced toward the shed but parked a safe distance away, some with roofs alive with lights and some unmarked with theirs hidden in grills or flashing from dashes. Trucks with various logos arrived bearing ladders, hoses, and equipment marked "Hazmat." Spotlights on poles were set up. Officials in different colors of uniform gathered in clusters, while others secured the site and checked in each arriving vehicle.

The scene swirled, and Aran drifted in and out of consciousness. During the times he was awake, he was only half-listening to what was being said. But the conversation between a Human male and female beneath his branch jolted him fully upright and completely alert. Both were about the same height, in dark suits with big tags hanging around their necks. Aran assumed they were official identification of some sort—he had seen Humans wear them before—but he couldn't make out any details.

"So how many went off?" the man asked the woman. He was taking quicks puffs of his cigarette and pacing four or five steps in each direction.

The woman cleared her throat, lit up her own cigarette, and spoke flatly, as though she couldn't believe her own report. "Four others just like this one."

"Wonder what happened here? Looks like some kind of fight."

"Don't know. I think it was internal, though—some falling out among them—not government. Maybe someone got cold feet. None of us knew this was happening. Freaking nuke, and we had no clue. How could that be? And stop pacing, will you? You're getting on my last nerve."

He stopped. "Heard it was some sort of eco-terrorist group."

"Yeah, but no one knows how they pulled off something this big. They had to have help, and apparently there's something weird behind the scenes. A video feed has been going out of this building for the last couple of hours. Someone tried to shut it down, erase it, but that didn't work."

"That's great, isn't it?"

"Weird thing is, it's been confiscated by Homeland. And they're not letting anyone look at it."

"Yeah, weird." Then he shrugged. "But they specialize in weird." He was silent a moment, then asked, "So what's the consequence? You know ... of four big nukes." The pacing started up again.

"It's bad, really bad. They were like this one—not really near big population centers but set up on volcanoes. The nukes went off underground, which sounds good, right? Except each was placed to activate a volcano, and three did right away. The fourth volcano hasn't blown yet, but the scientists say it could go any day. The three that blew spewed radioactive ash, rock, and lava for miles around them. And that was just how they started. Now they're pouring out ash and still erupting."

"Where?"

Before she answered, she tried to light another cigarette with the one she was finishing, but her fingers were trembling so badly she dropped the new one. She pulled another from the pack and lit it. "Indonesia, a super volcano like this one. Iceland, Ecuador, and Morocco. Don't know much about the last two yet, except that the bomb in Ecuador seems to have just irritated the volcano. It hasn't gone off yet. But if it does, there's a whole chain of volcanos that also will go. All the information's being gathered by satellites and drones, though, so no one's completely sure."

"How bad will it be?" He ground out his cigarette with the toe of his shoe and kicked dirt over it.

"Well, when I finish here tonight, I'm going home, packing up my family, and driving to my uncle's farm. I'm heading somewhere away from the cities, near some streams and farmland, and hoping we can make it. Maybe I'll report in, maybe not."

His eyes widened. "What does 'make it' mean?"

"Survival. Everyone, everything on the planet will be struggling to survive."

CHAPTER FOURTEEN

Scene 1

THEST (TROW)

"Status?"

Before Thest could speak, Xafar gestured to the other chair at the table. Thest obeyed. Other than as part of a meal, he had never sat in Xafar's presence, and he did not know anyone who had. He had heard advisors to the King's court had such privileges, but they did not consort with soldiers.

"All Trow have been evacuated from the Earth. We cannot return for approximately five Earth years, as the psychic trauma of mass extinction will be toxic for us until then. At that time there will be few Humans left. Also a fraction of the species that existed yesterday. I hope the Paerrie will die off as well. But if any are left, we will exterminate both them and the remaining Humans when we return. I had considered moving the remaining Humans to reservations to maintain a viable source of slaves, but I think they would be more trouble than they are worth. Biomorphing for art or entertainment will be banned when we return. No more Humans or Paerries will be made."

"And all went according to plan?"

Thest knew Xafar's spies would have already told him that was not the case. "One device did not go off, unfortunately in a technologically advanced North American country. Another went off but has not yet activated the volcanoes surrounding it. In the end it will not matter, as the effects of the activated volcanoes will be sufficient to wipe out food for most of the population in North and South America. They will die slowly like much of the rest of the world. We believe Paerrie interference occurred in North America. But we were successful in hiding Trow involvement from the Humans. Consequently, they will not die hating and cursing us, reducing the psychic trauma. Nor will they be prepared for us when we return. The Paerries ... well, that is why we raised the originally planned three years to five. They will know we were the cause of their suffering and death. We will have to test whether the Earth magic responds to this, or whether the fact that they are partly 'us' saves the Trow from consequences."

"Time at that scale is not an issue for us. And Faelen?"

"He was involved in several more fights and perhaps responsible for the successful disappearance of the Paerrie colony before it could be terminated. He was eliminated. My regrets for your loss."

"Hmmmm." As Thest expected, Xafar acknowledged the sentiment with minimal emotion. "I understand you had your own loss. My regrets. Do we know how Paerries managed to wipe out a squad of Trow, led by someone of Demist's stature?"

Thest paused. Depending on how Xafar choose to interpret the events, Thest had failed to eliminate the Paerries, and Xafar could kill both him and his son. "I believe that Faelen trained them, just as he did the shaman Aran."

"Then my regret is intensified by my responsibility. You will be rewarded for your service and your sacrifice. Your son has prospered here at my court. He will continue to do so, whether or not he chooses to stay."

"As always, your kindness toward my son is greatly appreciated. The reward that I desire is to lead our triumphant return to Earth in five years. We should assume there will be Paerries left who have the knowledge to perform Trow magic. I want to remove their race from existence."

"Then it shall be. In the meantime, you shall be the guest of honor in a series of dinners."

Thest had tried to mask his feelings about Demist's demise, but despite the typical Trow difficulty in reading emotions, Xafar seemed to notice. Perhaps the doorway had read them. "But not tonight, Thest. I know you mourn. I am sure the dinners are not what you will want to do, but you must, later this week. I need you to show the flag of triumph on my behalf."

Thest knew the victory on Earth would cement Xafar's rule in the Land. The dinners were the opportunity for the Trow court to acknowledge that power and reach that conclusion. They were also Thest's opportunity to rise in Trow society, to become part of the court. Demist's aspiration, not his.

"As you wish," he replied. At Xafar's nod, he bowed and left.

Thest's walk through the government palace was a blur, as was the walk down the road to his own home. Demist had been proud of the station represented by the proximity of their house to the palace. Thest did not care. Instead of greeting him as he entered, the servants kept to the shadows, making their presence known but not engaging him in conversation.

He closed the door to his sanctuary, a room where only he was allowed. In the sparse light, he sat down at his work table and picked up a small, hand-painted portrait of Demist, done in much younger days. Her voice back then had been the sound of a beautiful stream. He was different then as well.

He slammed the painting on the desk, refusing to get caught up in memory. Instead he sought the solace of anticipation. He thought about the extinction of the Paerries, hoping Aran, Storng, and their colony would survive the next five years just so he could end them. He tried to keep his mind on this even though thoughts of his own loss left him awash in loneliness.

He had to prepare the house for the arrival of his children. Trow custom required that they return to the family estate and remain there in "mourning," though they would not truly mourn Demist's passing, any more than they would mourn his when they returned upon his death. It was not that Trow children were without love for their parents—in normal families, there was deep affection. But families like theirs, where both parents had spent years in the contamination of Human technology, were not normal. The children would not grieve and would be astounded by his level of sadness and anger. Shocked that he mourned.

And his anger? Was it over her death or that she had died at the hands of vermin? He tried to drive sadness out with thoughts of revenge, but it was an imperfect process. It had not been enough to kill Faelen.

He needed to destroy the Paerries and make plans for retaking the Earth. But he had plenty of time, five Earth years would be a very long time in the Land

Scene 2

Joss (Human)

Joss and Kate were on a major supply run. They'd gone into San José and were stocking up everything they could fit in the big truck they'd borrowed from Joss's friend. One of them stayed with the vehicle while the other went in to buy supplies.

They bought spare tires and car batteries, strapping them to the roof. They purchased big containers of toilet paper and boxes of canned goods, as well as equipment for growing food indoors, canning, and preparing it. They bought equipment for the horse they did not yet own. As they filled the truck and arranged for delivery of more items, they tried not to attract too much attention. Few others seemed to be stocking up on any more than the usual weekly supply runs.

Joss ducked into a nearby bookstore, where she could still see the truck, and grabbed every book on raising chickens, farming, canning, and survival skills. When finished, she waited for Kate by the truck. She spent the time remembering the call from Brophy that had touched off their shopping spree. Because she hadn't recognized the incoming phone number, she was surprised to hear Brophy's voice.

"I didn't set off the bomb," he said, *with none of the preamble of small talk or flirting she would have expected. "I was supposed to, but I helped stop it instead. With the help of a ... and I know this sounds completely crazy ... a parrot-man! Can you believe that?"*

When she tried to answer 'yes, I can,' the words would not come out. Storng's spell.

"And it sounds even crazier, but Angel turned out to be an alien—a bad Faerie."

"That actually doesn't sound crazy at all," she said, since Storng had told her that as well. "I never liked her. Weird and scary gal."

"Wait ... you accept that she was a bad Faerie? I'm not sure I believe it. You are so ... so unpredictable. Anyway, no time for that. I can't stay on the phone long."

He outlined the consequences of the volcanoes activated around the world. He said the governments had to know by now and must not be talking about it to avoid panic, but it was going to be awful—maybe extinction kind of awful. Theories had started to bubble up on the internet, but no one was taking them seriously yet.

He told her that he and his group had studied the anticipated effects of the Yellowstone volcano. The consequences set in motion by the Faeries was meant for something different. If the Yellowstone volcano had been triggered with all the other volcanos there be would be mass extinction of most species on Earth. Because that bomb didn't go off and the Ecuador volcanoes had not yet erupted, a mass die-off would still happen. But perhaps there was a chance for survival. No matter what, life was about to become extremely difficult for the entire planet.

"You need to stock up on everything," he insisted. "Chances are it's all going to run out."

"What about you? Where will you go?" she asked.

"I'm on the run. I'm using Angel's phone, but I assume this call is being monitored. They think I'm responsible for Yellowstone. But I was set up to be the fall guy, and like I said, I helped stop the bomb. At first, I thought it would be okay for Nature Now to be associated with trying to activate it. But now that I know what actually happened, I don't want *anything to do with it. Much of humanity will die hating whomever they think did this."*

"Turn yourself in."

He laughed. "Somehow I don't think my story of alien Faeries and talking-fighting parrot-men will convince them I wasn't part of what happened. They'd think I was going for an insanity defense. Just wanted to let you know it wasn't me. And to warn you to get ready for what's coming."

"Brophy, take care of—" but the connection was broken.

Kate came through the parking lot, pushing a flat dolly loaded with supplies. A young man trailed behind her, pushing a similarly stacked cart. Guns and rifles, bought at the hunting and fishing store, were carefully balanced on top.

"Hey, Joss. I was telling Max here about the store we're opening, how hard it is to round up all the items for it. He was saying that many of the small stores stock up here at their big warehouse store. Warned him we'll be seeing a lot of him."

"Great to meet you, Max." If Brophy was right, Joss thought she and Kate probably would never see Max again, which seemed unfortunate as he was enjoying comparing tattoos with Kate. In the last few days his future had changed dramatically, and he was totally unaware. She envied his blissful ignorance.

On the way to their next stop, Joss outlined how they would set up a network of contacts in the rainforest biology stations and villages near their compound. All day Joss had witnessed Kate flip back and forth from denial to skepticism to fear. She called her brother in New Orleans and asked him to join them right away, while he still could, but he had been doubtful of her apocalyptic predictions. Regardless of which mode she was in, however, she had been willing to humor Joss in gathering the supplies. She joked the worst to happen might be that they really would have to open a store to sell all the stuff they were gathering. Considering the supply run was causing Kate to drain her bank account, she was being pretty understanding.

Joss watched some children in the little playground they passed, imagining a specter reaching for the children, its clawed hand just inches above their heads. Like Max, they had no idea. She wanted to stop and shout at them, "Run!" But run where? Do what? Should she be racing through the city streets telling everyone about their future? Go on a local talk show and spread the word? Someone else would do it soon enough.

In the meantime, she wanted to save a very small part of the world—her beloved patch of rainforest and its residents, Human and other. Other. She recalled the wounded Silth she'd taken in. Was Aran the one who helped Brophy stop the Yellowstone bomb? Probably. Who was he, and was he still alive? What were the Silth? Storng had told her that they were born on Earth but fathered by the aliens—Faeries like Angel. Who were the aliens and what would they do next?

As she thought about Storng's magic, preventing her from talking about the Silth, she alternated between being angry and grateful. She'd like to talk to Brophy and Kate—of course, Kate would have no idea what she was talking about. She promised herself that she'd find the Silth and help them survive. Maybe they could help her as well. In the dark times sure to follow, she wasn't sure she and Kate would survive by themselves.

She considered the irony. She had spent most of her adult life trying to protect animals from loss of habitat accompanying Human prosperity, and to stop slaughter stimulated by the rich's willingness to purchase a jaguar pelt or a wild-caught parrot. Now she would end her days dealing with the consequences of Human hunger and desperation as they killed everything for food and burned everything for the fuel they needed to survive.

Scene 3

ARAN (SILTH)

In a tree above the shack where he'd fought Angel, Aran knew he was dying. He'd been there through the night and most of today, as different officials came and went. Though his wounds were serious, they didn't seem life-threatening. Nor was this simply the exhaustion of his magic reserves, which should have recovered with rest. It was more like the flame in the center of his being was guttering and about to go out.

He couldn't work up the energy to do anything about it. He couldn't think or make a decision, and he fought sleep, fearing he wouldn't wake up. Still he lost consciousness from time to time. When he awoke, he'd ponder where he should go if he could manage to move. Although the colony had exiled him, perhaps the subsequent events had changed his status. But where would the colony be if Storng had relocated it before the Faerie attack? He'd like to see Storng and Merit before he died, and he needed to make sure they knew about the other volcanoes and the Faerie plans. If Faelen was dead, only Aran could pass on any more Faerie magic. That thought finally rallied him to action. He had no clue if anyone would be at the Kawran Colony, but at least he could try.

Using the technique he'd learned from Faelen, he flickered, blinked out of the tree, and reappeared exactly where he had hoped to, in the courtyard where he and Merit had stood before the council. The space was empty, and no sounds came from the nearby buildings. The scars of a Faerie battle were all around him—the signatures of Faerie bolts were on the walls and trunks of surrounding structures, and a few arrows and spears lay on the ground. He saw no Silth or Faerie bodies. His legs buckled and he collapsed, closing his eyes.

"So you just give up?" came a familiar growl of a voice.

"Not much left to give up, I'm afraid." Aran forced open his eyes.

Storng smiled down at him. "I thought you might come back here. Come, sit up—it's too dangerous to stay. The Faeries who attacked here were beaten, so I expect them to return with a bigger force."

With Storng's help, Aran struggled to a sitting position and gasped, "There won't be … any more Faerie attacks … for a while. And I don't think … I'll be going anywhere else."

Aran described what he was feeling, and Storng broke in with, "What was the last magic you performed before these symptoms began?"

As soon as Aran told him about using the tree roots to crush Angel, Storng flew off without a word. Aran's mouth fell open. Was what he'd done so abominable that his friend wouldn't even say goodbye? He crumpled back on the small stones of the courtyard and awoke with a shudder at the sound of flapping wings. Storng stood over him again, arms filled with shaman paraphernalia.

"Your condition is very serious, but I know what's wrong. You have been poisoned."

"But how could Angel have—?"

"No, not Angel. You poisoned yourself. Remember, there's a price for all magic. Normally it's just our energy and it recharges when we rest, like every other life system that supports us. But when a type of magic is misused, the force of using it causes serious injury. Somewhat like tearing a muscle, but this muscle is deep within us and a part of what gives us life. You used Earth magic to violently take a life. You used roots, the givers of life, to kill."

"Not like I had much choice," Aran muttered.

"Decay occurs in the world as microbes eat away at things, and there is violent food-taking like a jaguar snatching a baby javelin. Roots do not do these things. Sudden violence such as the taking of a life is against their nature. Forcing them to do so poisoned you. Be quiet so I can work."

The shaman spread his tools around him. He began to draw with colored sand and chant an alignment song.

At some point Aran lost consciousness and woke up completely disoriented, sweating and shaking. Except for the nearby fire, darkness surrounded him. On the opposite side of the fire, Storng poured a cup of water onto hot stones in the fire. Steam burst upward, filling the sweat lodge where Aran lay. He had no idea how he had gotten there, the location of the sweat lodge, or how much time had passed. The lodge was barely big enough for both them and the fire, ringed by rocks that hissed and crackled.

Storng began talking as though there had been no interruption. "You'll need treatment for a week. Every day this lodge and these herbs." He pointed to a pile of nasty-looking herbs on a piece of cloth. "But you'll live. Sleep."

Aran closed his eyes but sleep didn't come. Although he was no longer in pain, he was weak, and his flesh seemed to be roasting on his bones. Despite that, he roused himself so he could let Storng know what he'd learned.

"The Faeries have left the Earth." Aran was shocked at the

sound of his voice—while raspy before, it hurt to hear the whisper that was now the most he could manage. "They expect that the Earth will be uninhabitable for them for the next five years. Then they'll return … to exterminate what is left of the Silth and enslave or kill the remaining Human population." Pausing frequently to catch his breath, Aran told Storng about the volcanoes and their consequences, as well as an account of the fight at Yellowstone.

Storng said, "So the Yellowstone volcano wasn't set in motion. Nor the one in Ecuador. This means the world may not necessarily be the place the Faeries anticipate when they return. It's a small opportunity, but more than we would have had without your intervention. Thank you."

Aran ignored the praise—he felt neither heroic nor like he'd stopped anything—but he had a clear idea of what the Silth needed to do to survive. "Storng, with no Faeries coming to the Earth, there'll be no more Silth either."

"That's right," Storng agreed. "The ones in the clutches now will be the last."

"We must bring the Silth together to protect the animals and places upon which we depend. The Humans will become desperate. They'll use anything and everything to try to survive. Remember the stories of the last time the great ice came upon us? Many creatures including the mammoth, giant sloth, and others did not survive Human desperation. We need to open a dialogue with the Humans to avoid war among us and prepare for the return of the Faeries. And we need to train all Silth in what I've learned from Faelen, so we can defend ourselves. Any sign of Faelen, other than the hologram? Angel said …" Aran swallowed hard against the lump in his throat and tried again. "He said they killed him and left his body in the rainforest."

Storng told him how Faelen had trained Merit and her forces. "But we haven't seen him for several days. Or found his body."

"He was the real hero. The one who stopped Angel. He must have set up the interference while they were moving the bomb."

"You'll need to compose the song to tell his story to those who follow …" Storng's voice trailed off. Aran wondered if, like him, Storng was contemplating the end of the Silth.

Aran had used up all his new-found energy. He fell back onto the mat of leaves and grasses Storng had made, deep enough to accommodate his folded wings as he rested on his back. He watched Storng tend the fire. In the dark, Storng's black eye seemed like an empty socket, making him resemble some long-dead Silth still moving around. Aran awoke with a start, the vision of a living-dead Silth vivid in his mind.

Storng sat silently for most of a day before leaving the lodge. When he returned a short while later, he said, "I've called the other shamans. I told Tellick to bring the colony and the council back, and I summoned the shamans to meet in seven days. We'll present a plan to both for how we should move forward. Now I must sleep, and so should you. The first few days after you emerge from this lodge will decide everything. Until then, you have a long journey of healing."

Scene 4

Aran (Silth)

Storng was right—the week Aran spent sweltering in the lodge seemed more like years. He had vivid dreams, and when awake he often hallucinated. The confusion began to sort out after several days.

Finally, his strength returned. His thinking was sharp. He was ready for freedom, but he wasn't ready to deal with everyone's questions. Or the council.

As soon as Storng pronounced him well, he soared out of the lodge and up through the canopy, expecting to break into a blue sky. As he emerged instead in a grey, overcast one, he reminded himself he awakened in a new world where sunlight was rare and temperatures much lower than before the volcanos. He couldn't help but find the changes depressing.

He flew to a hillside waterfall and stood at its base, watching the water as it struck the bottom and cascaded over moss-covered boulders. The sound of the falls, the moist air created by the ricochet of its crash on the bottom, and the beauty of its plummet lifted his spirits. He stripped and ducked into one of the smaller falls surrounding its base for a much-needed shower. He scrubbed off the sweat from his week in the lodge using tree leaves with a slight peppermint smell. As he lifted his face into the water, an arm encircled his chest, and an unquestionably female form pressed itself against his wet back. He said nothing, merely leaned back and relaxed back into the embrace.

A familiar voice whispered in his ear, "You've come a long way from sneaking into houses."

He turned and kissed Nadara for a long time before they slid down on the rocks and lost themselves in one another. The bliss ended as she, straddling his hips with her wings spread above her head, cried out and sent nearby birds up into the dark sky.

As they lay drying in the grass beside the stream, Aran asked, "Was this an experiment or the beginning of something?"

"A question Heartless would never have asked," Nadara replied, stroking his arm. "All I can tell you is that I have the same question."

"Aren't you a long way from home?" he asked as he dove back in the pool below the waterfall and surfaced to watch her dress. "Why are you here?"

"A question for Storng." She unfolded her wings and rose, hovering over him a moment. "See you soon."

When she was a mere speck in the distance, he put on his clothes. He'd just finished when another familiar voice floated down from a nearby tree.

"Hello, Shaman Aran, hero of the Silth!" Merit was squatting on a limb surrounded by vines and the forest flower-parasites. Next to her on the branch was Stalbon, her harpy eagle. The creature cocked its head and peered at Aran quizzically.

He joined them. "How long have you been here?"

"Not so long that your modesty is threatened." She paused, then, "Though you might recall—"

He laughed. "How'd you find me?" He scanned the area looking for her guards. "You aren't still having me followed, are you?"

"To protect you from what? I think you've shown you can protect yourself from almost anything."

"Almost anything?"

"Almost."

The wink she gave him was unexpected and most disconcerting. What does that mean? But then she abruptly asked, "Are you ready for the council?"

"While I'd prefer to fly in the opposite direction, I suppose I have to face them." He thought about the last time he'd stood before them and wondered how this time would go. Better, he hoped.

"Storng has been talking to them for several days. Bringing them up to speed on what happened. What you did and what it means. And what you plan."

"What I plan? I told Storng what I thought should happen next. No plan, just the ramblings of a delirious Silth."

"Well, the ramblings of a delirious, irresponsible and impulsive Silth, whose last 'plan' and the one before that almost got him killed," she said with a sudden seriousness. But then she smiled, with the awkward half face smile that she rarely showed. "But your 'ramblings' were still better than anyone else's ideas. You have the authority of one who just saved the world, together with the mystery of someone who cannot be challenged for the details. Then there is the power of your magic, already spawning an entire legion of storytellers. And maybe a few of us got together before Storng presented the 'plan' and added a few … um … details."

"Ahhh." He checked out the canopy around the waterfall and pool and spied a thick limb with a good view. "Perhaps we could sit up there. You can tell me 'my plan' before I go talk to the council."

Mist floated around the falls, cool and moist in his lungs. He paused to soak up the noises that were the voice of the forest—they told him it was alive. As Merit spoke, he studied her. Her good hand, so graceful given the warrior she was, moved constantly, and she turned her smile on and off as she described different interactions. A new trait, that reminded him of a different time. At times he reminded himself to actually listen to what she was saying.

They talked about the council, about Faelen and how he'd helped Merit prepare for the battle with the Faeries. She told him they'd evacuated the colony and hurriedly trained the warriors in Faerie-fighting technique. He noted ruefully that warrior Silth, even without magic practice for years, were much quicker studies on battle technique than he. They'd waited in the colony, and when the Faeries attacked, the Silth ambushed them and wiped out the whole group.

They talked about the days ahead. About what their future would be, making no mention of the two of them sharing any of it. Was that because it was all too uncertain, he wondered, or were there other reasons? Did he have any idea what he wanted?

"Tell me more about the council's current state."

"It has several new members. Storng now serves as the shamans' representative. Your brother's no longer on the council, having rejected the proposed plan out of hand. He argued that we should continue to hide from the Humans and petition the Faeries for peace and forgiveness. Now that the Silth have seen the true face of Faeries and that we can stand up to them, he got little support except from some of his New Faerie congregation. He resigned in anger and is trying to hold the last of his group together as the practitioners of New Faerie ebb away. He has moved all who would follow him to the old colony. By the way, I moved all of your swag to a cave. Too much traffic at the colony to leave it there. You'll need to move the egg though."

"Thank you. You know, I've been trying hard to forgive my brother and to forget his betrayal. I'd like to justify his behavior toward me as him doing what he thought best for the colony. But our problems began long before that. And I think he may have been spying for the Faeries. Something Thest said—he knew I'd been banished." Aran took some small seeds out of a pocket, offered some to Merit and began eating. "What will the council do next?"

"Storng says they'll hand out assignments when they meet with you. He's tasked with leading the shamans in opening a dialogue with the Humans. Many have talked to and interacted with Humans by phone for years, it turns out, even if the Humans didn't know who was on the other side of their conversations. The council wants the Fortress Colony to train all the Silth in the new skills we can access, to prepare to battle the Faeries upon their return. I may need you to teach me a little more before I show others. Faelen only taught me 'hide, shield, and attack.'"

He chuckled, thinking that Faelen would appreciate the sparseness of that characterization. The clearing beside the waterfall reminded him of the place where he trained with him. "I'll miss him. He's the one who saved us—from the Faeries and the bomb."

"You, Aran Shaman, know something about storytelling. Sing his story and it will join all those that define who we are."

They sat quietly a moment before she continued. "They want you to rally the Silth around the world to one cause. Because you can do that disappearing-transport thing like the Faeries, it means you can travel the world to mobilize the Silth. Most don't know what's happening, nor what's on the horizon. We need for them to train. Storng summoned the Tiki Crew to travel with and assist you. We must find a way to rally the Silth to fight for our future and that of other creatures on Earth as we deal with the Humans and the Faerie. And we need them to understand that every Silth life will be precious because we're the last."

He broke the silence that ensued by saying, "We'll treat that as a challenge rather than accepting it as a given."

"You're ready for your 'hero's welcome'?"

"I'm not a hero," he protested.

"But you need to be. The Silth need a hero and a leader. They're scared. There's so much to do, and we're not organized to accomplish these sorts of things. The tasks appear too big. And not enough of us are saying powerful things like—" she dropped her voice to mimic his gravelly one—"'we'll treat that as a challenge rather than accepting it as a given.'"

He felt himself blush below his hather as she went on. "You cannot be modest and tell them you aren't a hero. You simply must become one."

I can't pretend to be a hero, but I can sing Faelen's hero song, and I can lead.

When it was time, they took off. As they flew above the trees, he drifted a little higher and looked down at her. The green forest flowed by beneath her, dark beneath the grey sky but verdant nonetheless. He eyed the scar that snaked over her shoulder and partway down her back, among the curves with which her body framed it. He saw the powerful muscles of her back flex with each flap of the wings. He watched her colors flash along above the deep green and floated down next to her so the tips of his wings just brushed hers.

He laughed inwardly. I go to help lead a people who just a few days ago banished me. I have no qualifications to lead other than I'm famous. I'm famous for saving Humans, a species I don't particularly like. We live in a dying world where we may kill one another for the scraps to survive until an unbeatable force arrives in five years to end us all.

At that moment he realized to his chagrin, and perhaps slight shame, that he was unafraid of the future. It seemed arrogant not to be. But not only was he proud of the Silth and their role in what had happened so far, he also was confident they could have a role in the Earth's future. If he had to pick a word for what he felt right now, it would be ... excited.

But perhaps that too should remain his secret.

Continue the adventure
in Book 2 of The World of Paerries Series:
Refuge in the Pandamonium

ACKNOWLEDGEMENTS

THANKS TO:

Wayne Stubbs, who in July of 2013 was the Executive Director of Port Panama City U.S.A. and gave me a tour of the Port; Matt Smith of Project Perry – The Central Virginia Parrot Sanctuary (projectperry. com) for the special tour and information; Martha Slone, my wonderful wife who encouraged me, served as my typist, my copy editor and in many instances editor as well; my beta readers for their input and encouragement; my classmates at the Algonkian Conference for their helpful ideas, and Doug Waits, a biology professor at Birmingham-Southern College, for introducing me to the beauty of Costa Rica and the threats to the future of that beauty.

A PORTION OF THE PROFIT FROM ANY SALES OF THIS BOOK IS DONATED TO THE PROTECTION OF HABITAT FOR AND REINTRODUCTION OF PARROTS.

Made in the USA
Middletown, DE
24 January 2019